In A Timely Manner

In A Timely Manner

Kelley Dean Walker

iUniverse, Inc.
New York Lincoln Shanghai

In A Timely Manner

All Rights Reserved © 2004 by Kelley Dean Walker

No part of this book may be reproduced or transmitted in any form or by any means, graphic, electronic, or mechanical, including photocopying, recording, taping, or by any information storage retrieval system, without the written permission of the publisher.

iUniverse, Inc.

For information address:
iUniverse, Inc.
2021 Pine Lake Road, Suite 100
Lincoln, NE 68512
www.iuniverse.com

ISBN: 0-595-32225-5

Printed in the United States of America

For Bridget and Brendan, who are everything to me.

I would like to give special thanks to the following people for their support:

Mike and Linda McShane, Mark Lease, Sandie and Bob Kline, Erin McShane, Daniel and Angela Walker, Wendy and Frank Guzman, Timothy McShane, Ann Nagle, Shelby Willitts, Jim Kline, Carl Bjorklund, Mick Walker, Norma Hutmacher, and Melanie Brox.

I know I can rely on all of you for your first impressions, honest assessments, and observations. Without your input, I would be lost. I cannot thank you enough.

Chapter 1

▼

"Are we supposed to do anything special for him, or what?" Lou asked, staring down at the flight confirmation. "I mean, I never met a guy like this before."

"Neither have I," Andrew Daisley admitted. He tucked the airline schedule into his jacket pocket and the two men advanced towards the arrival gate. "They don't come more highly recommended, though, so just be cool with him and give him plenty of room."

"I guess I can do that," Lou replied with a shrug.

Louis Poklatar shrugged a lot. More than most people. Though it gave him a look of being aloof, the fact was that when he shrugged he didn't know the answer to the question or really didn't care what the answer was. In this case, the thirty-six year old police officer was simply at a loss as to how he was supposed to treat a professional killer. This was all new to him.

"We're going to want to move this along as fast as possible," Daisley reminded him. "Getting his ass over to the hotel is all I care about right now. We're in a wicked hurry already."

It was true that he was anxious to get their passenger out of the airport and into the safety of the Bonaventure Hotel, but he had other concerns as well. Just being seen with the man by the wrong person had the potential to destroy his career. At forty-two, the detective was happy with things the way they were and couldn't imagine life as a security guard or private investigator. Since that's exactly what he would become if given the boot from the force, Daisley was going to be extra cautious on this one.

"Dark blue suit and glasses, right?" Lou asked, scanning the first of the passengers as they disembarked.

"What did I tell you five minutes ago?"

"Dark blue suit and glasses," Lou replied, nodding as if to confirm it to himself.

Staring up at him, Daisley blinked several times. "That's right, Lou. Nothing's changed since then."

"So he'll be wearing a dark blue suit and glasses, right?"

"*Jesus*, Lou. Dark blue suit…glasses…that's right. You want me to write that down for you?"

Louis cocked his head to one side and looked down at his temporary boss. After a moment, he realized that Daisley wasn't really going to write anything down. "So I was right the first time?"

"Yeah, Lou…you were right."

"Then why didn't you just say so when I asked you?"

"Because I just *told* you what the guy was wearing five minutes ago," he answered, praying to be done with the sad dialogue before their man showed up. "I know you heard me, so let's drop it."

Louis didn't look quite done or ready to drop it. "How do you know?"

"Know what, Lou?"

"That I heard you? You said you knew that I heard you. How do you know that? Maybe I didn't hear you the first time."

"But you did. You heard me say it."

"How do you know, though?"

At this point, Detective Daisley had to pause and check himself. He'd only known Officer Poklatar for about a week and wasn't sure if the man was putting him on or not. Either way, it was becoming unbearable.

"I know you heard me because you know what he's wearing. Since you knew what the man was wearing when you asked me, I have to assume you heard me the first time. You did, right?"

"Yeah, I guess I did," Lou replied.

"Good. He should be out in a second. Do me a favor and try not to speak, okay?"

With the first sign of any understanding and logical thought, Louis simply nodded.

"Thanks. He'll have some carry-on luggage and he's supposed to be a pretty big guy. When you see him, just hold up the card."

Looking into his hand, Lou seemed almost surprised to see the large white piece of cardboard in it. It simply read: John Smith.

Of course it was just a pathetic alias—the least original alias ever known to man—but it was how they would make contact with him. In Chicago where the man was from, the name Terrence Fisk was synonymous with death. The word around law enforcement circles was that he was the most lethal man in the business and the last guy you wanted holding a ticket with your name on it. As far as Daisley knew, nobody had even seen his face.

"Okay, hold it up," he blurted out suddenly. Craning his neck around the passing people, Daisley had found his man.

"I don't see him yet." Lou held the card up higher.

"Turn it around, Lou," Daisley said quietly, squeezing his eyes shut tight for an instant. "The card...turn it around."

Complying quickly, Lou didn't have enough sense to look embarrassed as he flipped the cardboard sheet over. "Where's he at?"

"He just walked down the ramp. The tall guy. See him?"

"Which one?"

"Next to the blond with the red hat," Daisley whispered back. "He's got a black briefcase and he's holding a newspaper."

"What's he wearing?"

"He's in the dark blue suit and—" Daisley stopped talking before the rest of the sentence could spill from his mouth. "Just put the fucking sign down, Lou."

Exhaling loudly, he took a quick glance at his temporary partner and walked away, wading into the crowd of people. It was becoming obvious why his new associate was still a regular cop and not a detective like himself. At first he was surprised to learn that someone so close to the street was involved in this particular job. But then he got a look at the guy. When he had first met Louis, Daisley figured him to be the quiet, deep thinking behemoth that he appeared to be. Over the last week, he started to suspect there was less thinking going on than he had imagined. It wasn't until right now that he was sure that his partner Louis was a complete idiot.

He was a fairly big character at six-foot four and two hundred-forty pounds, so Daisley understood his usefulness, but looking back at the slack face and zoned out eyes, he couldn't help but be disappointed. And the poor dumb bastard was still holding up the card.

"Mr. Fisk?" Daisley asked quietly as he neared him.

The large man—smaller than Louis, but big nonetheless—turned slowly and looked the policeman up and down before extending a hand.

"Detective?" he said with a nod as they briefly shook hands.

They eyed each other for a moment before heading to where Lou was still standing with the card held high. He seemed to snap out of a daze as they walked up.

"Any luggage I can get for you?" Lou asked as he straightened his back, elevating himself an inch or two over their new company. He made no move to shake hands with the assassin.

"No, this is it," Fisk replied, nodding toward the briefcase in his left hand. "How far to the hotel?"

"We'll be there in twenty minutes if we leave now. Louis, bring the car around, will you?"

"Sure thing," he replied, turning away without making any eye contact with Fisk.

The detective couldn't tell if it was fear or disgust that had Lou shaken up. They had kicked around a few rumors about the man but hadn't discussed any particular feelings on the subject. From a layperson's standpoint, Daisley could understand the public's fascination with hit men and organized crime in general, but as a cop, the genre was less than enthralling.

Losing its luster after years of informers and turncoats, organized crime was becoming more of a novelty than a serious threat; especially on the West Coast where it had failed to thrive like it did in the east—publicly anyway. The only real entertainment value left was in the hit-man, which had always kept the audience in their seats. Andrew Daisley found it hard to share the public's enthusiasm about paid killers.

On one hand, they pretty much stuck to killing their own, which was fine with him. On the other, anyone who does a serious amount of killing is eventually going to miss and take out a civilian, which was not so fine. Though it was mostly the amateurs that missed the target and took all the fun out of gangland killings, the professionals were hurting as well, often taking jobs outside of the organization to supplement their income. That was where Terrence Fisk came in.

He was just one of the names tossed around as a possibility for the job at hand and, going solely by reputation, it was no contest. Unfortunately, reputation was all they had to go on aside from a few nuggets of information from insiders that may or may not have been true at all. If the rumors were true, they were dealing with a man with incredible talent. He was also the only person available for the tight time frame that they'd been forced to deal with.

"How was the flight?" Daisley asked, unsure of the protocol for their odd relationship.

"Fine," Fisk replied without looking at him. Apparently small talk wasn't in the contract. He walked with no expression as they exited the terminal and headed for the loading zone.

"Here we are," Daisley said as Lou finally pulled up. The silence had been uncomfortable but conversation had even worse possibilities.

Offering, or rather insisting that Fisk rode up front, Daisley prayed that Lou would keep his lips sealed. It was obvious he was rattled by the man's presence and in a situation like this he might be tempted to shoot his mouth off a little. Some people clamed up under pressure. Others got excessively glib. With any luck, Lou would remain the silent man he'd become accustomed to.

It was a nice surprise that Lou didn't talk as they edged their way through the crowded streets of downtown Los Angeles. Grabbing an occasional glimpse of the man in the passenger seat, his level of anxiety was slowly rising with each mile that passed. Fisk hadn't moved an inch since he climbed into the car and seemed happy with staring straight ahead. It wasn't until Lou began to whistle that Fisk turned his head for the first time.

Staring at the driver of the unmarked police vehicle, the assassin's eyebrows went up slowly and something close to a smile crossed his lips. He seemed to chuckle lightly as he faced forward again. It wasn't a pleasant sound.

"You can't whistle worth a shit, can you, big guy? Were we supposed to recognize that?"

"You didn't?" Lou replied with mild surprise. "It was the theme from *SWAT*."

Fisk shook his head and cracked his knuckles one at a time. "No it wasn't. I know what *SWAT* sounds like and that wasn't it. Not even close."

"Sure it was," Lou insisted. "I saw the show a million times."

"Then you were watching the wrong one because that was *CHiPs* if it was anything."

"No, it was *SWAT*, man. Here, listen again."

But he didn't get the chance.

Before he could purse his lips again, Lou heard his name quietly called out from behind him. Taking a glance into the back seat, he could almost feel Daisley's stare before he saw it. It was pretty much what he'd expected. The scowl was telling him to shut up and to do it now. He did so and turned back to the road.

They drove in silence for at least two minutes before he started whistling again.

Fisk's stifled laughter was nearly as loud as the groan that came from the back seat. Together, the sounds almost obscured Lou's off-pitch mewling, which stopped quickly.

"What's wrong?"
"Where should I start?" Fisk replied as they slowed to a stop.

Chapter 2

▼

Terrence Fisk was in heaven. If they knew that this was a vacation for him, they probably wouldn't have been paying him so much. The target they'd lined up was so pathetically simple that it was almost an insult to his skills. Even the fact that it had to be done within thirty-six hours didn't faze him in the slightest. It made no difference to him.

Spending a couple of weeks on the west coast was exactly what he'd been needing; plenty of sunshine, beautiful women, and a completely different train of thought. California looked like Mars compared to Chicago. It showed in everyone's attitude, clothing, speech patterns, and especially their faces.

What the fuck is everyone smiling about?

As far as Terrence Fisk was concerned, he was the only one with reason to smile. The fifty grand they were paying him was chump change considering the couple of million he had squirreled away off-shore, but at least it was cash. The last two payments he'd received were in the form of corporate checks with "Resource Management" written on the memo line. It was much different than the world he grew up in where everything was on a cash-only basis. Only a decade earlier, the thought of accepting a check for services rendered would have been a joke. Now it was commonplace.

As his former employers organizations were disintegrating, Fisk was busy digging up more clients…and then burying them. It wasn't just crime families that wished lightning would strike a competitor. He quickly found that practically every aspect of the business world craved his services and were willing to pay top dollar for them. More often than not, they also used it as a tax write-off and typically paid him with a company check, stock options, or other negotiable items.

For some reason he missed those good old cash days. Even though he was being paid more for his effort, there was something about a huge stack of hundred dollar bills that excited him more than the number of zeros written on a check.

And speaking of zeros, he thought. *How about the two zeros driving me around right now?*

The whistling moron and the uptight detective were not the types he was used to dealing with. They weren't LAPD—that much he knew. His previous jobs on the west coast were in LA and San Francisco and he'd always felt comfortable in both places. These guys were from further south in a tiny little place called Corona. He'd never even heard of it.

From the brief description he received, Fisk gathered that nobody on this job knew shit about anything. He knew that the detective was the lead man as far as action was concerned, but he wasn't the one who made the call and arranged for the meeting. That was some lawyer named Ratcliffe.

The lawyer talked loudly and full of confidence but it was a farce. He didn't know what he was doing any more than the two cops he was with at the moment. So far, they all seemed weak, naïve, and wildly uninformed. Fisk's first clue that the gentlemen were in over their heads came when they'd made their offer to him: One hit—fifty thousand. There were no guidelines to follow and no special requests; just a lot of money for shooting straight.

Special requests were usually reserved for a personal hit so he guessed this one was purely a business deal. Sometimes the people writing the checks wanted it to be painful. Now and then, some guy might even want an enemy or an ex-partner to lose a few fingers or toes before his lights were put out. And on occasion—especially when insurance policies were involved—they wanted it to look like an accident.

When someone made a special request, Fisk's usual reaction was to look as though he was pondering it but not thrilled with the idea. Eventually they'd throw more money at him and he would accept. The only thing that he could have charged extra for on the current job was the speed at which it had to be completed. It wasn't really an issue but most people needed a little more time to prepare for a perfectly clean assassination. For Fisk, is simply wasn't required.

The guys from Corona had offered him the money as a flat fee to get rid of a nuisance. For a job like this, an amateur would get maybe five grand tops. A pro would demand ten, but that's if he even wanted to waste his time with such a small-time operation. He suspected that the cops in Corona had watched one too many mafia movies on cable.

He'd take their money, though. That was a certainty. Being paid by the police to kill a guy was had a nice ring to it. It could also come in handy down the line if he ever found himself in trouble. If nothing else, he could blackmail the department into giving him a rock solid alibi if he ever needed one.

Fisk could just see himself under indictment for a hit in Florida or some other place. With one phone call, he'd be able to provide paperwork showing he was in a California jail at the time being booked for public drunkenness or some other load of crap. Yes, this would be a sweet score with more benefits than he could count.

For starters, the women out here were all gorgeous with blond hair and big tits. When the job was done, he planned on several debaucherous days of R & R.

Eyeing a particularly stunning specimen as they came to a stop in front of a towering glass building, he was surprised to see her approach the car and pull his door open for him. She wore her hair back and dressed sharply. Her smile and body language gave away nothing other than the fact that she was a knockout. It was the look of caution in her eyes when she saw him that let him know she was just another police officer.

Fucking cops. He scooped up his briefcase and exited the vehicle.

Chapter 3

▼

Though she didn't have any idea what to expect from their VIP, Qiana Schwartze could sense from his face alone that he was as bad as she'd heard. There was a coldness in his eyes that gave her chills and she suspected his voice would have the same effect. This wasn't how she pictured it at all.

The idea had seemed almost funny at the time it was first conceived, but now it was anything but hilarious. Even though she'd prepared herself for it, she still found it hard to believe that she was in the presence of a man who would make others die in exchange for currency.

"Room fourteen twenty-six. You can go right up," she stated firmly, pulling the door open wide. "Mr. Ratcliffe is waiting upstairs for all of us. It'll be a short meeting and we'll be heading out immediately afterward. Leave your luggage in the car."

"I didn't bring any," Fisk replied dryly. "Everything I need has already been shipped."

She pointed to the only item he had brought with him. "What's that then?"

Amused by the female officer's terse way of speaking with him, Fisk looked down at the briefcase in his hand and moved as if to hand it to her. As he lifted it up, she took a nervous step back. He loved the reaction.

"Relax, it's just personal stuff."

"What kind of 'personal stuff'?"

"It'll be easier if I show you," he replied. "It's locked but I've got the key right here."

When he finished the sentence, Fisk let the case drop from his hand and land loudly on the sidewalk. With uncanny speed and agility, he pulled open his jacket with his left hand and brought his right hand up quickly. Reaching into the left hand side of his jacket, he watched Qiana Schwartze's eyes go wide.

As if in slow motion, the two men who had picked him up from the airport were struggling to exit the vehicle and immediately began falling over themselves. The woman in front of him took another few steps back and moved a hand to her left hip, then to the right. Not finding what she was looking for, she reached around to the small of her back with both hands as Fisk took a lunging step toward her. Fighting to keep her balance, she nearly fell over backwards before he threw his left arm around her waist, effectively immobilizing her.

In a frozen state of panic with both hands stuck behind her, she watched horrified as he calmly brought his right hand to her hip and ran it up her side. As the killer's hand rolled over her left breast then the shoulder-holstered gun she'd been fumbling for, she was only seconds from yelling for help. When he held the key up in front of her face, she was glad she didn't.

"You still want to see what's inside?" he asked, his mouth only an inch from her ear. She had no reply aside from quickly pulling her face away from his.

As he gently released the woman into a safe and upright position, he could hear the three officers begin to breathe again. The detective looked less than amused as he ran a sweaty hand through his hair while the whistling idiot was still trying to free himself from the seatbelt he was tangled in. They were all looking at him with serious unease.

No, these were not the streetwise cops that dogged him in his earlier days.

"Are you guys nervous or something? I thought you were going to fall on your ass for sure, honey. You're lucky I was here to catch you."

The female detective looked ready to explode as her eyes narrowed and her top lip began rising above the gum line. It was her standard snarl and could usually scare anyone in the room. To Fisk, it was merely a very sexy look.

"Back off, Quartz," Daisley ordered, stepping between the two. "Lou, how about walking Mr. Fisk upstairs. We'll be right behind you."

Slowly unraveling himself from the seatbelt, Lou nodded with an unhappy look of his own. As he climbed from the car, he checked the revolver in his holster and unhooked the snap that held it in place. The killer may have startled the girl, but Lou swore to himself that he would be ready if any more funny stuff went down. With a simple tilt of his head, Lou beckoned the assassin to follow him. Picking up his briefcase, Fisk did so, taking a quick look back at the incensed woman who was busy straightening herself out.

Scared her, embarrassed her, and groped her too. This is turning out to be a hell of a day. He followed the big man into the hotel.

Staring into her reddening face, Daisley gave her a compassionate look that told her not to feel too badly. They were all a little on edge and Fisk could have chosen any of them to mess with. It was just her bad luck that he picked her.

"Are you okay?"

"I'm fine," she replied, unable to hide the humiliation. "I don't know what I expected but I sure didn't think he'd pull anything so juvenile. Someone with an itchy trigger finger—or someone who remembered where their gun was—could have blown him away easily for that shit, Andrew."

"I don't guess he gets many chances to screw around with the police to their faces. He's got to be loving this, Quartz. Don't take it personally."

The name Qiana Schwartze had been cut down to Quartz within her first few days on the force back in Riverside where she had started. Qiana was a pretty name but sometimes in police work, three syllables in a first name was just too much. Quartz was a lot easier to scream out in an emergency than Qiana anyway and she wore the name well.

"I swear, I thought he was going after your gun for a second," Daisley said with a sorrowful look. "If we weren't paying this guy, I bet he could have gotten it really easy. If he was being paid to do it, he probably could have taken us all out in a couple of seconds."

"Don't worry about that," she told him as she readjusted her holster. "It wasn't the gun he was after. The fucking pig totally felt me up."

Her humiliation was turning back to rage while he watched. More than messing with her holster, Daisley was getting the feeling that she was actually trying to brush the man's touch off of her breast.

"I'm sorry about that, but there aren't exactly any kind of rules dealing with a guy like this. Is there anything I can do?"

"Aside from squeezing the other one to even it out, you mean?" she asked, pulling open the right side of her jacket briefly. "No, I'll get over it. But let me warn you; if I get the chance, I just might bust his fucking head open."

"Hey, be my guest. If you think you can get away with it, go ahead and kill the prick. I wouldn't complain about it."

"Ratcliffe would, though," she reminded him, losing her sarcasm quickly. "We'd better head on up before Lou says something stupid and scares him away."

"Something tells me this guy isn't going to scare so easy. A few minutes alone with Lou might make him suicidal. But *scared*? I don't think so."

They entered the hotel lobby and went straight for the elevator. While they waited, Quartz fiddled with her holster and bra strap some more, grunting angrily with each tug. Only once they had entered the elevator did she speak again. When she did, she spoke in a whisper even though they were alone.

"You don't think he really killed Hoffa do you? It sounds like a bunch of crap to me, but Lou was saying that the guy—"

"Hoffa disappeared in seventy-five, Quartz," he said, cutting her off. "Fisk is a couple of decades too young. Do me a favor, will you?"

"Sure."

"Don't listen to anything that Lou's got to say. I mean, I like the guy, but he's so fucking dumb it's scary. I'm not sure why he's in on this but I'd take everything he says with a grain of salt. Okay?"

"No problem there," she agreed, thinking that the Hoffa bit sounded lame to begin with. The stories she'd heard about his other more colorful mob hits seemed more than real, though. At least one of them was confirmed by Detective Daisley himself.

"You can blow off any of the bullshit that Lou's been saying, but the guy's still plenty dangerous. You've already seen how fast he can move."

"Yeah, I've seen it," she agreed angrily.

A moment later, the bell signaling their arrival on the fourteenth rang softly. As the door opened, Quartz looked up to the ceiling and exhaled several times, trying to rid herself of any lingering uneasiness.

"Are we ready for business?" Daisley asked, wiping off the foamy piece of spit that had formed on the corner of his mouth. "I don't have any shit in my teeth, do I?"

Quartz examined him closely. "Looking good. What about me?"

"Wipe that gunk out of your eye and we're good to go."

He straightened his tie and stepped onto the fourteenth floor. Quartz followed behind, nearly tripping as her heel dragged along the ground.

"Perfect!" she spat out, rolling her eyes as she looked down at her favorite pair of shoes. "This is just what I needed. The goddamn tip of my heel came off."

"It looks fine, Quartz." Daisley viewed the damage and could see that a tiny piece of rubber smaller than a dime had been stripped from the bottom of her best pair of high heels. "Do you think we'll survive or should we just call the whole thing off?"

His sarcasm wasn't appreciated. Not only was her shoe now damaged, she knew that it had most likely been wounded during her brief scuffle with Terrence Fisk. The shoe could be fixed—it was only a tiny piece of rubber that could be easily reapplied; she simply hated the idea of her right foot teetering around on a pointy nail all day long. Now she really wanted to kill him.

Chapter 4

▼

As they entered the room, Daisley was aware of Fisk's eyes on Quartz and could tell that she was avoiding looking in his direction. She nodded briefly to the others in the room that she recognized, then crossed the room to take her seat near the window. Halfway to her seat, a popping sound began to follow her as the nail sticking from her shoe snagged on a piece of carpet.

Pop-pop-pop. Each step was punctuated by the sound as the carpet unraveled beneath her feet. A small sigh and an uncomfortable smile was all she could manage as she lifted her leg and freed herself from the loop of tangled fabric. Eventually, she was seated, though it didn't go without comment from a voice that was crude, cocky, and had taken over a year for her to get accustomed to.

"Smooth as usual, detective. Graceful as a fucking hockey player."

"Not now, Michael," the man at the head of the table warned. The lawyer who had summoned them all didn't bother to hide his disdain as he surveyed the strange collection of people in front of him. "There isn't going to be time for the usual pleasantries."

Donald Ratcliffe was about to begin the trial phase of the most sensitive case of his career and wasn't about to let the loudmouth cop have the floor. Once Mike Blash got to talking, it usually required an injunction from the superior court to get him to shut up.

"Are we all here?" Ratcliffe asked of nobody in particular, signaling the start of a short meeting that he could barely believe was actually taking place. Since the five seats were filled, he began without waiting for anyone to speak up. "This is going to be brief. Listen up and save your questions until I'm done talking."

Almost immediately, Lou's hand began to rise.

"Put your hand down, moron," Mike Blash snapped quickly. "He said to wait until he was finished talking."

"How long'll that be?" Lou asked in a loud whisper.

"When he's done, you'll know how long," Blash replied. "Then you won't have to ask."

Detective Daisley had met Mike Blash at the same time he'd met Louis Poklatar and the pretty, dark-haired one they called Quartz. Though Louis and the girl were genuine down to earth characters, he had his doubts about the other police officer. The guy was a different story entirely. He seemed to fill the cop role very nicely but talked like he'd been undercover too long. He said he'd worked the West Coast from San Diego up to Seattle but didn't make any mention of what types of guys he had to blend in with.

From the way he spoke, Daisley suspected that Mike Blash had maybe played a bouncer in the restroom of a whorehouse behind a truck stop somewhere in the desert. He had that much class.

"First I'd like to thank you all for meeting here," Ratcliffe continued, staring down at each individual with the exception of the assassin. Even the lawyer seemed to be a tad put off by his presence. "I know LA's a bit of a trek for some of you but this is where my office is located. You've all met Mr. Fisk, so I'll start with—"

"I haven't met him yet," Blash interrupted, seeming to be the only one willing to meet eyes with the man. And he met them dead on. "I've been busy setting this bullshit up and nobody's even been polite enough to introduce us properly. We're shelling out fifty thousand to the guy. I think it would be the courteous thing to do."

Though he seemed to be addressing everyone around the table, Mike Blash hadn't taken his eyes off of Fisk for a second.

"Mike, this is Terrence Fisk," Daisley said with a tone of resignation. "Good enough?"

"Fucking splendid. I'm sure the folks in Corona are gonna feel real safe now—"

"Michael," Donald Ratcliffe cut in, sorry for letting him talk in the first place. "That's quite enough. You gentlemen can get to know each other on your own time, but at the moment you're on my time and my time is pretty expensive. Since we won't be meeting together after this, I'll need your full attention now."

The lawyer spoke in a very even tone, sounding like the charismatic, attention grabbing man that he thought he was. The others were silent as he talked, but only because they were too busy sizing each other up to care what he was saying.

They'd already heard it or ran through it in their heads hundred times over the last week.

"I know first hand that this room is safe to talk in so I'm going to speak as bluntly as I feel I need to be. We all know why Mr. Fisk is here. I'll just say it out loud for you so you know what you're getting yourselves into."

They all knew the job and, aside from Terrence Fisk, none of them were too keen on the idea. With false calm expressions they listened to the attorney lay out his case, knowing it was too late to do anything about it now.

Instead of lining up a murder, the man sounded like he was narrating a slideshow.

"Over the last week, we've all become familiar with one Christian Roche. Mr. Fisk has had his portfolio for three days. He says it won't be difficult."

"And it won't be," Fisk reaffirmed confidently.

"Roche relocated to the Riverside area recently from Baton Rouge, where he had several small operations dealing mainly in narcotics and weapons. What made him choose the city of Corona as his new home is beyond me. If he was thinking retirement then I guess he changed his mind because he's been back in business for the last eight months."

It was just a quick rundown on the facts that they already knew—unoriginal facts about an unoriginal felon. The four officers stared apprehensively at each other, knowing what came next. Ratcliffe spelled it out for them anyway.

"Based on the figures I've come up with, this is the cheapest and most expeditious route to go. The way I see it, the county can spend countless man hours and money prosecuting the man and chance failing…or do what we've decided to do."

Once again, they gave each other knowing looks that asked the same thing. *What we've decided to do?*

"In as timely a manner as possible, Mr. Fisk is going to solve the problem permanently. Christian Roche will be eliminated sometime tomorrow evening and discovered shortly thereafter. Naturally, it will look like some bad element finally caught up with him, meaning there will be very few questions for you to deal with."

He was looking specifically at Daisley as he spoke. Being the only cop in the room who actually worked in Corona, it made sense. Just the same, he didn't like being singled out from the others.

"The following day, the rest of your payment will be made here in LA," he continued, looking at Fisk this time. "After that, our business will be concluded and I don't expect to ever hear from you again."

Fisk nodded with a smile, knowing it was what the lawyer wanted from him. Of course, upon leaving the hotel, the first thing he would do was make a list of the names of each person in the room. They would go into his "Get Out of Jail Free" collection. It wouldn't surprise Fisk at all if Donald Ratcliffe did hear from him again.

"I've got a meeting across town in half an hour and should have left five minutes ago. I'll give you a minute for questions."

"I've got an easy one for you, Don," Blash blurted out. "Who pulled *this* guy's name out of the hat?"

"He was referred to us by people who would know about such things. He has a certain reputation in the field that I'm sure you're aware of."

"Yeah, I've got awareness falling out of my ass," Blash said, shaking his head incredulously. "I'm just curious as to how a lawyer contacts a professional like this."

Fisk seemed oblivious to the conversation that surrounded him. He ignored their discussion of him and focused on woman across the table instead. Though she wouldn't look up at him, he knew she could feel his stare.

"You're going to have to ask Detective Daisley about that one, Michael. Incidentally, he's the boss from here on out. If you've got any bugs to work out before you get started on this thing, I suggest you do it quickly. We're in a big hurry and I don't want any mistakes to come back and haunt us."

Slowly, Lou raised his hand.

"Sorry, Louis," Ratcliffe said dismissively. "Out of time. I've got to go."

Instead of heading straight for the door, he walked into the bedroom of the spacious suite. A few seconds later he returned with a large manila envelope. Without a word, Fisk tossed his briefcase onto the table. He reached into his pocket and pulled out a key, giving Quartz a sideways glance as he did so. It was a small key that she had seen up close only a short time earlier.

When he unlocked the case and flipped it open, no one was surprised to find it was empty, though it didn't stay empty for long. He tore open the envelope and transferred the contents into the briefcase, quickly counting the small stacks as he piled them on top of one another. Since Ratcliffe had mentioned Fisk returning to Los Angeles for the balance of the payment, the police officers each assumed correctly that the twenty-five thousand dollar down payment was being made right in front of them.

While each pair of eyes shifted uncertainly from face to face, nobody said a word as the contract was sealed. When Fisk slammed the case shut, they all knew that their time to back out had just left the building. They were committed. They were all criminals now.

As though fleeing the scene of the crime, Ratcliffe started for the door the moment the briefcase was closed. Before he could make his quick exit, Terrence Fisk surprised the other members of his new team by calling out to the lawyer with a question of his own. It wasn't asked in a polite or even businesslike manner. He already had half the money. Being nice was no longer required.

"What kind of law do you practice, Mr. Ratcliffe?"

"The criminal kind," he answered, not missing the irony of his own words.

"Would that be prosecution or defense?"

The lawyer had just mentioned that he wanted to save the county the time and expense of prosecuting Christian Roche. But Fisk knew a lie when he heard it. He also knew a defense attorney when he saw one.

"I'm making a transition into the prosecution side of things," Ratcliffe replied, seeming to enjoy answering the assassin's questions. "In six weeks I move into the district attorney's office here in LA."

"What are you doing until then?"

"Well, since you're so curious, Mr. Fisk, my final case as a defense attorney is supposed to begin about…" The lawyer looked down at his watch. "…ninety-six hours from now."

"I take it this client of yours paid a retainer for your services?" Fisk then asked, figuring more out in ten minutes than the others had in a full week.

"He sure did," Ratcliffe replied. "He paid cash, too."

"Let me guess how much."

Chapter 5

▼

"So we're taking out his client?" Lou asked, unable to find the logic behind it.

"That's right, Pokey," Blash answered in a quick burst, typical of his pattern of speech. "It sounds like this Roche fellow went and got himself the worst possible lawyer he could have found. The loser's paying for his own hit and he doesn't even know it."

"Well, that's crazy," Lou protested in a whining manner. It was all he had in the way of an argument. "And don't call me Pokey. I hate that."

Growing up with the name Louis Poklatar, he had adjusted to being called Louie, Loop, Loopy, LP, and occasionally Poke. He didn't like any of them but lived with it simply because he had to. But there was always some smartass who would call him Pokey and that was crossing the line.

"Well, I'm sorry, Mr. Poklatard. I was just trying to answer your fucking question."

"Cut it out, Mike," Quartz said with enough familiarity to make it clear that she often spoke to him in such a tone. "Acting like an asshole isn't going to help us right now."

"Certainly not," Fisk agreed. "Why don't you all pull in here and let me explain how this is going to happen. I don't want to have to say it ten times."

Taking his place where Ratcliffe had been sitting before, Fisk looked prepared to take over completely. Instead of open ears waiting for their instructions, he was treated to several blank stares. Quartz finally said what was on all their minds.

"Ratcliffe said that Andrew was in charge, so I'd really like to hear what he has in mind before we commit to anything."

"I don't think so, Ms. Schwartze," Fisk replied dismissively. "I heard what Donald Ratfuck said too, but he's not here, is he?" Daisley stared uncomfortably at the ceiling while the others eyed Fisk with looks of distaste and mistrust. Quartz appeared ready to walk out but Fisk knew that she wouldn't. None of them would, no matter how poorly he treated them. "I should really let you folks know something right off the bat. I'll be running this show from now on and you'll be backing me up; not the other way around. In fact, all I really need from you people is to stay out of my way."

He spoke rapidly and with purpose. Sounding more like a motivational speaker than a hired killer, he took the floor and spelled it out for them.

"If the unlucky target is where he's supposed to be when he's supposed to be there, this will be a very quick job. I'll take care of the messy stuff while you three—" He nodded specifically to Lou, Quartz, and Blash. "You'll be keeping an eye on the surrounding property. That's total overkill for this thing, but if I've got you, I may as well use you."

The idea of being used by Fisk wasn't going over too well and it showed in their expressions. Daisley's face simply looked vacant as Fisk was currently making him obsolete.

"When it's over—which will be a minute or two after we start if everyone does exactly what I tell them to do—we'll leave the scene and go our separate ways. It doesn't get any easier than this."

"What about Andrew?" Quartz asked.

"He gets the discovery of the body, the fucking up of the evidence, the falsifying of records—the usual cop stuff. You don't have a problem with that, do you, detective?"

For a moment he didn't answer or even look up. Still coping with the fact that he'd been declawed and castrated in front of his fellow officers, he was floundering for a face saving solution. What finally came out was nothing short of total agreement.

"I have no problem at all. I'm the only one here who works for that department anyway. Nobody else even has jurisdiction. We've always known that."

He was trying to sound calm and unconcerned with Fisk's overbearing personality but didn't feel as smooth as he'd hoped for. When the job was completed, he knew that he wouldn't be seeing Terrence Fisk again so his concern had nothing to do with the man at all. It was his embarrassment in front of the other three that weighed much more heavily on him.

"I appreciate your cooperation, detective, and I'm confident you'll be able to clean up after me just fine. Now let's talk about accommodations."

Daisley had no trouble filling him in on this one. "I've got you booked into a motel less than a mile from Roche's house. It's pretty small—a shitty little place, actually—but I'm sure you'll manage."

"I suspect I will," Fisk replied, giving Quartz a suggestive leer that he knew would make her blood boil.

Over the years, Qiana Schwartze had to force herself to ignore being gawked at. There was just something about women in uniform that men found curiously attractive and she'd been putting up with the phenomenon for years. She was certainly pretty enough to qualify for all the attention but guessed it was more of an authority issue. The stares she got were fewer since she was promoted to detective but they were still a common occurrence.

Quartz liked the comfort and freedom of working in plain clothes but had to admit that she felt much sexier in the old black uniform. The first day she put on her starched shirt, skirt, hat, and sunglasses, she became so aroused with her own reflection in the mirror that she was ten minutes late to work.

But the way Terrence Fisk was currently looking at her had nothing to do with her eyes, hair, or makeup. The detective looked as dazzling as ever but she knew it was her occupation rather than her beauty that attracted him. He was just itching to screw a lady cop. It was obvious.

"Okay, it's almost noon," Fisk said, moving on to the next bit of business. "I want to have a full day to get used the surroundings, which means we'll be leaving right now. How far is it to your this city of yours?"

"It's a couple of hours," Daisley replied, checking his own watch. "I figured we'd grab some lunch here and then head out."

"Well, you figured wrong, detective. I already ate on the plane and I'm sure not going to sit around and watch four cops stuff their faces. If you're so hungry, we'll stop at a drive-thru and you can eat on the way."

By the time he finished the sentence, Fisk had already picked up his briefcase and was stepping away from the table. He paused in the middle of the room and turned back to the four who hadn't moved an inch. Tapping his watch, he nodded toward the door.

"*Today, people.*"

He wasn't as angry as he sounded, though, and he wasn't even in a hurry. In reality, he was just messing with the nearest figures of authority to him and shrinking them down to an acceptable size, which wasn't so hard since fucking with the authorities had been a hobby of his for years. He hadn't had this much fun since the time he was pulled over for speeding while hauling three bodies in his trunk over three years earlier.

Covered in red splatters from head to toe and bleeding from a gunshot wound in his shoulder, he had told the officer a ridiculous story about becoming disoriented when he ran over a woodchuck. After five minutes of describing how huge the rodent was, he was told to drive slower, watch out for woodchucks, and was sent on his way. He guessed the highway patrolman was almost as dumb as the four officers in front of him.

The whistler and the loudmouth were the standard cop fare he was used to. Both were big and none too bright. They were probably a couple of decent fellows but their occupations secluded them from any sort of normal life. Sure, they probably had plenty of friends, but they'd all be cops too. It took a certain kind of person to go into police work and these guys fit the bill perfectly.

The detective was another story. The fact that he let the meeting be taken over by a hired hand didn't say too much for the man's character. His lack of balls and leadership skills left Fisk almost feeling bad for him. Almost.

As far as he could tell, the only one of them with any brains was the woman. But after several long stares and a handful of her left breast, her intellect was the last thing on his mind.

Quartz they called her. *Cute name. Just give me some time alone with that one.*

When the four of them finally went into motion, he knew he would easily lord over this particular group. He'd given them orders and spoken to them in ways that wouldn't have been considered remotely respectful to the average person, much less to a police officer. They'd taken his shit and were now falling in line without argument.

This is going to be a lovely vacation, he thought as they climbed from their seats and headed toward the door. Though they still walked with a swagger and wore semi-confident faces, Fisk could see that their heads were hanging low on the inside.

Like a boy getting a shiny new bike for Christmas, he beamed at the gift that had been given to him by the slimy lawyer. Four shiny new cops of his very own.

"After you," he insisted, gesturing with his hand. They were inept and dangerously stupid but he wasn't going to turn his back on them.

I own your ass…thanks for playing, a voice in his head said as Daisley walked past him.

That's right…yours too, came the voice again as Louis lumbered by.

The voice was silenced momentarily as Officer Blash bumped shoulders with him and continued walking. It was an insignificant gesture but Fisk appreciated the effort. At least he was trying to play the tough guy.

Quartz was the last in line and gave him a wide berth as she maneuvered around him, knowing that if a stare could be felt, her ass would be on fire. Pausing at the door, she turned to see how close behind her he was, suspecting he would be right on her tail. But she was surprised to find him still standing in the center of the room watching her. He was smiling at her with an expression that could not be misinterpreted.

Oh, what I would love to do to you, young lady.

Being caught in mid-stare didn't disturb him at all. His head cocked slightly as his eyes moved slowly over her body from her face to her ankles.

Quartz's teeth began to grind against each other as she looked back, noting his reluctance to divert his eyes or even act in a civilized manner. She could feel her eyebrows coming together in a scowl as he actually took a step back to take in a full picture.

Damn, this is one fiery bitch, he thought comically, expecting her to lunge at him at any moment. She didn't. Instead, she watched angrily as he cocked his head to the other side and brought his hand up to his chin, nodding his head at her as if she was a piece of art being looked over by a critic—or a piece meat being sniffed at by a hungry diner. Though it was only a cheap thrill, Terrence Fisk was enjoying himself on many levels as she seethed for him. Playing on the rage that was amusing him so much, he retreated another step back and prepared a final insult. It was going to be the rudest, most crass thing he could think of.

He couldn't get the words out fast enough, though. Fisk's mouth had stopped moving at the same time his right foot did.

With all of his weight moving backwards and his left foot way out in front, he began to wonder how he would steady himself without looking foolish. The quick thinking assassin simply didn't have the time to ponder his escape route from the embarrassing scenario. He was falling backwards and he knew it. With one hand holding the briefcase and one leg unable to move, he was left with a foot that was out of position and an empty hand that was good for nothing but flailing wildly.

An instant later, his head smashed into the edge of the solid oak table that he'd just been sitting at.

"*Jesus…*" she uttered in quiet amazement, watching the formerly graceful killer stumble and fall over. Even though she had nothing but rabid hate for him, she still couldn't help but wince at the sound it made when his head and the table introduced themselves to each other. Bringing a hand to her mouth, she approached cautiously, hoping he wouldn't get too angry about the smile she was trying vainly to conceal.

The hand dropped and her smile vanished when she drew closer and realized that their fifty-thousand dollar hitman was dead.

Chapter 6

▼

"*Quartz! What the hell did you do?*" Daisley shouted, shoving his way past Lou and Blash, who were staring at the floor with unhidden amusement.

"I didn't do *anything*, I swear," she replied. Her eyes were the size of silver dollars as she looked to each face for an explanation of what had just occurred. They were giving her the same look right back. "He was just standing there…then he wasn't."

Daisley was the first to act, kneeling down and laying two fingers across the man's throat since nobody else had stepped up. He wasn't a doctor by any means but was aware that without a pulse, a man simply couldn't live. Though he wasn't thrilled with the idea of touching the dead man, he was happy that Fisk didn't suddenly jump to life when he checked for signs of life. He would have had a heart attack.

Looking over their crumpled hitman, the detective started doing his job and searched for a clue. It didn't take long for him to find the culprit and begin assigning blame.

"Quartz, you killed this guy," he informed her, looking up from his kneeling position.

"I didn't do a fucking *thing*…."

"You were the only one still in the room with him," Blash pointed out.

"Yeah, Quartz, what'd you do?" Lou jumped in, wiping a sudden wave of sweat from his forehead. "He was kind of a jerk, but you've got to ask somebody before you do something like that."

"I didn't do *anything*," she protested again, her voice rising. "One second he's standing there looking at me like I'm an ice cream cone. A second later, he's falling back and—"

"His right shoe came off," Daisley said, noting the exposed black sock. "He got caught on your carpet, Quartz."

With a gasp, she craned her head behind her and bent her right leg. She could still see the point of the nail that had snagged the strand of synthetic fiber. Kicking off the pair of deadly shoes, she shrunk down to five-foot four and slowly made her way to a chair where she could sit down and think. It was a hard thing to do at the moment.

"We're so screwed," Lou said, whining deeply and bringing both hands to his head. "We are *so* screwed."

"Not me," Blash countered, already making for the door. "I knew this job was going to be crap, but I didn't know it would be this crappy or that the crappy part would start so soon."

"Hold up, Blash," Daisley ordered. "You're not going anywhere."

He stopped instantly, but not because of anything that the detective had said. As Blash was preparing his exit, he was grabbed gently on the back of the neck by the biggest cop in the room.

"He said to hold up, Mike," Lou muttered, unsure of how heavy handed he should get. He was quite sure of the chain of command, however, and decided to fall back on it. If nothing else, he could still follow orders and he expected everyone else to do the same.

"What do you suggest, then?" Blash asked, nearly giving himself whiplash as he violently pulled himself from Lou's grasp.

"Well, I don't suggest leaving this room yet," Daisley answered. "And I think one of you should close the door before someone walks by. We've got a dead guy here."

Realizing that Detective Daisley spoke the truth, Lou and Blash raced each other to the door. While Blash was worried about who might have walked by or be walking by, Lou was more concerned with getting the door shut fast. If they'd gotten their priorities straight sooner, Blash wouldn't have been painfully crushed when Lou slammed it with almost everything he had.

"*God...damn!*" Blash cried loudly as he fell to the floor, wrapping his arms around his chest. "Jesus *Christ*, man. How many of my ribs are you trying to bust, you stupid motherfucker?"

When he saw what he'd done, Lou grimaced and looked to the floor, stepping away from the door and the man he'd nearly broken. More sweat poured from him as he, like Quartz, searched for a chair to drop into.

"Damn, are you okay, Mike?" Daisley asked, unable to focus on any one thing for more than a second or two. "Why don't you lay down on the sofa and...*Jesus!* Would *somebody* shut the fucking *door* please?"

Now the door was hanging open with two men sprawled out on the floor.

Wanting to make herself somewhat useful, Quartz forced herself out of the chair and walked shakily past Blash, who was struggling to massage his lower back. With one finger, she gently pushed the heavy wooden door into a closed position. Letting out a bewildered sigh, she wandered back to her chair.

Daisley stood up and surveyed the three remaining members of his team, then sighed loudly himself. Ignoring Lou, who was sitting with his elbows on his knees and his head in his hands, he checked on Quartz. He watched her hands tremble as she dug around in her purse for a pack of cigarettes. He sincerely hoped she would find some.

Blash still had his pain face on, but had at least pulled himself up against the sofa. It was obvious he was hurting but it didn't look hospital worthy. From what he had seen of the man so far, Daisley guessed that it would take a punctured lung to get him into an emergency room.

"We're screwed," Lou repeated, shaking his head in a complete daze. "I think we're all screwed and we're going to jail. It's right to jail for all of us."

"Quiet down, Lou," Daisley said, attempting to sound relaxed and in control. "Quartz, toss me one of those, will you?"

"Sorry. Last one." She looked up at him with sad eyes as she threw the empty cigarette box to him. She then proceeded to quickly suck down the final cigarette while he watched. Judging from her enthusiasm, he assumed that asking for a drag would have been inappropriate.

"I wonder if this place is paid through the rest of the day," he then mused out loud, hoping that somebody would know. He was beginning to agree with Lou's assessment of the situation; he certainly felt screwed and the jail he'd mentioned was very, very real.

"Checkout's at eleven," Quartz informed him. "It's past noon, so I'd guess the room's solid until tomorrow. Thank God for that."

"Thank God for *what*?" Lou asked, whining again. "They're gonna find us up here with a dead hitman and we're gonna be screwed and we're gonna go to jail. He goes to the morgue—we go to jail. Screwed, screwed, *screwed*."

Blash ignored his pain for the moment and explained the scenario to the big man. "She's saying that we've got twenty-three hours to figure this out, stupid. That's plenty of time for us to get him out of here."

Lou seemed to calm down as Blash's words began to make sense. Maybe they *were* in a hopeless situation—a tougher-than-average spot of trouble, certainly—but they had almost a full day to eliminate or control the damage. It wasn't much comfort, but should have given them a little room to breathe. Unfortunately, Daisley's expression hadn't changed a bit.

"Sorry to contradict you, Mike, but we don't have that kind of time. If all I was worried about was getting his dead ass out of here then we'd be fine. It's not that simple, though."

"*Why not?*" came three voices, almost simultaneously.

"In case you forgot, we've got about a day and a half to kill a guy."

As they looked at each other it was apparent that they had indeed forgotten all about it. On top of disposing of one notorious hitman, they still had only thirty-five hours to turn Christian Roche into a corpse. If it didn't happen in the time allotted, a prison cell would be waiting for each of them.

Chapter 7

"I say we split the work up," Daisley suggested, hoping for a volunteer. "I'll take care of Fisk and make sure he's tucked away in some—"

"Now, *that's* a load of shit," Blash jumped in forcefully. "Why don't the three of us do it while you're burning Ratcliffe's client?"

Daisley could only shrug his shoulders at him. He wasn't sure how it would go from this point on, but being an assassin's replacement simply wasn't going to happen.

"What about splitting into two teams?" Lou offered.

"That might work," Quartz agreed. "As long as I'm on the team that stays here."

Working backup to a hired gun left a bad enough taste in her mouth as it was. If anyone was expecting her to take the lead on a sanctioned murder, they were fooling themselves.

"Me too," Lou agreed, nodding a little too vigorously. "I'll stuff this guy in a bag and carry him down to the dumpster if I need to. Hell, give me something sharp enough and I'll put him in two or three bags. But really, guys—I'm not killing anybody."

"I'm with Lou on this," Blash chimed in, giving Daisley the *What now?* look. "The only prick I was considering taking out myself is laying right there on the floor."

"Well, *someone's* got to do it." Daisley reminded them. "One way or another, this thing has to get done."

"*I know*," the three officers said, almost at the same instant. Staring at each other awkwardly, it was apparent that they seemed to have the same goals.

The question of killing Christian Roche wasn't really a question at all. They all knew it was essential that he didn't make his court date; not necessarily essential to them, but from their individual meetings with Donald Ratcliffe they could tell it was of the utmost important to him. That, in turn, tossed the problem right back into their laps.

"So who's going to do it?" Daisley asked, checking each pair of eyes for a glimmer of interest. "If this doesn't happen, I'm fucked. I'll tell you that right now. I'll be fucked and from the looks on your faces, I'm guessing you'll be fucked too."

Their expressions told him he was right.

"Blash?" Daisley said, holding his palms up flat in an almost pleading gesture. "Come on, man. What do you say?"

"No way, Daisley. And I know what you're thinking. Just because I've burned a few bad guys doesn't mean that it's my job to do the dirty work. And that's what this is, you know. It's dirty as hell."

"There's no doubt that it is, Mike. But we all know you're the one who could pull this off. You've done it before and—"

"Uh...*wrong*," Blash objected. "I've never done *this* before. Yeah, I've killed a guy or two, but I was defending myself and that's a totally different thing all together. I'm not going to blast some unarmed guy who wouldn't even see me coming."

"So that guy Kendall had his sights on you, did he?" Daisley asked, knowing it would draw some kind of response from him.

Mike Blash almost flinched at hearing the name but should have known to expect it. Jonathan Kendall had been the subject of a statewide manhunt only two years earlier and it was just dumb luck that he ended up in Riverside County looking for a fake ID in his effort to flee. He was already wanted for killing one state trooper, but another officer died before Blash had been awarded the honor of dropping him with three shots.

"Kendall was a dangerous man," Blash replied, looking strangely vacant for an instant. "And yeah, he was aiming right at me when I shot him. It was a clean shoot. You can ask around."

"I'm sure it was, Mike, and we can make this one look just as clean."

Blash lifted his shirt and ran a hand over his rapidly bruising ribcage. "Nope, I'm feeling fucked enough as it is, thank you very much."

"Louis?" Daisley begged.

"I can't do it," he replied, but rephrased his answer quickly. "I won't, I mean. I could do it if I had to but I'm not gonna plan ahead for it. And Mike's right—this is too dirty for me to touch."

"The guy's a fucking drug dealer, Louis. And we're not just talking weed either. Coke, heroin—stuff that does nothing but fry young brains. You know how many kids he's killed with his recipes?"

Daisley hoped that he wouldn't ask how many since he was just making it up as he went along. So far, his little pep rally wasn't gathering much steam.

"I don't care, man," Lou replied sadly. "I'm sorry, but I don't. Ask me to bust him and throw his ass in jail—no problem. But I'm not gonna end his life because some lawyer wants me to."

"What would it take, Louis?"

"A fucking act of God, man."

It was clear that Lou wasn't bending. For a man who'd had more than his share of "incidents" with suspects, his principles were pretty tight. Daisley didn't see why the Fresno police officer infamous for breaking arms and legs couldn't simply move higher on the anatomy and break a neck this one time.

"So we're just going to roll over and forget about this?" he asked, looking back and forth between the two men. "Well, that's fine then. You were right, Louis. We're screwed and we're going to jail. Thanks for pointing that out."

This time it was Daisley's turn to flop down into a chair, totally resigned and ready to face the music. He knew that an embarrassing arrest, ugly trial, and prison time would be coming for him as soon as Ratcliffe discovered how badly he'd dropped the ball. Now seemed as good a time as any to get used to the idea.

"What about me?" Quartz asked, crushing out the cigarette that had at least three good drags left on it. "Aren't you going to try to needle me into doing it?"

She'd already basically said she wouldn't, but the fact that he pitched it to the two men so hard left her feeling a little insulted. No, she wouldn't do it, but the least he could do was try to talk her into it.

"Would it help?"

"No, it wouldn't," she admitted. "I already know what I'm capable of and this isn't even close. But with all of our options, I don't see why you're ready to throw in the towel so fast."

"What options? Do you want us to draw straws or something?"

"No, I don't," she replied. "But who says it has to be one of us? I don't know anybody that I'd consider truly knowledgeable in the murder department, but I might be able to think of someone willing to give it a shot. Maybe you guys too."

Seriously, between the four of us, we must have arrested thousands of scumbags. I've got informers and people who owe me one all over the place."

"Me too," Blash blurted out, suddenly looking less beaten. "I'm not saying I've got a name to throw out there, but she's right. If we only had the time to set it up."

Daisley knew immediately that Quartz was right, but he knew Blash was right too; time was the only problem. He could think of several names right off the top of his head. In fact, the more he thought about it—and he didn't need to think very hard—the more names, faces, and various charges jumped out at him. And the true beauty of it was that the charges didn't even matter. Experienced murderers wouldn't be required.

He hadn't cultivated any working relationships with cold-blooded killers lately, but Daisley, as well as the others, knew about a hundred junkies and crack heads who would suck the shit out of a dog's ass if the price was right. He only hoped the ones he was thinking of were still alive, not currently in prison, and were easily accessible. But even if he could get his hands on them, there were still plenty of flaws to the idea.

"Let's say we can find somebody to do this," he began cautiously. "The only reason we know these people is because we've arrested them or even sent them up. How anxious are they going to be to help us out?"

"The guys I'm thinking of would rather see me dead," Blash said, already losing faith in the idea. "That or they'd turn me in to my own department."

"Well, I might know someone," Lou quietly interjected. "There's these two guys I busted just a few months back. Real whack jobs from what I hear. One of my other perps was in a cell with them and tried to make a deal."

"What kind of deal?" Quartz asked as she looked down at the cigarette she had just extinguished and considered relighting it.

"He said they were talking loud about some gangster they killed and he was hoping for some kind of immunity if he'd testify against them. A couple of real nasty characters, I've heard."

"What happened?" Daisley asked.

"Nothing," Lou answered with a shrug. "My perp's lawyer got the charges dropped, he took off without another word about it, and everyone went home. These guys don't really stick around unless you've got something that they want."

Lou's statement was as true as Blash's observations. Most of the criminals he knew weren't on standby, waiting for the day they could offer a favor to the man that had arrested them.

"Well, I don't see any problem with getting a few candidates," Quartz said, surprisingly upbeat. "And I think this whole issue with time can be worked out if we keep our heads on straight."

Daisley wondered if Quartz had even been listening to them talk. "Do you have some magic potion that's going to turn their hearts to gold and make them help us out, or something?"

"No," she replied, climbing out of her chair and stepping to their former killer's body. "But we've got a twenty-five thousand dollar donation towards a new employee. I don't think Mr. Fisk will mind too much."

I wonder if he smokes, Quartz thought as she began rifling through the dead man's pockets.

Chapter 8

▼

Room service was expensive but money was no object today. Before doing another thing, they decided to eat some lunch. Regardless of how things went, they were definitely going to need some strength to get through the next day and a half since just cramming Fisk's body into the ridiculously small bedroom closet seemed to take a lot out of the group.

After eating the rich hotel food at a sickeningly fast pace, it was time to fish around for some information. Following a trip to the gift shop for some much needed cigarettes, Quartz and Blash retrieved every piece of equipment they had from the one car they had driven. A quick inventory revealed their four individual cellular phones and two laptop computers.

"I hope you've got some high priority access," Blash commented as they plugged in the modem cable and fired up one of the laptops. "That database is huge and takes forever to spit anything out."

"Well, we're not going to be doing random searches, Mike." Daisley had to speak up to be heard over Lou and Quartz who were already busy working the phones. "You just give me the names and I'll give you their status."

"Try William Bishop. He's a desperate fucking loser junkie, but kicking ass for dollars has been his game for a while now. Last I heard, he relocated south somewhere but you never know. He might have come back to LA or Orange County if—"

"He's dead," Daisley stated as the information hit his screen faster than it should have. "The dead files come up quicker since the information never changes. It didn't happen very long ago. Gunshot. Drug related. Sorry, Mike."

"Yeah, I give a shit—try Drake Melton," Blash continued without even blinking. "His last address was in Norco I think."

The detective pounded on the small keyboard and hoped for the best, though the news he ended up with wasn't very good at all. At this point he was just happy to get the bad news at lightning speed.

"No, it was Upland. Drake's dead too, pal. Give me another one and get me the names of Louis and Quartz's top guys. Maybe we can save some time."

"Try, uh...Baker. Tim or Jim—something like that. What was that dude's name?" Blash quietly interrupted Lou. "Your top five choices—give them to me."

Lou cradled the phone uncomfortably in his ear and wrote down five names for him. When he was finished with the call, he scratched another name off of his own list. "Well, that one's back in prison. Man, I told that boy to keep his nose clean."

The irony of his statement made Blash's ribs hurt worse than they already did. He took a look at Lou's list of four felons. "We'll check these for you. Keep going, though. They can't all be dead or locked up."

He asked Quartz for her top five then ran back to Daisley. "John...I'm sure of it. John Baker. Give it a try." He bounced right back to Quartz to grab her list.

"There are forty-seven John Bakers in here, Mike. Where's he live?"

"Chino back then and I haven't got a clue about the fucker now. I busted him for distribution, but I think he also committed some armed robberies. He moved around a lot so I can't be sure if he's still local."

"Oh, he's local all right," Daisley said as the information rolled across the screen. "And he's still in Chino. Right in the men's correctional facility. Give me some of Lou's names."

The tension, volume, and anxiety rose steadily for the next two hours as the lists began to run dry. Finding a live felon with a history of some sort of violence was very easy. Finding one that they had arrested made the job a little harder. Finding one that they felt they knew well enough, or could at least control, was proving very difficult. With two hours behind them, the short list of candidates wasn't very promising. Aside from Lou, nobody was left with their first choice.

Amazingly, Lou's pair of psychopaths weren't in prison and, in fact, had no rap sheets whatsoever. Aside from their short stay in a jail in Fresno where Lou had picked them up, neither had spent a single day behind bars. Even then, they hadn't been charged with anything and were released. This told him two things. They were incredibly smart and they could handle themselves well enough to stay alive and out of prison. They sounded perfect and were given to Lou as his assignment.

"I can't guarantee anything with these guys," Lou said with his usual shrug. "But they ought to be a good place to start. I've got two names and two addresses. I hope it's enough to find them."

It better be, Daisley thought as he gave Quartz a hard look and confirmed her assignment. "Are you sure yours will be up to it?" he asked, trying hard not to sound like an enormous asshole. "She doesn't look like shit on paper."

"Netta's a bad girl," Quartz replied, hoping to say as little about the woman as she could get away with. "You'll have to trust me on that. If that address is correct—and it probably won't be—I'm pretty sure she'd work for us. She's a looker, too. That might make it easier."

"She's never been picked up for anything other than…let's see…possession, vagrancy and breaking and entering." Daisley wasn't sounding too enthused. "Are you sure that she's—"

"I know a few things—the kind of things that wouldn't appear on a rap sheet, if you know what I mean."

"Good enough. She's all yours."

Quartz let herself relax momentarily. They were nowhere near out of the woods yet but she had an assignment and that meant they were moving forward. As long as they could remain active and busy she felt like there could be hope for them.

"Blash, is this the best that you can do?" Daisley asked, reading the specs on their final candidate. "Walter Van Staadt? Are you fucking kidding me?"

"Why not?" Blash asked, pretending not to know how desperate his last choice seemed.

"We're looking for killers, Mike. I don't see where this guy's different from any other dealer out there."

"There's a big difference. I know this one and I can control him."

"But what can he do for us?" Daisley asked, seeing nothing on the man's sheet to indicate a violent streak. "A couple of drug busts doesn't tell me anything."

"Just leave him to me. If Walter can't figure it out, I'll tear off one of his arms and beat Roche to death with it."

It would never come to that, of course, but the man he was thinking of didn't need to be violent to be effective. He also didn't need to be informed about every little detail of what he was doing or why he was doing it. Sometimes ignorance was bliss…and just as effective.

"He'll come up with something," Blash said, wishing he sounded a little more sure of himself.

Daisley was hoping for solid solutions, not three sets of improvised madness. Realizing that they were relying on the assistance of four uncertainties, he decided to stay out of the recruiting business and stick to command and control.

"Does everyone have their phones?" he asked as he closed up his laptop. "I'll be running around like mad and I'll need constant updates."

Quartz, Blash and Lou held up their cellular phones so he could physically *see* the devices that they had all been talking loudly on for the last two hours. Quickly, they scrawled each cellular number on four sheets of paper so anyone could be reached at a moment's notice.

"What'll you be doing?" Lou asked, curious as to Daisley's lack of a candidate to track down.

"I'll be getting you guys what you need. Depending on how this goes, we may need some extra supplies or things we haven't thought of yet. You can also bet that I'm going to do my best to defuse this thing before it even gets started."

"Wouldn't that be nice?" Quartz sighed wishfully.

"Yeah, keep dreaming, sweetie," Blash replied. "I don't know if I'd be able to pull this off if I had a week to do it. Even if I started right now, it would be iffy. As it is, we've got a two hour drive just to get back to our cars."

"Crap, I forgot about that," Lou said, thinking that it was the worst news he'd receive for at least another ten minutes. He was wrong.

"Not you, Louis." Daisley was checking his watch. "You said something about carrying Fisk down to the dumpster?"

"Whoa, guys—I've got shit to do now. And this is a big fucking hotel. Ditching a body here isn't a one man job."

"Do what you've got to do. Whatever it takes."

"But I don't have a *car*."

"I'm sorry, Louis. You've got plenty of cash for a cab ride. You just do whatever you have to."

"Thanks, guys...really." Lou could do nothing more than shake his head as they filed towards the door. "Not even a garment bag to wrap the son of a bitch up in. Great."

"We'll see you sometime tonight," Daisley said, hoping he was speaking the truth. "And remember, Louis. Fisk was never here. You do whatever it takes."

A fucking act of God, Lou thought to himself for the second time in a day. *That's what it's gonna take.* The door closed and he was suddenly alone.

Chapter 9

"That was cruel and not too smart, Daisley." Blash watched the tall building get smaller as they drove away from it. "We should have stuck around and done it together."

He could see where Blash was coming from but keeping his eye on the big picture was what concerned him at the moment. He didn't like the idea of leaving Lou there either; it was a simple matter of realistic expectations. "Louis's guys are a pipe dream. It's not going to happen. I don't think he could even track them down, much less get them to accept an offer from him. What would *you* think if a cop asked you to kill someone?"

"I guess I'd suspect a setup," Blash replied dryly, then looked back to Quartz. "And we're both going to run into the same problem."

"We might," Quartz agreed. "But my girl is smarter than most. She knows what we can and can't do legally. I don't know about you, but I'll be able to convince her that I mean what I say."

"I'll just have to put enough fear into my guy so he doesn't question anything," Blash replied. "If I can find him, I'll put his ass to work. I've got almost two hours to think about what I'm going to do, but I'll tell you what's bugging me right now."

"What's that?" they both asked.

"I'm wondering what Lou's going to do with Quartz's stiff."

"I told you, Mike. I wasn't even near him."

"Would you guys shut up please?" Daisley begged. "It wasn't anyone's fault. Bad luck—that's it."

"Bad luck for *Lou*," Blash uttered quietly and stared out the window.

"He's the only one big enough to carry the guy down twenty flights of stairs if it comes to that," Daisley pointed out. "I know it'll be a little tough on him, but what else could we do? Have the four of us each grab a limb and carry him through the fucking lobby? We can't afford to waste time on things that won't work."

"And leaving Lou to dispose of a body achieves what?" Quartz asked.

"It fixes a problem and gets his dumb ass out of the way while we go to work." He'd already let Quartz know how he felt about Louis anyway. Checking Blash's expression, he was satisfied that they were all in agreement. "Now, how about you two getting busy? Use your phones or the radio and find out what these people of yours have been up to."

Chapter 10

I can't believe it took them so long to leave. With Officer Blash and the two detectives gone, Lou felt relieved for the first time since Fisk had fallen and couldn't get up. He had been condescended to quite enough this morning and was happy for some peaceful solitude. Thinking a little alone time with their VIP was just what he needed, he grabbed Terrence Fisk by the lapels of his jacket and lowered himself to within inches of face.

"Hello there, handsome," he said, grinning at the man who, only a half hour earlier, had made light of his limited whistling skills. "How fucking stupid do I look now?"

Yanking him violently with two larges hands, Lou pulled Fisk unceremoniously from the small closet and let him drop to the floor. With more room to work now, he hoisted the man up and tossed him face down on the bed.

"You're lucky they left you with me, pal. That guy Blash would probably be fucking your ass right about now. He didn't like you too much, you know."

He only chuckled a little bit at the sick visual that played in his head before deciding it probably wasn't funny at all. He shook off the disrespectful image before stepping to the window and checking around the edges for any kind of hinge. Judging from the way the building looked from the outside, he assumed that the glass was merely cosmetic, giving the structure a shiny uniformity. He found he was right since none of the windows were made to open up.

"You know what I was just thinking, don't you? Sure you do, my poor suicidal friend. I wouldn't do it from here, though. You know that, right? I'd take you a few floors up to someone else's room—like it matters now."

Fisk had no response for him as Lou paced around the room.

No problem...no problem. There's got to be a million ways to do this. Moving back to the bed, he flipped the man over and grabbed him by the collar of his shirt.

"Out with it, asshole," he ordered, shaking Fisk's head back and forth. "What would *you* do in this situation? You're the professional. Just give me a clue."

Once again, Fisk had no reply and it made him happy. The job was probably already permanently botched, but at least he had the satisfaction of humiliating the corpse of a truly bad individual. Not just a little bad, but *truly* bad. Bringing his arm back, he slapped Fisk once across the face.

"How do you like that shit, tough guy?"

He felt more powerful than usual as he hovered over the body and guessed it was the same way his older brother had felt when he used to pin him to the floor and torture him. Remembering it like it was only moments ago instead of thirty years, he climbed onto the assassin and picked up two limp arms. After waving them around for a moment, he slammed a semi-fisted dead hand down onto Fisk's nose.

"Why are you doing that?" he asked, roaring with laughter as he did it. Then he did it again. And again and again. "Why are you hitting yourself, dummy? *Stop it. Don't do that.* You'd better quit doing that before someone gets hurt."

The cheap thrill of forced self-brutalization only lasted for a minute or two since harassing a target that didn't fight back lost its appeal very quickly. It also brought on the realization—thirty years too late—that he could have avoided a lot of humiliation from his older brother if he hadn't struggled so much.

"Okay, seriously now," he sighed, crossing Fisk's arms across his chest. "You're an important man, buddy. I can't just stuff you under the bed like a dead hooker. We've got to think of something good. I've got people counting on me and you're holding me up."

What would a mob shooter do? Think mafia. Think serial killer. Or how about thinking like a cop for a change? What would Starsky and Hutch do? Or Steve McGarret from Hawaii Five-0?

Most people probably didn't even remember those guys but Lou had always liked the old TV show cops. His interest had been renewed a few years earlier while he was laid up with an injury after taking down a suspect. It was just a groin pull and a sprained ankle but he couldn't work, which gave him little to do beside spending two weeks in front of his TV.

He hadn't even thought of *Kojak* since he was a kid, but there he would be. Telly Savalas; alive and on his television screen. The bald man was decades out of date but Lou didn't care. Likewise, Robert Blake from *Baretta* was still walking free and helping to put the bad guys away instead of being put away himself for shooting his wife in the head. They were all cardboard cutout throwbacks from eons ago but he'd felt like calling the TV station and thanking them personally for the privilege of viewing them again.

Starting with *The Streets of San Francisco* at eleven, he'd eat lunch and then watch Tony Baretta solve a crime. At one o'clock, Kojak kept him busy until Starsky pulled up in that nifty red car with the big white swoosh across it. By three in the afternoon he and Detective Hutchinson had found a clue and saved the girl. After that he'd do an hour's worth of prescribed stretches and move about slowly. He didn't really care for *Ironside* anyway and he couldn't just sit in one place all day.

Lou had never liked watching Raymond Burr push himself around in a wheelchair even though it had made him feel better about his own situation at the time. As painful as his injuries were, having a twisted ankle and tweaked nuts was preferable not being able to walk at all. He was sure that his current assignment would agree wholeheartedly.

"Some people would tell you that you were lucky, man—to be dead, I mean," he clarified. "A shot on the back of the head like you got could have caused a spinal injury. Then where would you be?"

Just like Ironside. Legs getting all shriveled up from doing nothing all day. Arms tired all the time from rolling after the bad guys. Having to look for an access ramp if the perp he was chasing happened to step up onto a fucking curb. Stuck in a goddamn wheelchair while all the other guys had—

Lou, you fucking moron. Though brilliance was years beyond Lou's capabilities, he knew a good idea when he heard it; even when it came from his own head, which wasn't terribly often.

"You just hang tight, pal. I know this isn't a hospital, but they've got to have something like that around here someplace, don't you think?"

It seemed simple enough. If he was lucky enough to find a wheelchair, all he'd have to do is toss the guy into it and roll him right out the front door. Once he had him in the car, his options would be endless.

"What do you think, loser? Can I trust you not to take off on me?" he asked, shouting into the bedroom from the doorway. Hearing no response, he walked back to the bedroom and poked his head in. "You still dead over there?"

Still no response.

"Okay, I'll quit asking. Just stay that way and we're cool."

He checked the time and walked out of the expensive suite for what he hoped would be a very brief jaunt around the hotel. He paused outside the door for few seconds, getting the feeling—a very familiar sensation—that he was about to fuck something up really bad. Sometimes the feeling arrived a few hours too late but this time, fortunately, it came upon him a couple of seconds early.

Only a moment before the door could shut behind him did he realize that no one had left him a room key. He stopped it with his foot and went back inside, knowing that if he wanted to go out and forage for a wheelchair, he was going to have to leave the door ajar while he did it. Stepping back into the suite, he returned to the bedroom for a rare brainstorming session and was unhappy with what he saw. Terrence Fisk was exactly as he had left him—and he looked really, really bad.

More than that, he looked really, really dead.

He pulled back the covers and dragged Fisk towards the headboard and when his head hit the pillow, Lou bent his legs in and turned him on his side. As he tucked the killer in, he left an arm hanging out for maximum realism, hoping that it would pass inspection if something unthinkable occurred.

As he walked to the desk on the far side of the room he made sure that the hitman under the sheets looked like a sleeping man from every possible angle. It was perfect.

He began to whistle as he dug through the desk drawers and by the time he located a roll of scotch tape and had applied a few strips to the door latch, he was feeling like it was all going a little too smoothly. He couldn't deny that the whole thing had been a disaster from the start, but Lou could sense that his end of the disaster was holding up nicely.

Chapter 11

Walking the halls of the fourteenth floor, he was amazed at how much everything looked alike. Each hallway led to another hallway that looked exactly the same as the one before it. Even the vending machines and ice makers were situated the same way at every intersection. For a man who became confused easily, the fourteenth floor was scarier than a cemetery at midnight.

Not finding anything other than closed doors, he decided that the lobby would be the next step. He hadn't been on any other floors yet but figured they'd look just like this one. He would have been right.

Fortunately, he didn't have to check out the other floors or even the lobby. Before he could locate the elevator to go downstairs he found exactly what he'd been hoping for. It wasn't one of the swanky electric ones that could practically drive itself but it would do the job just fine. As long as it could roll, it would do.

Though he didn't have a shiny detective shield, his regular police ID made the wheelchair acquisition a piece of cake. It was given up with hardly a struggle at all. Guiding the beast through the hallway took some getting used to.

At first he tried to push it like a shopping cart and it simply wasn't cooperating. By the time he figured out that it was the front wheels that did the steering he was almost back to the room.

He could feel that it was close. It was the one that would push open without needing a key. That was all he had to go on considering he'd already forgotten the room number.

Beginning to panic, he felt slightly better when he remembered that it started with the numbers one and four. It should have been enough to go on but, amazingly, every room on the fourteenth floor started with those same two numbers.

Lou was beginning to feel sicker to his stomach with each turn he took and no matter where he went, the same hallway was there to greet him. It was the same thing over and over. That was when he parked the chair and started running.

Giving a light shove on each door that he passed, Lou prayed that the next one would be his. After the first twenty or so wouldn't budge he picked up the pace, determined to make it out of the hotel in the next ten minutes. Five minutes and thirty-five doors later he was still out of luck as he ran back into the wheelchair he'd left behind. Somewhere along the line he had turned around without realizing it.

"How many rooms does this goddamn floor have?" he asked himself louder than he meant to.

If I'm gonna find room fourteen twenty-six I need to find the elevator that I came up in and try to remember which way I turned after I—

Fucking moron. He rolled his eyes and wiped more sweat off of his forehead, furious with himself but grateful that information could fly back into his head as quickly as it had disappeared.

Fourteen twenty-six. Fourteen twenty-six. Fourteen twenty-six.

He retrieved the chair in a hurry and was elated to find that his room was just four doors down from where he'd left it. If this was what passed for luck, he was happy to get it. With one light push, the door swung open and things were as he'd left them. By now he felt it was a miracle that he didn't find a chambermaid flipping Fisk's inanimate form over so she could change the sheets.

"It's time to go," he called out, closing the door behind him. "I've got, like, two minutes to get you downstairs, so quit screwing around."

Feeling good that nothing incriminating had been left in the suite, he uncovered Fisk and threw him into the wheelchair, which wasn't as hard as he thought it would be. Making him look natural was another story. Just keeping the man propped up was a chore and even after a good amount of twisting and maneuvering, he still looked like a dead guy in a wheelchair.

Returning to the desk, Lou picked up the scotch tape and got to work.

In less than a minute Fisk was bound and sitting semi-straight, strapped to the chair at the ankles and wrists with long strips of the cheapest adhesive on the planet. He still looked dead, but in motion he'd at least be somewhat animated. It also helped that his eyes were slightly open. It was terribly gross from Lou's point of view but from an outsider's perspective, Fisk would look like a mildly drunk quadriplegic.

The eerie sight would also help distract any curious onlookers from the parts of scotch tape that couldn't be hidden by sleeves or pant legs. He gave the chair a shove and they rolled into the hallway.

"Now, try to keep quiet until we're outside," Lou suggested, feeling that this was one request that would be respected.

*   *   *   *

The trip through the lobby was as uneventful as he'd hoped. Aside from a few impolite stares, nobody seemed to mind sharing their space with a man who would probably begin to decompose very soon.

Even though he knew from experience that his passenger wouldn't start stinking badly for a while, Lou appreciated the fact that Fisk didn't foul himself when his body ceased functioning. More than a few of the dead people he had the misfortune of discovering had been found with crap in their trousers. He was always embarrassed for the poor lifeless bastards and prayed that when his number was up, his body would have the decency to hang on to whatever shit was in the on-deck circle…at least until he was in a box.

Let's do our best to keep our turds a private thing if we ever get capped, was his main thought as he rolled Fisk out through the main entrance. Since ditching their VIP within the hotel itself had never really been any kind of realistic option, Lou decided to put some distance between himself and the last place that Fisk might have been seen before planting him in an out of the way location.

He started for the car but only got ten feet down the sidewalk before suddenly remembering that he was several minutes over on his wheelchair rental—though it was only a minor issue when compared to the fact that he couldn't remember where the car was. After a full minute of jerking his head back and forth between the lobby, the street, and the hotel's parking structure, he recalled Detective Daisley saying something about calling a taxi.

At the time, he hadn't been sure if the comment was intended to be sarcastic or not. He was pretty sure he knew the answer now.

Well, here we are on a crowded sidewalk in front of the Westin Bonaventure in broad daylight. Me, one very exposed dead guy, no wheels. He spun the wheelchair around and went back the way he came.

As he reentered the lobby, he was already scanning the room for a telephone book. It was apparent that a cab would solve his immediate problem of transportation but it wouldn't do a thing for his situation with Fisk. What he needed was a vehicle that would afford him some freedom of movement and privacy. He pushed the chair to a bank of courtesy phones, having only a rough idea what he was looking for, and prepared to call somebody for a ride. That was when one of the several dozen stickers posted around the telephone jumped out at him.

It wasn't an ad for a cab company or shuttle service. It was a rental agency.

He was familiar with Avis, Enterprise, and Hertz, but this wasn't one of them. He'd rented cars from each of them and was usually pleased with the mid-sized sedans they set him up with. These guys were different, though. The name said it all.

High Performance Rentals, huh? I'll bet they're expensive.

Chapter 12

By the time Louis Poklatar finished thinking the word *expensive*, he had dialed all seven digits and was speaking to a rental agent. Pending verification of his identification and other information, he could expect his car to be delivered in front of the lobby of the Westin Bonaventure Hotel in roughly twenty minutes. It was all the time Lou would need before he set off to track down two young men he had arrested almost a year earlier while getting rid of one pesky dead man at the same time.

For this part of it, Fisk would be forced to fend for himself while Lou made the best use of the few minutes he had.

After only a few subtle adjustments, the assassin looked human enough. He had been stripped of his scotch tape without so much a sideways glance, then was seated in the lobby, appearing to be dozing.

Just from a quick look around, he could tell that the business travelers and tourists alike chose their spots so that they would be as far away from anyone as possible while they made their calls and arrangements. Maybe in smaller towns people were more comfortable with huddling together as they worked, but this was LA. Being in close proximity with a living, breathing person was something that most of them would rather not have to put up with.

The fact that Fisk was dead might have even encouraged a native Los Angeleno to draw closer. As it was, he was in the middle without a soul within ten chairs on either side. The hope was that he'd be safe enough for a little while at least. Looking at his watch for the tenth time in five minutes, Lou drew in a deep breath, abandoned the man he was responsible for, and started pushing the chair again.

It took about four more minutes for him to get back to the fourteenth floor. Sharing the elevator with several busy city dwellers, he felt badly for taking up so much room in the enclosed space while people were trying to get on with their lives.

The feeling only lasted until he got his first dirty look.

Lou supposed he could have done a better job folding up the chair up to make room for a few more of these insensitive imbeciles, but felt much less inclined to do so with the first glare from an impatient businessman who had to separate from the rest of his party. It meant a delay of a whole minute and a half for the man, which apparently warranted a tiring sigh and a smug glance.

"Sorry about the size of this thing," Lou offered with an apologetic smile and one of his more pathetic shrugs. "I couldn't fold it up right."

Expecting a sympathetic gesture in return, he was met instead by a blank face that had a look of superiority painted all over it. The man looked at his watch and rolled his eyes while tapping his foot. If not for the five other people in the small elevator, Lou knew deep down that he would have dismantled him right then and there. With a brief look in the man's direction, his eyes told him exactly that.

In a somewhat surprising gesture, the businessman in the charcoal gray suit caught the look and stared down with a light smile. He shook his head in a fashion that Lou heard loud and clear.

You wish you could get a piece of me, you dumb fucking retard. If you lay a solitary finger on me, I'll sue your ass off.

He actually *heard* it in his head. And not just the words, either. He heard the tone, the pitch, the inflection—everything. It was one of the main reasons for his participation the day's happenings.

When the elevator stopped on the seventh floor, it cleared out almost completely. Shoved in the corner with his obtrusive wheelchair, Lou watched all but one of his comrades depart. He could see the wheels turning as his uptight businessman considered bailing out a few floors early. For some reason—probably an assumption that Lou wasn't about to go right out of his mind—the man remained.

The instant the door closed and they were isolated from the rest of the world, Lou calmly stepped forward and hit the *Stop* button. Then just as calmly, he turned to the only other occupant and shoved his ID into the man's face, causing the look of self-imagined strength and power to melt away before Lou could complete a blink of his eyes. It was clear he had so much he wanted to say but, for some reason, he couldn't quite get the words out.

Lou could speak just fine, though.

"Let's start with who the fuck you think you are. Can't you see I've got a wheelchair here? Does that tell you anything?" There were sounds in response, but nothing that resembled words as the man floundered for an explanation. "How about I take your dirty looks and shove them up your ass for you? How'd that be?"

"I'm sorry, officer. I didn't think this was—"

"I didn't ask for an apology," Lou barked, bringing his face close as he cornered the man who had already effectively cornered himself. "And I don't care what you thought. You see this chair?"

The man looked at it quickly then nodded.

"What do you suppose it's for?" Lou asked, trying a technique that had been used against himself more times than he could count.

He had learned over the years that when asked a question that was painfully obvious, it was best not to answer. If you answered in the positive, you received a smack in the head and a look that told you that you should have figured it out sooner. If you answered negatively, you were smacked in the head and corrected quickly.

"I don't know. I guess there's someone that needs a—"

"—a wheelchair," Lou finished for him. "That's exactly right, smart guy. Somebody needs this. I'm taking this thing up to them and…you…you…you're giving me the eye like I'm taking up your valuable space or something. Am I invading your personal space? Is that what I'm doing?"

"No…no, officer. I just…"

It wouldn't have mattered what the man said. Lou could feel a painful itch developing deep in his skull. It was the same itch he had every time he lost his cool and shattered the bones of some unfortunate, foolish person who'd said the wrong thing at the wrong time.

But his businessman was guilty of nothing more than sheer arrogance—even Lou could see that. And as quickly as it came, the feeling subsided.

Once he was satisfied that the scare would stick with the man for at least a couple of weeks, Lou stepped back and released the *Stop* button. "I've got a person upstairs who needs this. Do you think it's too much for me to ask that I get this thing up there without any shit from a fucking nobody like you?"

"No sir, not at all," the man stammered.

Lou turned his back on him and finally accepted the apology. "Thanks, that's sweet of you."

He could still hear the man in the charcoal gray suit breathing heavily behind him as the elevator shifted into life again. When it ground to halt at the twelfth floor, Lou barely glimpsed a gray blur fly by him as the man scooted swiftly from the glass box of death he was sure he would be trapped inside. Dashing to a meeting that he was still early for, he was gone in a flash.

Though Lou would never know about it, his arrogant businessman would require over forty-five minutes of self-motivation and a serious talking to by his boss before he could engage in any business negotiations. Even after a valium and a double-shot of rum, he was still essentially unable to function without shaking visibly. In short, his day and a deal worth forty-million dollars to his client went down the toilet because he was rude to the wrong guy.

By the time the double doors closed and the elevator was moving again, Lou had already forgotten about him.

Thirty seconds later, the doors opened on the fourteenth floor. Looking left then right, he bolted from the elevator and ran towards room fourteen twenty-six. It wasn't the room he was looking for, but the set of vending machines just down the hall. They were the third set of machines to the right of his old room if he was remembering correctly. Fortunately, he got this one right.

Breathing a sigh of relief, he paused as he pulled up next to the ice maker and locked the brakes of the wheelchair. Gently, he extended a hand downward and smiled as nice as he could.

"I can't even begin to tell you how much I appreciate this, ma'am. You've been a life saver, lady. A real life saver."

"You don't need to bother with any thank-you's, son," the elderly woman replied as Lou lifted her up and expertly guided her into the chair. "If I had more to offer you in your police work, I'd give it up in a second, young man. I hope it helped you."

"It helped out a lot, ma'am—more than you know. Really."

Her sweet smile and gentle eyes made him feel deceptive. Here was the sweetest old lady in the world and he'd lied to her to get his hands on her only means of transportation. It was only for a little more than fifteen minutes but he felt filthy as he unlocked the brakes and wheeled her away from the row of vending machines.

"Which room is it again?"

"I'm right here in one-four-three-three," she answered, pulling out her key. "I can't wait to get home and tell my grandkids about this."

She appeared to be in her late eighties at least and, though she'd been left for a quarter hour on an uncomfortable bench-seat in a hotel hallway, she seemed enthralled with the whole ordeal. Lou had been in a hurry and made up a story for her on the spot, unable to even remember exactly what lie he'd told her.

He smiled pleasantly and held the door for her as she rolled into the room. "Once again, ma'am—I truly can't thank you enough."

"I was glad to help, Officer Poklatar," she replied, waving off the overabundance of gratitude. "And I hope you were able to get that dead man out of your room without anyone being the wiser."

With that, the door closed behind her, leaving Lou alone in the hallway to marvel at the latest depths of his own thoughtlessness. Knowing there wasn't much time for marveling, he took two big gulps of air and dashed back to the elevator.

Dead guy in the lobby. Dead guy in the lobby. Don't forget about the dead guy in the lobby.

He repeated the words in his head, hoping he wouldn't get distracted by anything in the two minutes it would take him to get back downstairs.

Chapter 13

▼

"Score one for me," Blash muttered with minimal enthusiasm, pulling the cell phone from his ear as he turned to Daisley. "I just got the word. Walter Van Staadt is still at the same address he was when I busted him before. It's just over in Norco. When we get back to Corona, I can be there in a flash."

"I know you *can* be, Mike, but it's whether you *should* be that's bugging me. How sure are you about this druggie friend of yours?"

"Not sure at all," Blash replied bluntly. "And Van Staadt is as much a friend of mine as that fuckhead lawyer Ratcliffe is a friend of yours, so let's not hear that shit again."

"That's not what I was saying."

"Well, that's definitely what I was hearing. Did you hear that, Quartz?"

"Yeah, I heard it too," she replied from the back seat. "But that's not what he meant and you know it. Like me, he's just curious about what a non-felon, non-violent offender can actually do for us. Right, Andrew?"

"Exactly. It's nothing personal, Mike. I think it's great that we've got something solid to work with—I'm just not holding my breath, if you know what I mean."

It was true; as nice as it was to have made a little progress, Daisley didn't think that Van Staadt would add up to anything. None of them did. But it would only be Mike Blash's waste of time and as far as Daisley was concerned, anything that would keep him out of earshot for a few hours could only be described as a good thing.

"And don't get me started on Ratcliffe," Daisley continued. "That guy's not a friend to anyone; especially cops."

Quartz leaned forward, putting herself between them. "But I'll bet he changes his tune when he starts working for the DA's office."

"There's no doubt he will," Blash agreed, staring out the window. "Which means we're the last batch of good guys he gets to treat like shit on his shoe. Does that make us special or something?"

"It sure does," Daisley replied. "Special in the worst way possible. But you know the benefits. It'll all even out when this thing's over."

With gritted teeth and as much patience as he could muster, Blash turned slowly to the detective behind the wheel. It was the first time anyone had mentioned the benefits of the job they were given. "What do you know about it?"

"Specifically…I don't know anything. But I know Ratcliffe wanted you for a reason. He wouldn't have given me your name if he didn't think you'd say yes."

"In case you don't remember, I said *no*."

"Sure, I remember, Mike. But here you are. I know *I* didn't talk you into it—I'm not that good a salesman. Should I assume you changed your mind all on your own?"

"Do me a favor and don't make any assumptions about me, okay? The way I see it, Ratcliffe had you pitch the job to me because you said no to him first. And if that's the case then there must be some good reason you're still involved."

"Listen, Mike…"

"Let's not bullshit each other here," Blash continued, twisting in his seat so he could address both Daisley and Quartz at the same time. "Here's what should've happened: Ratcliffe hits you up to whack out a client who's sure to botch his perfect record. You say 'Fuck you' to the guy and contact the DA's office yourself. Hours later the fucker's suspended. A month later he's disbarred. Maybe a few months after that he goes up for conspiracy to commit murder." Blash was practically spitting the words out, moving his eyes from Daisley to Quartz rapidly. "This motherfucking lawyer should be in prison but somehow not only does he *not* go to jail, but now he's got me, one big retarded street cop, two detectives, and a real live professional killer working for him. Well, make that a real *dead* professional killer, but that's beside the point."

"Then what *is* the point, Mike?" Daisley asked.

"I'm just saying…" Blash paused, feeling that Daisley hadn't earned himself an answer to anything just yet. Turning to Quartz, he spoke directly to her instead. "It's obvious that we're all doing something that we don't want to do and, for one reason or another, we're doing it anyway. I just want you to know that I'm not dirty. Even if Daisley is, it's important to me for everyone involved to know that I'm not. Daisley doesn't know me—you do. A minute ago he implied that Ratcliffe might have evidence that I was dirty and was using it against me so I'd help out on this job. Tell the detective here that it isn't true."

She didn't hesitate. "He's right, Andrew. Mike's a good cop."

"I never said he wasn't."

"No, you didn't," Blash allowed. "But you *implied* it and I'm just letting you know that you're wrong. I'm not in the mood to explain why I'm here, but you'd better know it's not because I'm a piece of shit dirty cop who's playing both sides."

"Well, I'm sorry then." The short sentence had all the makings of an apology but Daisley's tone wasn't anywhere near conciliatory. It wasn't exactly sarcastic, but wasn't penitent either. "I'm sure we've all got our own reasons for being in this and if I implied that you weren't on the level, I didn't mean anything by it."

Blash had no reply for him and didn't waste his time trying to think of one.

Not enjoying the uncomfortable silence, Daisley decided to make sure they were all on the same page and spoke again. "And just so you know, I've got my own reasons for this too. Ratcliffe doesn't own me."

There was still no immediate reply. Blash remained silent for over a minute before bothering to acknowledge the detective again. His response was uttered softly, as though he was whispering the words to himself. But he wasn't.

"Fucking liar."

Chapter 14

Mike Blash hadn't even thought about Walter Van Staadt since the day he'd personally walked him into the station. Suddenly, the little man was back in his head again, though he seemed slightly more important than when he had been arrested during a narcotics sweep over a year earlier. If he was remembering him correctly, Walter was more of a danger to himself than to others. But he had potential.

He'd been pulled in with twenty-six others who happened to be at the same club at the same time, all doing roughly the same thing. It seemed like a pretty standard drug bust at first; grass, coke, heroin, meth—all the usual suspects. Then there was Walter. He was a little different.

* * * *

"Okay, I've run this through every test we've got," the man in the lab coat told him, holding up a small vial of clear fluid to the light. "And I don't know what the hell it is."

"It's drugs, though, right?" Blash asked, hoping the man understood that in order to arrest people for possession of drugs, a certain amount of drugs had to be present. The other twenty-six that were caught with their misdemeanor-sized stashes on them were already in lock up. There hadn't been anything going on with the group that he considered to be serious but he knew the number *twenty-seven* would sound impressive to whoever heard it. He was becoming impatient with his final holdout.

"It's not like any of the stuff that the rest of them had," the man noted, daring to take a whiff from the tiny bottle. "Smells like water to me. It acts like it too.

It's pH is at seven it's perfectly clear and has the same density as tap water at room temperature."

"What does that mean?" Blash asked, not feeling ignorant in the slightest. Usually he didn't care about such things since it wasn't his job, but this one was making him angry.

"Basically, there are all kinds of ways to tell what a certain fluid is. I'm talking about inside the lab. Basic stuff like checking for cloudiness, weight…."

"*Weight?*"

"Yeah, weight, density, salinity, chlorine and fluoride levels. It can tell a lot about your fluid here. This stuff is pure. But pure *what?*—I don't know."

"This is exactly the kind of crap I didn't want to hear. What does it mean?"

"It means that if this is something that's supposed to be on the Schedule I controlled substances list, I can't tell you what it is. If it's a narcotic or hallucinogenic, it's camouflaged big-time. Was there any more of it?"

"He was the only one carrying the stuff."

"Has he peed for you yet?"

"You know we can't make him do that," Blash replied. "Aside from guilt by association and that bottle there, we can't even hold him. That's why I'm here with you, genius."

Though the highly educated man wasn't used to being spoken to in such a fashion, he lowered his voice to a whisper anyway and pitched Blash the same offer he gave to every other cop he'd done work for. "If it's really important that you hang on to the guy for a little while, we could always dummy this up with a little—"

"Man, would you shut the fuck up?" Blash spat out, shaking his head angrily at the lab tech who didn't appear to have any issues with manufacturing evidence. It had always been a touchy subject for him. "It's not like I'm gonna tell your supervisor about this—lucky you—so you may as well stop shitting your pants and just do your fucking job. Now, be a sweetheart and tell me what's in the bottle."

"I would if I could," he replied, hoping his sigh of relief wasn't too obvious. "If we can get some urine, we might have a clue what he's taken. Then, if we can isolate what he's on, then we'll know what to look for. It's our only shot at this point. Ask him to pee and see what he says."

"I can't force him to."

"Just ask him," the tech replied, wishing he could just put a few traces of cocaine into the solution and make their jobs easier. Instead, he would have to wait for a probable drug dealer to subject himself to a chemical screening that he was in no way obligated to participate in.

Amazingly, Officer Blash had no trouble at all getting what he wanted out of their man. He pulled him from the holding cell, dragged him into the nearest restroom, and told him what to do.

It wasn't a very formal arrangement.

* * * *

"Now you understand that you don't have to do this and are submitting to this test of your own free will, right?" he asked of their current oddity, figuring it would be enough to cover his ass if the test came out positive. After that, his man could be charged for what was in the vial then be tested again for anything the courts would use against him.

"Yes, sir," the neatly dressed and very polite arrestee replied. Walter Van Staadt smiled at his captor as he unzipped his pants. "I'll do anything I can to clear up this matter for you, sir."

Watching the short, twenty-eight year old man get into position, Blash couldn't help but notice the anticipation on Walter's face. It wasn't anxiety, but something closer to excitement. He'd never seen someone so enthusiastic about taking a piss before.

"Yes, sir. We'll clear this right up for you." Walter began to urinate into one of the few cups that were set aside for him. He took a quick glance at Blash to make sure he was catching the show.

"Jesus fucking Chr—"

The barely intelligible response confirmed that he was most definitely catching it.

Practically gagging on the profanity that began streaming from his mouth, Blash leapt back quickly and slammed into the stall door behind him. With no more room to back up, all he could do was watch; and watch he did. Walter Van Staadt turned to the cop who'd arrested him and smiled wider still as Officer Michael Blash's face twisted and contorted in utter disgust.

"Yep, it's getting real clear now, huh?" Walter then paused and corrected himself. "Well, it's not exactly clear, I guess."

He was right—it wasn't clear at all. And it wasn't yellow either.

Walter's urine was black. Black as night.

In an instant, the standard urine test procedure was set aside. Normally, the officer would hover around the suspect and make sure that they weren't substituting someone else's urine for their own or diluting it with water. Actually seeing the urine flow from the subject was technically required. But all Blash needed was a quick peek for confirmation that he was seeing what he thought he was seeing.

There was no denying it. Walter was peeing a stream of something that looked like used motor oil. Instead of waiting for him to finish, Blash ran from the room and waited outside.

* * * *

"You weren't lying to me," the lab tech said, examining the urine sample. "This is black. *Really* black."

"Yeah, black—like I said," Blash replied, still feeling shaky but soothed by the fact that his technician wasn't scared by it. "What else can you tell me?"

"It's urine, that's a fact. Blood-alcohol level is point zero-zero. Not even the tiniest trace of nicotine, which is pretty much impossible."

"Why's that?"

"Because he was arrested in a bar and probably inhaled half a pack's worth of secondhand smoke. But there's nothing. No coke, no heroin, no THC. This is really weird. According to this, the guy doesn't even have any caffeine in his system."

"So?"

"So everybody does," the tech explained. "Think about it. Just about any soft drink with color has caffeine in it. So does coffee, tea—even most brands of aspirin have it added."

"Why are you looking for caffeine?"

"It's not standard. Sometimes we get a real twitchy perp who swears he's not high. He says he just drank too much coffee, right? Then I show him that he doesn't have enough caffeine in his system to give a hamster the shakes. It isn't anything we can use in court, but it cuts through the crap if the perp's an idiot and hasn't lawyered up yet."

"Why check this guy for it?"

"Because he should have some in his system, even trace amounts. He doesn't. My guess is he's using some sort of masking agent."

"The same stuff people use to pass drug tests at work?"

"Kind of," the tech answered, shaking his head. "It's like one of those chemicals that athletes use to hide their steroid use. Other drugs too. But this is different."

"How?"

"*Everything's* hidden or it's properties have changed enough to be unrecognizable. But this—the guy's piss looks like black coffee. I've seen chemicals that you can put in a person's drink and it'll turn their pee bright orange or purple. You know, as a prank. But this I've never seen. I don't know what it is, but this guy would be screwed if he had a medical emergency now."

"Why?" he asked, feeling like he'd reached his quota for questions already.

"Any medical tests would be skewed by whatever he's using. It could be dangerous for him."

"Yeah, I give a shit. Can we charge him or not?"

"Not for a vial full of nothing and a cup of black piss. It's weirder than anything I've ever seen, but it's not illegal that I know of."

Blash snatched the small sample from the tech's hand and headed for the door. "I think I'll get a second opinion if you don't mind."

Less than an hour later their man of mystery was released. Though Walter didn't know it yet, he was going to be that second opinion whether he liked it or not.

Chapter 15

The small house hadn't been anything special but it couldn't be described as a dump either. Not knowing a thing about Van Staadt, he'd decided to make a stop at his residence first, seeing as how the surprise drop-in by Officer Blash was always a big hit with the narcotics crowd. He loved the looks on their faces when he showed up at their doorsteps without any legal reason for his presence. No warrant and no subpoena—just a personal visit into their personal business at the most personal place imaginable. If the house had been too nice, he would have had have to change and shave first since he was still in his street clothes. At the moment, he looked more like a junkie than a cop.

He didn't like dressing poorly, but that was the job and, regrettably, he wore it quite well. Having the ability to slip in and out of seedy environments with little difficulty wasn't something he would ever brag about no matter how good he was at it. And why would he? As it was, he already had to remind himself daily that his nasty appearance was simply a ruse like any other, designed to make access to dirtbags that much easier.

In this case, it was access to Walter Van Staadt and his objective was simply to talk to the man. Nothing official. A casual conversation between a serious police officer and the one that got away. And even though his own bust that had netted twenty-six offenders was hardly an embarrassment, on the inside he still felt cheated. If it could happen once, it could happen again.

Blash knew that if another suspect slipped through his fingers because of some new product that was on the street he'd only have himself to blame. And he hated taking the blame for anything; even when he was guilty of it.

"No, I'm sorry, Walter's still at work," was what she told him.

It appeared she had completely bought the line that he'd given her. Unfortunately, since he told her that he knew Walter from the office—wherever the hell that was—it made it much more difficult to ask where his place of business was actually located.

The lovely woman, maybe in her early twenties, didn't quite match up with what he'd been expecting. He figured Walter was a decent looking man, not magnificently handsome like Blash pictured himself, but from what little he knew about him, Walter and the pretty girl who answered the door didn't seem to be on the same level. Either he seemed beneath her or she seemed above him.

It was the first of a few inconsistencies that went against the profile that Blash had prematurely formed in his head. He made a quick mental note to drop a few of the educated assumptions he'd made about his quarry.

"So, where's he working today?" Blash asked, hoping a little vagueness would draw the information from her. "Is it the same place as before? I think the last time I saw him he was off-site at that one place…you know…that building…downtown maybe…."

Mike Blash had spent much of his life honing the skill of acting confused to dig for the information he needed. It worked wonders on some people, making them feel so sorry for him that they went out of their way to help him. The others simply got so irritated by his disconnected ramblings that they would eventually finish his sentences for him just to make him go away. It was hit and miss—not an exact science at all—but it was apparently working like a charm on Walter Van Staadt's housemate.

A look of sympathy spread across her face almost instantly. She seemed to understand his situation and was ready to provide everything he needed.

"You must mean Helmwood," she said with a very sweet smile and eyes that were almost sad. "But it's not downtown. It's just over on Flower Street, near the golf course. Do you remember it now? Flower Street?"

"Helmwood, sure," Blash said, smacking his forehead. "On Flower near the golf course. He gets off at five, right?"

"Actually, he's been working from noon until nine since last summer," she replied apologetically. "If you want to call him here later on, he usually answers the telephone until eleven p.m. That's eleven in the evening…at night. You can call until then."

On top of the odd few sentences, her annunciation of each word was peculiar as well. She was speaking very slowly and even a little loud; not in a rude way, but just kind of different. Only then did it occur to him that the poor girl might be challenged in some way. She was certainly nicer than the average human being, which was the big clue. In Mike Blash's cynical world, kindness for no apparent reason was the type of behavior that indicated some form of mental damage.

"Maybe I *will* give him a call," he said, smiling awkwardly at her. "Is your number still five-seven-three…wait…I mean seven, um, five…wait…three…wait…"

She ended up just giving him the number.

* * * *

It looked like a rest home but it wasn't. The first thing that tipped him off was the security; the way everything was laid out was almost like the first police substation he'd worked at in Montclair. It wasn't a jail, but it was certainly designed to keep it's occupants inside. From the moment he opened the front door, he could smell what kind of place he was in and he didn't care for it.

The powerful odor of industrial strength disinfectant reminded him of when he had to visit his great-aunt when he was a kid. Even at seven years old, he had felt that each trip to see her was like a ride into hell's septic tank. She lived at the place they would call "The Old Folk's Home" and though there were plenty of old folks, it didn't seem like any kind of home.

Before he'd ever been to visit her, Blash had always thought that every old person in the world was good, kind, and full of presents. But the old folks at "The Old Folk's Home" were strange looking, erratic, and scary. He was able to close his eyes when he couldn't stand the sights anymore, but his nose was another story.

It didn't take him long to figure out that the strange smell of "The Old Folk's Home" was actually just your average, garden variety, medicine-ridden shit. He never asked anybody about the odor since it would have been rude, but he had seen enough wet crap running down the backs of enough old folk's legs to take a wild guess. Since pinching his nose shut would have been rude, he tried breathing through his mouth for a while, which was a big mistake since the air actually tasted worse than it smelled.

With a shiver, he decided to forego the trip down memory lane and get back to the present. Shoving the thoughts back where they belonged, Blash stood in the lobby for several minutes taking it all in.

No, it wasn't "The Old Folk's Home". But it was close.

"Can I help you, sir?" the woman behind the counter hesitantly asked. The 'sir' once again freaking him out a bit.

"I believe you can," he replied, pulling out some ID before she could get the wrong idea and started calling for security. "I'm curious. What exactly is it that you do in this facility?"

"Of course, Officer...," she leaned in, squinting at his ID. "...Blash. This is the Adolescent Mental Health Services division of Helmwood. This particular building cares for children and teens with behavioral and developmental disorders ranging from mild to severe. Though we offer long-term care at our adult facility, most of our guests are evaluated and placed in the situation that best suits them."

She rattled it off as though reading right out of the brochure.

"How many residents do you have now?"

"From fifty to a hundred and twenty at any given time, but that's as specific as I can get."

"You don't even know?"

"I can't *say*, officer," she replied with a smile that dared him to challenge her. "It's really an issue of privacy. I'm sure you understand."

"Of course I do. But the thing I'm really curious about is the safety and security of a place like this. Would it be possible to get a tour of the building?"

"We give them all the time," she answered, turning to the computer screen on her desk. "The next one's scheduled for Thursday at ten a.m., but if you need—"

"I'd really like to see it now. In fact, I was hoping to have a walk-through with one of your employees. I know that you're busy people around here but safety is a very important issue. I was told that a Walt...let's see here...." He let her hang on his words for a moment as he pretended to search through his pockets. "I think it was Walter Von...something."

"Van Staadt," she confirmed for him. "Walter's an orderly on the fourth floor."

"Yeah, that's him. Do you think he might have some time for me?"

"I'll see what his schedule's like," she said noncommittally as she picked up her phone and punched in his number. As the receptionist spoke, her voice dropped into privacy-mode and couldn't be heard at all. Most likely, she was warning him about the cop that was here to see him. A moment later, she hung up. "He'll be right down. You can have a seat if you'd like."

Blash nodded but proceeded to wander around the lobby anyway. Making the woman as uncomfortable as possible was his new goal for the next few minutes but after a only very brief wait, he heard Walter's voice echoing through the lobby.

"Sir?" It was the exact same 'sir' he'd used on Blash before he peed the color of midnight and scared the shit out of him.

"Ah, Walter," Blash replied with a big smile. "It's really good to see you again. I'm glad I was able to catch up with you."

Anyone who wasn't aware of their dealings on the previous night would have suspected the two knew each other. To Walter, the cop's voice was nothing more than cruel sarcasm. It was clear he wasn't expecting a visit but he played it off without much trouble. He even managed a welcoming smile.

"How're you doing, Officer Blash? I'm sorry I didn't think to put you on the schedule today but I wasn't expecting to see you this early. Everything good?"

"It's great, Walt."

"Good to hear. Why don't you come on upstairs with me and we can get started right away."

Shifting his eyes nervously to the receptionist, it was clear that he didn't want any conversation to happen until they were alone. In total silence, they stepped into the elevator and waited for the door to close. When it did, Walter was the first to speak.

"I wasn't charged with anything, so what are you doing here? I have a phone. You should have at least called first."

"Sorry, man, I know it must seem rude for me to just show up like this. Invading a person's life at work can really screw things up, can't it? Next thing you know, all your coworkers are talking about the cop that came to see Walter. They're wondering why I'm here and especially why I'm here talking to *you*. You look nervous, Walt. Why are you so nervous?"

Walter didn't answer as the elevator doors slid open on the fourth floor. Stepping out and turning to his left, he walked down the long hallway with Blash one step behind. When they got to the end, Walter unlocked an empty room and stepped inside. Only when the door was closed behind him was he ready to speak again.

"I'm only nervous because you're here. Like you said, this is where I work. Are you trying to get me fired?"

"Not just yet," Blash answered, leaving the possibility open. "I just want to make sure that we're clear on a few things before you get on with your life, acting like last night didn't happen. Because I'm here to remind you that it *did* happen and I can remind a whole lot of other people too."

"Why would you do that?" Walter asked fearfully, fidgeting with his fingers.

"Because I'm thorough. You see, drugs are my business. They're my job. I know you thought you were being cute last night and you thought you had it all under control. But you're not cute, Walt, and trust me...you don't have any control at all."

"I know my rights, sir. And I know you can't harass me at work without cause. I'll get a lawyer if I have to."

"Go ahead and call one then," Blash replied calmly, nodding towards the phone that was less than a foot away. "Of course, in order to get the full picture, I may need to start interviewing some of your co-workers and see what you're all about. That receptionist was a real bitch. Maybe I'll start with her. Or maybe your supervisor."

Yeah, it would work. He could see from the pain in Walter's face that he was coming to the correct conclusion. He also looked ready to answer a question or two.

"What is it then? What's so important?"

"It's just one question. Real simple. All I need is one answer."

He seemed to relax at the idea of one question. One question could have always led to more of them but as long as the cop had something specific in mind then he knew it would come to an end eventually.

"Okay," Walter said cautiously, eyeing the officer with a complete lack of trust. "I'll tell you something if you tell me something."

Blash shrugged and gave him a nod.

"Why are you dressed like that? You look homeless. If I hadn't seen you last night, I wouldn't have guessed you were a policeman."

"Undercover, genius. That's kind of the idea."

"No, I get *that*," Walter countered. "But last night was last night and this is today. You're in the same clothes."

"Maybe I didn't feel like changing."

"Then I should let you know that Marla—the receptionist—she thought you might be one of our old patients. We get a few disoriented wanderers that come back every now and then."

"Is that right?" Blash asked, acting like it didn't mean anything to him. It did mean something, however.

Embarrassingly, he remembered the way the woman at Walter's house had spoken to him; especially the way she pronounced everything and spoke loudly and slowly. It was almost laughable considering he thought that she was the one with mental problems. He felt a sudden urge to shave or at least run a comb through his hair.

"I'm not trying to insult you, sir," Walter said, treading carefully. "I'm sure that in your line of work you need to blend in with a certain type of crowd...but here you just look like one of our sad cases."

"Flattery won't help you, Walt, and you can be damn sure that I didn't come here for clothing tips. You already know that, though, don't you?"

Yeah, he knew. He had to ask anyway, though. "What *are* you here for then?"

"The bottle, Walter—that little vial you had. I'd really like to know what was in it."

Chapter 16

"Well?" Daisley asked, his expression one of complete frustration. He had listened to Mike Blash spit a story out at him for the last twenty miles and still had no idea where he was going with it.

"Well, what?" Blash replied, playing impossibly dumb. He peered back to Quartz with a smile, enjoying the moment. Leaving the detective in suspense was the most fun he'd had in the whole miserable day.

"Well, what was in the fucking bottle, Mike? Unless it's privileged information or something, I think you should tell me. It's the only reason I've been paying attention to you."

"You may as well stop listening then," Blash responded coolly. "I almost busted a blood vessel in my head trying to understand when Walter told me what it was, so I won't even try to explain it to you. It was really interesting though. Really. Wild stuff, Daisley. You should have been there."

"Are you kidding me?" the detective complained, his voice loud enough to startle Quartz in the back seat. "I swear to God, Mike. You've been talking about this clown for twenty minutes now and you haven't told me a goddamn thing—well, other than the fact that he works at a mental hospital and pees black stuff. Thanks for sharing that, by the way."

"No problem. Let me know if there's anything else I can help you with."

"Mike, I don't give a shit if the guy's piss is carbonated and he blows bubbles out of his dick. I just want to know how he's going to help us." Daisley's knuckles were beginning to turn white as his grip on the steering wheel tightened. "What can he do? I looked at his sheet too and I didn't see anything that would make me believe he could help fix this for us. What's he been pulled in for? *Possession?* What does that mean to us?"

"His sheet doesn't mean anything," Blash replied. "He's afraid of me and he owes me one. A big one. So why don't you worry about what you're going to do and I'll take care of my end of things. When it's over, we'll know who was right. How does that sound?"

"It sounds like we're going to jail," he answered solemnly, hoping that the big man they left behind at the Bonaventure Hotel wasn't in jail already.

Chapter 17

When he entered the lobby area, Lou was relieved to find that Fisk hadn't budged and appeared to be unmolested. He took a seat and wiped a few ounces of sweat off of his forehead and neck, almost envious of the man next to him who hadn't perspired a single drop in over an hour. Fisk's stress and anxiety were a thing of the past, but somehow Lou still found it in himself to feel bad for the man.

Putting an arm around the killer, he considered himself to be his sole protector and like Daisley said, would do whatever it took to see the job to its completion.

"Sorry about smacking you in the face," he said quietly into Fisk's ear. "I know it wasn't too cool but you've got to understand that I'm in a fragile emotional state right now."

A fragile emotional state.

He'd heard his own lawyer use the phrase several times while defending him against members of his own police department. Based on those four words, Internal Affairs had agreed that the officer had been antagonized to the point of using excessive force and couldn't be held responsible for his actions. He had been warned and sent back out onto the street four times and it was pretty clear that one more incident would be the end of it for him. Treating common criminals with the same basic respect afforded the general public took too much getting used to. He didn't like it one bit.

From day one, Lou had been trained specifically to generate fear; not only to criminals but to any element that didn't quite fit in with the lower and middle class areas of Fresno where he got started. When the first training officers got a look at his size, he was marked for high profile duties where a huge man in a uniform would make an impression. Starting with crowd control, he eventually became a face recognized at almost every police raid in the county. Though his actions weren't integral to the workings of a drug or weapons bust, his size alone made a strong statement that the cops in his department were larger than life and best not to be messed with.

Never the first man through the door, he usually sauntered in after the first sweep of a house had been completed. Once secure, it was his job to stand around and scare the hell out of anyone they could locate in the suspect residence. At first it was like a game. He would stare down at them with the meanest face he had—which was hard when trying not to laugh—and within minutes they'd roll over on the next guy in line.

Most criminals, especially when drugs were involved, were more than happy to pass the blame around a bit. Some weren't. Some even thought they were tough and that was when the trouble began for Officer Louis Poklatar.

Thinking back on it, Lou recognized now that the first one wasn't a big deal at all and could have been avoided completely. At the time, however, it seemed plenty important enough. The bust was simple and went exactly how all the others had gone: A mad rush of cops through every door in the house, a lot of yelling, several guns pointed in many directions, and a finale that resulted in seven perps face down on the carpet. It was a standard outing.

What wasn't standard was the lack of cooperation they received from one of the suspects. A little resistance was expected—if nothing else, they had to prove to the other bad guys that they were unshakable and wouldn't roll over on anyone. He played the game well and made himself out to look very tough in front of his comrades. It didn't last long.

By the time the unfortunate young man blurted out his fifth "Fuck you" in Lou's direction, he found himself nearly folded in half. He'd been sitting in the middle of the floor with his legs out in front of him and his hands cuffed behind his back. When Lou's tolerance went south, a hand was placed on the back of the perp's neck and he was pressed forward. In a flash, his forehead was jammed against the carpet between his knees.

An ambulance was required to take the badly sprained man away while another kind of doctor was told to have a close look at Officer Poklatar. It was the first time he'd acted impulsively on the job and the checkup was merely a technicality. With a wink and a nod, he was sent back to work the following day.

Two years, two lawyers, and three incidents later, he was told that he was in a "fragile emotional state" and would require some time off. Looking at the man next to him, Lou guessed that his time off could have been spent a little better.

A fragile emotional state.

He was babysitting their killer and preparing to hunt down two more for work he chose not to do himself. At the moment he didn't feel very fragile and, in fact, felt quite powerful. He knew that Daisley had picked him for corpse detail out of desperation and lack of confidence in him, but that was expected. It wasn't a problem and he wouldn't take it too personally. He rarely did.

Hearing his own name being suddenly blared throughout the lobby was what snapped Lou out his deep thoughts and brought him back to full consciousness. He looked around sheepishly, wondering how long they'd been calling his name. He knew that it could have been quite a while before he noticed.

"I think our wheels are here," he said, removing his arm from around Fisk's shoulder. "Stay here for a minute. I'll be right back."

He walked casually—not too fast, not too slow—to the front desk where a young man was waiting. He was holding a clipboard and a set of keys. After furnishing the man with two ID's and a credit card, the keys changed hands.

"Enjoy your stay in Los Angeles, sir," the young man said, then headed out the door.

"Thank you," Lou heard himself reply dreamily as he examined the keys. He returned to Fisk and took a quick look around the lobby before a nervous but very brief pause.

Putting on his best nonchalant face, he kneeled in front of the seated body. He wrapped his arm around Fisk's waist then hoisted him up and, without a single hint of awkwardness, walked straight through the lobby and out the main entrance with the man slung over his shoulder. Not even bothering to avoid eye contact with anyone who cared to view the strange scene, he glimpsed a few faces watching him with amused interest.

I hope they think you're toting a drunk guy around, he thought as he stepped to the curb and fished in his pocket for the keys. *We just might look a little suspicious.*

He knew he was supposed to be in a God-awful hurry but found himself distracted. Parked at the curb just two feet in front of him, Lou gawked at the 1959 Porsche 356 speedster that he had rented. Since he was a boy he'd dreamed of owning one and it perfectly matched every picture he'd ever seen of the vehicle, which was all he had to go on since the low-wage cop from Fresno had never even been close to one before.

With shaking hands, he stepped to the rear of the automobile, getting ready to roll his newest friend into the trunk. He couldn't figure out which thought hit him first, but they were both pieces of bad news.

The realization that he couldn't just throw the guy into the trunk in broad daylight left him feeling suddenly exposed. Worse still, as he got his first look into the trunk itself, it seemed to be filled with all kinds of lovely machinery. He quickly recognized the 1600cc engine for what it was and decided to check the front of the car for luggage space.

Two steps toward the front of the vehicle told him that his boyhood dream of driving a Porsche 356 should have waited for a later date. He hadn't even opened it yet, but one look at the front compartment made it clear that the bulky Mr. Fisk would have to ride shotgun for a while.

More sweat poured from his face as Lou unlocked the passenger door. He received a few double-takes from people but no direct stares as he placed the man in the leather seat and gently buckled him in. Locking the door, he slammed it shut tight and headed around to the driver's side door.

Noting that he didn't have the keys in his hand anymore, Lou said three Hail Mary's before tugging on the door. It opened easily, allowing him to take his first seat in the car of his dreams. He took the keys out of Fisk's lap, where he'd inadvertently left them, and fired up the engine.

He'd heard it was very fast. He'd read that it handled incredibly well. He'd seen pictures of its elaborate beauty.

But sitting down, all he could think of the Porsche 356 was that it was tiny. Really fucking tiny.

*   *   *   *

"Hey...carpool lane," Lou noted as made a quick lane change across the double white lines. "You're a pretty handy guy to have around."

So far, the speed and maneuverability of the small Porsche were a complete waste in the LA traffic. From the moment they pulled onto the freeway Lou felt crippled in the speedy automobile that wasn't permitted to break the fifteen mile an hour pace that was set by the cars in front of him. Not until he discovered the swift moving carpool lane did he finally get to open it up a bit.

"Why in the hell would anyone want to live in a place like this?" Lou asked his passenger as they flew by hundreds of cars full of irate travelers. "What's LA up to? Seven million...eight million...*ten* million people crammed in here? I mean, I'm no country bumpkin but I'll tell you something, pal. People need space. Lots of it."

Turning to Fisk, he could hear the question being asked through unmoving lips.

"*Why do they need so much space?* I'll tell you why," Lou answered, pulling a pair of sunglasses from inside his coat pocket. "Because an overcrowded community will gobble itself right up. I swear to God, Terrence—you don't mind if I call you Terrence, do you?"

Fisk's lack of response told him that using his first name would be just fine. Sliding the dark black sunglasses onto Fisk's face, he adjusted them slightly and continued to speak.

"Anyway, too many people stuffed onto too little land is a total mess. Especially if they're poor. It's not so bad if you've got buttloads of cash and if you choose to live with millions of other people, but if you don't have the money and have to live in some shitty apartment complex full of a thousand broke-ass guys just like you, it makes you frustrated. Frustrated, pissed, and competitive. Not a good combo, Terry."

Checking Fisk's expression, he didn't seem to mind being called "Terry" at all. It seemed the hitman was finally lightening up.

"Take me for example; I grew up out in Fresno," Lou explained, nodding his head back in the opposite direction they were heading. "It's a big place. Covers a lot of land. You know, farms, agriculture, and all that stuff. But we got our tight places too. Even in a city that's huge there are areas just packed with tons of people. About ninety-five percent of the crime in the whole county is committed on about one percent of the land. Guess what part of the land."

Lou suspected that if Fisk still had thought in his head, he would have guessed correctly.

"That's right, Terry. In the areas where the population is densest—*is that a word? Densest? Denser?* Well anyway, in the places with the most people is what I'm trying to say."

Even in death, Lou thought the man looked embarrassed for him and his lack of command of the English language. Getting the words right was only half the battle. Keeping his thoughts straight was the real chore.

"Now, I know it makes sense that since people commit the crimes, it follows that more people means more crime. I know that. I'm just saying that if you move all of those people into an area that's a little bigger…not a lot…just a little bigger, maybe give them an extra few feet of elbow room, it would cut the crime way down. Crimes against people, anyway. I mean, you're still gonna have kids tipping over cows and stealing cars but that's not personal."

Looking to his companion, Lou guessed that Fisk knew the difference between personal crimes and acts committed out of sheer boredom. As a hitman, he had probably told dozens of people that his killing them was "Nothing personal—just business", but even Lou knew that it was a very personal thing anyway.

"I'll bet Chicago's crowded, huh? *Much crime?*" he asked with a laugh, figuring his point had been made. "Yeah, I thought so."

Only ten minutes into their journey, Lou fell quiet, not sure what to talk about next. Driving in silence with the man had been intolerable from the start, but Lou didn't guess that they'd be together for much longer.

"Somewhere between here and Corona you're gonna need to get lost. This is southern California so you'll have some options. We got it all here, Terrence. I can leave you in the woods, in the desert, in the snow, on the beach, in the ocean…man, I could drive you up a freakin' mountain and throw you off. Anything you want, Terry. It's only a forty minute drive to any of those places from here."

Fisk didn't seem nearly as impressed as Lou when it came to the geographic diversity of the Golden State. He never even turned to check out the view.

"If you see something you like, let me know and we'll give you a nice little send off. If you weren't such a well known guy, I could probably kick you right out of the car and no one would say shit; at least while we're still in LA."

The thought struck Lou as funny, sending him into a fit of laughter. Realizing slowly that he was the only one with a case of the chuckles, he toned down the volume.

"We'll be in Long Beach before too long. That's another place I could just toss your ass out of the car. After that, it's Orange County and I'll tell you what; those guys start crying if you throw a freakin' *cigarette* out your window, much less a dead guy. Now, I know Orange County is a little out of the way, but that's where your replacements are. At least I think so."

It suddenly occurred to Lou that a few more phone calls might be a wise move. If time was of great concern—and it was—he could go east on I-10 and make it to Riverside a lot quicker. Assuming his boys were still beach-city dwellers, moving through Orange County first made sense.

He would be at his interchange in about ten minutes and was hoping for an answer before he got there. With his cell phone jammed against his ear, Lou was connected to the Fresno PD before being rerouted to the Orange County Sheriff's Office and then on to the Costa Mesa Police Department. After being transferred for the fourth time, he found himself on the line with what sounded like a young woman. Diving right in and speaking in an urgent tone, he probed for information. He could almost hear the smile on the face of what was sure was a rookie administrator's assistant. She was way too enthusiastic to be a real cop just yet.

"Yeah, two of them," he said, slowing his voice down on purpose, not wanting to annoy her and lose what valuable assistance she had to offer. "Sheridan, Joseph…" he paused as he could hear her pounding away on her keyboard. "…and Bautista, Alex. We have Santa Ana and Newport Beach addresses for them but they're not current."

Her keyboard jumped to life again as she entered the data. Though she didn't speak for over a minute, she was decent enough not to put him on hold while she waited for the information to appear across her screen. A moment later her smiling voice reemerged and gave him some good news.

"A parking ticket, no kidding?" he asked, pretty sure the officer wasn't just pulling his leg. "Just two months ago? That's beautiful. Let me have it."

As he pulled a small pad of paper from his coat pocket, he had the insane urge to put one of Fisk's hands on the wheel and let him steer so he could write more clearly. Instead, he drove with an elbow while he wrote down the last known address for Joe Sheridan.

"Nothing on the other guy? Okay. No, don't apologize. If this address gets me to Sheridan, I'll be able to find Bautista really easy." He wasn't sure if it was true or even if the two men partnered around together anymore, but his experience led him to believe that partnerships that involved killing usually lasted until one or the other was dead or imprisoned. "Thanks for all your help, miss."

As was his nature, Lou thanked her two more times before signing off. He closed up his phone and turned to Fisk.

"It looks like we're headed to Costa Mesa. I guess Sheridan parked in front of a hydrant or something and had to pay off a ticket. We've got an address and even what kind of car he drives…well, the one he got the ticket on, anyway. Either way, we're styling now, Terry. All we've got to worry about is driving straight for the next hour or so."

He couldn't believe it, but he'd actually located the pair. Lou was only doing what he'd been told to do but, like the people who had given him the assignment, he didn't really expect to get any solid results. Then again, he didn't expect to be driving around in a Porsche with an infamous paid killer in the passenger seat either.

Chapter 18

They had been driving for more than thirty minutes without a word from anyone. Daisley stared straight ahead, only occasionally looking into the rear view mirror and nowhere else. With at least an hour left to go, he supposed that no talking at all beat the hell out of screaming at each other, which was probably the only other option.

Blash had been silent since their conversation about Walter Van Staadt and didn't look ready to get very talkative anytime soon. Thinking of how he was going to handle the man once they reached Corona took all the brain power he had.

Quartz, who was still waiting patiently for a call back regarding her part of the job, was more than happy to have it quiet for a while. After watching the two men in the front seat butt heads over the smallest things possible, she felt lucky to be left out of it. She was also glad that no one had bothered to ask her about her own disaster waiting to happen.

Nanette Lalonde. *Netta.* That girl again. She wasn't a sure thing by any stretch of the imagination but she *had* to be better than Blash's guy.

Quartz could easily see why Daisley was getting upset with Mike and fortunately she had been left out of their bitter exchange. She knew the shots they were taking at each other were based on nerves rather than any real disagreement since it was all a huge gamble anyway, but taking sides would have made it infinitely worse.

Waiting for her phone to ring, she watched Daisley drive and could see the wheels of his mind spinning wildly. Though she and Mike were about to be very busy rounding up people with the potential to murder for cash, Daisley was doubly frustrated since he'd already gone through the same thing locating the finest killer that money could buy.

She hadn't been present when the deal with Ratcliffe had been made, but a week earlier when Daisley had mentioned that Terrence Fisk would be the designated hitter, she couldn't help but be impressed.

* * * *

"*Terrence Fisk?* Sure, I've heard of him," Quartz had told him, nodding enthusiastically as she dragged on her fourth cigarette of the hour. "But he's not real. He's like an urban myth or something."

With a slow shake of his head and an expression of complete sincerity, Daisley was about to let Quartz in on an irrefutable truth. They were sitting together at an outdoor table of a low key café, the mood much less formal than the previous meetings they'd had with the other members of the team. This one involved a meal, coffee, and conversation outside the job they'd been given. It didn't include Mike Blash or Louis Poklatar and from some viewpoints could have been considered a date.

"He's real enough, Quartz, and there's no doubts about his capabilities," he replied, lowering his voice a notch. "If I hadn't seen his handiwork roll across my desk back in Chicago I probably wouldn't believe it myself. He's racked up quite a portfolio. Real high profile stuff."

It was true enough, all right. Though he was never in a position to investigate the man, information on him traveled pretty freely internally through the department. Fisk was almost like an inside joke, tallying more verified kills than the old Murder Incorporated boys back in the thirties. The joke of it, of course, was that the majority of his hits were directed towards the kind of people that didn't exactly take top priority when it came to investigating their demise. Most of his victims were already in one kind of dead-pool or another before they met him up close.

"Is he invisible or something?" she asked, still not convinced. "Someone must have some kind of ID on him or at least a fingerprint. If you know about him why hasn't he been locked up?"

"For a lot of reasons." He quickly confirmed that there was no one was within earshot before continuing. "Mainly, it just because he's quick and clean. He never hangs around after he's done and never leaves anything behind."

"Then how do you know for sure that he was involved in those particular hits?"

This was the sketchy part. He hadn't been affiliated with the Chicago PD in years but still knew how it worked. Telling her the facts was potentially dangerous. Fortunately, he knew he could count on her discretion if nothing else since her ass would be on the line as well as his.

"Usually, when a semi important hit went down," he explained, loving the fact that the beautiful detective was hanging on his every word, "I could get at least a little information on it within twenty-four hours. Sometimes, if I was really curious, I could get it even sooner."

"How much sooner?" she pried, suspecting she knew where he was headed.

"Well, one time—just one time...I might have heard about a guy who was about to turn. You know, roll over on a few associates and make things easier for himself."

Quartz nodded, understanding as Daisley knew she would.

"The thing is, the detective who mentioned it was busy filling out a report on the deceased *while* he's telling me about the guy. Now, this detective—he didn't get all the details one hundred percent right, but he was definitely talking about a man who's getting ready to flip on his crew...while jotting down the details of his murder. How many gunshots, location of his wounds—two in the head, one in the chest—pretty specific stuff."

"Before the guy had even been killed?" Quartz asked, shocked but seemingly enjoying it to a point.

"Two days before he got burned, that's right," he replied. "And it went down almost exactly the way he wrote it on the report. Coincidence?"

"Not too likely, Andrew," she said, suddenly realizing that the man in front of her looked even better than he did only minutes before. It was also the first time she'd referred to him by his first name. It didn't feel bad at all.

"I'm sure you're right, Qiana."

"That's sweet, Andrew," she said, almost wincing from the way her exotic name fell out of his working-class mouth. "But let's not call me that anymore, okay? *Quartz* will do just fine. It's easier, anyway."

"Anything you say."

"So, how did you end up meeting him?"

"I didn't," he answered, wishing that he had met the killer as he watched his female counterpart's eyes lighting up. "And I still haven't. I expect we'll all meet him at the same time. He's not even flying in until the day before the job takes place."

"Pretty confident, huh?"

"I guess so," he answered back with a shrug. "He says it'll be a breeze."

"So you've talked to him?" Fisk was finally becoming a real person instead of the mythical figure she'd heard about.

"Just once—yesterday. Other than that, everything's been handled by a few friends back in Chicago."

"What did he sound like?"

Andrew Daisley glanced around intensely before speaking. She was practically on the edge of her seat.

"Unfriendly," was the best answer he could come up with.

* * * *

It had only been a few days since their lunch together but for some reason seemed quite a bit longer. It was panicked and busy as hell...but longer regardless. Excited at first by Terrence Fisk's involvement, Quartz remembered feeling guilty for it only a day later. It wasn't like her to get star-struck over a criminal. Initially, she justified it by the experience of watching how the man worked—theoretically, making her a better and more knowledgeable police officer. But she was lying to herself and she knew it.

He was a famous killer and she simply wanted to see him in the flesh. It wouldn't exactly be like meeting Al Capone or John Gotti, but more like working with Frank Nitti or Sammy Gravano—their respective enforcers. Not glamorous...but still pretty neat.

But by the time the LA meeting was set to take place, her excitement about Fisk was completely dead and had even started moving in the opposite direction. Maybe it was because he was real now; or that the job was real. Either way, it had all become very real, very quickly and wasn't quite the game she'd been imagining.

It only got worse when she finally made eye contact with him. The word that Andrew had used to describe him was right on the mark.

Unfriendly.

Regardless of the straits they were currently in because of his unexpected demise, Quartz still couldn't help but feel that justice had been served to some point. It wasn't just because of the way he looked at her or even when he'd felt her up and embarrassed her in front of Lou and Andrew. It helped a little but that wasn't the reason she was grateful that he was dead.

As a rule, fear was Quartz's least favorite emotion. The man had made the mistake of scaring her and that was more than enough to warrant the venom she had for him. Unfortunately, she had only killed Fisk indirectly, leaving a good deal of hot blood pumping through a heart that was feeling blacker by the second.

It wasn't enough to change her mind about personally pulling the trigger on Christian Roche, though she was slowly warming to the idea.

With any luck, her phone would ring shortly, leading her to a woman who might not share Quartz's frailty when it came to taking a life. If she was still local and using the same name as before, Nanette Lalonde would soon be given a chance to prove her suspicions true. Never imprisoned in the states and never detained for more than breaking and entering, her attitude alone had put Nanette in a class of her own.

If Quartz had to use one word to describe the strange European woman that she had arrested what seemed like an eternity ago, *Beautiful* would have been in the running. So would *Manipulative*, *Deceptive*, and *Beguiling*. There was another word that sprang to mind but Andrew had already used it describing someone else.

Unfriendly.

She wasn't always unfriendly, though. Quartz knew that one from experience.

She was still dwelling on it ten minutes later when her phone began to ring.

Chapter 19

▼

"I arrested them up at a construction site just off the freeway," Lou said, answering Fisk's unasked question about his possible replacements. "Alex Bautista and Joe Sheridan, I mean. That's why I know these guys. It was a long time ago, but I never forget the name of a guy I've busted."

Sneakily, Lou shifted his eyes towards Fisk to see if he was buying it. No dice. Even his new friend Terrance knew he wasn't being totally honest.

"Okay, I'm lying. I don't remember much of anything really but I definitely remember those two guys. I remember them because of what that little peckerhead Bobby Cress told me. You see, Bobby—a little turd if I've ever seen one—was caught in a public park with an ounce and a half of weed on him. I was just cruising, doing my regular nightly thing when the call comes through. There's a complaint about some kids drinking in a park in a residential neighborhood. You know, screaming and yelling and all that. So I roll up on them real quiet like. It was hilarious because with all the noise they were making, they didn't even hear me pull up within ten feet of them."

Lou's face grew animated as he told the story. His favorite parts of police work were when he punched in and when he clocked out. Arriving to work, he got to hear all the stories that had occurred during the previous shift. After his own shift ended, it was his turn to report on the criminal geniuses of Fresno. Though the crime rate was fairly low for a medium sized city, the stupidity of the perpetrators was on a scale all its own.

"They were just a bunch of dumb kids, doing what kids do, but then the first joint comes out. Now, I've got no problem with the whole drinking in the park thing—I did it myself for Christ's sake—but I can't let them smoke grass right in front of me and *definitely* not on a playground where some little kid might find half a joint that some dumb-ass stoner dropped in the sand. Normally, in a situation like this I'd hit the lights and punch the siren once. The kids would scatter and I'd be drinking their leftover beers for the next few days. But in this case, they all scatter except one of them. And he's so stoned he can't even walk."

Looking over to Fisk, Lou observed the way his body was slack and in a terribly unnatural state.

"He looked kind of like the way you look. He was just staring off into space and didn't even notice that everyone else had split. Just smiling and all red-eyed. He knew he was busted but didn't seem to care at all. Anyway, I pat him down and find a bunch of weed. A bunch. Anything less than an ounce and it's no big deal, so I still don't understand why he was carrying so much. Probably just showing off to his friends, I guess."

Checking the gas gauge and odometer quickly, he estimated that they'd be to their destination in about thirty minutes and they wouldn't have to gas up anytime soon. Beaming, he was pleased with himself for even remembering to check the gauges at all.

"Now the idiot is gonna be charged with distribution instead of possession," Lou continued, shaking his head. "So I drop him off and he goes straight into a cell. It's a weekend night so he's got lots of company. You know, drunks and such. He's real stoned and pretty drunk himself so he starts shooting his mouth off. He's so whacked that he starts getting up in the other guys faces, like he's daring them to try something. This pinhead thinks it's like at school where a teacher will come along and break up any fights that get started. I'll tell you what, Terry…it ain't like that at all."

The Porsche had been purring along beautifully since they'd entered the carpool lane but was running a little hot for Lou's comfort. It was only luck that he peeked at the stick shift for a moment and the number five jumped out at him.

"How about that?" Lou said, slapping Fisk on the shoulder. "It's a five-speed, Terry. We've been in fourth for over an hour now. I swear to God I'm not as stupid as I seem."

He continued to laugh in a humiliated, though entertained, tone as he stepped on the clutch and shifted into fifth. Checking the stick one more time, he didn't find a number six so he assumed their gear ratio to be at its most efficient setting. He didn't think of it in those terms exactly, but it all meant the same thing to him.

"So anyway, Bobby Cress—the stoner guy I was just talking about—he starts screaming. Right there in the cell with ten other guys. He's screaming like mad and one of the guards goes to check it out. When he gets there it's all quiet. No one's saying shit and Bobby's gone. I mean *gone.*"

Fisk didn't look surprised in the least by Lou's revelation.

"So the guard—his name's Jimmy Tan…really good guy—starts counting heads and, naturally, he comes up one short. One by one, he clears the cell and checks off the guys as he moves them into another cell. When he's almost done, he's got three names left on the sheet and only two guys in the cell. The way Jimmy tells it, these two guys are sitting there on a cot, smiling like they're sharing a joke or something."

Lou hadn't been there to see it first hand, but if Jimmy Tan could see Lou's face right now, he'd say that it was a perfect match for the one the two men were wearing.

"So he's just standing there, waiting for the guys to move out of the cell when he hears something. Then he notices that one of the other cots is missing its mattress. Jimmy said that when these guys got up, they just walked out of the cell like nothing was going on. Then he hears the crying."

Holding his hand up to keep Fisk from ruining the punchline, Lou continued.

"He steps into the cell and flips the mattress off of the poor guy. He's gasping for air and all curled up like the shivering little punk that he is. And he's crying like a little girl. I guess Bobby started spouting off to these guys and instead of kicking his ass, one of the guys—Sheridan I think—grabs dumb-ass Bobby around the throat and pushes him down to his knees. Even though there's seven other guys in the cell, Bobby thinks he's about to be force fed a dick or two and starts squealing."

Sick as it was, Lou half expected his dead passenger to burst out laughing. It wasn't a nice thing to happen to somebody but Lou guessed that Fisk would see the humor in it.

"Well, the other guy—Bautista—he squats down next to the weepy little shit and starts whispering something in his ear." Lou started speaking with a loud, melodramatic whisper of his own. "Bobby Cress stops crying real quick. In fact, he stops moving and almost stops breathing. A few seconds later they toss him on one of the cots and Sheridan and Bautista take a seat on each side of him. They're not doing anything…just sitting there next to him and looking at him. Well, he starts getting all twitchy and whiny again, so they get up, grab another mattress, push him down, and cover him up. Then they sit down on the fucker. You ever seen a mattress in a Fresno County jail?"

Judging from Fisk's reputation as a solid professional, Lou suspected that he hadn't. An explanation was definitely in order.

"Have you ever been to camp and had to sleep on one of those tiny, thin little foamy things that smell bad even when they're brand new?" Even if his parents hadn't sent him to summer camp, Lou knew that Fisk understood completely. "Well, picture that same thin mattress covered in crap, piss, puke, boogers, blood, snot, and semen. Now you're in the Fresno drunk tank. It would be bad enough just to lay on top of the filthy thing, but here's poor Bobby, crying his eyes out, sandwiched in between *two* of them with two guys on top of him. By the time Jimmy peeled him out of the cot and got him into his own cell, he was already screaming for protection…and a lawyer."

Lawyers. It's always got something to do with them, doesn't it?

"No shit, it does. When Jimmy starts asking him what his problem is, Bobby says that they threatened to kill him. That doesn't surprise me. Guys are always saying they're gonna kill each other. What *did* surprise me though, was when Jimmy calls me in after my shift and starts asking questions about my boys.

"*Now* Bobby Cress is saying that Bautista told him he was gonna kill him *just like he killed Gabriel Marcos*. Now, I know that doesn't mean a thing to you or anyone outside of Fresno, but Gabriel Marcos was kind of a celebrity around here…in a bad way. He wasn't anything but a wannabe gangster and drug dealer, but his murder was big news for a couple of weeks. He'd been shot fifteen times and was cut up pretty bad after he was dead, so it was a big deal."

Looking to Fisk, Lou guessed that *he* didn't think it was such a big deal. Shooting a guy fifteen times and slicing him up a bit would probably be considered dull and unimaginative to the hitman.

"As far as I know, we didn't have a single lead in the case, so we jumped all over the two guys. And let me tell you, they were a couple of scary ones. Real cool. They didn't get rattled or even break a sweat; at least that's what I heard from the top. They don't let guys like me interview murder suspects, you know. I was the arresting officer but it didn't have anything to do with murdering anybody. Not that I knew of, anyway."

As he talked, Lou kept an eye on the road while occasionally watching the scenery. So far, today hadn't been the nightmare he'd been worrying about all week. In fact, he was rather enjoying himself. Nobody had ever let him ramble on the way Fisk did.

"By the next morning, they had every resource available snooping around the place where I caught them. It was a total mess because there was crap all over the place. I mean, it was a construction site, so what did they expect? They were only a quarter of the way done with the office they were building, so there were lots of tools, lumber, steel, and a ton of exposed earth that had been dug up. It was impossible to tell if there'd been any fresh digging, so they had all kinds of experts poking around for the reason they were there."

Once again, he could feel Fisk asking a question.

"What did I pick them up for?" Lou asked of his passenger. "Just theft. They had a big van and when I caught them they were loading some tools and other stuff into it. Nothing big. Just a couple of hammers, some plywood, nails, and some two by fours. That's what I busted them for. Simple theft. But when I told the detectives what they'd stolen, they nearly shit. They looked at me like I was a moron and said it looked like the guys were building a few coffins. I guess that could've been the case, but let me ask you something?"

Ask away, Lou, Fisk seemed to say.

"Whenever you had to get rid of a body, did you build them a coffin first?" Even Lou thought the question completely ridiculous. "I mean, if I'd have caught them with shovels in their hands, digging a hole at a construction site, I'd be a little suspicious of what they were burying. But from what I actually saw, though, they could've been getting ready to build a fucking treehouse, you know?"

Sure thing, Lou. You make a valid point and I agree with you wholeheartedly. You certainly are a very bright man.

"After a few days of checking the site, there was nothing to go on. It hurt like a bitch, but they had to let the guys go. Other than the word of a stoned idiot there was no evidence at all. And I'll tell you, those guys walked out of the jail like they'd never even been inside. They were laughing and pointing at all of us cops like they'd really pulled a fast one on us."

"And get this," Lou continued. "Not *once* did they call a lawyer. Didn't even ask for one. They just sat in room after room, answering question after question. They used their phone calls to make contact with someone in Bakersfield and never asked about calling anyone else. It was a freaky scene, especially since they weren't locals and never gave a good explanation why they were in Fresno in the first place. But off they went, leaving us with nothing but a shaky Bobby Cress. He'd been hoping that we'd find something to pin on the guys so he could have some leverage—maybe an immunity deal on his weed bust."

Throwing his hands up, Lou sighed and shrugged his shoulders.

"Nothing ever came of it, though. Somehow Bobby's ounce and a half of weed turned into about a quarter of an ounce by the time it made it into evidence. Either he knew somebody in the department or every cop in the precinct took a little piece for himself before it was logged in. It really doesn't matter. The point I'm making is that no charges were filed against the little shit and he walked away. We never found out if Sheridan and Bautista had killed Gabriel Marcos or if they buried someone at the construction site. If they did, they got away with it because the office is finished now and every other part of the site is covered with asphalt."

He wanted to ask Fisk what he would have done in a similar situation from the bad guy's perspective. How it could be done. How he would dispose of a body. How he would compose himself under questioning. He was curious about all of it except for the reason why. He already knew the answer to that one. It was money, plain and simple.

If his boys in Orange County were anything like Fisk, they'd do it for the same reason. He prayed they were still open for business.

"I hope they don't have day jobs," Lou noted as he looked at his watch. "The middle of the afternoon on a Thursday isn't exactly prime time for guys like these."

Turning to the only person who bothered to listen to him today, Lou knew that Fisk could see where he was coming from. He could feel that they had a connection. Not a living, breathing one—even Lou knew that was impossible—but like a partnership. A *silent* partnership.

"Okay, I'll be the good cop and you…" Lou paused, not finishing the sentence, knowing that Fisk was way ahead of him.

That's right. You get to be the bad cop, he thought as they exited Long Beach and crossed over into Orange County. Within fifteen minutes they were parked ten yards from a house listed as Joseph Sheridan's last known address.

Chapter 20

▼

"Gotcha, you nasty little thing," Quartz said, slamming her cell phone shut and leaning into the front seat between Daisley and Blash. "She tried to hide from me but I'm just too damn good, huh?"

"*Way* too good," Daisley replied, sounding both surprised and impressed.

"Yeah, just like Wonder Woman," Blash added. "But without those great big tits. I take it you're not going to have to jump a plane to fucking Singapore for her?"

"Los Alamitos," she informed him. "It's just south of Long Beach near Cypress."

"Where'd the word come from?" Daisley asked.

Quartz removed herself from between them and leaned back in her seat. "I'm not saying. Nothing personal, guys."

"Yeah, like I give a shit about your information pipeline," Blash responded, following her advice by not taking it personally. Everybody had their own hoops to jump through and their own way of jumping through them. Sometimes it was best not to ask and even better not to know.

Daisley merely grunted at the information, just glad that it was available at all.

"Is Thursday a race night?" she asked, seemingly confused by her own question.

"I wouldn't know," Blash answered with a sneer. "Los Alamitos sucks ass and I wouldn't be caught dead there. I go down to Del Mar or up to Hollywood Park whenever I feel like playing the ponies."

"Oh...*horses*," Quartz said, feeling totally uninformed. "I guess that makes sense. My guy in Orange County has her linked to a bookie and pimp named

Nestor LaGuardia. I've never heard of him. He doesn't sound like the kind of guy Netta would be hanging around with, though."

"Netta?" Blash inquired with a raised eyebrow.

"Nanette Lalonde," she replied with a harsh grin, wishing immediately that she hadn't referred to her in such a familiar way. "When we brought her in I was stupid enough to feel bad for her. I actually thought she was the most defenseless thing I'd ever seen. I'd good-cop her to death while the detective in charge took a break. The whole sympathetic, weak and kind-hearted, lady cop thing. You've seen me do it, Mike."

"Yeah, I've seen it. You'd make a great con artist. No doubt about it."

"Well, make sure you tell her that when you see her. She wasn't buying any of it. I thought she was at first, but she was just playing with me. Smart girl. Too smart, maybe."

"Hot though, huh?" Blash interjected. "You said she was a looker."

"Smokin', Mike," Quartz said as she pulled a small mirror from her purse and checked her own makeup. "You'd want to eat her up. Of course, she'd rip your nuts off and cap your teeth with them, but you'd still think she was pretty."

"Blond?" It wasn't important but he had to ask anyway.

"Redhead," Quartz replied, running fingers through her hair. "Not the kind you get from a bottle either. A real deep, dark red. I was jealous. I tried for a red like that once and it made my face look green."

"What is she...French?" Blash asked. "*Nanette Lalonde*. Sounds French."

"Sure, I guess."

If Blash had been more on the ball he would have caught her in the lie. It would have been obvious to even an untrained eye but distracted as he was, it got by him.

Being virtually ignored by both of them, Daisley listened and drove. Not having to play an active part in the conversation made it easier to follow and to tell who was full of the most shit. Since Quartz had never mentioned Nanette before, it was hard to figure why she felt compelled to hide anything about her. It didn't upset him to be out of the loop in regards to Nanette since, until now, he didn't care a thing about her. What was driving him slightly crazy was Quartz's glibness with Mike Blash.

It was only because they were the only ones on the team that had ever worked together before, but their familiarity was unsettling to him. Their rapport was fast, loose, and laced with sarcasm, which was exactly the way that Daisley had become accustomed to speaking with her. It was just envy; plain and simple.

"You want to step on it, Daisley?" Blash asked lightheartedly. "If I want a hot date with Quartz's redhead I'm gonna have to work fast."

"Yeah, Andrew, step on it. Mike's in a hurry to get shot down. Let's not make him wait too long."

It wasn't a serious suggestion but Daisley raised their speed to eighty-five anyway. With the hurdles of tracking down a couple of potential killers out of the way, the new priority was getting Blash and Quartz within reach of their candidates.

"Hey, when you do find her," Blash said, turning to Quartz with a smirk. "make sure she showers real good before you present her to me. I don't want some dirty frog stinking up my sheets."

"I've got you covered," Quartz replied. "I'll have her spit-shined before I submit her for your approval."

Blash flashed a nasty grin her way but it only lasted for a few seconds. "But seriously—she's as mean as a snake? Killer material for real?"

"She'd better be," Daisley said, jumping uninvited into the conversation. "I don't want to get her all set up only to find out she's a stewardess or something."

Quartz could only shake her head at the thought of her girl Netta in such a job. Helping others, even if she was being paid for it, didn't seem to be part of her repertoire. Hopefully the stack of cash they could throw her way would alleviate any qualms she might possibly have about offering her assistance.

"I hope you guys get to meet her. She's a strange bird but she doesn't mess around. The thing I'm curious about is this guy she's been connected with. I could see her associating with a bookie. But a pimp? I don't get it."

"She's not that kind of girl, huh?" Blash asked with a crude leer.

"No, not this girl."

Not my Netta, she thought to herself, the very idea making her feel sick. If there was one thing that Quartz could always depend on, it was consistency among her perps. If the toughest woman she'd ever seen was now nothing more than a hooker with a pimp, Quartz was about to get deeply depressed.

Not my Netta, she thought again, hoping that consistency still existed. She also hoped that the horses were running tonight.

Chapter 21

▼

"You should have pushed it to eighty-five as soon as we hit the freeway," Blash said, stepping from the car. "We would have been here half an hour ago."

Daisley didn't respond. Yanking the keys from the ignition and practically leaping from the vehicle, he paused only for a moment to open the rear door for Quartz. It wasn't necessary and probably wasn't even a good idea in front of Blash, but it felt like the natural thing to do. It was automatic.

"Thanks, dummy," she said quietly. "This is hardly procedure, you know."

Fortunately, Blash was busy stretching, bending his back left and right, creating sounds of bones grinding and popping. Of course, even if he knew of the two's relationship he would have only laughed anyway. They were on a special assignment that broke every rule there was. As far as protocol went, all bets were off.

"I think I'll wait until this thing's over before I start worrying about what anyone will say," Daisley replied. "With all that's going on, I don't think Mike would notice anyway."

"He's probably already noticed. But you're right; now's not the time to care about it either way. I've got the longest day ahead of me, Andrew."

"You and me both," he agreed as he followed her through a secured door into the rear entrance of the Corona Police Department.

Holding the door open, Daisley only had to wait fifteen seconds for Blash to round the corner and catch up with them. In the short time since they'd arrived back in Corona, Blash had already lost the look of frustration that had been a permanent fixture while they drove. Now he looked excited, anxious, and ready to tackle the problems they'd been presented with.

Heading straight for Daisley's office, Quartz took a seat immediately while Blash stopped at the door tapping his foot. In the middle of the desk sat a large package wrapped in brown paper.

"Is that what I think it is?"

"It sure would help," Daisley allowed, dropping into his own comfortable chair.

"Well, I'd love to stick around and see what the tooth fairy brought us, but I've got about a million things to do." Blash checked his watch against the one that hung on Daisley's wall. "If I get lucky, I might be able to catch Walter at work again and really freak his ass out. He won't be too happy about it but I'll see if I put a smile on his face. How much cash do we have between us?"

Pulling a bundle from her jacket pocket, Quartz tossed a stack of bills on the desk. Blash set his stack on top of it and started estimating.

"Right down the middle works for me, guys. That should leave me with about ten grand to flash to Netta when I find her. I hope it's enough."

"If she gives you any shit, just call it a down payment," Daisley offered, separating the pile into two roughly equal stacks of hundreds. "Unless you're going to be glued to her side for the next twenty-four hours, don't even give her the money yet. Just let her see it for a few seconds. Let her know we're serious. Same for you, Mike."

"The money's nice, but I'm thinking Walter will need more motivation than this." He wore a mildly evil glare as he spoke. "The *free* kind."

"Whatever it takes, Mike. Just don't go throwing that money around too freely. If I get ripped off by one of these losers I won't be happy."

"Trust me, neither will I," Blash replied, checking his pockets for keys. "Unless you've got anything else you want to talk about, I'm ready to split. I want to knock this thing out fast, so keep your phone handy. I'll be calling you soon."

He wasn't sounding very realistic but at least he had a positive attitude. Daisley suspected that he would hear from Blash some time this evening, but wasn't nearly as optimistic in general. "Sounds good. Go get him, Mike."

"Yeah, good luck, Mike," Quartz echoed.

"You too," Blash replied, offering Daisley a weak smile and Quartz a wink before sliding out of the office.

Daisley and Quartz looked down at the desk, then stared at each other for a full minute before Blash came flying back into the room. Winded and slightly embarrassed, he went straight for the desk.

"Gonna need this, huh?" he asked as he scooped up his half of the money that he'd left behind. Without another word he was gone.

Chapter 22

After realigning the black sunglasses on Fisk's face, Lou adjusted him and propped his arm up so that it hung partially out the window. Figuring it was as natural as the poor guy could look, Lou took one last glance at him before walking slowly to the front door of the residence.

Several knocks on the door later, Lou exhaled loudly and wiped a fresh layer off sweat from his forehead. As expected, no one was conveniently home, offering their services to the first cop who wandered to their doorstep. It wasn't a horrible setback considering Lou wasn't even sure if they'd be able to track them down at all.

Looking dejected, yet feeling surprisingly upbeat, he returned to the car and crammed himself into the tiny seat again. He still loved the Porsche, but now understood completely why large sedans were the preferred mode of transportation for the police. Especially for a guy his size.

"Now we wait," Lou said, trying to give Fisk a feel for what police work was all about. "I'd feel better about it if there was a car in the driveway. Then we could at least verify that we're at the right place. Do *you* think we're in the right place?"

It's a certainty, Louis. We're where we're supposed to be, doing what we're supposed to do. Now let's act like cops and sit on our asses for several hours and wait for something to happen.

"I agree," Lou replied, shifting his weight around violently as he tried to get comfortable. "All we've got to do is wait for them to come to us. We can wait all day and all night if we need to. Let me just make a call. I guess it would be cool to let the others know where we're at."

Good thinking, Louis. Communication is key for an operation such as this. You're a very smart man.

Dialing Andrew Daisley's cell phone number, Lou prepared to report his location and status to the detective in charge. He was also pretty curious as to how the others were doing and wondered if they were having as much fun as he was.

Fun...is that what we're having? Fisk asked, prompting Lou to hold a finger to his lips and shush him before Daisley got on the line.

Chapter 23

▼

After unceremoniously ripping the paper off of the large parcel, Daisley and Quartz were left staring at what looked like a large gray suitcase. Samsonite, it wasn't. The marking on the top read *Anvil* and looked about as tough as one. Flipping the two heavy-duty latches, he lifted it open.

"*Pretty*," Quartz said in a strangely sexy voice as she viewed the contents.

Reaching into the case, she unhooked the Velcro band and lifted out the largest handgun she'd ever held. Just seeing her reflection in the serious weapon made the hair on the back of her neck stand straight up.

"That's ridiculous," Daisley said, shaking his head as he viewed the obscenely huge firearm. "That's got to be for show."

"It'd knock something down, that's for sure. You couldn't conceal it worth a shit, though."

"That's what I'm saying. It's too big for general use. Maybe it made him feel extra tough."

"Or maybe Terrence Fisk just had a really small dick," Quartz offered, pushing the small office's door closed. "I'd be curious to see what kind of car he used to drive. I'll bet it was a Ferrari."

Turning to her left, then to her right, Quartz neatly flipped the gun around in her hand as though shooting from several angles. Blowing imaginary smoke from the barrel, she straightened up and posed with the shiny weapon.

"Am I hot, or what?"

"You sure are," he replied, though it was with less enthusiasm than usual. "I noticed you didn't check the clip or the chamber but…yeah, Quartz, you look really sexy swinging around a possibly loaded Desert Eagle .44 magnum in my office. Smart, too."

His sarcasm sank in as she lowered the barrel from her face and pulled out the clip. As expected, it was packed full of very large shells. Making sure the safety was on, she carefully placed it back in the case and immediately picked up the next one.

"Ah, the old standard," she said with big eyes as she held up a smaller .45 caliber pistol. This time she cleared the round from the chamber first. "I don't think I've seen one this nice, though. Looks like a custom job."

"I'll bet they all are," he replied, flipping open the next compartment of the case, exposing three more handguns. He half expected to find another compartment with knives, piano wire, some newspaper, and a dead fish, but found ammunition for all five weapons instead. "I think we've got a gun for every occasion in here. And all this ammo's special too."

He removed several boxes of various caliber shells from the bottom of the case and lined them up on his desk trying to make sense of them. Matching each gun with it's respective ammunition, he set them aside one by one. Each gun was packaged with two boxes of shells. One marked "subsonic", the other labeled "hyper-velocity".

"*Ooh*, this one has threads," Quartz noted excitedly, setting down the weapon she was holding. A threaded barrel could only mean one thing.

Digging through the case, she found what she was looking for in a side pouch. Considering the former owner's occupation, she wasn't surprised at all. With a few simple turns, the silencer fit snugly onto the barrel of a smaller .32 semiauto pistol.

"We're fucking deadly now, Andrew. All we're missing is a shotgun, a hand grenade, and…"

"…and someone to pull the trigger on these things," he finished for her, waving his hand over the small arsenal.

"Hey, we've got our feelers out and more than twenty-four hours to take care of business. I think there's a good chance that we might get lucky."

Looking hard at his partner, Daisley was amazed by her. Preoccupied with the silenced .32, Quartz was unaware of his gaze while she plugged away at imaginary bad guys against his office wall. Even after the day they'd had, she still found it possible to think that they might get lucky. It was one of the things that attracted him to her and kept his mind in balance during the longest week of his life.

"I'm sorry, Quartz, but for some reason I'm just not feeling that lucky today."

"Maybe we've already been lucky, Andrew. I mean, I know it's been a rough day, but compared to…let's say…*Terrence Fisk*, I think our day's been pretty tame."

A moment later, a phone began to ring. Getting a dial tone from the phone on his desk, Daisley reached into his jacket and pulled out his cell phone. Instead of talking, he could only listen to the voice that was blasting his right eardrum out. It was easy to tell who was on the other end of the line.

"What are you saying, Louis?" Daisley asked with disbelief, breathing heavily into the phone. "You're telling me we're covered? No problems?"

Chapter 24

▼

"Yeah, I took care of him," Lou said smiling, his hand resting on Fisk's shoulder. "He's in a safe place."

"No problems at all? I'm serious, Louis. Not one?"

"Not one," Lou repeated back at him, winking at Fisk. "I made a few calls on the way down here and…"

"Where are you right now?"

He had only said about six sentences but Lou was already unhappy with Daisley's demeaning tone. "I'm in Costa Mesa. I got some info on one of my guys and we're…uh…I'm just waiting for him to show up."

The line was silent for a moment as the detective wrapped his brain around the fact that big dumb cop from Fresno was already way ahead of everyone else. It was a start, though, and he was happy about any luck they were going to get.

"You're sure he still lives there?"

"Nope," Lou answered simply. "But a citation was mailed to this address about two months ago and the ticket got paid off. Someone wrote a check for him and if they're still here then…."

"That's great news, Louis," Daisley interrupted again, sounding suddenly upbeat. "Call me the second you make contact with either of these guys. If we can get them to…" Pausing, Daisley had to choose his words carefully. The line between what would confuse Louis and what he could say about their business over a cellular phone was very thin. "…you know…do that thing for us. We're going to have to be careful about how we pitch the idea."

"What do you mean?" Lou asked, winking at Fisk again. The detective's condescending words and constant interrupting were worth a small dose of intentional stupidity from the big man.

"Damn, Louis," Daisley whined, barely containing his anxiety. "I'm saying we've got to cover our...we've got to make sure that...fuck."

At this point, all he wanted was contact. Letting the street cop initiate and negotiate this kind of thing would be insanity considering that they never thought he'd get this far to begin with.

"What are you trying to say?" Lou asked, fighting to keep a lid on his laughter.

"Okay, here's the deal. You stay there and watch the place. If your guy shows up, don't do anything. Okay, Louis? Not a thing."

"No problem. I'll stay here. But what if he comes home then tries to leave?"

"If that happens, call me immediately," Daisley answered in the commanding tone that Lou was getting less and less thrilled with. "Depending on the situation, I may have you follow him. How well do you remember these guys?"

"I'd know them if I saw them."

"How much talking did you do with them? When you brought them in, I mean."

"All they did was answer questions," Lou replied. "They didn't try to talk their way out of trouble or anything. Didn't really get chatty with anyone except for each other. I think they knew better than to shoot their mouths off."

"Okay, like I said, you just stay there. If you see him, don't approach him. Just make a call."

"What if someone else shows up?" Lou asked, figuring that he'd have to be very lucky to run into Joe Sheridan at all. "You know, a roommate or something. If they could tell me where he works or where he's at, maybe I can...."

"No, Louis. Don't do anything like that," Daisley said harshly, busting up Lou's third sentence in less than two minutes. "This is more delicate than you know. If you lay eyes on him, I'll get over there as fast as I can and see what kind of deal we can come up with. Do you have anything on him?"

"On who?"

"Either of them. Is there anything you know about that we could hold over their heads? Maybe some evidence that was inadmissible or tainted. Do we have any leverage? That's what I'm asking."

"Nothing but suspicion and the word of some loser. I guess I could try to bluff them and...."

"Don't even think about it," Daisley charged in, shutting him down again. "No bluffs, no questions, and no talking to these guys. I'll handle that if anyone shows up. You just keep your eyes open."

"I will," Lou replied dryly, ready to toss the phone out the window if he was cut off by the detective again.

"Beautiful. Depending on how everything goes, I'll either be here in Corona or somewhere between here and Long Beach chasing down something for Mike or Quartz. I'll have the phone the whole time so I shouldn't be hard to find. We only got here about twenty minutes ago and Mike's already gone, but so far I'd say you're doing a great job, Louis. You're hours ahead of us."

Lou didn't know whether to take it as a compliment or a sign that they were all horribly screwed. Somehow, being the front runner didn't make him feel any better about their situation.

"You just stay on it, Lou. I'll expect to hear from you soon. And thanks again for taking care of that other thing. I know it must have been a pain in the ass."

"No problem," Lou replied honestly, patting Fisk on the back. "If I see either of our guys, you're the first call I make."

"Perfect, Louis. I'll be waiting for it. Good luck."

"You too," Lou replied as the phone clicked in his ear. Rolling his eyes, he turned to his right. "You hear that, Terry? The detective wishes us luck. Ain't that sweet?"

Chapter 25

"Hey, Alex, I got a question for you," Joseph Sheridan bellowed as he peered through the venetian blinds from his bedroom. "I'm probably wrong about this, but I want your opinion on something."

Stepping from the garage, Alex Bautista carefully wiped off his hands before entering the room. "What is it?" he asked in a soft and almost whispery voice.

If Joe hadn't known Alex for over ten years, he would have thought that the young man was extremely depressed; just like everyone else did when they first laid eyes on him. A look of sadness or deep concern seemed to emanate from his twenty-four year-old face and was a constant fixture.

"The guy outside," Joe said, motioning towards the opposite side of the street.

"Oh, him. What'd he want?"

"I didn't answer the door." He widened the gap in the blinds. "Check him out."

Moving to the window, Alex took a hard look at the Porsche and her occupants before stepping back and nodding. He then slowly walked out of the room and headed back to the garage.

"Well?" Joe yelled, hoping for more of an opinion than a nod.

From the garage, he could hear what sounded like words coming from his quiet friend. Knowing it would do no good to yell again, he did what he should have done in the first place and walked into the garage.

"What did you say?" he asked, watching Alex unload the back of the van. "I didn't hear you."

"I said you were right."

"Right about what?"

"Right about what you said you were probably wrong about."

"But...."

"Yeah, I know," Alex responded with what passed for a smile. "It's that stupid cop from out in Fresno. I told you we should have skipped that place and stayed on the interstate."

With that said, he returned to the back of the van and continued to unload it. Wordlessly, various pieces of stainless steel and copper were carefully stacked and moved about the garage. Joe waited patiently for elaboration until it became apparent that he didn't intend to say anything more on the subject.

"Okay, you're a fucking genius. Tell me why he's knocking on my mom's door and I'll be impressed. You don't think they've been watching us, do you?"

"No, we'd have seen them," Alex answered with a single shake of his head. "Next time he comes to the door, maybe you should answer it and ask him what he wants."

"Maybe I'll do just that. What if he's got a warrant or something?"

Alex seemed to think about it as he hopped into the van and looked for any little pieces that might have been left behind. "If he did, there'd be more than two of them. Now give me a hand with the hardware. I don't want to bump any of this stuff around."

"Why do we need to be so careful?" Joe asked, looking down at the reflective metal. "It looks tough enough."

"How tough do you think it will look when it explodes and kills the both of us? It's not rocket science, but it kind of is. There's a lot of pressure involved. Even a tiny crack would be a bad thing. Besides, we're going to make a ton of cash off of this and I'd rather have it fully operational."

Arguing with Alex's ungodly high IQ would have been pointless and most likely dangerous in the long run. Grabbing a side, Joe grunted as they lifted the device up off of the ground and set it on the work bench.

"I hope you know what your doing with that thing," he cautioned as Alex unfolded a blanket and covered the whole bench. "I know it doesn't have a lot of moving parts but it looks pretty fragile anyway."

"I'll special order a manual or something," Alex agreed, then walked out of the garage, leaving Joe to wonder if he was being sarcastic or not.

After waiting for over two minutes in the garage, Joe assumed that Alex was not coming back and went in search of him. Putting up with his constant disappearing acts was part of the deal if he wanted to hang with the smartest and most devious fellow he'd had the good fortune to know.

Alex Bautista was an acquired taste who could be the most impatient person in the world. At the same time, he could sit still for hours or days if need be, depending on the situation. Being an enigma of quirky and sometimes annoying behavior, he wasn't necessarily someone to be desired as a friend. As far as one on one interaction went, Joe Sheridan was the only person permitted deep into his oddly illogical world.

"What're they doing?" Joe asked, finding Alex perched in front of the blinds.

"The cop who arrested us is talking on the phone," he replied, straining his eyes to make out the other occupant. "The other guy's just sitting there. I've never seen him before. Nice car."

"*Too* nice, huh?"

"Too nice, too small, too clean—they look stupid in it," Alex agreed in a pondering tone. "You'd better get me the ears."

Without hesitation, Joe returned to the van in the garage and threw open the glove compartment. Finding two cellular phones, he grabbed the one wrapped in red electrical tape and ran back to the bedroom, slapping the beat up phone into Alex's outstretched hand. With a press of a button Alex started checking frequencies. The modified handset was more of a scanner than the two-way speaking device it was manufactured to be. He'd built it one afternoon out of boredom but seldom used it, though the potential for abuse was astounding.

The problem was that people's private phone calls didn't interest him in the slightest. He could tell that Joe had felt a certain thrill from invading another's privacy, but never got the same feeling himself. After the first few eavesdropping sessions, he was even more bored than when he built the thing in the first place.

It was less than a minute before the words coming out of the speaker aligned themselves with the movement of the police officer's lips. Even through the tinny ear piece they immediately recognized the voice on the line.

"Oh, yeah, that's the guy," Joe said, seemingly unimpressed with the speed at which they were able to tap straight into a police officer's conversation.

The brain power required to do so was still extraordinary, but over the years he grew immune to Alex's bursts of demented brilliance. As they listened in silence, the two young men eyed each other with confused looks. They were sure of what they were hearing but not so sure about what it meant.

"You want to roll tape on this?" Alex asked, mainly for Joe's benefit. Not everyone could be expected to remember every word that was uttered in their presence. "They're talking like a couple of idiot gangsters who know their line is tapped."

"Yeah, this is odd," Joe agreed, digging through a desk drawer for a small hand-held tape recorder. Once the recorder was located, he reached into a different drawer for the proper plug adapter. Alex waited as he loaded a tape and connected the plugs to their corresponding jacks. Joe wasn't quite the wizard that Alex was but felt happy that he had a few moments of his own from time to time.

As the conversation expanded, so did their confusion. From the way the intruders in the Porsche were speaking, it would have been impossible to tell that at least one of them was supposed to be a police officer. A minute or so later, the call was concluded.

"You know what I think?" Joe asked, his face scrunching into a disbelieving look.

"Yeah, I know," Alex replied. "They're looking for us…but it doesn't really sound like we're in any kind of trouble. It sounds important, though—well, to *them* anyway."

"And it doesn't have anything to do with the stuff in the garage?" Joe asked, hoping for some confirmation.

"I don't think so."

"Well, what do you think?"

Instead of answering, Alex searched his brain for an appropriate response. He wanted to say that he didn't know *what* to think, which would have been a first. After listening to the strange conversation again and then once more, Alex turned the small tape recorder off and calmly peeked through the window again. Joe, looking slightly more concerned, checked out the scene as well.

"What was all that crap about leverage and holding things over our heads?" Joe asked, mostly of himself.

"Well, he's a Fresno cop so it's got to have something to do with that whole thing that happened up there. That's the only reason he'd be here, right?"

He wasn't really asking Joe's opinion but merely bouncing the words off of him to see how they sounded and if they made any sense. So far, they didn't.

"But the guy's just a patrolman or something," Joe pointed out, the pitch of his voice rising. "He shouldn't be staking us out. It's not his job and he's out of his jurisdiction. Just a few months ago he was wearing a uniform and driving a cruiser out in Fresno. Now he's got a partner, they're wearing suits, and he's driving a Porsche—a nice one. This is bullshit."

"Sorry, man, all my fault," Alex told him, not really sounding very apologetic. "I shouldn't have said anything to that little fucker when we were locked up. I just wanted to see him shut up real quick."

Joe's face broke into a smile. "He did, didn't he?"

"Yeah, but I still shouldn't have said shit."

He could still picture the look on Bobby Cress's face when his knees had hit the floor of one of Fresno's uglier lockdown facilities. It was filled with more worry and anxiety than any human should have had to bear. Naturally, Alex had felt an urge to make it even worse. And he did.

"You don't think they found anything at that construction site, do you?" Joe asked with an amused look.

"Wouldn't that be funny?"

Chapter 26

"I take it Lou wasn't calling from a jail cell?" Quartz asked as she lit a cigarette, sensing Daisley's excitement.

"No, thank God. In fact, it almost sounds like he's doing all right. He couldn't give me any details about it on the phone but I'm guessing Fisk is out of the picture now. He said he's in a safe place. You know, you're really not supposed to smoke in here."

"Oh, I'm sorry," she said, dragging even more heavily, blowing smoke around his office. "But seriously…," she continued, taking another drag. "…do you think he stashed him really good?"

"He's safe. That's what Lou said. I'll have to take his word for it this time."

"What was all that other stuff? You said he was hours ahead of us. He's not really onto something, is he?"

"It's doubtful," he answered noncommittally. "He thinks he tracked down one of his candidates. He's just sitting there in front of the guy's house waiting for him to show up." He started to laugh at the thought of it.

"Do you think it's for real?"

"Frankly, I don't care and I'm hoping that nobody shows up. Right now, the safest place for Lou is right where he's at. If he sits across from the guy's house in a car all night long, I couldn't be happier. The further away from the action he is, the better I'll feel."

"He's not sitting there in a cab, is he?" Quartz mused, her eyes floating upward as she pictured the scene in her head. "I sure hope he didn't leave the meter running."

"Oh, *shit*," Daisley uttered, suddenly picturing the same thing. Fumbling, he reached for his phone again.

"Hold up, Andrew. I was just kidding—mostly. He probably rented a car. Even if he didn't and he's actually sitting in a taxi cab right now…how bad is it really? All we'd be doing is paying some poor cab driver an insane amount of money to baby-sit him. But I wouldn't even worry about it. He rented a car. He may be stupid but he's not retarded for God's sake."

"You sure about that?" he asked, certainly not sure himself.

"Positive, Andrew. I guarantee it," she answered, blowing smoke directly into his face this time. "I think he'll do the right thing." She only wished she meant it. With all they had to do before the day was out, the last thing she wanted Andrew or herself worrying about was Louis Poklatar. She hoped he bought it.

"Yeah, I guess you're right."

"Of course I am. And I'm also running late," she added, taking a look at the time. "Do you know where I can get one of those things that'll tell me what's happening at the track?"

"A racing form? I think Garden Liquor on Third Street has them. They should be near the front door, next to all those auto reseller magazines. It'll be big like a newspaper."

Yes, Daisley knew about racing forms. Though Los Alamitos was far below his standards, he made the time to visit at least one of the more decent tracks each year. If he didn't plan on being terribly busy for the rest of the day, he would have considered going with her.

"I guess I'll pick one up then. I've never been to a racetrack before. What do I do? Do I need to change?"

"Haven't you ever seen a movie or TV show that takes place at a track?"

"Sure."

"Well, Los Alamitos will be just like the ones you've seen on TV except it's like—on a budget. It's not like dog races in Mexico but definitely isn't Emerald Downs either."

"Emerald Downs?"

"Never mind, Quartz, you'll figure it all out once you're there. You can change if you want to but first I'd try to figure out how your girl Nanette will be dressed. If you think she'll be all dressed up then you might want to do the same. I'd bring an extra set of clothes—maybe a few—and change once you've ID'd her. She'll be more likely to sit down and talk with you if you don't stand out."

"Don't worry, I'll get her," she replied with a serious face. "She'll solve all of our problems and we'll never have to think about Christian Roche or Donald Ratcliffe again."

"Great. As long as we're fantasizing here, do you think she could whip up some breakfast for me tomorrow and maybe give me a back rub before she kills him?"

"I don't know, I'll ask."

Looking ready to crush out her cigarette on the floor, Daisley quickly grabbed the almost extinguished butt and opened his office door. Briefly exiting the building, he took the last filter-tasting dregs of a hit off of it before flicking it into the parking lot. By the time he returned to his office, Quartz had her jacket back on and looked ready to leave. He wished she didn't have to.

"Are you going to be okay?"

"Detective Andrew Daisley," she said, looking into his eyes. "You don't need to worry about Detective Qiana Schwartze. She's cocked and loaded. I'll be fine."

"Do you need anything? Last chance."

"I think I've got everything I need," she said, holding up her phone. "If I'm wrong, you'll be hearing from me."

Quartz buttoned her jacket, gave him a kiss on the cheek, and left the building. Within a minute she tore out of the parking lot, happy to finally have a bit of solitude. She enjoyed Daisley's company but had seen and heard quite enough of him today.

While Quartz was screeching from the lot, Daisley was mentally kicking himself back in his office. If he had been thinking, he would have offered her one of the guns from Fisk's case. They would all be unregistered and untraceable, which could prove handy in the event of an unauthorized shootout. Distracted by any number of things, he'd forgotten to bring it up.

It was only while he was putting the items back in the case that he noticed that something was amiss. He also realized that Quartz was no dummy—maybe a bit overzealous, but definitely not stupid. The largest handgun of the lot was missing. Along with it, a box of shells marked "hyper-velocity".

No, the little woman wasn't stupid at all.

Chapter 27

▼

"What're they doing now?" Alex asked from a reclining position on Joe's futon bed, figuring it didn't take more than one pair of eyes to watch two men sitting in a car.

"Same thing—nothing," he replied, beginning to take more notice of the car itself than the boring occupants. "Are you getting pissed yet?"

"For a while now," Alex answered quietly, rising from his seat. "I'm starting to wish you answered the door when he knocked. He knocked, right?"

"Yeah. A few times."

"Well, then they're not spying on us. And they're not trying to conceal themselves, so they don't seem to care if we know they're there. I guess it's the phone call that's bugging me."

"You want to go ask them what it was about?"

"Nah, let's ask them from right here."

Alex picked up his modified cell phone once again and punched a few buttons. He didn't even need a number. As easily as he'd plucked the officer's frequency from the air, he was now ready to transmit on the same channel.

Joe pried the blinds open again. "Make sure you tell them I said hi."

* * * *

When the cell phone rang to life Lou nearly jumped out of his seat. He'd been hoping for some news but hadn't expected it so quickly.

"Lou here," he said excitedly, smacking the phone painfully into his ear.

"Lou who?"

Lou who? Not in the mood for a crank call, he spit out his name, rank and serial number which would afford him the proper respect he was owed. "This is Agent Louis Poklatar, Federal Bureau of Investigation. Who's this?"

In this instance, he decided to go for a little more respect than he deserved. It didn't help.

"Louis? This is The Lord."

"Who...?" For moment—only a brief one—Lou could feel his heart going gimpy. "Is that you, Mike?" he asked after a few seconds of silence, figuring that Blash would be the only one with balls enough to impersonate God. "What's the news?"

"This isn't Mike, Louis," the voice said, followed by a series of whispers. *"And you're not FBI. Your windows aren't even tinted."*

Turning to Fisk with a quizzical look then checking his windows, he found that The Lord was indeed correct. In fact, there was nothing about the car that would indicate connections to any kind of law enforcement agency. Anyone who looked at the car would think the same thing. All they'd have to do was open their eyes.

The last thought clicked somehow and gave him a quick mental ego boost, not to mention a serious case of goosebumps. His eyes darted all around the car then settled on the house.

"You can see me, huh?"

"Yeah, Louis. We've been watching you for a while now," the voice said, fading back into whispers for a moment. *"Why so patient?"*

It was creepy as hell knowing he'd been spied on but at least it wasn't the Lamb of God doing the spying. If he'd have been staking out a church or a cemetery he supposed he would have dropped dead on the spot.

"I already knocked on the door a bunch of times."

"Well, knock again. You guys can talk to us on the porch. Nobody comes inside."

"Who am I talking to?" Lou asked, just to make sure that a choir of angels wasn't going to meet him at the door.

"Don't act like you don't remember me. Quit hanging out in the street and come up to the front door. You look suspicious out there...and...wait a sec...Joe says hi."

Joe says hi? What is that—code for something? If it was, Lou was unaware of it's exact meaning. Instead of wasting time thinking about it, Lou slowly rose from the driver's seat and rolled his neck around. After several loud pops, he started for the house.

"Okay, I'm on my way," he said, hanging up and folding his phone shut. Taking a look back at Fisk, he mouthed, *"Bad cop...remember, you're the bad cop."*

* * * *

"Here comes one of them," Joe announced as Alex clicked the phone off. "What's the other guy doing?"

Straining his eyes to view the man in the passenger seat, Joe didn't like the look of it. He was sitting completely still and stone faced. Though he was wearing dark sunglasses, Joe could have sworn he was staring right at him.

"He's hanging back for some reason. Keep the ears handy in case he decides to call someone."

Joe nodded and accepted the phone, stuffing it into his pocket as he quietly stepped from the room and headed for the front door. A moment later, Alex joined him and together they walked out onto the porch. As usual, their portrayal of amazing coolness was perfect and would certainly hold up to the likes of a Fresno street cop. It always had before.

* * * *

Only after stepping onto the concrete driveway did Lou remember something that the detective had said to him. It was something to the effect of *"Don't speak to them"*...only more rudely and condescending.

But the way Lou saw it, he was ordered not to initiate contact. He was only supposed to report when they showed up and then watch them from a distance. The detective didn't say anything about what to do if they made the first move or did something unexpected. Receiving a call on his unlisted cell phone seemed to qualify as unexpected.

"Fuck you, Daisley," Lou mumbled to himself and continued his short journey to the front porch.

Five steps later he found himself face to face with his assignment. Both of them.

Scanning the two young men, the uncomfortable silence wasn't too uncomfortable since they were looking at him in exactly the same fashion. He didn't mind and was even elated that they'd made an appearance at all. They were just like he remembered them. Well, mostly.

"Weren't you guys bigger?" Lou found himself asking before thinking of the words that came from his mouth. Correcting his bad etiquette, he quickly struggled for a recovery. "I mean, you know—*bigger*?"

And now he'd said it twice.

With amused glances, the two looked each other up and down. After it had been determined and silently agreed upon, the two men answered simultaneously. "I don't think so."

It should have broken the ice but it didn't. Lou couldn't think of a thing to say and was starting to understand the detective's motives for keeping him quiet. Luckily, they spoke first.

"So, Officer Poklatar from Fresno," Alex said in a calm and friendly manner. "You're a little out of your jurisdiction, aren't you?"

If you only knew how far, he thought before telling them, "I'm on a special assignment."

"What kind of special assignment?" Alex asked.

"You two guys," he replied. "You're my assignment. I was supposed to find you and…well…now I have."

Alex crossed his arms, scrutinizing the only man who had ever put him in handcuffs. "Keep talking, Officer Lou. You were supposed to find us and then *what*?"

"And then I was supposed to ask you something," he replied with a shrug.

But he wasn't. He wasn't supposed to ask anybody anything. He wasn't even supposed to speak. Lou hadn't uttered a single phrase about the job yet but could already feel the wrongness of his current situation spreading like poison in his mind. He could feel it moving outward from his brain and projecting itself onto his face. Worse still, he knew they could see it as much as he felt it.

Whatever justification he'd made for disregarding Daisley's direct order only minutes earlier had already been lost. It was gone. Like many of the other choices he had made in his life, Lou had no idea what in the hell he'd been thinking. He tried to hold his tongue as he searched for a way to back-pedal from what he had done.

"You see, guys, I've been authorized to extend an offer to you."

But you just had to fuck it up even worse, didn't you, Louis? He could practically hear Fisk screaming at him from the car. *Don't get me wrong—you sounded almost smart there for a second—but you haven't thought this all the way through, big guy. What kind of offer were you talking about? And who authorized it? That's the next question. You'd better have an answer.*

"Authorized by who?" Alex asked, as if on cue. "The Fresno PD?"

"Well…"

Careful, Louis. They're not as big as you remembered but they're still smart. Don't say shit about Fresno. In fact, don't even mention cops. If you hit them up with this as an officer of the law you won't even get your foot in the door.

"No," Lou finally replied with a simple shake of his head. "This isn't something that the police—"

No...don't say that. It sounds lame. Say this: "It's not a departmental matter". Stand up straighter and squint your eyes a bit. Not too much. Just a little.

"Well, let's just say it's not a departmental matter," Lou continued, rising two inches as he straightened his back. Then, as if warding off the sun, he let his eyes close slightly and shifted them back and forth between the two men. "It's not police business at all. And in fact..."

It's okay. Go ahead. Just make it good.

"...it falls outside what would be considered 'legal'."

Even better than I expected, Louis.

"Who is it then?" Joe asked, hoping Alex would jump in soon and drag it out of the cop already. "If you're not representing a department, who's making this offer of yours?"

"And what exactly is it you're offering?" Alex added, skipping right to the important stuff.

I told you they'd ask. Have you figured out how you're going to put this, Louis? Don't just spit it out. Think first. Or better yet, let me do the thinking on this one.

"We're talking purely hypothetical now, right?" Lou asked, his mouth saying one thing, his eyes saying something completely different. The two young men nodded, getting his point.

Perfect. If it goes badly, this conversation never happened. At least, that's what they'll think. Fucking brilliant, Louis.

"Well, hypothetically speaking," Lou began, peering over both shoulders and lowering his voice to a whisper. "I might know of a private party willing to pay a decent amount of money to make one of his problems go away. If we could talk inside, I'd feel a little better about—"

"Nobody goes inside," Alex interrupted, calmly yet firmly.

Be cool, Louis. They've got something in there that they don't want you to see. You're still a cop, you know.

"Okay," Lou paused, taking a deep breath and pulling in closer to them. "Let's say we've got this guy. He's a pain in the ass, right? A real piece of shit. Anyhow, this other guy—the man I represent—he wants the first guy I was talking about to stop doing the bad things he's been doing."

"What kind of bad things?"

"He rapes children," Lou told them, not realizing just how good—or just how bad—it sounded until the words actually came out. "The guy's a Level III sex offender who's back at it again. There's been at least three that we know of. Probably a lot more. And the one's we don't know about—they're most likely dead."

The looks on each of their faces told Lou that he'd struck a chord. A combination of distaste, shock, and curiosity emanated from both of them. They would want to hear more.

It's perfect. Where'd that come from? Lou asked himself in total amazement.

You're welcome, Fisk replied silently.

Chapter 28

▼

"So if you know who he is and where he's at, why isn't the fucker under arrest right now?" Joe asked, clearly unhappy with the workings of California's judicial system.

"You guys should know how it works," Lou replied. "He's got himself some hotshot lawyer who makes all the evidence unusable." He knew there was a technical term for it but couldn't think of it at the moment. "He's supposed to be arraigned on Monday for the latest one but it will probably just be more of the same shit. The man I work for doesn't want to bother with another trial that goes nowhere."

"What does he want then?" Alex asked, seeming to want to hear the words very badly. Lou didn't sense it right away but Fisk seemed to pick up on it immediately.

Okay, Louis. This is the important part. He wants you to spill it. Now, I don't know if these guys are for real or not but they're definitely interested. You can see it in their eyes. And get this…you haven't even mentioned money yet. Go ahead and say it. They want it, Lou. They're begging for it.

"My boss wants him dead by tomorrow night. It doesn't matter how it's done. It just has to happen."

Upon saying it, Lou expected a long period of silence as the pair absorbed the information that had just been dumped on them. There was none, though. Not a moment of it. The words had barely left his mouth before Joe Sheridan was asking the requisite followup question.

"What exactly is the offer then?"

"Yeah, we're curious," Alex agreed. "You're not just offering us the privilege of killing this guy, are you?"

Okay, now we talk about money. You've already pissed away a bit on the Porsche and you can bet your cop buddies aren't being too frugal either. Keep it low. Don't give it all away, Louis.

"No, you get to kill him *and* you get..." Lou paused, numbers flashing through his head. "...ten thousand dollars for your trouble."

"How much money do we get for going to prison when you turn around and arrest us for accepting this offer of yours?" Alex then asked, completely void of sarcasm.

"Or when somebody else does," Joe added. "What's *that* worth to you?"

"It won't happen like that," Lou explained. "Once it's done, another officer—a detective, actually—he'll be the first on the scene. All the evidence will make it look like a revenge job that no one would even investigate anyway. It'll be real clean. No problems."

"Why don't you do it yourself?" Alex asked, looking up at the cop who seemed to have gained some IQ points since their last encounter. He certainly looked capable of dismantling a child molester all on his own.

You should have seen that one coming, Louis. Time to get tough.

"Are you kidding? I begged him to let me do it. But this is a very important man who's footing the bill for the deal. He wants guarantees that it won't be tied to the department. *Any* department. That way, he's protected if things get out of hand."

Yeah, that's what I would have said. I think you're getting brighter by the second, Louis.

Alex gave Lou's face a measuring look. "If this is such an easy job, what makes you think it might get out of hand?"

Trying hard to think of what could make an easy job get ugly, Lou searched vainly for an easy answer. He didn't want to scare them off and certainly didn't want to explain that only a cold-hearted motherfucker would ever kill somebody for money. Telling them that he was still a good cop on the inside wouldn't have helped either.

But that's what you are, Big Lou, came Fisk's voice. *You're a good cop and this really isn't your thing, so I'm going to recommend letting the bad cop handle this one.*

"Okay, smart guy," Lou said, the words not feeling completely like his own. "Let's say I'm me. I'm a cop, okay? I just walked into the guy's place and blew him away really easy, right? Now let's say I'm giving the place the once over to make sure I didn't leave anything incriminating behind. But as I'm walking out the door, I slip on something and crack my fucking head on a table or something stupid like that. Now I'm a dead cop in a dead drug dealer's house and it's obvious that I just killed him. Next thing you know, the guy I'm working for is connected to it and everyone's screwed."

"What drug dealer?" Joe asked, responding to a quick glance from Alex. "You said we were talking about a—"

"It's just an example, guys," Lou said tiredly, looking away from them.

Nice recovery, stupid. Try to stay in character, will you?

Alex already had a few opinions of his own but asked Joe for another one anyway. "What do you think, man?"

"I think he's still fishing for clues about that Gabriel Marcos guy in Fresno. It's a weird way for a cop to do business, but that's my two cents. I think he's still digging."

Alex listened and nodded while Lou was treated to two pairs of leery eyes.

We're losing them, Fisk's voice came again, more urgent than before. *It's time to throw your nuts out there and let them know who's shitting who.*

"Okay, do you know what entrapment is?" Lou asked, staring hard at Alex.

"I'm familiar with the concept."

"Well, how does *this* work for you?" Lou asked, reaching into his coat pocket. Watching their eyes grow wide, he removed a short stack of bills wrapped in a thin band. They were all hundreds.

"Here's the deal. I give you a name, a picture, and an address…and ten thousand dollars. All I want you to do for the money is to take out the man that we've been talking about. You can shoot him, strangle him, fire him out of a cannon, or burn his fucking house down—I don't care. Whatever works for you. Now, what would it be called if you accepted my offer and I turned around and busted you for it?"

Excellent, Louis. They know the answer.

"Yeah, that'd be entrapment," Alex replied with half a grin. "Even a shitty lawyer could beat that. Let's see the money. Hand it to me."

As Lou did just that, it was Alex's turn to peek over both shoulders. Once the cash was firmly in his grip he ran his thumb across the end of the stack as though counting it insanely fast.

"There's only about five grand here," he noted, tossing the money to Joe.

"Half now," Lou said, not really sure how much he'd just handed over. Hopefully, it was enough. They weren't being very scientific back at the hotel when they split the money up in the first place. Everyone simply got a pretty good handful and walked out of the room. "Are you *still* worried about being arrested?"

"I guess not," Joe said, smiling as he played with the money. "But just to be on the safe side…we're still talking hypothetically, right?"

"That's right."

Hypothetically. These guys are cracking me up, Fisk whispered into his ear.

"Good," Alex said, straightening up. "Then me and my friend will do some hypothetical talking and discuss your hypothetical offer."

"How long do you need?"

"Give us a few hours. We've got your number. We'll call you. And don't park across from the house next time. You look suspicious."

* * * *

"That whole entrapment thing—is it true?" Joe asked as they watched the Porsche make a three point turn and head off. "And I'm not too sure on all this *hypothetical* bullshit. It doesn't really protect us, does it?"

"No way," Alex answered quickly. "If he recorded the conversation and played it for a jury, the word *hypothetical* wouldn't mean anything. They'd know we were talking seriously and that's all that matters. We'd be screwed. He's right about entrapment, though. That whole thing with the money and asking us to kill somebody—he's not allowed to do that."

"Then why would he take a chance like that? With us, I mean. Why are we so special?"

"Because we killed Gabriel Marcos when we were in Fresno," Alex answered as though it was obvious. "Shot him fifteen times and whacked him up like a birthday cake. We'd be perfect for something like this."

"Yeah, I guess. But we didn't do that."

"I don't think that matters," he replied, completely unfazed. "As far as they're concerned, they're using a couple of bad guys to kill another bad guy. Only the bad guy they want us to kill is a *real* bad guy. If they didn't think we killed Marcos, they wouldn't have gone through the trouble of asking us. They must be pretty damn sure that we're guilty."

"Is that a good thing?"

"Up until fifteen minutes ago I would have said no," Alex answered, looking out to the street. "But ten grand? It could go a long way. Think of all the shit we could actually buy instead of stealing."

"Don't forget there's a job attached to that money."

"What—killing a pedophile?" Alex Bautista's eyes narrowed. "I've always wanted to do that anyway. I just haven't had the time."

Chapter 29

▼

She didn't remember him even after he showed her his badge and told her his name. Though it had been over a year since she'd last seen him, Blash expected at least a tiny glimmer of recognition from the uptight receptionist at Helmwood. He didn't get it.

"Yes, ma'am. Walter Van Staadt," he repeated, glancing around the lobby that hadn't changed a bit. "I was hoping to speak with him."

He already had all the information he needed so he didn't have to act like a confused idiot this time. The only thing he wasn't sure about was what Walter's reaction would be when he saw him. Unlike the receptionist, Walter would certainly remember him.

While she punched in his phone number, Blash watched with interest as she lowered her voice and turned away from him. Just like she did over a year earlier, she slipped into privacy-mode to warn Walter that a cop was here to see him. At least she was consistent.

"He'll be right down," she said, turning back to him with the first smile he'd seen on the woman. He preferred her without it.

Only two minutes later, Walter Van Staadt strolled into the lobby. Unexpectedly, he was wearing a smile as well.

"Mike!" he nearly yelled, beaming and walking with an outstretched hand. "It's been way too long. How are you?"

Expecting the opposite reaction from the man, Blash searched for an appropriate response. Unable to think faster than Walter was walking at him, he threw on a smile of his own and grabbed the hand that was offered to him. Shaking it roughly, he slapped Walter on the shoulder.

"I'm doing great," he said back excitedly. "I was back in town and I thought I'd see what was happening in your end of the world. You're looking great." He felt like a first-class asshole.

"Thanks, Mike. I'm in between patients right now. You want to come on up and tell me what's been going on?"

"You bet," Blash answered, following Walter who'd already turned away and started walking. Only after the elevator door had closed behind them did Walter speak again. Amazingly, the lighthearted expression on his face remained intact.

"You know, I'm actually glad you're here. I knew you'd be back but I didn't know when. It was killing me. So, how are you, really?"

It was a very odd question from a very odd man.

"I'm fine, Walter," Blash answered awkwardly, nodding his head slowly. "And I like your attitude about this. I really thought you were gonna shit when you saw me."

I was hoping so, anyway.

"No, I'm due. I know it. It's been like sleeping on a bed of nails. You couldn't have picked a better time."

"Why's that?"

The elevator doors slid open on the fourth floor. After stepping into the hall and making sure no one was around, Walter led him to an empty room.

"Because it'll be one less thing to worry about. It's been a pretty crazy few months for me and knowing you'd show up one day was just making it worse. With my wife in the hospital and...well...the other things I've been working on, it's been hectic. I was even considering calling *you*."

"What for?" Blash asked, taking a seat while Walter closed the door.

"There's this group of meth freaks in Upland I've been hanging with on Tuesdays and Fridays. It's like a convention, I swear. There's the guys who cook it up, the distributors, the street dealers—name it. I'm pretty much done with them, so—"

"No, Walt. Why was your wife in the hospital?"

"Oh, she was having all kinds of...you know...woman problems. But she's cool now. Taking it easy."

"What was she diagnosed with?"

"Pregnancy," Walter answered simply. "See, her uterus is a little tilted and the lining has—"

"It's okay, man, I get it," Blash said, holding a hand up before he had to hear about the woman's last three menstrual cycles. "Congratulations, though. I hope she's okay."

"Thanks, I'm sure she'll be fine," Walter said, looking like he was still trying to convince himself of the fact. "But like I was saying; this group—there's fifteen of them. They're the main movers of crystal in the area and I've got them all lined up, just waiting for you."

"Listen, Walt—" Blash started, but was cut off by Walter, who was too excited to stop talking.

"I can set it up for Tuesday or we could even do it tomorrow night. I think that will make us just about even."

He didn't want to rain on the man's parade, though a fifteen dealer drug bust did sound pretty sweet. It just wasn't what he was after this time. It was roughly what they'd agreed on over a year earlier, but the priorities had changed in the course of a single afternoon.

"Listen, Walt. I've got some bad news."

Finally, Walter closed his mouth and listened.

Chapter 30

▼

"What are you expecting me to do?" Walter asked with an anguished face. "I mean, I can check the guy for injuries and maybe patch him up a bit, but that's about it."

"No, Walter. I'm saying the guy's dead. Like, permanently dead. There's no patching him up."

With a squinty eyed look that wouldn't go away, Walter stared at Blash trying to figure out what the man was asking for. If the person he was referring to was already dead then Walter didn't see where he could be of any assistance whatsoever.

"Okay, he's dead. What do you want me to do? Throw some rice over my shoulder, dance in a circle and start chanting? It won't bring him back if he's all the way dead, you know."

"I know it won't and that's not what I'm asking you to do. I'm not even finished talking yet, man. The guy I'm talking about—the dead one—he was all set up to do a job for us. A very important job."

"Undercover type work?" Walter asked, taking an educated shot in the dark.

"Yeah, that's exactly right," Blash said, slowly nodding. "Undercover work. But it's the kind of work a cop can't do himself."

Staring down at the small, fidgety man, Blash found himself feeling sorry for him; not in the conventional sense, but on more of a personal level. Though he hadn't figured Walter out yet, he stood apart from the usual crowd of drug fiends that Blash often had to associate with. The whole "good-guy, bad-guy" thing didn't even apply to Walter as he was really in a class of his own.

"Isn't that what private investigators are for?"

Apparently, Walter knew a thing or two about the way it worked. When most people thought of a private investigator, they pictured anything from Sam Spade to Magnum P.I. Stand up guys with a soft spot for a woman in trouble. Back in the real world, though, the private investigators that Blash knew fell somewhere between a repo-man and a peeping tom. Most of them only got their licenses in order to carry a firearm legally. He knew there were good investigators out there, he just hadn't met a single one of them yet.

"Sorry, Walt. We can't use subcontractors on this job. It's too important and it's better if we don't involve someone who works with us regularly."

"More important than the fifteen meth dealers I'm trying to hand you?" he asked, disappointed and confused as to what would make Officer Blash care so little for such a righteous bust.

"Oh, we'll get their asses—don't worry about that. It's the other thing that's important right now. Then you and I will be a done deal. Even Steven. Hell, I'll owe *you* one when this is over."

"What do I have to do?" Walter asked, becoming aware of an increasing level of discomfort from the cop. "Make a buy or something?"

"No, nothing like that, man—nothing like that at all. We're gonna need a change of venue before I can get too into it. Any chance you could scoot out of here for the rest of your shift?"

"I've got a guy who could cover me," Walter replied. "Do you mean now? Right now?"

"Yeah, Walt. *Now*. Can you get off or not?"

"No problem," he answered then picked up the phone.

* * * *

It was only a short ride back to Walter's house with Blash tailing behind him. He had found someone to cover his shift in record time with no complaints from the administration. The fourth floor orderly seemed to carry quite a bit of weight with the staff. That, or maybe they just forgot that an orderly is supposed to empty bedpans, hand out little cups of pills, and be available at all hours of the day and night. Somehow, he seemed above it all, though he didn't act it.

Even the car that Blash followed behind didn't fit. It was a tiny orange sedan that looked slightly older than dirt. At first glance, Blash guessed it was an old Nissan. Only after they hit their first stoplight did he see the insignia on the rear of the vehicle.

The guy's driving a fucking Datsun, Blash thought, hearing the brakes grind and squeal as the car stopped. The vehicle looked like it could fall apart right there at a dead stop and looked even worse as Walter struggled to get the car back in gear. With another squeal—the alternator this time—he stepped on the gas and proceeded through the green light.

Blash wasn't exactly sure what year it was when the Datsun name rolled over to Nissan, but it was definitely forever ago. To actually see one on the road was like finding a four leaf clover…and not in a lucky way, either. Just the same, Walter looked happy enough driving the monstrosity the short distance from his job back to his residence.

The house hadn't changed at all from what Blash had seen a year earlier but this time—after a much closer look—he realized that it was actually pretty nice; not nice like it was bought that way, but in a fixed up sense. It had the potential to be a real shithouse but was kept up nicely, most likely by Walter himself.

The car was another matter, however, and he had to jiggle the handle several times before the door would even open for him. After peeling himself from a seat that was in tatters, he got out of the car and brushed bits of foam and seat cushion from his clothes.

Stepping from his own vehicle—the typical low-profile mid-sized sedan—Blash winced as he watched Walter close his door. Then again. Then again.

"Watch this," Walter said, laughing as he slammed the door again. "Fourth time always works. I don't know why."

He was right. It finally stayed closed.

"You want me to fix that for you?" Blash asked with a smile as he held open his jacket, exposing his revolver.

"What is that—a thirty-eight?"

"Yep," Blash answered, patting the gun with his hand.

"It won't work then," Walter said dryly. "You need a 9mm."

"Why?"

"This is a Japanese car. It's metric."

Blash began laughing and immediately felt bad for it. Laughing and joking around with a man that he was about to use was dangerous and stupid for more reasons than he could count. But he laughed anyway and continued to do so as they walked to the door together.

"Do we have to be anywhere soon?" Walter asked.

"Nope," Blash replied, still chuckling. "Unless I get a bug up my ass to pull in these meth dealers you're talking about, we're solid until tomorrow night. I just need some time to lay this all out for you."

"Good. Are you thirsty?" he asked as he pulled his house keys from his pocket.
"I might be."

Chapter 31

▼

Nanette Lalonde. What a name, Quartz thought as she shuffled hangers around in her closet. With a few hours before the races started for the evening, she wanted to look perfect. Unfortunately, she wouldn't know what perfect was until she got a look at the one who'd been calling herself Nanette. She'd only heard the woman's real name once and had always found it strangely beautiful.

It was a good name and by Quartz's way of seeing things, it was a shame to butcher it down to the horribly French sounding alternative. Even Blash had thought it sounded French, making Quartz think that Netta must have picked the name specifically because it sounded that way. The easy answer was that she changed it because she was hiding from something. Of course, if that was the case, she would have most likely chosen something a little further from her real name. The girl was an enigma right from the start and she only got weirder from then on.

Looking at everything from jeans to long dresses to miniskirts, Quartz picked one set of each and hoped it would be enough options. She'd start with the jeans considering the way Daisley and Blash had talked about the track. If she got lucky she wouldn't have to change once she got there.

Tonight was harness racing, whatever the hell that was. She'd heard of quarter horses and thoroughbreds but anything to do with a harness was news to her. Feeling like an amateur, she wished she had time to do some homework on the subject.

Not this time, baby. We'll wing it and kick ass like we always do. She lit up a cigarette and poured herself a short glass of wine.

Netta, Netta, Netta...what have you been doing with yourself?

She hadn't seen her since her arrest in Cerritos but had always been curious. Curious about her Netta and what she was doing with herself.

* * * *

Her accent was thick, though not French in the slightest. Trying to pass herself off as a western European was working fine with just about every detective in the precinct. To the other officers, she was a stunning, exotic, and coldhearted piece of Euro-trash. To Detective Schwartze, she was just another Ukrainian.

The woman's voice, attitude, and even her facial structure told Quartz all she needed to know about her ethnicity. The harsh, yet striking features were as obvious on Nanette Lalonde as they were on Quartz's own mother.

While she watched the senior detective rip into the uncooperative woman, Quartz remained silent, blanketing her face with the most compassionate expressions she could come up with. With every word that he barked at the woman, Quartz responded with a visible and uncomfortable flinch, rolling her eyes when he wasn't looking...and when Nanette *was*.

"So what you're telling me, Miss...Lalonde...," Detective Sarzo began, spitting out her name like it was a dirty word. "...is that you broke into the house. We're clear on that, right? You broke in through a sliding kitchen window and went straight for the bedroom."

Dragging on a cigarette that Quartz had offered her, the quiet woman shook her head slowly. She looked at the huge Italian detective with a stare that seemed to go through him.

"I went into the big room with the television first," she said, the *W* in *went* sounding the same as the *V* in *television*. It was so extreme that it sounded fake. "Then the bathroom. Then the bedroom."

"When we searched the house, the living room had a large screen TV and several thousand dollars worth of A/V equipment in it," Sarzo said, never losing the scowl that he wore during every interrogation he was involved in. "Let's see here...CD, DVD, three VCR's, a couple of cameras and a shitload of computer hardware. Why didn't you take any of it?"

"Because I am not drug addicted," she answered, putting out her cigarette then holding out her hand for another one. "I only wanted the things on the wall. I have no use for the shitloads of a computer."

Her answer was laughable and disjointed but at least it showed she was paying attention.

"So it was the paintings you were after?" Sarzo asked, drifting in between disbelief and impatience. "That's your story? You broke into the house at three a.m. to steal some paintings and nothing else?"

"They were copies…prints…not real paintings," she said, dropping her eyes to the floor. "No value. Worthless."

"Now, where were they located?" Sarzo asked, knowing perfectly well that they'd covered the subject many times. She hadn't changed her story once yet.

"Big room…bathroom…bedroom," she said for the fourth or fifth time since they began questioning her.

"And that's where you found him," he stated, reading directly from the report in his hand. "Was he face up or face down?"

"Same as you found him," she answered with tired eyes that shut tight as a visible shiver wracked her body. "I did not touch him. He was my employer. I had never seen him dead before."

"And how long did you work for Mr. Kadouris," Quartz asked in a voice that was soothing and calm. Basically, the complete opposite of the way Detective Sarzo spoke to her.

"I was a maid for no longer than a year," she replied, seemingly embarrassed by her former position. "I stopped the work last month."

Sarzo leaned towards her, getting close to her face. "How long was it before you called us? And why didn't you call 911?"

"*911?*" She seemed confused by the question. "I called police instead. Correct?"

"How *long*, Miss Lalonde? I'm asking you how long you waited to call the police after you discovered the body. Can you answer that?"

"Very fast," she answered quickly. "I was afraid. I did not care about pictures after that."

It was quiet for a full minute as Sarzo stared down at her. When she finally looked up, her eyes were brimming with tears. The fear she felt was apparent in them as well. After a brief look from Quartz, Sarzo slammed his paperwork on the empty table in front of him.

"You just sit tight," he said, jabbing a finger at the shaken woman. "Detective Schwartze, come with me."

Rising from her chair, Quartz left her pack of cigarettes and a lighter on the table for her. As Sarzo stepped from the room, she placed a hand on the woman's shoulder. Instead of looking up, her head went down as she sobbed loudly.

"I'll be right back, Nanette."

Shutting the door and joining the senior detective in the room adjacent to the interview room, they were silent for a moment as they watched Nanette Lalonde from behind the two-way glass. Puffs of cigarette smoke were forced out of her mouth with each loud sob that shook her violently.

"She seems pretty solid," Sarzo said, glad to let the muscles in his face relax for the time being. Looking angry and impatient was the job. Actually being either of the two wasn't required. "I'm not saying she's being straight about everything she says, but I'm guessing she wasn't the one who put all the knitting needles in our victim."

"The call?" Quartz asked, knowing what he was thinking.

"Yep, I can't figure it out," he said, sipping on his cold coffee. "Either she's real smart or real dumb. If you were committing some insignificant theft and ran across a body, would you call the cops or split?"

He wasn't asking her to get into the woman's head but merely wanted an opinion. He already decided himself that he would have bolted from the house and let the body rot where he'd found it.

"Well, if I was her…," Quartz began, pausing as she considered all the possibilities. "…I'd make the call. Here's why: She went from the living room to the bathroom to the bedroom in that order. She said it four times for God's sake. She'd probably already taken the first two frames off the wall and was going for the third when she found him."

"Then what?" he asked, studying the brand new detective's intuition and attention to detail.

"Then she freaks out. Her first reaction was probably to run. But she stops because she's already yanked down two frames and leaned them against the wall in the hallway. She starts thinking about other things she might have touched. And with a body in the house, now she's not just worried about fingerprints. She's wondering if she might have stepped in some blood or if one of those long red hairs fell out of her head while she was in the house. Taking a pinch for burglary doesn't sound like too much to sacrifice to avoid being mistaken for a murderer. That's if she's smart."

"And if she's dumb? What's the scenario like?"

"If she did it and then called us…yeah, that'd be dumb," Quartz answered. "Maybe she kills the guy, then realizes what she's done and feels guilty about it. She calls us then changes her mind about it but it's too late. I'm not really leaning towards that, though."

"Me neither," Sarzo agreed, going over what little information they had about her. "She's a weird one. It says here she emigrated from Belgium back in ninety. Full citizen now. She didn't know what 911 was. Did you get that?"

"Yeah, she called us direct," Quartz said, watching her gather herself together in the lonely interview room. "Belgian, huh? So that's what they look like."

Belgian. Not likely, Miss Lalonde.

"Hell, I thought she was French," Sarzo admitted. "Anyway, she's as close as we've got to a witness so let's keep tabs on her. Go ahead and be her best friend for a while before you send her on her way. Just in case."

"I got it," Quartz said, taking a deep breath, preparing to go over it all again.

Ten minutes later she was sitting across from her once more. Standard procedure would have been to plow through the same story she'd already heard several times, only smiling instead of scowling. Deciding to blow off procedure for the sake of her own curiosity, Quartz chose another direction. Instead of going over the story again, Quartz wanted to hear about life in Belgium. *All* about it.

Starting with the places she'd lived and the schools she'd attended, Nanette Lalonde told startlingly vivid stories of growing up in Europe and the diverse culture of the continent. The sights she'd seen and the people she met were very well covered as was detailed information on her family and why they happened to come to the states. It was all very entertaining.

Nodding, smiling, and occasionally laughing, Quartz took in all the bullshit she could handle and then some. Though Nanette calmed down throughout the final hour of the interview, she still managed to cry at times and moan loudly when it was appropriate.

Quartz had heard more than enough to know that the woman was a fantastic liar and was quite prepared to tell Detective Sarzo all about it. But before she could excuse herself to make the call, Detective Sarzo called her first.

"Okay, you can send the Belgian cat-burglar home," he said, chuckling light-heartedly. "The coroner just called. Kadouris has been dead for at least thirty-six hours. We'll have to start looking elsewhere."

"Charges?" Quartz asked.

"Fuck it—let her go for now," Sarzo said, caring very little about the woman he'd broken down over several hours of questioning. "Just make sure you remind her that we can always pick her up for the breaking and entering. And don't apologize to her for me being a prick, Quartz. You're a detective now. We don't apologize. Got me?"

"I got you, detective," she said, hanging up.

Turning to the shaky woman at the table, Quartz raised an eyebrow and stood up from her chair. "Well, Nanette from *Belgium*." She said it with enough sarcasm to drag a mild flinch from the other woman. "I'm afraid we're going to have to cut you loose. Do you need a ride home?"

"No," she said immediately, rising from her chair, looking ready to run a sprint out of the station. Instead, a light but firm grip was placed on her arm.

"*Nyet?*" Quartz asked, repeating the word, only in a language that she thought might be understood slightly better.

For over five hours, Quartz had watched her work every human emotion like an artist paints on canvas. As Nanette's eyes darted up, meeting Quartz's in a cold stare, a tight but genuine smile crossed her lips.

"*Da*," she said once, nodding to Quartz, who led her from the room.

* * * *

Two hours and several shots of vodka later, the interesting pair sat face to face at a small table with a single candle on it. Nanette Lalonde was no longer present.

"*Nanetta Lalanskaev*," Quartz said aloud, raising another tiny glass of vodka which was tapped lightly in response by her red-headed counterpart. "*Netta*…I like the sound of it."

"And so do I," she replied, swallowing the fiery liquid a great deal easier than the detective. "But when we left from Kiev, the man who moved us said that it was a bad name for where we were going. Very much too ethnic. Quartz is pretty too."

"It's just a nickname," Quartz answered with smiling eyes that were getting heavy and glassy. "My last name is Schwartze. My grandfather was from Germany and my grandmother from Uzbekistan."

"*Quartz Schwartze?!*" Nanetta cried loudly, howling with laughter and shaking her head. "It is like a bad rhyme. Your parents—they are not nice."

"*Nooo,*" Quartz said, laughing as well, mildly confused as the alcohol seeped into her brain. "Nickname…nickname—not a real name. I was named Qiana, after my grandmother. Qiana…Schwartze…Quartz. Get it?"

"Yes, I see," she answered, understanding but still laughing smoke and vodka fumes into the detective's face. "So, you are Uzbeki…Uzbekistanian? Or whatever your fucking people are called."

"Partly," Quartz replied, ignoring her vulgarity. "I'm an American. We're from everywhere. My mother comes from the Sevastopol region and she said—"

"You are *Ukrainian?*"

"Well, I'm not fucking Belgian, sweetie." Nanetta nearly fell from her seat. "As soon as I heard your voice I knew where you were from. You sound like my mother and she's not Belgian either."

"*Belgium*—it was on the passport I was given," she said chuckling tearfully while trying to explain. "And it was so long ago. The idea was bad one. Very dangerous for my family."

"You mean you defected? From the Soviet Union?"

"Yes, it was a very bad mistake. Bad and expensive." Nanetta rubbed her thumb and forefinger together.

"What's so bad about living in the states? I've met a lot of immigrants—a whole bunch from the east. They all agree that life's far better here. Why not for you?"

"No, it *has* been good," she argued. "*Very* good. But one cannot see the future. We did not know what would happen."

"And what happened?"

Quartz could sense embarrassment pouring off of the woman in waves. Several times, she stopped and started, finally laughing and spitting the words out.

"We don't like Ukraine…we want to leave," she said, tossing her hands into the air. "Father saves money for smuggling…we leave. Go from country to country until we land in New York. Busy days."

"What was the problem?"

"There is no problem," Nanetta said with a shake of her head. "We begin the new life. It is very good. Two months after, our Soviet Union is no more. It is gone. It is fucking *gone*, Qiana."

It ees fawking gone, Qiana. Quartz repeated the sentence in her head and, for the first time in her life, thought her name sounded good coming out of someone else's mouth.

"Now you come and go as you please. No papers, no checkpoints. Now anyone can do this. You. Me. *Anyone*."

Instead of laughing outright, Quartz covered her mouth as best she could. Nanetta was somewhere between furious and hysterical; it was hard to tell with her. Apparently she understood what *irony* meant.

"Yeah, that's definitely some bad timing," Quartz agreed as she opened a new pack and shoved two cigarettes into her mouth. "But at least you had a head start over all the other people who left when the borders opened. That's a good thing, right?"

"Fucking Americans with the glass always filled up half of the time," Nanetta jokingly complained. "Why can't we just be sad?"

"Because sadness is so...un-American."

Quartz lit both cigarettes dangling from her lips simultaneously. Removing one from her mouth, Quartz noted the dark lipstick stained filter as she offered it. Rolling it between her fingers, she did her drunken best to wipe it clean before Nanetta snatched it from her.

"*Spasibo*," she said, lighting the tip up like a bonfire as she dragged insanely hard on it.

"You're welcome," Quartz replied, barely aware of what language they were currently speaking. If it was the international language of inebriation, they were doing just fine.

Sitting, smoking, and drinking into the night, they traded stories and dreams until the bartender yelled that it was the last call for alcohol. Though she was having a surprisingly good time, it was last call that Quartz had been waiting for to ask a simple question. She guessed they were both finally drunk enough.

"Netta?" she asked, slurring the letter "N", which she didn't think was even possible.

"Qiana?" Nanetta replied back in the exact same fashion, giggling profusely.

"What was it like working for Mr. Kadouris?" she asked, expecting Nanetta's demeanor to change instantly. It didn't.

"It was like any job where your employer tries to fuck you all of the day. He was a pig." Though her eyes narrowed slightly, her smiled had widened. "He did not die hard enough."

Stumbling arm in arm from the bar, they waited for a cab while Quartz tried to forget, or at least explain to herself what she'd heard. There could have been any number of interpretations of what Nanetta had said. Before she could come to a conclusion, alcohol pushed the thought far enough back in her head so that it was hidden from sight. As she teetered around on wobbly legs, it occurred to her that she probably wouldn't even remember it anyway.

What she would remember distinctly was Nanetta herself. More than anything, she would remember the smell of her hair.

* * * *

Confused and mildly horrified, Quartz awoke in a bed with the scent of *Finesse* wafting into her face. The distinct aroma—an aroma made even more distinct by the circumstances of the current situation—would now be forever tied to a vague, sensory memory that would only come back to her in very short, semi-vivid clips. Some of the wilder segments she explained away as the imagination of a drunken woman deep in the throes of REM sleep. But there were other parts of it that she couldn't explain at all.

Slowly, she unwrapped her leg from around Nanetta and freed her hand from the woman's hair. Buried deep near the scalp, the assumption was that she'd passed out while running her fingers through it. She glanced around the room and thanked God that everything looked familiar; at least she was at home and in her own bed.

Then peering down at herself, eerily unsure of what she might find, she gave thanks to God again. She still had most of her clothes on. So did Netta.

Climbing from the bed as quietly as she could, Quartz tiptoed into the bathroom. She jumped into the shower and took her time under the hot water, knowing that no matter how slow or how quick she was, it wouldn't have been fast enough to catch Nanetta Lalanskaev gliding from between her sheets and slipping out her front door, vanishing on the detective who taken a possible murderer home with her.

Though the disappearing act had been expected and was appreciated for its lack of required explanations, she couldn't help but be curious what those explanations might have been. For months afterward, Quartz would wonder about her Netta and what she was doing with herself.

Chapter 32

"What'd you call this one?" Blash asked, pointing to one of many numbered cylindrical containers that their drinks were coming from. They were both sitting comfortably in Walter's basement.

"That one's a pale ale," he replied, taking a few sips from his own cup. "The first one was stout. What did you think?"

"Thick, man. That's the only way I can describe it. Good, though. What's next?"

Walter handed him another small cup, noting that Officer Blash was developing quite a collection of them. "I use orange peels in this one. You can't really identify the taste, but it's in the orange peels. Weird, huh?"

"Not weird at all," he countered, sampling the light colored brew. "I'd have figured it out eventually. You are definitely a mad fucking scientist, Walt."

"Aren't I?"

Upon entering the Van Staadt residence, the first thing Blash had noticed was the cleanliness factor. Though it looked comfortable and lived in, it also had a feeling of sterility. The walls were unmarred and the pictures that hung on them were perfectly level. There was order in every corner of the room from the ceiling down to the floors. Either the carpet was brand new or it got vacuumed every single day.

It also looked bigger on the inside than from out in the driveway. Each and every wall in the house was painted a bright hospital-white, giving all the rooms a huge feel to them. It reminded him of the way Walter's mental institution looked; especially when they got to the basement. It looked like a lab of some sort, which made him uneasy at first.

He was anything but uneasy now. Far from it.

Rising from his chair, Blash took another cup from Walter and wandered about the room, examining the stacked, two-foot high cylinders that lined the wall and appeared to be fastened firmly to it. He knew what the first few of them contained—the fine beers he was tasting had come from them—but the others were still a mystery.

"God *damn*, this is good," Blash said, swishing the fluid around in his mouth. "And you make all of this yourself?"

"It's a hobby," Walter replied while filling another cup. "I started brewing a few years ago. At first I only made one kind—a malt liquor—and it was pretty good, but what I really wanted to do was come up with something unique. So one day I just went to the grocery store and bought every kind of fruit and vegetable they had. I tried all of it."

"For beer?" Blash asked, trying to imagine what a beer flavored with bananas would taste like. It made him shiver.

"Anything that ferments and makes booze, really. I was thinking about trying a wine or sherry, maybe a cognac. You know, I actually made one out of avocados once."

"Beer or wine?"

"I don't know what the hell it was," Walter replied with a laugh. "It tasted like shit, though. You never know 'til you try."

Wandering further down the wall, Blash stopped at the first one that didn't have the same tap as the others. It had a small, thin tube that looked capable of dispensing only drops at a time.

"Is this the real stuff?" Blash asked, knocking once on the cylinder, which rang quietly. It was labeled #10.

"It's real but it's old," Walter replied, pointing to the labels. "Anything that doesn't start with the number one is some kind of beer."

"And if it does?"

"Then you sure wouldn't want to drink a whole cup of it…or maybe you would. I don't know yet. I'm only in phase three, so I haven't gotten into that."

"How much does it take?" Blash asked, noting the size of the container.

"I'd been using a Visine bottle for the second batch. That little glass vial was too conspicuous—thanks for pointing that out—and I've never done more than two drops at one time. When I'm finished, I want the dosage to be no more than one."

Looking back at the cylinders, Blash eyed the labels numbered ten, eleven, and twelve. There were no higher numbers. "So what's the difference between these guys?"

"Well, phase one—that's number ten there—it was good, there's no denying. But it turned out to have a bunch of properties that weren't necessary at all." Walter switched from brewer to chemist instantly. "It actually had a tiny buzz factor, which I try to steer clear of."

"What kind of buzz?" Blash asked, feeling completely out of his element. "Like an alcohol buzz or heavier?"

"Like you just drank some NyQuil. A few said that their scalps tingled and their legs got restless. I fixed that, though. That's what phase two was about."

While Walter went on about adjustments he'd made to correct the unwanted effects, Blash was busy thinking of what to say to him. Watching him get excited explaining how his pet project was going was almost too much to bear. *Oblivious* would be a good word for it since that's exactly what Walter was. Totally oblivious to the reason for Officer Blash's sudden reappearance.

Here he was, thinking that he'd have to make a drug purchase to even it out with the one cop who knew his secrets; he was even happy to do it. But if he knew what Blash was thinking, he probably wouldn't have been nearly as thrilled.

But like Walter said himself: You never know 'til you try.

Waiting until the moment was right, Blash remained content listening to Walter talk about drug analogs, dosages, neuron receptors, mood enhancers, and serotonin inhibitors. In short: the same stuff he'd been spiking people's drinks with for over a year.

Chapter 33

"What's so special about this third batch?" he asked, more than a little curious but afraid the answer might twist his brain around even more than it already was.

"Well, barring any disasters, it should be finished," Walter replied, looking plenty proud of himself. "It's pretty much what I set out to do but I'd say it turned out even better. The side-effects, which aren't really side-effects at all, make it perfect for it's purpose. Plus, the potential for abuse is nil. Zero."

"Just because you made it work without a buzz?" Blash asked, knowing that anything that could be ingested could and would be abused.

"No, because this stuff takes you in the opposite direction; another interesting side-effect I hadn't expected. That time you busted me—you remember why I picked that group?"

"Sure, you said something about how you wanted to test it out on people with motor-skills disorders, right?"

"That's right," he replied, glad the cop had been paying attention. "But I don't have access to those kind of patients, so a bar full of drunk and stoned people would have to do the trick. It's not quite the same thing, but in regards to reaction times and reflexes, it helped a lot. Real world scenarios are what I'm all about anyway." Pausing for a moment, Walter stepped to a container labeled #06 and filled another cup. "I used parsley in this one. It'll get you trashed and make your breath fresh at the same time. But anyway—my third batch. *Phase Three*."

"Yeah, *Phase Three*," Blash repeated, downing his drink.

"I started out like I did with the first and second batches. You know how I do it." He received a nod in reply. "I picked a bar in Fontana—totally random—and made the rounds just like with the second batch. But something weird happened."

Watching Blash's brow furrow, Walter held up a hand and shook his head.

"No, nothing like that. Nobody got hurt. I was being really careful, keeping track of everyone who got a dose and watching them. Now before, it was always the same. I could notice subtle differences in their behavior. Nothing big. The whole point of this is to test it on all kinds of people regardless of their gender, weight, or physical health. But this time I noticed something about each and every person who got it."

"And what is it, man?" Blash whined, starting to feel the beer kick in. "You're fucking torturing me over here."

"In a loud bar full of drunk and rowdy people, I watched seven people change in less than a minute," Walter answered. "How ever much money they spent on alcohol that night was completely wasted. They went from totally wasted to razor sharp in a heartbeat. Now, I wasn't in their heads or anything, but I could swear they all enjoyed the experience."

"Sobriety, huh? And they liked it?"

"Well, it's like sobriety...but not. After the initial shock of losing their buzz, they all started looking around like they were wondering what they were doing there. All of them. It wasn't like they didn't remember going there or anything. It was like they were asking themselves the same question."

"What was the question?"

"Why?" Walter answered.

"Why what? What do you mean?"

"Just *Why?*" Walter repeated, trying to explain it but doing a very bad job. He'd consumed as much of his beer as Blash had and was feeling its effects. "It's not a really specific question. They were asking themselves *Why?* The best way I can explain it is that they just got real...contemplative, I guess. And after about half an hour, they started finding each other."

"Lost me again," Blash said, returning to the container full of the stuff made with orange peels.

"Okay, the seven people who got a dose," Walter began, making sure that he had Blash's attention this time. "They all started making eye-contact with each other. I know it sounds pretty out there, but in a bar full of fifty people, my seven were scoping each other out within fifteen minutes. And it wasn't just because they were the only sober people in the place, either. There were a few designated drivers hanging out and they didn't even get a glance from my subjects."

"They only saw each other?"

"No," Walter struggled to explain. "They were still totally cognitive of everything else around them too." He paused, hoping for a glimmer of its significance from Blash but didn't get one. "They were hyper-cognitive, Mike. I think they could feel something inside themselves but wouldn't have been able to describe it to save their lives."

"I still don't—"

"But they knew it when they saw it. And in this case, they each saw it in six other people that they didn't even *know*."

"Yeah, but—"

"Two of them sat at the bar and talked all night and two of the others left with each other. I'll tell you, there were some wild connections going on."

Blash took it in, finally looking somewhat impressed with what he'd been hearing. "What about the other three people?"

"Well, one of them was this college kid who'd been shot down by every girl in the place. The dose I gave him didn't get him laid or anything, but he stopped making an ass out of himself and *really* started kicking ass on the Asteroids machine. The other two guys shot pool like Minnesota Fats for a couple of hours before they decided to go outside and kick the shit out of each other."

"What in the hell for?"

"I didn't see a valid reason," Walter replied, seemingly happy with the violent result of his actions. "All I can tell you is that they were a couple of guys who, no matter what, were never, *ever* going to get along with each other. Sometimes clarity clears up a little too much, I guess."

"You're not saying it made them smarter, are you?"

"Jesus, what a score that would be," he mused as though it would be no less spectacular than the holy grail. "But no, it just made them *aware*. If they'd taken it before they started drinking they probably wouldn't have felt a thing; not unless they had problems to begin with."

"Mental problems?"

"Could be. It really depends on the disorder and what chemicals are out of kilter. And the real beauty is that dosage levels aren't even an issue. This stuff..." he said, tapping on container #12. "...only has one speed. 'On'. There's no increase or decrease based on dosages that I can tell and there's no fluctuation in moods once administered. As far as I can tell, it does one thing and one thing only; it makes you think as straight as you're capable of. If you're an idiot, it won't make you any smarter—but you might realize for the first time just how dumb you really are."

In a sort of awe, Blash took a long look at the containers and the equipment used to create what they held. "This is a couple of years worth of your life here, Walt. Why would you take the time and effort to do something like this? Is some pharmaceutical company going to pay you big bucks for this stuff?"

"No, it's too illegal and works way too good," he replied, disgustedly. "I've got forty-two kids on my floor right now with various mental illness or behavioral disorders; big-dollar patients that'll be taking twenty pills a day for life. About half of them would see an immediate improvement and that's exactly the reason it won't ever go public."

It was clear that Walter was a zealot on the subject. Though Blash didn't understand most of what he was referring to, he decided to side with Walter anyway.

"As a doctor, I wouldn't be allowed to prescribe them anything but FDA approved garbage. But as your friendly neighborhood orderly, I can pretty much give anybody any damn thing I want. So that's what I do."

Walter was becoming belligerent as the alcohol took over but it wasn't without reason. He could see the officer's curiosity grow with each slurred sentence he spit out.

"I'm beginning to see your point," Blash replied, finishing off another tiny cup of beer that suddenly didn't feel so tiny. "Jesus, how much alcohol's in this?"

Mike Blash had been drinking beer since he was twelve years old and was always aware of how much he could consume before falling on his face. At this particular moment, though, he was doubting his judgment. Based on what he'd had so far, he suspected he should be feeling mildly lightheaded. He was way beyond it.

"You're not going crazy—it's pretty potent stuff. Are you spinning yet?"

"Not yet, but I've got a mean...wait...yeah, I'm starting to spin," Blash admitted, sniffing suspiciously at the drink in his hand. "How are you doing?"

"Blasted," Walter laughingly replied, wiping a string of drool from his chin. "I'm worse off than you because of my size, but you should be pretty well crippled in a few minutes."

"Promise?" Blash asked with a chuckle, returning to his beer.

While his brain cooled its heels in homemade liquor, Blash watched as Walter unlocked a desk drawer and removed a tiny bottle from it. He couldn't read the label but the bottle looked very familiar. He knew that at one time it used to contain Visine.

"It gets the red out," Walter quipped as he leaned his head back and let a single drop tumble onto his tongue. "Whenever you're ready."

Blash nodded with a crooked smile as he poured himself one more drink. It was the parsley concoction this time.

"Let me just freshen my breath and I'll be right with you."

Chapter 34

Daisley watched the clock roll over to six p.m. and groaned at his lack of ability to find even the smallest amount of positive motivation. Still seated at his desk, he hadn't moved or even picked up his phone since Quartz had driven away. Though he'd told the others he would be spending his time trying to defuse the situation, staring at the wall was all he could manage. He didn't even know where to begin.

He knew where it had begun, though. With an admission of guilt—a confession that should have withstood all boundaries of the attorney-client privilege. It didn't, though, and in retrospect he wished he'd chosen a priest instead.

Unlike the lawyers that Andrew Daisley had met earlier in his pockmarked career as a law enforcement officer, Donald Ratcliffe was the only one who seemed to want the real truth from him. So much, in fact, that he went so far as to ask for it. Before then, all of his previous lawyers had reminded him of a picture of three monkeys he used to have. One had his eyes covered, another his ears, and the last was covering his mouth. These were the lawyers he was used to dealing with.

I sure miss you guys, he thought, never imagining that he'd long for his days back on the force in Chicago. Days where the lawyers hired to protect him didn't need the truth and, in fact, despised it. No, his monkeys were long gone and had been replaced by a shark.

At first, it was like a godsend. The shark devoured all who opposed it. Evidence was eaten and holes were chewed through witnesses. A feeding frenzy always followed the first sign of blood and, after a meal, the shark would gracefully swim away completely unscathed.

It was fun…for a while. He could feel some of Ratcliffe's arrogance spilling over into his side of the pool, and *why not?* To walk around feeling completely bulletproof was almost addictive. Unfortunately, the addiction was exactly what the shark had been counting on and Daisley found out the hard way just how difficult it was to put a leash on him.

If the man was a dog—and Daisley had met plenty of them—the standard, lawyerly collar would have fit just fine. Leaving it loose for a while, his attorney would get comfortable wearing it and if he ever needed reigning in, a good hard yank on the chain usually did the job. On Ratcliffe, however, the collar never took. In fact, it had slipped off and been neatly sliced in two by the dorsal fin only seconds after it was put on.

Whether by design, coincidence, or a cruel act of God, Daisley's escape from Chicago wasn't nearly as clean as he'd hoped and he wasn't too surprised to find that he had company.

It wasn't so strange a move. Hell, it was almost cliché.

When the detective moved west from the wild side of Chicago to the relative calm of Corona, he was following in the footsteps of his first captain, first partner, as well as the detective who had trained him years earlier. They weren't the only ones either. They'd all burnt out in one way or another and ended up in smaller towns far away or in the suburbs of Chicago. Some went to warmer climates while others followed money and dreams of cities with no crime to speak of. Basically, the easy life. But Daisley was actually running away and had no trouble admitting the fact to himself.

Sure, working Corona was the very definition of the easy life, but easy wasn't part of the plan. It was a bonus but not the goal. The goal was simply avoidance of prosecution and with the assistance of Donald Ratcliffe he'd been safe so far.

According to the deal—a deal which had been made very deeply under the table—as long as he remained outside the state of Illinois, he could count on no problems from his department, the city, or the state itself, all of whom wanted a small piece of Detective Andrew Daisley. Of course, deals made under the table were never notarized and were always subject to change or negotiation and when Ratcliffe made his own move west, it was only a matter of time before he was ready to renegotiate.

Something Daisley had noticed about him after weeks of trial preparations and hours in cramped quarters was that Donald Ratcliffe hated to lose. Sifting through the contents of Terrence Fisk's case of weapons, he now fully understood how much.

He could have made a call and checked how Louis or Blash were doing. He could have gone for a drive and tried to round up a candidate of his own. He could have called Ratcliffe and begged for mercy. But he didn't do any of it.

He concentrated on the wall instead and stared right through it, waiting for somebody—anybody—to take the initiative and make things right. If there was one thing he knew about himself, it was that he could talk the talk pretty well, but couldn't actually be relied on for anything remotely important.

Something as important as *this*?

Forget about it, he thought dejectedly as he lowered his head into his hands and shut his eyes tight. He was glad Quartz wasn't still around.

Chapter 35

The first post was at six fifteen. Quartz wasn't sure exactly what it meant but it certainly sounded like something was going to start about that time. She thought buying the racing form would clear up a lot of questions she might have but, unfortunately, she hadn't seen a more confusing piece of literature since she tried to make sense of the stock quotes in the business section once.

There were regular sized numbers followed by smaller ones. Then even tinier print. And fractions. On top of that, everything was abbreviated. And what the hell was a *furlong*, anyway? Standing in the huge parking lot, Quartz was intimidated by just about everything she saw.

Once inside, she was treated to large echoing rooms filled with endless chatter, video screens visible from every angle, and lines of somber looking people waiting to piss away another paycheck on a horse that would never come in. Choosing to follow the lead of the more experienced folks that surrounded her, Quartz stopped and purchased a book that seemed a great deal easier to read than the racing form she'd long since given up on.

As she wandered out to the stands, which was nothing more than row upon row of benches, she was startled by a booming voice from a loudspeaker. If she'd heard it correctly, it was five minutes until post time.

Post time. At least that was making sense now.

As if the voice in the speaker had suddenly woken the crowd from its stupor, the lines of men grew suddenly longer and a strange pitch seemed to fill the air. Turning herself around in a circle, Quartz surveyed the stands, something called a tote board, the concession stands, and finally the people themselves. Though it was an entirely different sport—if it was even referred to as a sport—she felt like she was at her first major league baseball game.

As the pitch rose yet another notch, Quartz quickly tore open her new little racing book and easily found the first race. Running to grab a place in a line, she read each of the horses names and started searching her purse for money. As she waited, she was very careful to listen to each word said by the person in the front of the line.

They were betting on winning, which she understood; placing, which she guessed was just shy of winning; and showing, which she didn't understand at all. They were betting on exactas, too. Some of them were even boxing their exactas. *Boxing?* They were betting across the board, guessing the pick-six, and watching the odds as they changed rapidly.

It was all very confusing. But more than that, it was exciting.

Looking at her form again, she decided to go with a horse called Lord Nathan. She'd known a guy named Nathan once and couldn't see herself wagering on a horse named Suckers Bet, Nut'n Toulouse, or Plato Shrimp.

A lucky observation was that none of the other people in line referred to their horse by name. It was always the 'Two horse' or the 'Five horse'. She could imagine the man at the window rolling his eyes at her if she didn't at least pretend to know what she was doing. The person in front of her stepped aside and Quartz found herself at the betting window.

"The four horse," she blurted out shakily, laying ten dollars on the counter. "I want the four horse. I want it to…show. I want the four horse to show," she repeated excitedly.

The man smiled and casually punch numbers into what looked like a huge, old adding machine and a ticket popped up in front of her right out of the counter she was leaning on. Thanking him, she took her ticket and headed back out to the stands. It was early still and the place had only begun to fill up. She felt lucky that she could just move right up next to the rail separating herself from the horses by less than ten feet.

Looking around giddily, she hoped her body wasn't giving away what she was feeling inside. She really did feel lucky.

Suddenly, the lights grew brighter, which was odd since there was still daylight, and a trumpet began to sound. Yes, she'd heard the tune before. It was just about the most recognizable sound a trumpet could make. Any time she had seen an advertisement for horse racing, the same tune blared from the TV speakers. A chill was forming at the base of her neck.

It was then that she saw the horses for the first time and it wasn't what she was expecting at all. She'd seen it before as well, but it wasn't called harness racing. She was picturing something out of *Spartacus* or maybe *The Ten Commandments*.

Oh my God, she thought as they began to circle the field. *I'm about to watch a fucking chariot race.*

Every horse was running but it became clear that the race wasn't on yet since there was a big white Cadillac speeding ahead of them. Attached to the back of it was some sort of wide gate that the horses nosed closer and closer to. Eventually, they all seemed to be running at roughly the same speed and had lined up almost perfectly. A second later, the voice from the loudspeaker was back.

"There they gooooo!" he said, sounding as though he was enjoying it as much as Quartz was.

The Cadillac sped way up, leaving the horses far behind. The race had only started moments ago but her horse was already in the lead.

Lord Nathan—her number four—was cruising right along, dragging the straight-legged driver behind him in what looked like a two-wheeled cart of instant death. Each of its steps were short and calculated. Quartz wanted to scream for him to pick it up but didn't know how appropriate it was to do so at this point in the race. Her body was shaking and her hands were gripped onto the rail very tightly. A moment later, she found out why Lord Nathan wasn't hauling ass the way she wanted.

As Plato Shrimp tried to pass on the outside, he did a funny thing; he started to run the way Quartz would have wanted *hers* to run. His short, careful steps were suddenly changed into a gallop, completely altering his gait. As the horse began to bounce up and down, the driver started to pull on the reigns until it slowed and veered to its right. Once cleared of the other horses, the driver led Plato Shrimp off of the track.

From what she could gather from the mumbling of the crowd around her, the horse had gone off stride—whatever that was supposed to mean. Quartz didn't understand what had happened or why it was important but she didn't care. All it meant to her was that Plato Shrimp had made room for her Lord Nathan to destroy the competition. He was pulling even further out front as they made the final turn.

In the last few seconds as the horses came out of the turn, the lights got suddenly brighter. The crowd got even louder. It had an electric quality to it that she simply couldn't explain; not even to herself.

Now that her horse was way ahead of the others, Quartz found herself asking him to maybe slow it down a bit. After watching Plato Shrimp get too excited and blow its stride, she was afraid Lord Nathan might do the same. It didn't happen, though, and Lord Nathan powered through the finish line without another horse within twenty feet of him.

She hadn't realized it but she was screaming. Just like every other person around her, she had become part of it. She had been screaming "Nathan!" and "Four!" for over thirty seconds without noticing.

What she did notice out of the corner of her eye, though, was the rest of the horses coming in. A few were pretty far back, yet still seemed to be fighting for a piece of the victory. They wouldn't get it. Instead, what they got was the poorly performing six horse heading diagonally across the track. Quartz wasn't sure what caused it, but number six ran straight into the driver of number one.

It only nudged him but it was enough.

As his two-wheeled sulky—a term she would learn later—overcorrected and went tumbling, the two horse directly behind him seemed to want to jump over him as opposed to squashing the little man. The driver of number one flopped out onto the track and lay still while the number six horse continued its sideways rampage and got caught up on the rail. Bailing out, the driver of number six leapt from the sulky and ran to the driver of number one.

After a great deal of painful thrashing, the six horse managed to make it half way over the rail and fall over on her side. The sulky was mangled.

The crowd went silent as the ambulance, which was standing by, rushed towards the fallen horse and driver. Watching with breath sucked deep in their lungs, they waited for the outcome. As they carefully loaded the driver onto a stretcher, she could see what had to be the owner of the other horse. He appeared to be crying.

There were educated murmurs from the crowd saying that the horse would probably have to be put down. It certainly wasn't looking too good.

For a moment, Quartz watched the scene in horror and felt almost like crying herself. The driver had fallen very badly but didn't look nearly as bad as the horse. Even with all of the confusion and pandemonium on the track, she couldn't help turning to the nearest person to her and speaking her mind.

She didn't know the man, but grabbed his arm anyway. She screamed right into his face. *"This is without a doubt the coolest…thing…I…have…ever…seen!"*

Chapter 36

▼

"And there you have it," Walter said with a very straight face, watching Officer Blash's eyes clear up. "That's what the big deal is."

If something was supposed to happen, he sure wasn't feeling it. Aside from complete and total sobriety, there didn't seem like much else to be had. There might have been something else—a very small something else—but it wasn't anything he could put his finger on.

"Weird," Blash said, waving his fingers in front of his face. Only a couple of minutes earlier his eyes were having trouble tracking the very same hand. "It's like...."

"Waking up?" Walter asked and answered at the same time. "I've heard that a time or two."

"Well, that's a fact. But without all the grogginess of waking up. Should I be feeling anything else?"

"Nothing," Walter answered with a shake of his head. "Unless stupidity counts. You're a pretty trusting soul for a cop, you know. You're lucky I didn't poison you with cyanide or something."

"I'd say *you're* the lucky one, Walt," Blash replied, walking the length of the room and trying out his legs. They worked just fine. "The last person who tried to poison me lived to regret it."

"Divorced, huh?"

"Yeah, she couldn't cook worth a shit."

As the pair chuckled away, Blash got to thinking about what Walter had said. Thinking clearly and deeply, as Walter had told him he would, he did begin to wonder why he would allow himself to ingest something based solely on the man's word.

It wasn't just the drop of *Phase Three* either. Looking back, he knew it probably wasn't too bright to even accept a drink from him. Just the same, he never had a doubt about Walter. Until now, he didn't even know why. But looking at the overachieving orderly as he wallowed in his own cleverness, Blash made a snap judgment—an executive decision.

He decided that Walter was one of the good guys. Not just a good guy, but a genuinely good person who was probably being befouled at this very moment simply by being exposed to Blash himself.

Why in the fuck am I thinking this?

As a man who made a hobby out of ridiculing other people, self deprecation had never been a habit and was usually to be avoided. Even as a child he had been raised to respect himself above all others.

Why then? Why do I feel guilty for being here in the man's house? he asked again as Walter picked up two large cups and began to fill them with water.

"You'll want to drink a few of these," he said, handing one to Blash. "I know you don't feel wrecked at the moment, but your body still has to deal with it. If you went to sleep right now you'd feel great until you woke up."

"What then?"

"Hangover time. You've still got every drop of that alcohol in your system. Just because you don't feel it doesn't mean it's not there. Eating will help too. No Tylenol, though. With alcohol, it's really bad for your liver."

Oh my God, the genius actually cares if I get a headache or not. I don't even care. Why should he?

Following doctor's orders, he drank the whole cup of water, then another. He thought about the water and what Walter had said. As he drank, he looked at the cylinders against the wall and wondered what kind of metal they were made of. Looking at the taps where the beer flowed from, he wondered how many gallons per second could squeeze through the small hole. He wondered if Walter could make beer out of heroin or hallucinogenic cacti.

What kind of fucking metal? How many what? Gallons per second? Peyote Genuine Draft? What the hell am I thinking about this shit for?

He was confused...but not.

The questions came at an amazing rate, yet were dealt with very easily, usually with the answer *It really doesn't matter, does it?* But the questions were there and that in itself was highly unusual. Blash was beginning to fear that if he walked outside he might stop to smell a flower.

What am I—a fucking hippie now? Did Walter turn me into a pacifistic pussy-boy or something? I don't care if he did, but a fellow should get a little warning beforehand.

"You were saying that food would be beneficial?" Blash asked, suddenly famished. "I haven't had a bite since before noon and I was thinking—"

"Don't worry about it," Walter said, shrugging the suggestion off. "Jessica will be home any time now. She'll fix us something decent."

"Isn't there a hotdog place over on Fourth?"

"Yeah, it's been there for years and it's great. But unless you can find someone to drive us there, we're out of luck."

"I'm fine, Walt. Really."

"Me too, but we're both *way* over the legal limit," he replied, pulling another small bottle from his desk drawer and holding it up. "I can hide any number of things in a urine sample, as you can attest to. But a breathalyzer—I can't do a thing. Drinking and driving is illegal anyway."

"It is, huh?" Blash asked, trying to measure the exact level of irony of the statement. "Just *how* illegal is what you've got here? And what are you trying to hide with that masking agent? You don't seem like a big-time recreational drug user."

"But I am...sometimes. I've got to be. What if my latest batch interacts with speed or even a sedative? The kids on my floor are on a hundred different types of anti-anxiety, antidepressant, anticonvulsant, anti...whatever drugs. I've got to know what it's going to do to them."

"So you try it out on yourself first? That doesn't sound too smart."

"Actually, I've never been the first one to try anything," Walter replied, keeping an eye on Blash's expressions. "There's always got to be someone who goes first. I just make sure it's someone who wouldn't be missed too much if something went wrong. It's never gone bad, though."

"Yeah, I give a shit. What kind of things do you check for? In the testing phase, I mean."

"Mostly interactions. That's why I needed to hang out with those meth freaks I was telling you about. Same goes for the night you busted me," Walter added, feeling as though he needed a good excuse for the company that he often kept. "I've seen every drug imaginable used with *Phase Three*. Tried most of them myself. Except for heroin and acid, it works the same as it does with alcohol."

"Why not heroin or acid?"

"Well, with LSD, the receptors I'm working with are already busy. *Phase Three* gets overridden—you shouldn't ask the reason why if you want to hang on to any deniability about this. And I don't know about heroin at all. I've never done it and I can't stomach being near junkies. With coke, meth, the usual pain pills, or weed, I can do them with whoever I'm testing that day. Nobody gets suspicious that way. I'll bet you do the same thing."

Blash only shrugged. As an undercover cop, his job often required him to ingest, smoke, or snort illegal substances for the same reason as Walter. Nobody gets suspicious if you're doing the same drugs they're doing and they get *really* suspicious if you don't. It was hardly department policy and had a lot to do with the deniability Walter had just mentioned.

"So heroin's still a bit of a mystery," Walter said unhappily. "Naturally, I've tested it against all kinds of opiates and other legal forms of morphine, so it should be okay. I just like to know for sure how it's going to act under any possible scenario."

"But this stuff is detectable?" Blash asked, referring back to the bottle of masking agent. "How can they detect something they don't know exists?"

"No, not the *Phase Three*," Walter explained. "I can take it all day and it won't leave a trace unless they come up with a test specifically for it. They'd need to use a needle for that, by the way, and it would go into a place that hurts really bad. Like I said; don't ask. I only use the masking agent so I don't get arrested or fired from my job for all the regular drugs that go through my system. I'm still working on getting it to work right without turning my urine black. I thought it was funny at first, but you cured me of that."

"It *was* funny," Blash noted with a disgusted grimace. "But in a real sick and weird kind of way that made me want to throw up."

Walter suddenly peered up towards the ceiling of the basement. Light footsteps could be heard moving from one end to the other.

"Jessica's home."

"The pregnant one you were telling me about?"

"No, the Indonesian concubine I keep in a cage," Walter replied sarcastically, looking at his tiny Visine bottle then back to Blash. "I told you that it doesn't make you any smarter."

"Shut the fuck up and feed me already."

Chapter 37

"Daisley's gonna be pissed, huh?" Lou asked, giving Fisk a sheepish look. "I pretty much did everything he asked me *not* to do."

Ask yourself this, Louis: Who's the man getting all the results?

Is it Daisley? Nope. We would have heard something by now.

Is it Blash? I don't think so. He's not a people-person, is he?

Maybe Quartz? I don't even want to think about that bitch right now. My head has a big dent in it in case you hadn't noticed.

That leaves Big Lou. The man who gets it done. Hours ahead of everyone else. The detective even said it himself. I wouldn't worry about anything if I were you.

"Okay, I'll try."

Darkness was closing in as the streetlights turned on one by one. The few hours that Alex Bautista and Joe Sheridan said they'd need had now stretched into the evening. When the phone finally rang at seven-thirty, Lou wasn't even sure who'd be on the other end of the line.

"Lou here."

"Okay, we'll do it," Alex Bautista told him. "What now?"

Good question, he thought, turning to Fisk who had no answers for him at the moment. "How about I swing back to your place and give you some details?"

"We'll be waiting."

*   *   *   *

"Joey! There's a man at the door for you!"

The yelling startled him but it was the embarrassment of his mother screaming his name that made him flinch the most. He was twenty-four but hearing the voice made him feel eight years old.

"It's only been ten minutes," Joe whined, climbing from the back of the van.

"You should really get a place of your own," Alex replied, feeling bad for his friend's humiliation but enjoying it nonetheless. "You should also bring him in here before that idiot tells her why he's at her house."

"*Joey!*"

"I'm coming! *Jesus!*" Joe yelled back as he clinched his eyes shut and pinched the bridge of his nose between two fingers.

Alex chuckled lightly as Joe ventured into the house to retrieve the man. The thought that he shouldn't be laughing crossed his mind but only for an instant. Unlike Joe, he did have a place of his own, but it was such a small and cramped apartment it couldn't provide nearly the room they needed. Even with Joe's mother around—probably even because of it—he liked their place a lot better than his.

A moment later, Joe led Officer Poklatar into the garage. Only a day earlier, the idea of letting a cop into the garage would have been unthinkable. The multitudes of stolen merchandise amounted to nothing less than grand theft and maybe a few other felonies on top of it. Somehow, that didn't seem to be a problem anymore.

"Nice lady," Lou commented as the door swung shut behind him.

Alex said nothing but agreed wholeheartedly. Sure, she was forty-six, divorced, and the mother of his best friend, but that didn't mean he couldn't lust after her. Though Joe wasn't onto him, Alex had been thinking nasty thoughts about her for years. As far as he was concerned, Joe's mom was the hottest thing since Mercury—the planet closest to the sun; not the stuff in a thermometer.

"Here you go," Lou said, pulling out the stack of bills again. "It's only forty-eight hundred but I'll get you the rest when it's done. That'll be—"

"Fifty-two that you owe us," Alex said, not feeling like waiting for the cop to do basic math. "What else have you got?"

"I've got a name, an address...no picture though. But there's a description in there."

Unfortunately, when they were splitting up the money and everything else in Fisk's briefcase, Daisley had kept the photo. No Xerox machine was available at the time so copying the information by hand was their only resort. Luckily, Lou had remembered to do it.

"What's all this crap?" he asked, finally noticing a certain strangeness about the garage.

The large, shiny objects were scattered about the entire room. Looking similar, but distinctly different from one another, it was obvious they were all the same thing but maybe different versions of that thing. It still didn't help him figure out what they were.

"That's not an appropriate question to ask, Officer Pok—" Alex began, then paused. "What the hell do we call you anyway?"

Without warning, Fisk vaulted back into his head.

Well, for starters, don't let them refer to you as anything resembling a cop. It's not wise. From here on out, I think letting them call you "Lou" will be fine. A completely fake name would be even better but I don't want you getting confused about anything. Sorry, Lou. I didn't mean for it to come out like that.

"Just call me Lou," he replied, seeming a tad dejected for a moment. "And I don't give a shit about all this stuff. I was just curious."

"Don't be. It's private."

Sensing that the officer wasn't appreciating the cold brush-off, Joe quickly changed the subject. "Let's figure out how it's all going to work before it gets late. We've got plans tonight."

"What kind of plans?"

This one he wasn't just curious about. What he really wanted to know was how they could be thinking of anything else beside the job they had just accepted. It was a very serious matter. If their evening was to consist of something frivolous, he was ready to be scared.

"It's fight night at The Pond," Joe answered back with a smile.

"The Pond?"

"Yeah, The Arrowhead Pond," Alex explained. "The Ducks play there."

"The Ducks?"

"Hockey, Lou," Joe responded, amazed by the man's lack of sports knowledge. "The Mighty Ducks. You've heard of them, right?"

"Yeah, a bunch of kids. I saw the movie."

"Okay, slow it down, Lou," Alex suggested, waving off the last few sentences of their conversation. "The Ducks are a hockey team. A *real* team owned by Disney; the guys who made that movie you're talking about. The Ducks play at a place called The Pond. Cute, huh?"

Lou's look told him that the word "Cute" wasn't even in his vocabulary tonight.

"But we're not seeing The Ducks tonight," Alex continued. "Costa's fighting a former champion from Bangkok. I don't know who's on the undercard."

"Costa?" It was occurring to Lou that eventually he would have to at least start acting like he knew what they were talking about.

"Oh, *Lou,*" Joe replied with a sound of despair. "*Gianni Costa.* Bantamweight. He's only the best fighter in the western hemisphere. He doesn't get as much press as the other big names but he's a god. My mom's work got a bunch of tickets for it and hooked us up. I'm not missing it."

"Me neither," Alex agreed.

Lou sighed and decided not to argue. He knew it would have been futile anyway.

For the next thirty minutes, they discussed the particulars of their job, locations, timeframes, and target. Their coolness in dealing with the subject was astounding as well as frightening. At one point Lou caught Alex yawning, which reminded him of the brazen way Fisk had acted when they were back at the hotel. He hoped it would be as easy as they thought it would be.

An hour later, the four of them went to the fights together and watched Gianni Costa beat the crap out of some poor little guy from Thailand. It was one hell of a fight.

Chapter 38

By the sixth race, Quartz was up three hundred dollars and watching the tote board like a hawk. For someone who had never been to the track before, she caught on very quickly. It only took her until the end of the second race to realize that picking a horse based on its name was just plain foolish. Likewise, gut feelings weren't to be trusted as well.

For the first several races, everything she looked at seemed like a sign; even during a quick trip to the restroom. It just happened that the number six was scrawled on the stall door in pencil. Thinking it might mean something, she immediately ran out and placed a bet on the six horse, who ran second to last and cost her a whole ten dollars. She wouldn't make that mistake again.

With only five minutes before race six would start, she was scrutinizing the odds on the tote board. As the numbers changed, so did her potential wager. Torn between two horses that fell somewhere in the middle of the odds, she watched and waited to see which would pay more if they had the decency to at least come in third place.

Her latest strategy was to bet heavy on a mediocre horse to show. *Heavy* meant twenty bucks. The most she'd won so far was on the fourth race when she accidentally bet on the horse with the fifth worst odds to *win*. She picked the horse she wanted but had only expected it to show. Instead it won and she very nearly peed her pants.

As she checked her watch, she decided to place the bet on the sixth race. It looked like the odds wouldn't change much between now and post time so her decision was made. Approaching the betting window, the nerves she'd had before were gone completely.

"I'd like a two dollar exacta on…horses two, four, and five…boxed," she said, trying to fire the words out before they closed the window. "Also, twenty on three to show and…let's see. Oh, screw it—fifty on four to win."

She didn't know where it had come from but that was how it worked at the betting window. It was almost like an impulse buy at the grocery store—a fifty dollar impulse buy. Not exactly a pair of fingernail clippers or a tube of Blistex. By the time she was seated again the race was about to start. She was already used to the pattern. Depending on the length of the race, one could expect about a minute's worth of extreme excitement; especially if you came out on top. Regardless, when the race was finished there was the obligatory thirty minute wait until the next one.

She felt like a crack addict. A wicked high followed by a period of doldrums. But unlike cocaine, the user could name their own price for the rush. Minimum bets were only two dollars. Even if she lost all night long she could still afford it…and still enjoy it.

With another enthusiastic "There they go!" from the announcer, race six was on.

Watching the Cadillac speed away, Quartz was suddenly aware of a partition of the track off to her right. She had noticed the people on the other side of the fence but only because they were the lucky ones who could stand right at the finish line and watch the horses as they crossed it. Other than a tinge of jealousy for not having as good a view, she hadn't given them another thought. Now she was giving them a great deal of her attention.

It was a close and very tight race. Though she had more money on this race than all of the other races combined, she missed it completely.

Instead, her eyes were locked on the stunning redhead who was standing in the doorway of the restaurant on the other side of the partition. For six races, Quartz had been sitting in general admission, only fifty feet or so from Nanetta Lalanskaev, who had been dining at a place called the Vessel Club.

Spying Netta having an after-dinner smoke, Quartz looked down at the pathetic box of nachos in her hand and felt cheated as well as dumb. If she had been only half as curious about the rest of the facility as she was about horse racing, it wouldn't have taken her long to find the clubhouse. She'd been sitting in the cheap seats for almost three hours and hadn't known the difference.

She hated feeling like an amateur. She also hated being underdressed, which she definitely was. Netta's clothes were sharp but informal. She looked almost like a beatnik, dressed in tight-fitting black from her neck to her ankles, wearing sunglasses though it had been dark for a couple of hours.

Damn, she looks good, Quartz thought, dropping her nachos and heading for an exit. Only pausing long enough to hear the results of race six, she ran back out to the parking lot and changed right in her car. Sliding into black nylons and a miniskirt, she began adding up her winnings in her head.

Her fifty dollar impulse buy had screamed through the finish line with the two and three horses trailing behind. She'd picked the winner, picked who would show, and nailed the exacta on top of it. As charmed as she felt, Quartz hoped that Netta would keep her winning streak going.

Chapter 39

"Sure, I remember you," Jessica Van Staadt said, shaking hands with Blash. "How could I forget you? I thought you were a patient and I gave you directions to my husband's office so you could harass and threaten him. You look much better now."

"Almost nice, even," Walter added, grabbing a seat at the dining room table. "You didn't get all dressed up just for me, did you?"

"Yeah, right," Blash answered, looking down at the suit he was wearing. "I feel like an idiot in these clothes. Ordinarily, I would *never* dress like this in public, but I had this thing today in LA at a real ritzy hotel. They probably wouldn't even let me through the door in my street clothes, so here I am."

"Was it a convention or something?" Walter asked, curious as to what kind of events the officer was willing to shave and clean up for.

"No, it was a meeting with this lawyer…what a dick this guy is. He has the four of us—that's me and three other cops—drive all the way out to LA to meet with him and an associate. This clown rents a top notch suite at the Westin Bonaventure for a meeting that's going to last ten minutes. What a showoff."

Taking his jacket off, Blash hung it on his chair and watched Walter's wife move about the kitchen. She was as pretty as he remembered her and it didn't seem strange this time. He could see how, if given the chance and the timing was right, she could easily fall for a smart and funny guy like Walter. It was amazing how a little bit of perspective repainted the scenery.

"So, what does he have to do?" Jessica asked, yelling to be heard over the water that was running.

"*Do?*" Blash asked, genuinely unsure of what she was asking.

"She knows the deal," Walter said, gesturing quietly towards her. "She's just worried that if I help you make a bust, the guys that get arrested might come looking for a little payback."

Holy shit. I'm supposed to ask Walter to do something for me, huh?

Only seconds earlier, he was describing his meeting with Donald Ratcliffe and didn't think about Terrence Fisk or his job at all. Whether it was his desire for food, a side effect from the *Phase Three*, or some residual alcohol in his system, he hadn't given any more thought to his current dilemma. Watching Walter's pregnant wife cook dinner for them, he was tempted to push the subject from his mind completely.

"I wouldn't worry about anything coming back to haunt you, Walter," he assured.

Checking to make sure everything was cooking properly, Jessica retired from the kitchen and joined them at the table. Now that dinner was started she took up a position between the two men, looking back and forth between them.

"He doesn't have to worry about it, Officer Blash, because I've been doing enough worrying for the both of us." She spoke in a leery tone, yet maintained a pleasant smile. "Like I told my husband, I understand and appreciate what he's working towards…up to a point. Prison or even just a nasty arrest is enough to put him out of work and you know he isn't making any money off of his hobbies in the basement. If he loses his job, we lose our insurance."

"He's not going to lose his job, ma'am," Blash replied, feeling quite the jackass for referring to her as though she was just another citizen. "And he certainly isn't going to be incarcerated for anything."

"What about protection for him then?" Walter rolled his eyes as his pregnant wife with the tilted uterus took over entirely. "He's been done with his Friday night group of speed freaks for months now. The only reason he keeps in contact with them is for you. You know that, right?"

Blash could only look at her with a blank stare. He knew Walter had wanted to get him off his back, but associating with dealers for no other reason was going beyond the call of duty.

"Honey, I think that—" Walter began, but the words were cut short.

"Hush, sweetheart. I don't like it. I don't like it at all, but if that's the deal—if that's the arrangement you had—then let's get it done. How's tomorrow night for you, Officer Blash?"

Tomorrow night. Oh, Jessica, if you only knew how tomorrow night was for me.

Blash rubbed his temples with his fingers. With his mind still running at one-hundred and ten percent, he also took the time to think that Walter and Jessica made a nice couple. With his brains and her balls, they could go far together.

"Call me Mike," he suggested, looking her in the eye. "Tell me, Jessica. What does your husband do exactly? What's he really, really good at?"

It was merely a stalling tactic since he wasn't sure what to say to her just yet. He'd spent hours with Walter today already and the man hadn't pushed the issue at all and, in fact, seemed more than content just pouring beer and chatting with the cop. His wife was a completely different story but just as smart, it appeared.

"He's a registered nurse with a masters in chemistry from UC Riverside," she answered. "He's the smartest and dumbest person I know. He could get a job at Dow Corning or Monsanto if he wanted to, but he works at Helmwood in a job that pays next to nothing. He loves it, though, and that's fine. Helping people, Mike—that's what he's good at. Now, how's tomorrow night for you?"

She seemed to have a great deal of experience taking the bull by the horns. Judging from Walter's lack of confrontational skills, Blash guessed it was another reason that they were made for each other.

"Tomorrow looks good, Jessica," he finally answered. "And you can forget about any dealers paying you visits."

Her eyes narrowed slightly as she stared at Blash then checked her watch. Looking to Walter, then back to the stove in the kitchen, she gestured towards a large pot. "Keep stirring."

Dutifully and without question, he rose from the table and made sure the spaghetti sauce didn't thicken too much. Standing over the pot, he looked prepared to mix up the ingredients until she asked him to return. She was ready to talk in earnest.

"Promise me," she said, dropping her voice to a harsh whisper and grabbing tightly onto his shirt sleeve. "Promise me that nothing will happen. Promise me that ten years from now, we're not going to have some drug dealer who just got out of prison show up on our doorstep with a machine gun. Can you do that?"

He thought hard about the question and prepared an appropriate answer. Looking to Walter, who was still stirring like mad, then to the pregnant woman in front of him, Blash made another executive decision. For a very brief period, he was beginning to wonder if he would use Walter at all. But that time had passed.

Now he was sure of it.

Chapter 40

So, here I am defusing the situation, Daisley thought, almost laughing to himself. Ordinarily, a bottle of plain label whiskey from the supermarket would have done the job just fine. Tonight it was Chivas Regal. He didn't even use a straw.

It was only an hour earlier that his paralysis had broken, giving him the strength to finally climb out of his chair at the station. Mostly, it was because his ass started feeling uncomfortable, but after hours of thinking and getting nowhere, he decided to liven up the party and get more productive.

Productivity involved a bottle, a glass, and at least one active participant. By the time he got home to his apartment two miles from the station, he was ready to get started.

Yes, the situation is getting defused, he thought, drinking his fifth shot on top of the glass he was sipping from.

At least he wasn't panicked anymore; that was the worst. It was one thing to be totally screwed and remain decisive. But when panicked, the smallest decisions seemed like huge ordeals that needed to be approved by a committee.

Finally, back in control. Those other guys are lucky I'm on top of this thing. Any minute now, a great plan—a perfect plan—will fly right into my head and this mess will be behind us before we know it. I'll take care of it. Defuse, Andrew. Defuse.

Even the words in his head had stopped making sense.

Quartz...Louis...Mike...good luck. But don't worry about a thing. Detective Daisley's got you all covered.

Upon finishing the thought, he threw up onto his carpet and fell forward into the mess that his stomach had created. He would lay in his own vomit for several hours.

Chapter 41

"Hands up," Quartz said, sliding slowly behind the woman in black.

She didn't even flinch. Instead, she took a long drag off of her cigarette and crushed it out on the floor before turning slowly. Even behind dark glasses, Quartz could see her eyes light up.

"Qiana, my comrade," she said, flashing teeth that had been recently capped. "You are not here to arrest me, no?"

Before Quartz could even make sense of the question, she was enveloped by Nanetta's thin but muscular arms. Either her excitement was real or she intended to crush her to death in front of a few hundred people.

"No, Netta. No arrests tonight."

The Ukrainian had a certain aura about her. Nanetta wasn't the same woman she'd interrogated before and she certainly wasn't the prostitute Quartz feared she would find. No, this woman had strength and appeared to be on top of things.

"I missed not seeing you," Nanetta said, putting on a frown but in too good of a mood to keep it for more than a second. "But now you are here. Come with me to my table and tell me why it is you are here."

Grabbing Quartz by the hand, Nanetta led her to the back of the small clubhouse to a booth in the darkest corner. Two other women were already seated at the table and immediately stopped talking as they approached.

"Leave us," Nanetta said with a familiar scowl, gesturing towards another table.

Without hesitation, the two women climbed from their seats and scooted by them. Neither made eye contact with Nanetta but both gave Quartz shifty glances. From what little she'd heard from them, Quartz surmised that they were both Russian or possibly Latvian. One thing was for sure, though: if she came to the track expecting to find any hookers, she had definitely found them.

"Sit, Detective," Nanetta offered, turning towards the bar and gesturing again. "Sit with me and tell me why I am seeing you after so long."

Taking a seat, Quartz found herself searching for words. Relieved at first by the fact that Nanetta wasn't a prostitute, her suspicions were rekindled by the women she had just chased away. Though it was merely a distraction and didn't have anything to do with Quartz's business for the evening, she was suddenly unhappy anyway.

All she really knew about the woman was what she'd gotten out of her during a bullshit filled interrogation and whatever else popped out while they were drinking. She decided to be cautious.

"Look, Netta, this isn't exactly a social call. I'm here to talk to you about something. Something important."

Nanetta's easy facial expression hardened a bit but remained cordial. It was her turn to be suspicious. "Important business with the police?" she asked, running her eyes over Quartz's distinctly informal outfit.

"Partly," she replied, steeling herself for what she would say next.

Even with the money involved, Quartz knew that a certain amount of leverage would need to be applied to get the desired response. Fortunately, her old associate, Detective Sarzo, was more than forthcoming with what little information he had on her. She knew that the key would be the pimp and bookie that Nanetta had been linked to, but when Sarzo told her about him, she had more questions than he had answers.

"I'm wondering why I'm hearing your name mentioned when I ask about a man named Nestor LaGuardia."

Lighting a cigarette—completely ignoring the fact that she was in a restaurant in California—Nanetta tilted her head and stared at Quartz with squinty eyes. "It is an interesting question you are asking of me. Why are you concerned with Mr. LaGuardia?"

"Because I've been in contact with my old department in Cerritos and they tell me that you've been a busy girl. In the last few months they've had over twenty prostitution arrests involving native Russian women. When the same person pays their bail every time, we usually notice things like that."

"And what else?" Nanetta asked, knowing that there was more.

"And that you dropped off the checks and signed each of the women out."

"You think that I am a *whore*?" Nanetta asked with a look of disbelief. "You did not come here to tell me this, did you, Qiana?"

No, she didn't. She was just getting started. "I just wanted you to know that a case is being built against him. When they catch up with him he'll be charged with felony pandering. Not prostitution, but *pandering*—there's a big difference in the eyes of the law. Over twenty counts, Netta. He could go to prison for just one count and we're talking *twenty*. You do the math."

She seemed to do exactly that while Quartz watched. Lines formed on her forehead as she broke eye contact. "When?" she asked, looking down at the table with a grave expression.

"Whenever they want," Quartz answered. "They're adding more counts and more charges every day," she said, glad to finally have the upper hand. "By the time he's brought in…."

"No, Qiana. That is not the question."

"When *what*, then?"

Slowly raising her hands to Quartz's face, Nanetta shook her head as they locked eyes. She was smiling again.

"When did my Qiana become such a very bad liar?"

Though she had been stopped in her tracks mentally, Quartz allowed her mouth to answer back with perfect timing, taking an embarrassing risk.

"About the same time you became a man named Nestor LaGuardia. That's one ugly fucking name, Netta. You could have picked something better."

It hadn't necessarily been an educated guess, but the look in Nanetta's eyes easily confirmed her suspicions. It was an indifferent glance that asked the question *What of it, detective?*

"So you are here to arrest Mr. LaGuardia, no?"

"No, Netta, Mr. LaGuardia doesn't concern me in the slightest." Quartz calmly lit a cigarette of her own while thanking the heavens that she'd guessed correctly. "Even after my old boss was through telling me all about him, I didn't say a word. It's still your secret…or *our* secret, rather."

Nanetta took a quick glance around the room before turning back to Quartz. Even while searching for the police officers that she was certain would be there to arrest her, Nanetta kept her amused expression. Following her lead, Quartz took a look around as well. When it was clear that no officers were waiting on standby, she shrugged and dragged on her cigarette.

"Told you," she said, raising one eyebrow.

"This is good," Nanetta said. "It is nice to have secrets. I like it that we have one to share."

"There's more."

Laughing loudly, Nanetta dropped her cigarette into what was left of her drink. Placing her hands flat on the table, she cleared her throat and waited for it. Her smile was still present. "You are silly with all your games."

Instead of another accusation or helpful tip about what the police already knew about her, Quartz began digging through her purse. A few seconds later an envelope was placed on the table between them. Once again, Nanetta glanced around the room before reaching for it.

"Do I have to open this? *Then* you can arrest me?" she asked, eyeing both Quartz and the envelope with suspicion. "I will not be happy."

"You might be," Quartz offered, trying to guess which expression would cross her face once the contents were revealed. "Go ahead and open it."

Quartz watched, totally absorbed in the woman's eyes as she opened the fat envelope and began leafing through the bills. As she counted, no indication was given as to her thoughts. Her face was all business.

"This is a lot of money, Qiana."

"Yes it is."

Yet again, Nanetta looked around the room before leaning over the table towards Quartz. Meeting her half way, Quartz leaned in as well. A moment later Nanetta's lips were pressed against her ear.

"Is it a woman or man that you want me to kill?" she whispered, then leaned back and reached for another cigarette. She was still smiling.

Chapter 42

"Man, that little guy sure knew how to bleed," Joe said, the excitement of the fight still hanging with him. "I'm sorry your friend wasn't feeling up to it."

"Yeah, he missed a hell of a fight," Lou agreed. "He's been feeling crappy all day long. Headache."

"He's lucky he skipped it then," Alex noted. "I can't even watch a fight on TV if I've got a bad headache. It hurts like hell every time they connect really good. I know it shouldn't since I'm not the one getting hit, but it still does. It's a psychological thing."

"Speaking of your friend…" Joe started asking the question but was quickly jabbed in the ribs by Alex. "…uh…tell him I hope he feels better."

It sounded weak but it was obvious that Alex didn't want him going there for some reason. Though he was curious and knew Alex was too, he'd let it lie until his brainier counterpart gave him his opinion.

"I'll do that," Lou said, seemingly appreciative of the gesture.

Stepping to the side as a few thousand fight fans exited the ritzy venue, they finished their four dollar drinks rather than throw them away. Noting a similarity in the people filing out of the arena, Joe was unable to remain silent.

"Did someone swing a big bag of *ugly* around in there or something?"

It was just a little joke, but very accurate. The amount of physical ugliness that walked out through the doors was absolutely uncanny. It wasn't long before Alex joined in.

"Whoa, look at that one," he said quietly, careful not to be too obvious. "There's a face that could make a cat bark."

It was an old line that he'd been using since grade school but it seemed appropriate. Immediately, Lou began to cough and gag. Wiping his nose on his sleeve, it was easy to see that a buck's worth of his four dollar cherry coke had blasted out of his nostrils.

"There's one that could make a freight train take a dirt road," Joe added, pointing to another brutal face, then watched Lou's eyes clinch shut as the carbon dioxide from his drink burned his nasal passages. He was laughing painfully but didn't seem to mind.

Go ahead and yuck it up with these guys but don't let your guard down, Louis, Fisk's voice blasted back into his head. *That guy Joe was about to ask about me, but Alex shut him up. I know you saw it, so don't play stupid.*

Lou didn't know if he was trying to hurt his feelings, but he didn't like it. Unfortunately, Fisk's advice had been pretty good up to now so he'd put up with it for the time being.

Cut these guys loose for the night and get some rest. If they ask about me, just tell them not to ask. Tell them you'll call them tomorrow and give them the final details. And quit being so damn comfortable with them. I'm sure they're a swell couple of gentlemen but they're going to kill a guy tomorrow and I think you're being a little too friendly with them. That's just my opinion. Do what you want, Louis.

His internal dialog went unnoticed as Alex and Joe were busy critiquing the facial structures of the less fortunate fans. And Fisk was right; he was feeling too good about his two temporary employees and not acting enough like their handler. It was just his style, though, and he couldn't change his personality for Fisk or anyone else. Plus, it was hard to look threatening with cola dribbling from your nose.

"Well, I'm going to hit it, guys," Lou said, stretching his back and cracking his neck. "I've got a long day tomorrow and so do you. I'll call you at noon and let you know how it's going down. It could happen any time between eight and midnight…I'm not sure yet, but I'll let you know when to be there."

"Whatever," Alex said with a shrug, busier watching a pretty blond exit the building than listening to Lou.

"Yeah, Lou," Joe agreed, distractedly watching the same girl who looked like a goddess swimming through a sea of bad complexions and greasy hair. "No problem. Anytime between eight and twelve. We'll be there."

"Your help's appreciated," Lou said sincerely as he walked away from them. "And thanks for the fight," he shouted quickly before he disappeared into the crowd.

Both Alex and Joe nodded and waved before turning to each other.

"Now, the guy in the car…" Joe waited for an explanation.

"Sorry I shut you down but I didn't want the cop to know we were onto him. The guy who's been hanging out with him all day—he's got to be the money man. He has to be. If I was going to be paying to have a job done, I'd tag along and make sure it got done right too. I don't know why he keeps hanging back, but I would guess he's just laying low. Maybe he's supervising the deal."

"You're probably right," Joe agreed, nodding. "Where do you want to crash tonight?"

"We'd better stay at my place. It wouldn't be too cool for your mom to overhear us talking about this and I think we're going to be talking about it a lot. I know the guy's just a fucking child molester but I'll probably need to get seriously psyched up for this."

"So *you're* going to do it?" Joe asked hopefully.

"I know we hadn't discussed it, but when it comes down to it…I think I should pull the trigger on this piece of shit. It's not that I don't think you could do it—"

"Oh, I wasn't thinking that," Joe said, lying through every tooth that he had. "I just wasn't sure if we were going to flip a coin or something. But if you want to do it, be my guest."

"I think it's settled then," Alex answered, taking a certain amount of pleasure from letting his nervous buddy off the hook. "Let's go home and see if we can get in the right mood for this thing."

"Sounds good. Nervous yet?"

"Queasy as all fuck. What about you?"

"I'm probably gonna puke any minute now," Joe replied as they headed for the van.

Chapter 43

"Any questions?" Blash asked as he threw his jacket back on.

It was late and both Walter and Jessica looked ready for a little sleep. A call had already been placed to let the people at Helmwood know that Walter would not be coming in to work tomorrow. He didn't even bother to try to sound sick.

"Yeah, just one question," Walter answered as he walked Blash to the door. "Is it that you're insane or just stupid?"

"Ask my doctor," Blash responded, winking at him. "I'll give you a call tomorrow morning and let you know how it's going to happen. I'm thinking I should pick you up."

Walter caught the look that Blash was giving to his Datsun and had to agree. "That works for me. If you change your mind about any of this, don't hesitate to—"

"Sorry, Walt, I'm really pretty committed to this thing. I appreciate what you're doing for me here and I won't forget it."

"Well, I'm here for you, but you should think hard about this one," Walter said, pulling a Visine bottle from his pocket. "*Really* hard, Mike. Just think about it."

With a light flick of his wrist, the bottle was tossed into Blash's open hand. He put it in his pocket and made a mental note not to accidentally leave it in his medicine cabinet. "I'll take it under consideration. Get a good night's sleep."

* * * *

Only ten minutes later he was home. Winding his way through the maze of mobile homes, he stopped in front of the one that he was just sure had to be the ugliest piece of crap on the lot. He'd picked it out himself after all.

"*Honey, I'm home,*" he yelled as he opened the door.

Hearing no response, he knew he was in the right place. Immediately upon closing the door, he pulled out his cell phone and tried Daisley again. He had made the first call as soon as he pulled away from Walter's house and received no answer. He took it as a good sign. If Daisley wasn't answering his phone it was probably because he was too busy trying to straighten the whole thing out.

With luck, the hours spent with Walter would be nothing more than a waste of time—and a pleasant waste of time at that. He *sincerely* hoped that Walter wouldn't be necessary at all.

Comically, the first stop he made was at the refrigerator to get himself a beer. Only after he removed the cap did he realize just how futile the endeavor would be and, for the first time in his life, Blash drank a beer solely for the taste. With his mind spinning in several directions, he considered taking a valium but knew it would have as little impact as the beer.

After a quick shower and another answerless call to Daisley, he decided to follow the last advice he gave Walter and try to get some rest. He wasn't fooling himself; it wouldn't be easy.

On any normal night, the ritual was to turn on the TV, sit in front of it, and hope to wake up on the couch the following morning. It didn't always happen that way and in some cases, sleep simply never came. But in all cases—every single time—the morning came whether he slept or not.

He felt it worse tonight than any other in recent history. Sometimes he was up for days at a time…sometimes more. It had mellowed lately with the passage of time but Blash knew the pattern and what to expect. All he could do was pray that Walter's *Phase Three* would talk his brain into sleeping for real tonight.

Fucking demons, he thought, laughing to himself. The laughing wasn't exactly appropriate but it was preferable to crying. Prayerfully, he closed his eyes and hoped for the best. Before he was even done hoping…he was asleep.

Chapter 44

▼

"So then Costa—you wouldn't believe the speed of this guy—he whacks him with a left, a right cross, then goes back for a double left hook to the guy's rib cage," Lou explained excitedly in incredible detail. "After two in a row to his side, the guy finally lowers his right hand to block the body. Guess what happened next."

Fisk remained silent, indicating that he wanted to be told.

"That's right—a *third* left hook right into his ear. *Bam!* And that was just the second knockdown. It wasn't until the fourth round that the cuts started opening up. It was gross but it was fun."

I'll bet it was. I'm sorry I couldn't be there with you, Fisk said, sounding a bit neglected. *Thank God you're here to give me the blow by blow.*

Lou couldn't tell if it was a sarcastic statement or not. So far, they'd been getting along famously. "So, what do you think of my boys?"

I think they're shit, Louis. Amateurs, the both of them, but they'll do. For a guy working under as much pressure as you've had, I'd say you've done an exceptional job. They're not professionals but what can they expect on such short notice? Try calling Daisley again.

"I already called him twice," Lou complained as they pulled up in front of his hotel room in Corona. "He's not answering."

Call him again. Let it ring this time. Let it ring a long time. That way, when he finds out that you disobeyed his direct orders, you can tell him how many times you tried to call him. He's going to be pissed anyway but this way you're covering your ass a bit more. Just do it.

Complying, he dialed the number again and let it ring. After seven rings he set the phone down, leaving it ringing. "I've got Mike and Quartz's numbers here too. Maybe they've heard something. Or maybe they've already got someone lined up."

Better than your guys? No way.

"But you just said my guys were shit."

Mike and Quartz are shit. I watched them in our little meeting earlier today. What did your buddy Blash call you? Was it moron? Wait…didn't he call you Pokla-tard? Like you were retarded or something? No wait…it was both. Fuck that guy, Louis. You can do better.

"No, man. Mike's cool. He just didn't like you."

Sounds to me like he didn't like you. You ever think of that?

"I don't even know those guys," Lou replied, not sure of the reason why Fisk was hacking on his crew. "But they seem real good. I'll admit, Daisley's a bit of a jerkoff but he's the boss. He has to act that way. It's the way we're trained."

That explains a lot. Is he a crook too? Or is he just in a fragile emotional state like yourself?

Before he even realized that the door was open, Lou found himself yanking Fisk from the car.

What are you doing, Louis?

"What does it look like?" Lou replied, enraged as they tumbled into the parking lot. "I'm kicking your fucking ass. Get up."

Uh…what?

"I said get the fuck up off the ground and…" It only took him a moment to figure it out. Frantic, he scanned the parking lot for moving cars and people before pulling Fisk up off the ground.

Sorry, Louis. I was just screwing around. Relax.

"Shut the fuck up before—"

Hurry, Louis. I can make myself heavier, you know.

And he did feel heavier as Lou began cramming Fisk back into the passenger seat. Only now did he remember how hard it was getting the man into a decent position the first time. "God, this is ridiculous. I swear I should have kicked you out back in Long Beach…fucking shooter…big time hitman…punk ass little…."

Shhh.

"*You* shut up," was Lou's slick reply.

Shhh. You've got to quiet down, Louis. We're going to get in trouble. And quit jerking me around so hard.

"Stop talking then. Can you do that? I just need it quiet for a few minutes.

And what am I? Noisy?
"Just shut up for a minute...*please.*"
See, there you go again.
"Goddamn it!" Lou yelled, slamming the passenger door.

Walking around to the driver's side, he climbed in and slammed that door too. Once seated, he went right back to straightening up Fisk, who still didn't look quite alive. In total silence, Lou propped him up and buckled him in. He even smoothed out his tie.

Thanks, Louis.
"Shut up."
I'm comfortable now. I appreciate it.
"Shut up," he said again, gripping the steering wheel tightly.
What are you feeling, Louis? Fragile? Emotional? You're not in a state, are you? Just kidding...I'm sorry.

"Man, that does it," Lou said, exhaling loudly. "As soon as I talk to Daisley, I'm going to find out what hotel he had you booked in. I know it's nearby because he said it was within a mile of Roche's house. I'm going to check you in somehow and leave you lying on the floor next to the nightstand. It'll look just like the accident that it was. Different location; same stupid accident."

Lou nodded to himself as he spoke. He wasn't even speaking to Fisk at the moment, but was just going over it out loud to see how it sounded. It was starting to sound good.

You're not really going to do that, are you?
"Count on it, smart guy."
Why?
"It's my job," Lou replied, staring at him. "It's nothing personal."
That's my line, Louis.
"I know it is, Terry. How does it feel?"

Chapter 45

▼

"You are right, Qiana," Nanetta said as she climbed from her chair and motioned for the other two women. "This is not the right place for such a discussion,"

Stepping away from Quartz, she spoke quietly to the two prostitutes and seemed to dismiss them with a wave of her hand. Sharing more quiet words—with the bartender this time—she nodded and returned to Quartz.

"I am yours. We will go wherever you like," she said, eyeing Quartz's purse which currently held roughly ten-thousand dollars of Fisk's money, plus the eight-hundred or so that she'd won so far.

"Perfect," Quartz replied as she pulled the purse closer to her body and held onto it like a football.

Grabbing Nanetta by the hand, she led her in the opposite direction of the exits. It wasn't just the fact that she felt Nanetta might mug her before they got to her car—it was the intermittent screams from the cheap seats that were currently calling to her. She'd already wasted races seven and eight while in the confines of the restaurant. She wouldn't miss anymore.

"No, no, no, Qiana," Nanetta complained as she was dragged towards what seemed to be the ultimate humiliation. "Not in the general admission...*please*. At least not on the ground. Up...we go up."

Pointing to one of the higher levels that Quartz hadn't gotten around to checking out yet, Nanetta clearly didn't want to be seen in the bench seats with people who worked for a living. It was cute in an elitist kind of way, but not Quartz's. She'd sat through five races with these same people and liked the way they got excited. They weren't afraid to show how happy they were when they won, even if it was just a two dollar winner. In the clubhouse, on the other side of the partition, they were so subdued that it was hard to tell if they were winning or losing.

"I think I'd like to sit here," she said, sliding into a bench seat. "Come on. Sit with me."

"No, Qiana. We cannot." Nanetta's voice was serious as she pulled back on Quartz's hand. It was a strong grip.

Planting her feet and readying herself, Quartz applied twice as much pressure to Nanetta's hand and yanked her in. As she was pulled, Nanetta's feet slid on the ground as though she was a spoiled child being pulled from the toy department. After a moment of looking and feeling asinine, she relented and dropped unhappily onto the hard wooden seat.

"Okay—race nine," Quartz said, leafing to the correct page of her program. "It's an eight horse race. I'm looking at Wheezy. What do you think?"

"*Wheezy? The four horse?* She is a dog," Nanetta said, looking away from her in a childish manner. "She is six to one. She will not win."

"But if I bet her to place or show—"

"Then you might win some money. Bet your money, you win a few dollars. When you collect your winnings you can buy more chips and a drink to go with it."

Nanetta's sarcasm was greeted with excitement rather than it's intended effect. "Well, then I'll bet twenty and get us both a chili dog. Should we bet the favorite to win? The long shot? How about a little help here."

With a heavy sigh and a roll of her eyes, Nanetta snatched the program from Quartz's hands and scanned the page quickly. Once again, she was all business. "Give me one-hundred dollars," she said, circling the five horse.

"Star Sailor? She looks like the second to worst horse on the field and I haven't bet more than fifty on anything. Why Star Sailor? And why would somebody give an animal such a *horrible* name."

"The names—they are all very bad and mean nothing," Nanetta explained, pointing to another name on the program. "Do not bet on the horse. They are stupid animals. Bet only on the driver."

"Billie Mayer?" Quartz said, reading the name that had been pointed out. "Is he any good?"

"*She* is very aggressive," Nanetta corrected. "With harness racing the driver must be in control. If you let the horse run too slow you will lose. If you let it run too fast you will lose. Mayer is most controlled."

"She'll win? Are you sure?"

"Nyet. Give me the money and we will see."

"Whoa, Netta, that's a hundred dollars. What if we lose?"

"Then we get no money back," Nanetta stated as though it should have been obvious. "Have you not wagered before?"

"I get that," Quartz replied in an exasperated tone. "I just think a hundred is a lot to bet on one horse. I don't care how controlled you say your driver is. There aren't any guarantees."

"Of course not. Give me five-hundred dollars," Nanetta said, holding her hand out again. "You like to wager?"

"Yes, but five-hundred is too much for—"

"You do not like to wager," she replied, shrugging as she pulled her empty hand away. "You have no stomach for it."

"I *do*, Netta. It's just that five-hundred, hell, even *one*-hundred is too much of a gamble—"

"How much have you won tonight?"

"About eight-hundred." She immediately felt as though she shouldn't have said a word.

"Give me one-thousand dollars, Qiana. This is your last chance. I will leave if you do not."

She looked serious.

Checking the time, she stared at Nanetta and stalled for as long as she could afford to. Frustrated yet curious, Quartz opened her purse and carefully pulled out ten one-hundred dollar bills. Her hands were shaking.

"Come," Nanetta said quickly, grabbing the money and rising from her seat. "I will show you how to wager. Is this more money than you can afford?"

"It's more than I've won tonight and it cuts into the ten thousand that I'll be giving to you," she replied, realizing that Nanetta was correct. It was more than she could afford.

"Good," she said, smiling for the first time since she was dragged to the cheap seats. "You have begun to wager correctly. Now it will be fun."

"Fun?" Quartz echoed. "There's a good chance I'm about to lose a thousand dollars."

"See, it is fun, no?"

Just in time, they made it to the betting window. In silent horror, Quartz watched Netta fork over a grand to the man behind the window. He was indifferent to the amount, which gave Quartz a little pause. But at least he didn't shake his head and laugh.

"One-thousand dollars on the four horse to win," Nanetta said as though she was telling him without a doubt which horse was going to cross the finish line first. Handing the ticket to Quartz, she watched the detective's eyes go squinty, then very wide.

"*Netta!*" she shrieked. "We were talking about *Star Sailor…Billie Mayer*…the *five* horse. You just put all my money on fucking *Wheezy!*"

"That is what you thought the first time, no?" she asked, happily watching Quartz's face go pale. "She was your gut feeling?"

"Yeah, but you talked me out of it. Wheezy's a dog. You said so yourself."

"I know I did," Nanetta replied dryly. "Now you are *truly* wagering. Enjoy it."

Quartz nearly fainted.

Chapter 46

Half in and half out, Blash's sleep came on quick but it was unlike any sleep he'd experienced before. He was thinking about the afternoon meeting and all that had occurred. It may have been a dream since he felt like he was in as deep a sleep as he'd ever been, but the events were very un-dreamlike and pertained only to actual occurrences.

In other words, there weren't any monkeys clinging to the walls getting whipped by a simian dominatrix in tap shoes—a dream he actually *did* have once.

No, this seemed to be almost an exact replay of the events as they transpired. Mostly it was pretty uninteresting—he'd already done those things today. It was after Fisk had fallen into a heap on the floor that it started to get interesting. Fortunately, while replaying the scene where Louis Poklatar had squashed him with the door he didn't feel any pain.

He watched as Daisley went straight for him and practically begged him to kill Christian Roche. Blash watched himself flatly refuse. He then watched Daisley continue to try to sell the idea. He went so far as to bring up the fact that he'd killed before and, therefore, shouldn't have any trouble killing again. He even mentioned Jonathan Kendall by name.

He could still hear Daisley saying that they could make Roche's killing look just as clean as Kendall's. The words he used and the tone in which he used them—even the look on his face while he spoke made Blash uncomfortable. That was when the dream changed. He was no longer in the suite at the Bonaventure. It was just as real and was being replayed verbatim as the events had occurred.

It was suddenly dark and he was in the back of a truck unloading case after case of stolen whiskey. The group he had infiltrated was strictly bottom drawer and he knew he would be pulled out soon. Undercover work was the greatest if one was truly up to it and could blend in with the other felons. They weren't a bad bunch of guys—just a crew of six who needed help from time to time moving stolen merchandise.

*   *   *   *

They took to him quickly without much in the way of any kind of background check. They simply liked his crass style and thought he'd make a great member of the team. It also didn't hurt that he initiated contact by beating the crap out of their leader over a slight rub of shoulders in a bar. After a ten minute ordeal of taking punches he didn't have to and throwing punches that could have landed much harder, he and the man ended up on the ground and spitting blood, too tired to lift their arms anymore.

A good bloody fight in which no man gave any ground was almost always a basis for a lifelong friendship. Especially when there was no discernable winner.

In the end, drinks were poured and the two men congratulated each other on having balls made of steel, stone, brass, or in some cases, titanium—it really depended on the size difference of the two men. In Blash's case, his balls were brass; just shy of titanium, which disappointed him a little.

Of the six men, three—Gage, Wills, and Johanssen—were professional hijackers. They trolled the freeways between Riverside and Barstow for victims and had an infinite number of scams to keep the merchandise flowing in. Always threatening, though very charming when it was necessary, they were the main target of the investigation.

The leader who'd scuffled with Blash was a man named Palowski. He was the brains of the outfit, which was a little spooky since Blash thought the man was as dumb as a turd. He was a likeable fellow, though, and that seemed to carry more weight than his intellect. He was also the biggest, and in some circles it was enough to earn the title of boss.

A man they simply called Henry was the fence. He went to bars and warehouses in every desert community and pawned stolen booze, watches, clothing—anything that they happened to steal. The hijackers weren't always aware of what was in the truck they were stealing, so often it was a surprise when they opened them up.

Then there was Sparks; a real wormy type with thick glasses who acted as their forger. He could create bills of lading, invoices, and inventory sheets, but specialized mainly in fake ID's. Not the kind of ID's that an eighteen year old would use to buy alcohol with—the risk versus price ratio wasn't worth it to him—but he worked mainly with green cards, travel visas, and drivers licenses that stood up remarkably well under official scrutiny.

It was only a week and a half before Palowski's six man empire was to be taken down. But in a curse of bad timing and plain bad luck, a man named Jonathan Kendall rolled into Riverside looking for an ID that would get him as far as Nogales, where he hoped to slip into Mexico.

The APB on Kendall was statewide yet rated hardly a mouse fart in Blash's world. He'd heard the bulletin and read the report on the cop who had been killed up north; he just didn't see where it would involve him. Undercover work didn't give a cop enough freedom to simply drop what he was doing and go after a guy, effectively destroying months worth of groundwork. This one, however, fell right into his lap.

* * * *

"Are you Sparks?" the large man asked, his voice echoing in the nearly empty trailer. Dropping a case of whiskey, Blash leapt from the back of the truck. It was late and had been dark for several hours.

"Sparks is inside. What the fuck do you need him for?" Blash asked rudely, playing his role perfectly.

"Papers. I have cash."

"I'll get him for you. Wait right here and don't touch a fucking thing while I'm gone. I know how many cases are in there."

His first instinct was to drag the man to the ground and call for assistance, but since the only help he could get would come from a few other felons, he decided to stall him by helping him out.

"Sparks!" he yelled into the back of the bar that doubled as their warehouse. "Get on out here and earn a paycheck!"

"What is it, man?" Sparks asked tiredly, cleaning his glasses.

Walking him to the trailer, Blash pointed to the fidgety intruder. "The man needs papers."

As the two introduced themselves and prepared to negotiate, Blash turned from his work in the trailer and headed into the saloon instead. Boldly, he took a seat in the middle of the crowded, noisy bar and pulled out his cell phone. He made a call.

"Clark's Auto. How can I help you?" the female voice asked.

"Yeah, Clark. I've got a set of wheels over here and I can't rightly tell you what the make or model is. I'd like to move them, though."

"Are you in a position to discuss it right now?"

"I'd better be," Blash replied, hating the way he sounded while trying not to be conspicuous. If he would have stepped outside to use the pay phone it would have drawn more attention than just talking in the middle of everybody. Hiding in plain sight always gave him a rush anyway. "They're gonna move fast so I don't have the time to worry about it."

"Okay then. Let's have it."

"They're on that ATV I bought the other day."

"The APB on who?"

"Yeah, the original tires were all shot. They were those cheap-ass Kendall's that they used to put on three-wheelers."

"Fuck me. Jonathan Kendall?" the voice asked, changing in pitch.

"I'm pretty sure. I saw a black and white picture of the thing and the basic specs match up but I need some confirmation."

"Okay, let me see," the voice said, pausing. *"He's got a tattoo on the inside of his right arm. A snake coiled around a heart."*

"I already read that and it's not visible," Blash said, trying to hurry the voice along without giving himself away. "Anything else?"

"Other than what's in the report, there's nothing that you could see with his clothes on, Mike."

"Okay, I'll do what I need to do," Blash said, feeling that his undercover status might have to take a sidestep if this guy was his man.

"Keep in touch if you can. Just say the word and I'll send in the troops. This guy's a cop-killer, Mike. Be careful."

"I'll be cool, Quartz. Don't worry about me…it's not your job." He hung up.

Though worrying wasn't part of her job, he liked it that she did. If it was anyone else he would have been mad at the thought of it, but with Quartz he'd make an exception. She was a decent cop and pretty tough herself—for a girl, anyway.

Pocketing his phone, Blash nodded to a few familiar faces before heading out the back again. With a nonchalant walk he made his way to a trailer in the back corner of the small lot. Noting a figure by the trash cans, Blash took a quick look and moved on. The man appeared to be taking a piss against the dumpster. Not too uncommon an occurrence in his little corner of the world.

Of the seven halogen lights that covered the rear lot, only one hadn't been shot out yet and the whole area looked as though it was being lit up by a candle. He took another look back at the man before approaching the door.

"Sparks!" he yelled, knowing it would rattle the nervous man, but would go over better than banging on the thin aluminum door.

"Come in!" Sparks yelled back, which Blash considered a good sign. Aside from the one guy by the dumpsters, nothing seemed out of the ordinary.

Walking into the filthy trailer, the first thing he noticed was the man in the black long sleeve shirt sitting comfortably across from Sparks. He looked tired, like he'd had a very long day. He also looked just like the man in the photograph of Jonathan Kendall.

"How long's this gonna take, man?" Blash asked. "I've still got eighty cases to yank out of that fucking truck and I'm not doing it by myself."

"This'll take about an hour, I think. And when I'm done I'm not helping you anyway. It's not what I get paid for. Get one of the other guys. I'm busy in case you didn't notice."

Looking around the makeshift office, Blash let his eyes settle on the man in the black shirt. The man stared right back.

"What about you? What are you doing?"

"I'm just sitting here, man," he replied defensively.

"Well, you don't look handicapped. The cases don't weigh much but there's lots of them," Blash said, wiping imaginary sweat from his forehead. "I'll give you twenty bucks if you unload them and I'll wheel them in...or I'll unload them and you wheel them in. I don't give a shit."

He wanted to offer more than a measly twenty dollars but anything over that would have been suspicious. If this was his man and he was on the run, he'd be looking for any cash he could get his hands on. More than that, though, he wanted the man to roll up his sleeves.

"I don't think so," he replied, shaking his head with an insulted look on his face.

"We're talking about ten minutes worth of work here," Blash added, suddenly thinking of a better way to get his sleeves up. "But if you're too pussy to lift a couple boxes, then I'm sorry I asked. I'll find someone else."

In an instant, the man was on his feet.

"Maybe I'll lift your skull right out of your fucking skin," the large man said in a deep voice, stepping towards Blash. "This is the wrong time and place to be fucking with me. You don't know who you're talking to."

"Sure I do," Blash said, backing up as he slid out the door. "I'm talking to a big, girly faggot who's afraid of breaking a nail if he lifts something heavy. Isn't that right, sweet pants?"

As expected, he was coming at Blash slightly faster now, who was still back pedaling into the center of the parking lot. Smiling cockily at him, Blash stopped.

"You change your mind about helping out?" he asked, pulling his sleeves up, taking a defensive stance, hoping the larger man would follow suit.

"Helping you out of this world maybe," he replied, removing his shirt completely, exposing Blash to a very muscular body. "You should have just kept your fucking mouth shut."

His eyes had a familiar crazy glare in them that Blash recognized instantly. It was the same crazy look *he* gave to people he didn't think he could physically handle. It seemed ridiculous at the time, but Blash was almost certain that the man was afraid. Not necessarily afraid of him…but simply scared. He looked like he'd been scared for a while now and was tired of it.

Of course, the reason he was scared was because he killed a cop and had been on the run for over a week. The look on his face said it as much as the snake tattoo on his arm did. It was clear as day. The man was frustrated, desperate, scared, and now very, very angry. And it was obvious he was preparing to take it all out on the big-mouth in front of him. A big-mouth who seemed strangely optimistic about his near future.

"You know, I'm gonna rip that smile off your goddamn face," he said, moving slower now, stalking Blash who wasn't backing up anymore, but moving from side to side.

"That's funny, you believing that," Blash replied, dispensing with the smile. "It's sad too. It almost hurts for me to do this to a fine gentleman like yourself."

In a quick motion, moving both arms behind his back, Blash stepped backwards a few feet. His hands reappeared just as quickly but they weren't empty anymore. *Priceless* was the word he would have used to describe the look on Jonathan Kendall's face when he saw the gun pointed at him.

He started to say something but was seemingly distracted by something behind Blash, creating a very tough decision to make with so little time to think about it.

To look or not to look.

The first reaction would have been to turn and at least take a quick peek. That's what most people would have done, which is why it was called "The oldest trick in the book". There was also a good chance that Kendall was gleefully watching a car that was about to run over the man who was pointing a gun at him.

Regardless of the dilemma, common sense took over quickly and Blash stepped to his side. Keeping the gun on Kendall, he twisted himself and glanced back quickly. Feeling foolish, he saw the same guy who he'd seen before he went into Sparks' trailer. He was taking a piss.

"Turn around, Kendall," Blash said, turning back to him. "Get your hands out where I can see them. When I tell you to, I'm gonna want you to step to—"

Taking a piss? How long does it take for a guy to...?

Before he even finished the thought, Blash spun around quickly. He was just in time to see the gun come out. Quickly, he stepped further away from Kendall and pointed the weapon to his left at the formerly peeing mystery man. Before he could even get a shot lined up, Blash could see Kendall go into motion on his right. Two guns were being drawn and he was stuck in the middle.

Left or right? Left or right? Shit...shit...shit...someone's about to get shot, he thought, waiting for instinct to take over and do the right thing. It didn't fail him.

The man on his left was to be the unlucky one—the first one, anyway. Before he was even aware of having a straight shot, Blash's gun discharged twice. Without waiting for a body to fall, he swept to the right and dropped to a knee. Kendall was slow on the draw but was still bringing his weapon up. It was a horrible mistake; not the first of the evening. Two shots whizzed by Blash's head as he leveled the gun at Kendall. His eyes still looked scared and desperate as Blash put three rounds into his chest.

He had just killed a man. Maybe two of them. With so many thoughts fighting for attention in his head, common sense was looking to take over again.

Sparks had run from his trailer and was looking at the men on the ground. He held a large revolver in his hand. Customers, many of them armed, were beginning to come out into the parking lot to see what the commotion was. Even Palowski came running out back. He was carrying a shotgun. So were the men on either side of him. It seemed that everyone was carrying a gun.

"*Jesus, Mikey!*" Palowski screamed at him. "What happened? Who are these guys? *Sparks! Call 911!*"

This time, the sweat was real. When he saw all the firepower that was suddenly in the parking lot, he thought he was a dead man. Only then did it occur to him that the gun in his hand looked as natural as everyone else's. He appeared to be responding to the situation appropriately.

"*Mikey!* What the hell happened?" Palowski was still yelling. "Did you see anything?"

"Yeah, barely," he answered shakily. "I was in the back of the truck when I heard them yelling. Next thing I know they're shooting at each other."

As rattled as he was, Blash was starting to get the feeling that his undercover job was still solid. He felt badly for thinking of such a thing after possibly taking the lives of two men and didn't feel quite right congratulating himself.

Dropping the shotgun, Palowski ran to the man laying next to the dumpster. Even as he flipped the man over to check for a pulse, Blash could see that he was dead.

"This one's gone, I think. Check the other one," he said, motioning towards Kendall. *"Sparks! Call 911 goddamn it!"*

"I did, man," Sparks replied, running from the trailer. "They're on their way."

The gun was gone from his hand and he was carrying two blankets instead. For a small crew of criminals operating out of a biker bar, they seemed pretty efficient at caring for the wounded. Sadly, it didn't take them long to find that there were no wounded to care for.

Checking them over thoroughly, Palowski and the other two searched for ID's. After carefully covering the men with the blankets—only up to their necks until a paramedic could confirm what everyone already knew—Palowski grabbed Sparks by the elbow and dragged him back into the trailer. Blash didn't have to guess what they were talking about. A few minutes later they emerged. Palowski grabbed his two shotgun men and ran straight into the bar. Sparks approached Blash.

"Mikey, we've got to tear down the shop. The bar's cool but the stock room's still full of swag. We've got to get rid of it before the cops come."

"What for?" Blash asked, not ready to watch a whole room of evidence just drive away. "It looks like some kind of personal thing here. The cops aren't going to check in our stock room."

After taking credit for dropping Kendall, he'd have plenty of time to explain to the department what happened to all the hijacked merchandise. Since he was still part of the crew, he was sure to know where the merchandise would end up and could simply arrest them all at a later date. Realizing this, he started to breathe a little easier.

"They might check the whole building, Mikey," Sparks said, looking ready to cry. "Palowski says this place is gonna be crawling with a million cops in a few minutes."

"Relax, Sparks. I know we've got a killing here, but it's not going to bring a million cops."

"Listen, Mikey. I gotta tell you something," Sparks said, pulling him away from the others. "The guy…the dead guy over there…."

Oh shit. He knew it was Jonathan Kendall when he was making him the ID's. He fucking knew it. Oh, Sparks, I am going to fuck you up so bad when....

"...he's a cop, Mikey. I don't know who the big guy is, but Palowski dug this out of the other guy's pocket."

Blash felt a spike of pain shoot through his left shoulder when he saw what Sparks was holding. It was a badge not too different from his own.

* * * *

This was usually about the time he would wake up from the dream.

Some men might have woken up screaming from such a vivid nightmare. Some might have even woken up crying. With Blash it was always the same thing every night. He woke up apologizing.

Checking the clock on the coffee table, he noted the time. 11:38 PM. He'd been asleep for only ten minutes. It didn't surprise him. There was plenty more where that came from.

Chapter 47

"It's about eleven-forty," Lou said, slipping from the driver's seat. "I'm going to go grab some sleep. I can't believe this day's finally over."

Aren't you forgetting something, Louis?

"What—the duct tape I was going to put on your mouth?" he answered, feeling surprisingly witty.

What are you going to do with the body?

"What body?" Lou asked, not even looking at him. "I don't see any body."

Don't ignore me, Louis. I was just busting your chops earlier. It was funny. I'm a funny guy. I can't help it.

"Yeah, keep trying to make me laugh," Lou said, collecting the cell phone and his jacket from behind the seat. "You've got me giggling my ass off over here."

I'm sorry, Louis. Wait. Please...just wait.

"Can't do it, Terry. I'm tired and I'm done playing with you today."

Why? It's still early. What are you, an old lady or something? It's not even midnight yet.

Lou ignored him and slammed the door, locking it up.

You can't leave me out here. What if someone sees me?

With the door closed, Fisk's voice became muffled and distant. Looking around, Lou made sure no one was nearby and answered him.

"Then they won't steal my rental car. You make a great car alarm, Terry. And thanks for the free ride in the carpool lane."

It was probably the best zinger he'd come up with all day and it was directed at a man who wouldn't respond verbally. It was a cold thing to say. He felt bad for it.

Don't feel bad, Louis.

"Goddamn it," he muttered, returning to the car. He unlocked the door and got back in the driver's seat.

Hi again.

"Terry, listen—"

Where to now, Louis? Do you bowl?

"Shut up for a second, seriously," Lou said, pinching his eyes shut. "We've got to talk."

About what?

"You. You and me."

What about us?

"You think I'm stupid, don't you?" he asked, staring out through the windshield. He was tired of looking at Fisk's face.

You're only as dumb as the next guy, Louis. I f seen much bigger idiots than you. Did that sound bad?

"That's what I thought."

It's not so bad, Louis. You don't have to be a genius for people to like you. I like you...even though you're stupid. What's that worth?

"From you, it's worth a lot. You want to know why?"

I'm on pins and needles.

"Because it means *you're* the stupid one," he said, nodding to himself.

You lost me, Louis. I thought you just said that I was the stupid one. How can that be possible? I'm as smart as a whip...whatever that means.

"I never understood that phrase either," Lou said, facing Fisk for the first time since he got back into the car. "Which proves my point."

Oh, you have a point, do you?

"Yep. You're just a dead guy and me talking to you is just about the sickest fucking thing I've ever heard of. I can't believe I've been driving around with you. I thought I was nuts at first but it's making sense now."

Is it? Fisk asked, the tone in his voice giving away his uncertainty.

"Yeah, it is," Lou answered seriously. "But I don't understand something."

There's a shocker.

"See, that's what I'm talking about," Lou said, pointing at him. "What you just said there. That was quick. It was sharp. It sounded good even though it was supposed to make me feel bad."

I'm talented. What can I say?

"See, you did it again," Lou said, wishing he had the words to express himself. "You've been doing it all day. It's like you're...on your toes all the time. I say something to you—it doesn't matter what I say—and you, you fire something right back that sounds ten times better than the ignorant shit that I just said."

Does that surprise you?

"More than you know."

Why?

"Because it means I'm able to talk and think just as fast as you. I've got to be."

How so, Louis?

"Don't be stupid, Terry. Who am I talking to? Right now, I mean. Who am I talking to?"

Me? Fisk answered, sounding very unsure of himself.

"You don't think I believe that, do you?" Lou asked, staring hard into his face.

Fisk was silent for almost a minute.

Had you going for a while, though, didn't I?

"Just for a little while," Lou said, nodding in agreement. "But I'm the one in control. Don't think that I'm not."

Sure, Louis. Total control. Whatever you say. Can't sneak a thing by you, can I?

"No you can't," Lou replied, feeling the smartest he had all day. He began to exit the vehicle again. A comfortable bed was waiting for him and he suspected that sleep would come very easy tonight.

Louis?

"What, Terry? It's late. You're staying out here and that's the end of the discussion."

What if I did already?

"What if you did *what*?" Lou asked, losing the smart feeling he had only seconds earlier.

What if I snuck one by you already?

"Oh Jesus...."

Sleep tight, Louis.

Chapter 48

▼

"Who is it, then? This person—it is a man, no?"

"Just *wait* a minute." Quartz felt as though an electrical current was running through her as the horses lined up. "My God, they're about to start."

"You must relax, Qiana. It is only one race. If you are truly asking me to do what I think you want me to do, then this race should mean very little to you."

It was a valid point.

"I know...you're right...but..." Quartz stammered, shifting her eyes from the horses to Nanetta very quickly. "...just a minute. After the race, Netta. *After*."

"There they go!" yelled the announcer. The horses were off.

Quartz screamed and grabbed Nanetta's arm, not realizing how hard she was squeezing. Star Sailor, driven by Billie Mayer was in the lead. It was still early, though, and one thing she'd learned from her first night at the track was that the races never seemed to finish the way they started.

"Oh my God, Wheezy's blowing it," Quartz nearly moaned. "Where is she? Fourth? Fifth? Christ, I can't tell."

"She is trapped on the rail. Boxed in. But it is early. They will circle the track again. Much can happen before it ends."

Quartz wasn't too sure since Star Sailor was several lengths ahead of the rest of the field but she couldn't deny that Nanetta was indeed correct about her horse being boxed in. With a horse in front of her, behind her, and beside her, Wheezy's options were looking slim.

"This isn't funny, Netta. How's she going to get out of there?"

"She waits," Nanetta answered, trying to stifle a yawn. "When they make the final turn she will try to break out."

"What's going to happen until then?"

"Nothing. She can do nothing until the six horse moves from her side. She will wait and move after the final turn if she can."

"Why not break out now and—"

"She cannot," Nanetta said simply, removing Quartz's tight grip from her arm. "We must wait and see what the six horse does. Look at me, Qiana."

Painfully, Quartz pulled her eyes away from the horses and turned them on Nanetta. She had lowered her sunglasses and was staring at Quartz, measuring her. She said nothing until Quartz looked back to the field. This time, it was Nanetta who grabbed her arm, spinning her around.

"I said for you to look at me," she said, sounding very serious. "Tell me his name."

"Who? Oh…it's Roche…Christian Roche," she replied in a loud whisper, struggling to keep from turning back around. "He's a dealer from Corona. What's happening, Netta?"

"She is still on the rail but there is still much time. How old is this man Roche?"

"He's…forty-two…he's…" Quartz paused and turned her head to look. This time her chin was taken in Nanetta's right hand and her head turned back.

"Look at me, Qiana. Is he a large man?"

"Uh…five foot eleven…about one-seventy. *What's happening?*"

Nanetta released her with a huff and allowed her to watch their thousand dollar bet ride dangerously close to the rail. The six horse was still blocking her in. Star Sailor was still far out front. Nothing had changed.

As Quartz watched, frustrated by the fact that her horse wasn't being allowed to move out of her position, Nanetta calmly pulled out two cigarettes and lit them. Nudging Quartz out of her hypnotized state, she gave her one. The horses were about to make the final turn.

"Breathe, Qiana," she said, watching Quartz suck down a quarter inch of cigarette in one drag. "Whatever happens, it will happen now. This is excitement, no?"

"I'm about to have a heart attack. They're all so scrunched up together coming around the corner. I can't see if…*oh, Jesus.*"

Quartz stopped talking as the field opened up. All three horses that were running out front started to separate and moved closer to the outside rail. The six horse moved to her right, trying to take advantage of the sudden gap. With that done, Wheezy edged to her right as well, suddenly free from the rail.

"What in the hell is Star Sailor doing?" Quartz asked, screaming in Nanetta's face. It was a good question and many of the other spectators were thinking the same thing.

The horse who'd been leading from the opening moments of the race was now nearly on top of the outside rail. Her young driver was doing everything she could to pull her back into the race. She was still leading, but angling to the side had cost her at least a length. A moment later, the three horse joined her on the outside and looked ready to fight her all the way to the finish line.

By now, the left side of the track was looking interesting as well. The horses that had boxed Wheezy in from the front and back seemed comfortable where they were at and didn't look ready to move anytime soon. With the rest of the stragglers hanging lengths behind them, the middle of the track was practically barren.

Wheezy filled the spot easily. She was in third place for about half a second. A moment later she was trailing the leader by half a length.

Quartz yelled until her throat was raw. It was a high, hysterical type of shouting reserved specifically for moments like these. She wasn't alone. Suddenly two arms were wrapped around her from behind and Nanetta was screaming too. It was now a two horse race.

It ended with a flash of light and silence from the majority of the crowd. There was still plenty of hollering from the folks who had bet either of them to place or show, but it was the people who bet to win who were waiting for some kind of result. It wouldn't be official for a couple of minutes.

"Is that what they call a photo finish?" Quartz asked, knowing she'd heard the term before but never quite knew what it meant.

"Precisely," Nanetta confirmed, pointing to a monitor. "Watch the screen. In a minute there will be two noses in the picture. One will be our horse. Did we win? I do not know. So you say this man is a dealer? A dealer in what?"

"Dealer? What?" Quartz asked as though she hadn't even heard what she had said. The question meant absolutely nothing to her. Her eyes were glued to the monitor. Everything else was merely static.

"I am asking you a question."

"Drugs, Netta," Quartz spit out rapidly, tearing her eyes from the monitor only for an instant. "Drugs and guns and…all kinds of bad stuff—lot's of it. In a couple of minutes we'll have all the time in the world to talk about this. You're killing me."

"Oh, I am bothering you. Perhaps I should leave." Nanetta started to turn away but was quickly grabbed around the waist and pulled tightly against the detective.

"You're not going anywhere, sweetie. We're standing right here until they tell us who won. My God, what if we won? Can you imagine?"

"You are so cute with your excitement," Nanetta said, as if only just noticing Quartz's manic state. "I am afraid of what you will be like when we win. I will need to hold you down."

"You just might," Quartz agreed through teeth that were chattering though it wasn't cold at all. The picture on the monitor changed causing both women to suck in their breath.

The crowd went utterly silent.

Quartz stood motionless, staring at the monitor. Nanetta, still pulled snugly against her, stared at Quartz. Her facial expressions told her more than the TV screen ever could.

The announcement was made.

"Winning is fun, no?" Nanetta asked loudly, vainly trying to shelter herself from the woman who was shaking her madly.

Chapter 49

▼

"Five to one. Five grand. Five G's. Five fucking thousand dollars. This can't be real. Wheezy, I love you."

Quartz was still giddy even twenty minutes after the race had finished. Though she was tempted to stay for the final races, she was happy to be back in her car. Compared to the benches in general admission, the seats in her Mustang were like sitting on clouds.

"You were going to bet on the five horse, no?" Nanetta noted with a toothy smile. "I think it must be *me* that you love."

"Oh, I've got plenty of love for you right now." Digging through her purse, she began emptying the contents into Nanetta's hands as she searched for her lipstick. Quartz trembled visibly as she handed her the first, second, then third stack of five thousand dollar bundles. Dumping the rest out, Nanetta couldn't miss the large handgun that plopped into her lap and was slowly slipping between her legs. It was a defining moment in their relationship.

Unlike Quartz, she was very businesslike with the weapon as she pulled out the clip and checked the chamber. "I am guessing you want me to use this."

"You don't have to use it. I've got a lot to choose from."

She pointed the large gun downward, checking the sights. "So, you are being serious."

"I'm still trying to think of a way to convince you just *how* serious I am," Quartz admitted, knowing the dilemma would eventually present itself. "Especially coming from me—or any cop for that matter. And I know what you're thinking. I'm trying to set you up, right?"

"Are you?"

"No, I'm not." She felt ridiculous even as the words came out. "But I know you're way too smart to believe me just because I say I'm telling you the truth. I wouldn't believe me either."

"Why not?"

"Because it's a harsh, immoral, and illegal thing I'm asking you to do."

"*Paying* me to do," Nanetta corrected. "*Paying* me fifteen thousand dollars to do…."

Well, there goes the five grand I just won.

"…and making sure that our friend Nestor LaGuardia is not arrested or otherwise harassed by the police…."

I don't remember promising that.

"…and keeping very, very quiet about the unfortunate Mr. Kadouris."

This just got very easy, she thought, finally confirming her suspicions. It was an important thing to know since it helped her immediate situation a great deal. At the same time, she'd let a murderer walk free because she was a big enough sucker to feel sorry for the poor woman.

She still liked her, though. That hadn't changed, which she found peculiar.

"Why did you do it, Netta? I'm just curious. You don't have to tell me."

"It was a mistake; I know this," Nanetta explained, looking earnest. "I did not mean to kill him so badly. Me—the other women too—all of the time he tried to make us work for him. He tried to get sex from us and sell it to other men like him. One day he tried too hard. That is all."

"That's all?" Quartz asked incredulously.

"He is dead and the women sell their sex for me now. What else is to know?"

Quartz wasn't expecting it to be put so bluntly, but blunt seemed to be all that the woman was capable of. "I'd like to know why you went back to his house. And to call the police yourself—that was a gutsy move."

"I wanted to call them before they called me," she replied, turning her eyes back to the money. "And they would have called me for certainly. I stole from him all the fucking days of the week and my little fingerprints were on everything."

"But still, Netta."

"It was less of a gamble than your Wheezy and you won, did you not? You helped me and now I will help you. We will continue to help one another, no?"

Let's see—fifteen grand plus a guarantee of no prosecution for pimping, pandering, and one small murder. How in the hell did I get here?

"Of course we'll help each other, Netta," Quartz answered as she finally applied her lipstick.

Nanetta watched intently as she smeared the dark red makeup across her lips and rubbed them together. Catching her gaze in the mirror, Quartz turned to her and blew an exaggerated kiss in her direction before closing up her compact. She had her full attention and was hoping to close the deal quickly. To her delight, Nanetta was already ahead of her.

"When will I meet this man—this Christian Roche?"

"Tomorrow," Quartz said tentatively, knowing that the tight schedule would be almost as big a problem as the job itself. "I'm sorry that it's so—"

"What time?" Nanetta asked, expertly slamming the clip into the gun and putting the safety on.

Maybe it wouldn't be such a problem after all.

Chapter 50

▼

"Okay, last time. Knock-knock," Alex Bautista said, standing in front of his bathroom door.

"Who's there?"

"*Fuck*, man, just open the door," Alex complained, growing frustrated with the dressed rehearsal. "He's not going to ask who it is. Nobody does that. They look through the peephole."

"And when he does?"

"He sees me standing on his doorstep in my Sunday best and he opens the door. Do it again. Knock-knock."

This time Joe pulled the door open. Before he could even say hello, the shotgun was pointed at his chest.

"Boom. Now, what's so hard about that?"

They had gone over it a dozen times, trying to counter each glitch in their plan with a proper response. Of the several scenarios they came up with, the knock on the door seemed the safest bet. It had already been agreed that anything as stupid as busting through a window or even sneaking around the guy's property at night was a bad idea.

"You know, this won't work really late in the evening," Joe said, checking his own watch. "It's about one a.m. What would you do if someone knocked on the door right now? Usually, you're not going to get any knocks at your door past eight o'clock even on a Friday night. If it's later than that—and it probably will be—the guy will be suspicious as hell."

"That's why I'll be decked out in the suit and trench coat," Alex said, knowing full well that he'd already gone over most of this with him. "I'll look real official.

Official *what?* I don't know and I don't care. He only needs to open the door for a second and he's all ours."

"That shotgun is pretty big. Are you sure the trench will hide it?"

Standing up, Alex threw on the trench coat for the third time of the evening and concealed the weapon. It was a big gun but was hidden adequately. "See? And what other choice do we have? The armory's looking pretty empty."

The armory was Alex's closet. If he was the owner of any other weapon than the single shotgun, he wasn't aware of it. It had been purchased from a pawn shop for fifty-seven dollars over four years earlier. He and Joe had shot some aluminum cans with it once. They hadn't even looked at it since then and had almost forgotten all about it.

"Okay," Joe replied, throwing his hands up in defeat. "What if he doesn't open the door? Shit, man, what if asks 'Who's there?' I know you're telling me that people don't do that...but what if he does?"

"Then I take a guess where the voice is coming from and blow him away right through the door."

"Some voice asks 'Who's there' and you kill it? That's a great plan. Maybe we should just plant a bomb and blow his whole neighborhood up. We could kill lots of innocent people that way."

"Yeah, you're right," Alex conceded. "A visual should definitely be a priority. We've got a good description but I'd feel better with a photo. The last thing I want to be thinking about when that door comes open is if I'm getting the right guy."

"No kidding. I could just see some poor guy standing there with a shotgun pointed at him while you're trying to figure out whether to shoot him or not. Talk about cruelty."

"Cruelty to *animals*, maybe," Alex replied quietly with a foul look. "Remember back in high school when John Ranz got fucked by Mr. Schuler?"

It was rhetorical question. Of course Joe remembered, as did everyone who attended the school that year. A very popular teacher had been accused of the worst kind of impropriety. Though the accuser was painted as a liar for over a year, the truth eventually did come out when some former students stepped forward. It made the papers when he was finally indicted.

"Yeah, that was too fucking sad," Joe replied, nodding. "And the bullshit part is that Mr. Schuler was my favorite damn teacher."

"Me too," Alex admitted. "That was the trick. He acted real cool and got your defenses down. He got John's down, anyway. I can't be the only person who wanted to kill him for that. I mean, John was a good guy. What was he, fifteen or sixteen at the time?"

"Just a kid like us. It could have been one of us really easy. I'm not saying he could've talked his way into my pants but I trusted him as a teacher. I really did. I guess you never can tell."

"You sure can't," Alex echoed, dry firing the unloaded shotgun. His eyes were going flinty as Joe looked on nervously. "You can't be sure about any-fucking-thing or any-fucking-body. Not a single fucking one of them. Never. But don't stress it. I'll make sure we've got some rock solid ID before I start blasting away. Or maybe…fuck it—you know what I'm going to do? I'm going to look this guy right in the eye and ask him his name."

"Just ask him."

"Yeah, I'm just going to ask him. How cool would that be?"

"That'd be wicked," Joe answered, smiling. It was only an external smile, though. On the inside, any good vibes he had were long since gone. His friend was acting in a manner that he'd never seen before.

In over ten years of knowing him, he had never seen Alex in such a heartless mood. They had broken many laws together and done other things that the average citizen would have considered to be off-color; things that were done for a variety of reasons. Sometimes for fun, sometimes for monetary gain, sometimes for almost no reason at all. This was different, though. It bore what looked to be an incredible amount of malice and it certainly wasn't about money.

It had an "avenging angel" quality to it that made Joe edgy. He decided immediately never to make any crude jokes about child molestation or anything even close to it. At this point, nothing would surprise him. He thought about it as he walked into the bathroom again and waited behind the door.

"Okay, last time before we call it a night," Alex said, checking his coat for a protruding gun barrel. It was hardly noticeable. "Knock-knock."

"Who's there…shit."

"*Fuck*, man."

"Sorry, bro. Let's try it again."

Chapter 51

▼

"I'll be following you, so don't go tearing through any red lights," Quartz warned as she dropped Nanetta off at her own car which was precariously parked in a tow-away zone. The white Corvette had not been touched or ticketed.

"I would not dream of such a thing, Qiana."

She then stomped down on her accelerator and, in a choking cloud of burnt rubber, she was nearly out of sight before the Mustang could even get back into first gear. If she wasn't still holding all of the money, Quartz might have been nervous. Apparently this was just more Ukrainian humor since the Corvette was waiting for her at the first light she came to.

Its engine was revving awfully high. By the time she pulled along side her, the car was off again.

Where's she running to? She knows I'm following her home, Quartz thought, stepping harder on her own gas pedal. Mercifully, the streets were pretty barren as would be expected on a late Thursday night. She wasn't too hard to follow.

Even while trying to call Daisley for the fifth time, the Corvette was never more than a few hundred yards ahead of her. After letting it ring fifteen times, she hung up and dialed again. She couldn't wait to tell him how much she had accomplished. She was tempted to call Blash just to brag a bit but decided not to as Nanetta made another unexpected turn and nearly lost her.

Where in the hell are you, Andrew?

Less than five minutes later, Quartz pulled in behind the parked Corvette in time to see Nanetta dashing into her apartment complex. The surrounding air still smelled like burning tires. She smoked while she waited. Every drag tasted like rubber.

Insane…insane…that's what this is, Quartz sang in her head, trying to keep her thoughts straight. It wasn't helping. Nothing was straight and it all seemed horribly insane. Noting the time of twelve-thirty, it occurred to her that she'd indeed had quite a day. She couldn't believe it had only been twelve hours or so since Terrence Fisk got snagged on her piece of carpet and hit the floor.

She kept thinking about what a rude thing it was for him to do to all of them, dying like that. If they could have just kept him alive for another couple of days it would have been a simple operation and they would have been able to bury the whole experience deep in the backs of their minds. It wouldn't have been pleasant and certainly not something to be proud of, but she promised herself that she'd get over it. They were probably all thinking the same thing.

It seemed to make perfect sense at first. Simplicity at its finest. The way it used to be done. And though it interfered with her own moral beliefs, the idea of having a professional killer take out their man didn't weigh so heavily on her. As long as she wasn't actually doing the killing, Quartz figured it was like being a witness to an execution and it could be morally justified. She'd just be making sure the job was done. No hands-on involvement was required. Even now, playing it over in her head, it still made a scary kind of sense.

Things were slightly different now that their killer was dead.

She didn't care for Christian Roche in any way, shape, or form, but was beginning to feel bad about it; not about killing him—she figured he had it coming—but about dragging Nanetta Lalanskaev into the mess. She remembered Nanetta complaining earlier in the evening about being confused with a whore. The irony, of course, was that Nanetta wasn't a prostitute at all but she'd been made into a whore over the last couple of hours. And now Quartz would serve as her pimp.

She was almost glad when she heard that Nanetta had really killed her former employer. At least whacking out Roche wouldn't be anything new to her. Justifying it in such a way made Quartz feel less like a corrupting influence, but she still felt like a pimp.

Finishing the thought as Nanetta reappeared, Quartz dropped her cigarette and got back into the car. Nanetta jumped into the passenger's seat and tossed her overnight bag into the back. Quartz was determined not to let her out of her sight until the deed had been done.

"Drive, Qiana," Nanetta said, pointing straight ahead. "We will start our sleeping party now?"

"That would be *slumber* party, Netta," Quartz corrected, pulling out of the apartment complex. "It's called a slumber party. And yeah, it'll start really soon. What do you feel like tonight?"

"I feel like having a drink with you," Nanetta answered. "Vodka?"

"Da," Quartz replied as she headed for the freeway.

Forty-five minutes later the pair of Ukrainian pimps walked through the door of Quartz's apartment in Corona. They opened a bottle of Stolichnaya and didn't shut up for nearly three hours.

At four a.m. they stopped talking.

At six a.m. they went to sleep.

Chapter 52

It was six a.m. when the phone began to ring. Unlike the phone in his apartment, the ringing apparatus on this one was truly obnoxious. It sounded like the old phone his family had when he was a kid. But there was a reason for it.

"Lou here," he said, trying to sound alert and fully awake.

Instead of a live voice, he was treated to a recorded message. It was informing him that it was time to wake up.

"It can't be today already," he complained, climbing from the bed quickly. It was a little early to be rising but requesting the wake-up call had been essential. He guessed it was mostly safe to leave Fisk in the car at night, but during the daylight hours it didn't seem like as good an idea.

Dashing straight to the window, he parted the curtains and checked on the car. It didn't appear that Fisk had taken it cruising at any time during the night as he was still in the passenger seat. Lou showered, changed, and made a call.

* * * *

There it was again. The ringing.

He almost destroyed the phone in a drunken rage several hours earlier but had decided against it. The only reason it remained intact and functioning was because he wanted it that way. With every chirp from the tiny phone he was reminded of what a fuck-up he was and how many people he was letting down. It wasn't total penance but it made his head hurt worse than it already did, which he felt he deserved.

Daisley wasn't really hung over. He was just still painfully drunk.

It seemed the little thing would never stop ringing. A few times—once around midnight and maybe a little later—he considered answering it and seeing how his people were doing.

My people, he thought. *What did you ever do to deserve having me as your fearless leader?* But already knew what they did. It was the reason they were called in the first place. They were all guilty of something and they were all being punished.

The phone was still ringing. He let it drone on.

If things had gone according to Donald Ratcliffe's master plan he wouldn't be waking for another few hours. Even on Christian Roche's execution day he would have been able to sleep in. He wouldn't have been involved until much later in the evening after Terrence Fisk had made short work of the pesky drug and weapons dealer.

If Daisley would have known how hard it would be to find someone willing to kill for money, he would have contacted Fisk much sooner. It was only after he was totally desperate and out of options that he made the call to an old friend in Chicago since he had already scoured Ratcliffe's database for prime candidates…not unlike the job those very candidates were doing now.

At least Quartz, Blash, and Louis weren't at the bottom of the food chain anymore. It was *their* candidates that assumed that position now.

Daisley liked it better when he was alone in the whole thing. Being the only one who was completely fucked had a certain nobility to it. He could have simply refused Ratcliffe's offer and gone to prison; it wouldn't have been forever, after all. Just a few years, or maybe a little more.

Or he could have turned Ratcliffe in, like Blash had suggested. It would have been the smart thing to do. He didn't do the smart thing though, and the snowball had started rolling from that point forward. Ratcliffe had defended so many bad cops that it was embarrassing. He hadn't defended them all personally, but he had access to their files and that was enough to get started.

Michael Blash was the first obvious choice. He'd killed three men while on the job. Only two were on the record, but that was beside the point. It wasn't bad intentions that killed the undercover police officer, just bad luck. Bad judgment then followed, placing himself firmly into Donald Ratcliffe's hands.

His answer had been an emphatic "No". Actually, it was something along the lines of "Fuck you and your mother" but his point was well taken. In the end it wouldn't matter either way. Even though his answer was in the negative, he was obliged to be involved. Even as a lookout, he could be indicted for conspiracy and that was more than enough to keep him in the fold. He couldn't be blackmailed into killing a man but he could be blackmailed into helping out. He wasn't an easy sell.

The phone was still ringing. He was slowly adjusting to it like he did throughout the night. Eventually, the ringing would stop then *that* would annoy him for a while. He tried to guess which one of them was calling now. Perhaps it was Quartz. That would be nice.

Maybe I could impress her with more killers that I have access to. It seemed to work the first time, he thought, knowing that she would see through his bullshit eventually. He wouldn't have a clue as to what to say to her at this particular moment.

The same went for Lou. Aside from an apology for leaving him with Terrence Fisk's body to dispose of, he had no special words for the large man.

Louis—what a horrible mistake it was to call him. He looked like gold on paper; almost as good as Blash. He had never tallied any official kills but that didn't mean much. Often, it was what *wasn't* written down in a police report that told the real story.

Unbeknownst to Louis Poklatar, he was currently under investigation for the murder of one Gabriel Marcos from Fresno, California. Though he had been put on temporary leave, he was blissfully unaware of his department's suspicions. They had told him some story about being in a "Fragile emotional state" and sent him home for a few weeks while they dug into what little they knew. For Daisley and Ratcliffe, the timing couldn't have been better.

After meeting with the man, Daisley was sure of two things. The first was that Officer Poklatar hadn't killed anyone. The second was that he was completely wrong for the job.

For a guy who had busted up as many perps as he had, Louis Poklatar had morals tighter than Mother Theresa. Unfortunately, the job had already been pitched to him and it was the kind of offer that couldn't be rescinded. After a long and torturous sales pitch at Ratcliffe's home in Los Angeles, he agreed to cover the back of whomever accepted the job. Like Quartz and Blash, he refused to accept a dime for his services. Even so, they didn't tell him about the ongoing investigation against him. It would have only confused and distracted him.

Daisley decided he would tell him everything he knew after Roche was dead. It seemed the decent thing to do considering he was the only one who was getting absolutely nothing out of the job. Other than protecting the interests of the public—which Ratcliffe had easily convinced him of—he had nothing to gain. It was kind of sad, really.

Though Quartz and Blash also had nothing to gain, they had plenty to lose. For Blash, facing his department, or any department for that matter, would have been unbearable if they knew that it was he, and not Kendall, who had put two bullets into another officer.

For Quartz, it may have even been worse. Though accidents happen—even fatal ones from time to time—they could only be compounded further by trying to escape blame. She was only trying to help. She shouldn't have.

He was really starting to like her, though. She was tough, beautiful and smart...most of the time. It surprised him when she began to show any interest in him. It wouldn't last and he knew it. He'd also knew he'd blow it eventually anyway and deservedly so.

Quartz, I hope that's not you calling me. I'd love to talk but I'm afraid I'm all out of bullshit right now. Slipping back into the blackness, Daisley let his phone ring unanswered and pinched his eyes shut.

✳ ✳ ✳ ✳

"Where in the hell is Daisley?" Lou asked himself, slamming the phone shut. Immediately, he grabbed the Yellow Pages and turned to the section with hotels listed. Luckily, this wasn't LA or Orange County so there weren't a million to choose from.

One of them was the place he was staying in at this moment. Though it was unlikely that he lucked into staying at the same hotel that Fisk had been booked into, he thought it couldn't hurt to ask. Losing Fisk would be his first priority of the day. He called the front desk and asked for Terrence Fisk's room. He was told that there was no one with a room reserved under that name.

Under that name. I'm screwed without Daisley, he thought, peeking back at the car. Fisk was laughing at him. He couldn't see it but he could feel it.

"Yeah, I know," Lou said, shaking his head. "He wouldn't have used your name to make a reservation."

So, I guess it wouldn't be too bright to call all the hotels in that yellow book, would it? What now?

"I'm not sure. You'll be history soon, though. I'll bet you're stinking up my car right now."

Whose car?

"The car I *rented*, jackass. You know—the one you're rotting in. It won't be for long, though. If I need to, I'll take you out further in the county and dump you."

Won't the coyotes eat me up, Louis?

"Yeah, birds too. I hope it works out for you."

There was no doubt. He was in a very bad mood today. He hated feeling fragile and emotional when it really mattered.

Chapter 53

He was in his bed now. Some time during the night Blash had woken up long enough to find his way into the bedroom and try for some sleep that wouldn't leave his neck feeling sore. His head was sitting comfortably against the pillow but the sleeping part was a joke. He guessed that he got a whole three hours of solid rest. It was better than most nights, though.

The red digits on his clock said 6:34. He decided to get up. Moving slowly to the bathroom, he paused for a long look at himself in the mirror. He smiled widely at his reflection and winked.

"It's a big day, loser. Don't blow it and don't hurt anyone you don't have to. Bad guys, Mike...only shoot the bad guys."

With that said, he washed his face and shaved carefully. He wanted to look good today; not necessarily fantastic, but just good enough so that if he died today he wouldn't die wishing he had worn better clothes. It was the last thing he wanted running through his head in the event of a minor disaster.

A major disaster would mean the death of one of his partners. A minor one would mean his own. He wasn't suicidal by any means but found that he was quite prepared to take one for the team if it came down to it.

"Yes, it is a big day."

After shaving, he took a long, hot shower and cleaned himself impeccably. He even cleaned between his toes, which was something he hadn't done since he was a child in his old bathtub. He clipped the nails on all of them, then did the same with his fingers. He filed down the edges until they were smooth.

Stepping to his closet, he moved several piles of clothes out of the way and dragged a large locked box into the light. It was his old army foot locker. The distinctive smell of the wood hit him as he lifted it open and started pulling his weapons out. They smelled good too.

It was a motley assortment of guns that he had collected from men he had worked with, men he had drank with, and men he had arrested. Often, they were the same person.

Some were gifts, like the .45 with the Hell's Angels emblem etched into the butt. Some had been confiscated and were simply too good to go into the evidence room. He picked three of his favorites and set them aside.

It was seven a.m. when he picked up his phone and placed his first call of the day. He wasn't surprised when there was no answer.

"Running like Jesse Owens, aren't you?" he asked of the man who wasn't present, not caring if he had hopped a plane to Istanbul, Taipei, or Cabo. It didn't matter to him. In Blash's way of thinking it was to be expected.

He wondered if the others had figured it out yet. He was sure they weren't getting through to him either, but wasn't sure if they would know what it meant. He didn't think that Lou would figure it out until the last possible moment. Even then, he probably wouldn't truly believe that Daisley had left them hanging. The big guy had a big heart and was most likely a stranger to outright deception.

It was Quartz he was worried about. She seemed to have a thing for the pathetic detective and that was fine. But he had to wonder how good she would hold up once she discovered that he had bailed out on them. Though it wasn't his problem at all, her reaction to his disappearing act could easily become a problem to all involved. He'd keep an eye on her just in case. With any luck the whole thing would be over before she knew it had begun.

He hated seeing her frantic and scared. Hearing it was just as bad. He'd heard it only once and that was enough for him. Amazingly, she was remarkably calm in the few minutes he had spoken to her after killing Jonathan Kendall. In fact, she was the first call he'd made.

*   *   *   *

"Jesus Christ, Mike. I've got a report of three 911 calls from your area," Quartz had yelled, trying to block out all the background noise around her. *"They all came from local phones and they're telling dispatch that they've got two men down. Where are you calling from?"*

He was sitting in his car with one hand on the phone and the other holding the key that had already been placed in the ignition. All it needed was a single turn.

"Kill the tape, Quartz," he told her, knowing it would sound extremely suspicious if it were ever played back to anyone. He heard a click. All contact to and from the undercover officers were recorded and it was standard for a deal like their current operation. But this particular conversation would need to be forgotten and buried if possible.

"I'm still onsite and your reports are right; we've got two men down. I haven't seen an ambulance yet but I'm pretty sure they're both dead."

"Thank God," she replied with a huge sigh. *"When I heard that there were two of them...I swear I...Jesus, Mike. I was scared for you. Can you talk?"*

"Yeah, but only really quick. I think I really fucked it up this time." His fingers still gripped the key in the ignition. "One of them is Kendall. Tagged him three times. He's dead as shit."

"Good for you. Now give me the bad news."

"I need to know if anyone was on his ass," he said, seeing the dead cop's ID in his head. "I've got a name here. Diaz. Alberto Diaz from Sacramento. If you can run his name through and tell me that he's not a real cop...that would make me happy."

"Wait, Mike. You're talking about the other guy? The other dead guy?"

"Yeah, that's what I'm talking about."

"Hang on," she said, finally grasping the urgency of the situation. *"I swear to God, if this motherfucker has killed another cop...shit...hang on."*

He could hear her fingers banging away on a keyboard.

"What is it?" he asked, knowing exactly what it was.

"Yep. There's a patrolman up in Sacramento with ID that matches your guy. I'll give them a call and see if—"

"Wait, Quartz, just hang on," he said, trying to wake himself up from the nightmare he was sure he was having.

"But if he killed another cop—"

"I did it, Quartz. I shot him." Blash felt that he was only moments from throwing up all over his dashboard. "I shot both of them. Kendall was going for his gun. The other guy already had his out. I guess he could have shot me if he wanted to. Maybe he made me for a cop and—*shit*. What now?"

Quartz was silent for several seconds then spoke in a rapid and calculating voice. *"Are you sure that everybody's who you think they are? Can you at least verify Kendall?"*

"Yeah, I saw the tattoo. It's him."

"What makes you think the other one's this guy Diaz?"

"I saw his badge and ID," he answered dryly. "His *photo* ID. It's him, Quartz. I'm sure of it. I fucking wasted him like he was a bad guy."

"Any witnesses?"

"No one saw anything. I was unloading a truck before I called you. As far as everyone here is concerned, they blew each other away. As a matter of fact I'm the only witness there is. When the local PD gets here, I'm the one they're going to interview. Even the leader of the fucking crew I'm a week from taking down says I've got to talk to them and make sure there's no confusion. He doesn't want to be caught up in this mess and I don't blame him."

"What about weapons?"

"What about them?" he asked, noting that all of his guns were accounted for.

"Have they been snatched yet? With all those unsavory characters around and two guns that two guys won't ever need again...."

"What are you saying?"

"I'm just saying that it's not unlikely that someone might pick up one or both of the guns off of them. There are a bunch of state police headed your way. If there aren't any guns then there won't be any ballistics."

"The slugs in both bodies are going to be from the same gun," he said tiredly, covering his eyes with a hand. "Isn't that going to seem a bit odd?"

"It sure will. I take it you weren't holding your service revolver?"

"No way," he answered quickly. "I was using an old forty-five that Palowski gave me when we hooked up. No serial number or anything."

"Switch them, Mike. If you've got the time, I mean. Do you have enough time?"

"Maybe a minute or two," he answered with a sigh. "I could probably get to them before...*oh, fuck this*, Quartz. This is totally my fault. I'm calling it in. I just plugged a cop. Shit like this happens all the time, right?"

"Sure it does. Usually during a raid and it's almost always some rookie putting a round into the back of the cop in front of him. It doesn't sound like you."

"No, I guess it doesn't," he replied, shifting uncomfortably in his seat. "How much time before the troops arrive?"

"Any time now. Go get their guns, Mike. Do it now before it's too late. If any local cops see you, just identify yourself and say you were policing up the evidence before it walked away."

"And if my crew sees me?"

"Just say you were stealing their guns. That's not unreasonable, is it?"

"No...but...."

"Get the guns, Mike. Hurry up and call me back."

With nothing to do but talk into a dead line, Blash pulled the key from the ignition and stepped from the car. While his crew was running around like crazy moving boxes from the warehouse to several waiting trucks, Blash walked calmly to the back parking lot to find both bodies surrounded by people. They were muttering to each other in muted tones. Whisperings about policemen could be heard.

He pushed his way to the body of Alberto Diaz and peered down at it like the others. The first thing he noticed was that Officer Diaz's gun was missing. It shouldn't have surprised him, but it did. He was less surprised when he viewed Kendall's body and noted another missing handgun.

Looking at the faces near to him, Blash felt surrounded by parasites. In this case, their scavenging would be helpful but it didn't make him feel any better about it. A minute later he was back on the phone.

"Okay, they're gone," he said simply.

"What did you do with them?"

"I said they're gone, Quartz. Don't worry about it."

"Sorry. Do you still have the one you used?"

"It's right here with me," he replied, staring at the ugly forty-five as though it were a live snake.

"Hang on to it. You're going to need to talk to the officer in charge when he gets there. No, wait, I'll take care of it from this end and talk to the lead man myself. You're going to be busy enough keeping your own crew off your back. You'll still have to talk to the first officer you see. Just make sure it's private."

"This is some devious shit, Quartz. It's not right."

"Hey...I talked to you only minutes before this thing happened. If I had been informed that someone was on Kendall's ass, I would have mentioned it to you. This guy Diaz was a patrolman giving out tickets and citations. He wasn't authorized to be there. The first cop that Kendall killed was from Sacramento, right?"

"I think so."

"Maybe Diaz was freelancing or something. Maybe the cop that Kendall killed was a friend of his. Either way, he shouldn't have been where he was at. And if he was on to Kendall and following him south he should have fucking said something to somebody. He should have called it in like you did. That's how cops get killed, Mike. It's not your fault."

"I like the way you're thinking, Quartz, but—"

"But nothing, Mike. Their guns are gone and you've got the weapon that did the shooting. It's totally clean, right?"

"That's what I said."

"Who shot first?"

"I did. Two into the cop and three into Kendall...wait...Kendall got off at least two shots at me before I got him. He missed though."

"So we've got seven shots total and five bullet holes in people. I think we can pull this off."

The rest had been too easy.

*   *   *   *

"Yeah, we pulled it off, all right," Blash said to himself, tucking three guns into three different holsters on various parts of his body. "We sure as hell did."

They certainly did pull it off. They pulled it off with some help that they shouldn't have accepted.

Having access to the only witness, Donald Ratcliffe had painted Michael Blash as an officer who was in the right place at the right time. A man who not only jeopardized months worth of undercover work, but his own life in order to assist an officer in peril. Unfortunately, Officer Blash simply wasn't fast enough to keep Jonathan Kendall from killing Officer Alberto Diaz. But he was just fast enough to disarm Kendall and kill him with his own gun during the struggle.

Lucky me, he thought sarcastically. It wasn't even a real investigation in the true sense of the word. It was merely a formality in the case of an officer involved shooting. There would have been an inquiry regardless.

Yes, Your Honor. I ran as fast as I could towards the two struggling individuals. I wasn't armed at the time due to my undercover status so I only had fists of stone and nerves of steel to deal with the situation. And yes...I am, in fact, a kung-fu master with enough skill and speed to fend off the largest of fully armed men even while being quite unarmed myself. Lucky for me he had a gun, otherwise I would have had to kill him with my bare hands and I thought that might be a little excessive.

It didn't happen that way exactly but the end result was the same and seemed just as ridiculous. He was cleared of any wrongdoing and a month later still managed to arrest the entire crew he had infiltrated. He found it strange that making eye contact with Palowski, Sparks, and the rest of the crew in court was a great deal easier than meeting his own eyes in the mirror.

That was part of the job, though. Blash would learn to live with it even if Officer Diaz didn't get a chance to. He had apologized to the dead man every day since it happened but forgiveness was still evading him. He knew it would never come from the man himself and that's what hurt the most.

I'll get over it. Sorry, Alberto.
His day was only beginning.

Chapter 54

▼

"Uh…Netta?" Quartz uttered painfully as her eyes opened to the daylight that was streaming though her blinds.

Her mouth was dry and her temples were pounding. Trying to guess the time of day would have been useless. It had no meaning at this point. Looking down at herself, she was reminded of another place and time. It was all too familiar. Like deja-vu, Quartz slowly unwrapped her leg from around Nanetta Lalanskaev and gently nudged her arm.

"Netta?" she asked again, receiving no response from the comatose figure. As she took in the scene completely, Quartz was glad that the woman in her bed was still asleep. There would be no thanks to God this time for still being fully clothed since she wasn't. Neither was Nanetta.

Confused, though strangely amused with herself, she crept gently from the bed. Aside from a skimpy pair of panties that she had never seen before, she was completely naked.

"Oh, what a nasty little slut I am," she sang quietly to herself, hiding a tiny smirk, though no one was around to see it.

And a lesbian too, it seems, she added mentally, not really sure if it qualified or not. She had never seen other women as anything but competition before meeting the felon she had fallen into bed with twice now. *Lesbian? Me? No fucking way.*

Quartz could have easily chalked it up to the alcohol in her system on both occasions but decided not to. It wasn't totally clear in her head what had transpired but she knew that even while hammered, she wouldn't have done anything that she didn't consent to. Judging from the way she her legs were feeling at the moment, Quartz assumed that she had consented plenty. The dull pain in her thighs brought another tiny smile to her face, which she again covered with a hand.

Throwing on a robe, she moved slowly into the kitchen and filled up the coffee maker with water. The directions called for three scoops of coffee. She dumped seven into the filter and turned it on, watching every single drop fall into the carafe. She stood motionless for at least eight minutes and waited for it to finish brewing.

The clock on her coffee maker revealed a time of 9:35 a.m. They were off to a pretty late start considering that Nanetta wasn't awake yet. Even after she was, there would be much to do before the two could walk out the front door. Fixing the pain in her head felt like a good place to start.

Quartz pulled a bottle of aspirin from a cabinet and set four of them aside. She took two of them with her coffee and left the others for Nanetta. Ordinarily, she would have taken more than two, but this particular bottle of aspirin had been purchased from a pharmacy in Tijuana and contained enough codeine to cure a week's worth of hangovers. Waiting for it to take effect, she picked up her phone and tried to call Daisley. She let it ring ten times before hanging up.

"I'm about to give up on you, Andrew," she whispered tiredly and returned to her bedroom.

The vision of Nanetta sprawled out across her pillow gave her a fluttery feeling in her stomach. Instead of heading straight for the shower as she'd intended, Quartz leaned against the door frame and watched the woman sleep.

Maybe I've already given up on you, Andrew, she thought silently.

It still didn't make her a lesbian, though—she was certain of it. The idea was silly and, as far as Quartz was concerned, the whole thing was a simple unexpected and unplanned experiment. Her bed just happened to be the laboratory.

I'm just a nasty, curious, little bad girl. A bad, bad girl and I'm not going to think about this right now.

And she really didn't want to think about it. She didn't want to think about all the things she had done last night and she didn't want to dwell on the alien, though very interesting smell of another woman on her sheets. And she definitely wouldn't linger too long on the fact that that same smell was all over her body right now.

Damn...I am such a dirty girl. Ha-ha-ha. Dirty, dirty, dirty.

She went right on staring at her, though. Nanetta had shifted slightly since Quartz had gotten up and looked comfortable enough to sleep through the entire day. The comfort looked inviting but she quickly swore to herself that a shower and some form of clothing would be next on her agenda.

She looks too comfortable, though. She'll need to be woken.

Waking Nanetta did seem like a good idea. And since speaking loudly or yelling her name out would have been rude, Quartz tiptoed to the bed and carefully slid back in beside her. She ran a gentle hand up and down Nanetta's exposed back, finding her skin much more familiar than she had expected. Though the details of the evening were still hazy, Quartz could tell she had spent a great deal of time in close contact with her flesh.

Oh yeah...I remember that, she thought as a cloudy memory flashed into her head. It explained some of the stiffness in her arms and soreness in her jaw. *It still doesn't make me a lesbian.*

Moving her hand to Nanetta's waist, she followed the slope of her hip and discerned through sense of touch that her Netta had lost every stitch of clothing she had been wearing. Her fingers moved lightly over all the skin she had access to before settling on Nanetta's left breast. Yes, that felt familiar too.

You'd better let go, Quartz. Ten more seconds of that and you'll be a dyke for the rest of your life.

Shut up, I'm just checking for a heartbeat to make sure I didn't fuck her to death last night. Besides, if she hasn't woken up yet, she probably won't even notice that I'm groping her. I'll bet Mike would agree. Now, there's someone who could really appreciate this. Oooh, what a story this would make if I had the guts to tell him. He'd have enough whack-off material to last him until....

That was when her phone rang.

Compared to the former serenity of her bedroom, it sounded like a four alarm fire and, to make matters worse, the phone was on the side of the bed of the woman that was currently being fondled. Quartz felt like diving for it before Nanetta could awaken but it was already too late. Frozen by the awkwardness of it, she could only smile sheepishly at Nanetta's sleepy but open eyes as she slowly peeled her hand off of her breast.

"Uh...*good morning?*" she said in a horrified state and eased away from her.

Her eyes rolled from the floor to the walls to the ceiling in an effort to settle on something that wouldn't stare back at her. When she bravely shifted them back to Nanetta she was greeted with the same face that she herself had tried to hide only minutes earlier. The smirk was what Quartz would have called a *dirty little smile* and, regardless of the horror she was experiencing, she thought her latest bunkmate wore it very well.

As uncomfortable as it all was, Nanetta made it doubly so when she slowly reached for the phone, which was on its third ring.

"Don't you dare…" Quartz started to say. She didn't need to finish the sentence, however, as the phone was already in Nanetta's hand.

"*Bonjour?*" she answered in a sleepy voice, sounding French for the first time since Quartz had met her. Her dirty little smile only intensified.

Chapter 55

Bonjour? What's this shit? Blash thought hard about the sensual voice in his ear and it didn't take much creative thought for him to come up with a scenario that was closer to reality than he could have possibly imagined. *Oh, get the fuck out of here, Quartz.*

"Well, hello there," he said as his face broadened into a smile that he couldn't have scraped off with a sharp rock. "May I speak to Detective Schwartze, please? If she's available, I mean. I don't want to interrupt her if she's busy."

He could hear what sounded like a brief struggle for the phone as he waited for Quartz. There was some giggling and a few loud whispers. He liked the sound of it.

"Quartz here."

Her voice was completely out of breath. He liked the sound of that too.

"Isn't it a little early to be having a pillow fight? I know Daisley said not to let her out of your sight but *Jesus*."

"You're such a pig, Mike. We just woke up. I found her at the track and thought it would be best if we both stayed local until this thing is done. I let her crash on the sofa."

The sentences were sputtered out in a fashion that Blash had years of experience with. He could smell a lie; especially one like this. "Oh, listen to your sad little self. You don't have to go telling fibs to me. I always knew you were cool."

"And you were right. But we're not talking about this right now, Mike. Seriously. Today's going to be weird enough as it is."

"I know it is," he admitted, satisfied that he'd get the real story out of her sooner or later. "I don't suppose you've talked to Daisley any time in the last sixteen hours or so?"

"*No luck here. I tried him a few times last night and once this morning. What are you thinking?*"

"I'm thinking we might be alone in this," he answered cautiously. "I haven't talked to Lou yet—I'm almost afraid to. I was going to try him after I talked to you. I guess I don't need to ask how your night went."

"*No, you don't. I know you'll ask anyway, but all you need to know right now is that I got her. How did you do?*"

"I scored. Walter was a real push over. He's ready to do anything I tell him to. So we're both solid?"

"*As usual. You want to track down the big man and give me a call back? I won't be comfortable until I know his status.*"

"Me neither," he agreed. "I'll call him right now and get back to you."

"*Sounds good.*" The phone went silent for a few seconds. "*Mike?*"

"Yeah?"

"*Why is Andrew leaving us all alone in this?*"

It was a good question that needed answering. Of the many opinions he had on the subject, nothing was good enough to qualify as a serious answer, which he thought she deserved.

"I don't know, cutie. Maybe he's just running a little late."

"*Sure, I guess. Go ahead and call Lou. When you call back, I want some good news. Got it?*"

"Yeah, I got it."

Chapter 56

Lou had Fisk under the arms and was pulling him from the car when his phone began to ring. He had cruised through the most rural areas he could find since leaving his hotel room over two hours earlier and had finally found a decent location for Terrence Fisk to relax. It was as secluded as he could find.

"Lou here," he said, releasing Fisk and answering it before it could ring a second time.

"*Hey, big guy. It's Mike. Where are you at?*"

Looking around, Lou couldn't answer him immediately. First of all, if he explained that he was dumping Fisk's body, he would have been in trouble for not doing it sooner. Secondly, he had been down so many roads this morning that he honestly didn't know where in the hell he was anymore. If he had to guess, he figured himself to be somewhere in Moreno Valley.

"I'm just out driving around. I didn't sleep too well last night and I thought I could use some fresh air. I was getting ready to call you."

"*Any word from Daisley?*"

"Nope, and I've been trying him since last night. You don't think he got in an accident or anything, do you?"

"*Umm…I don't know, Lou. I just got off the phone with Quartz. She hasn't heard from him and neither have I.*"

"What are we supposed to do then?"

"*Well, we're not calling it off—that's for sure. I tracked down my guy and Quartz has someone on the sidelines too. We're ready to move. How'd everything go with our friend from the hotel? You know who I mean, right?*"

Staring down at Fisk, who was still halfway out of the car, Lou knew who he meant. "Oh, that? I took care of that a long time ago. I wouldn't worry about that anymore. I haven't talked to my guys yet today but I'll be giving them a call when we figure out all the details."

"Whoa...what guys?"

"My guys." Lou dropped his voice to a near whisper for no apparent reason. "You had your guy. Quartz had hers. I got mine. But like I said, I haven't talked to them today yet and I thought—"

"Get the fuck out of here, Lou. You tracked your boys down?"

It was obvious that the idea hadn't even occurred to him. Even Fisk could hear it in his voice.

Not a whole lot of faith in you, huh, Louis? Now, why do you suppose that is?

"Yeah, I got both of them. What do you think I've been doing all damn night? I'd have called you but..." Lou paused, not sure of what he should keep quiet about. "...I didn't get in until late. I tried to call Daisley a bunch of times. Sorry I didn't call you."

"Yeah, I give a shit. Don't sweat it, Lou. You got both of them? For real?"

For real? Fisk echoed. *Like you're going to fucking lie to him.*

"Yeah, I got both of them," Lou repeated. "And they sounded really into the idea. Excited even. I told you they were a couple of mean sons of bitches."

"That you did. Here's what we're going to do. I'm going to call Quartz back and set up a place for us to meet. Have you eaten yet?"

"Not a bite. I'm dying over here."

"Good. We'll make it a restaurant and have some breakfast. I'm thinking in maybe forty-five minutes or so. I've got to swing by Daisley's place and see what's up. How's that sound?"

"If it involves food, I'm in," Lou answered, watching a car approach from the distance. It was the first he'd seen on this stretch of road all morning.

"Excellent. I'll call you back in a few."

They hung up at the same time.

"You hear that, Terry? Blash and Quartz both came up with their candidates. Just like me. All we have to do now is figure out who's going to walk point and who's going to cover their ass. Ten bucks says my boys do the dirty work."

Ten grand says they get their dumb asses killed before they get the chance.

"No way," Lou stated confidently. "They'll have a ton of protection on all sides. One guy? No problem."

What makes you think he won't have protection of his own? Didn't anyone think of that?

"Sure we did. That's Daisley's end. He's got the place cased from top to bottom."

And when was the last time you spoke with the gentleman? It sounded to me like those other two morons weren't able to reach him either...and they really count in this thing. You don't mean shit to them. Did you hear how surprised Blash was when you told him that you snagged my replacements? He was shocked for God's sake. If Daisley's not in touch with them....

"We'll scope the place out real good before anything happens. Don't worry about it. Daisley will show up."

I'm not worried about a thing. You'll be hanging back far from the action, totally out of harm's way. It'll be the other guys getting blown out of their socks by a few bodyguards that you didn't know about. Of course, none of this will matter to me because I'll be laying out here in the fucking sagebrush getting gnawed on by coyotes. Or maybe not.

"And why's that?"

Oh, I don't know. Why don't you ask the cop that's pulling up behind us right now? Maybe he'll explain it to you.

"What are you talking about now?" Lou asked, then stopped as he turned his eyes back to the road. Fisk was indeed correct. There was a black and white cruiser pulling off the road, moving in behind them. "This is perfect...just perfect. I should have seen this coming."

You did, genius. From about a mile away. But that was at least a full minute ago, so I can see how it might have slipped your mind.

"Shut up. I couldn't tell it was a cruiser."

Whatever, Louis. Can you tell now? He'll be out of that car in a second and I'm still hanging here looking mighty unhealthy. Either push me back into my seat or pull me all the way out. I look pitiful.

Fisk was correct again. He looked as though he had fallen out of the car. His back was laying flat on the ground, leaving his legs occupying the passenger seat. Fortunately, the cruiser was manned by a single officer and was parked at an angle, which obscured Fisk from view. Lou worked fast. He was used to it by now.

As inconspicuously as he could, Lou propped him up and belted him in again. After placing the sunglasses back on his face and brushing the dirt off of his suit, Lou was satisfied that Fisk wouldn't be giving him away. It was none too soon. The officer was already stepping from the vehicle.

Chapter 57

"That was one of my partners on the phone," she said as Nanetta walked out of the bathroom wearing the oversized T-shirt that Quartz usually wore to bed. "We're going to meet him and another guy in about forty minutes to go over what we need to do. And thanks for answering my phone. I really needed that."

"You are welcome," she replied, sounding sincere about it. "That man...your partner. He is police too?"

"Yeah, we all are," Quartz answered, watching Nanetta pull some clothes from her overnight bag.

"Why is it that the police cannot take care of their own troubles? I am not judging you, Qiana, but killing this man is unusual, no?"

"It's not the way we usually do things," she replied. "Frankly, the guy means nothing to me. I'd just as soon arrest the idiot and let the courts go to work on him, but his lawyer has other plans. He's the one behind this mess."

Walking into the kitchen, Quartz fixed Nanetta a cup of coffee and poured herself another. Nanetta downed both of her aspirins with a single gulp of the scalding hot liquid. She stared at Quartz with a calculating look.

"Why is this lawyer wanting to have his client killed?"

As a paid employee, Quartz figured Nanetta didn't need to know any of the reasons for her participation. On the other hand, it gave them something to talk about instead of gawking uncomfortably at each other. Since all bets were off anyway, she decided to share a little.

"Because he's guilty as sin—it's that simple. I guess he doesn't want to lose a case. He never has before and Christian Roche is *definitely* going to lose."

"If you do not care about it, why would my Qiana be involved in such a thing? And the other policemen too?"

"It's complicated, Netta. None of us want this. We even told him we wouldn't be involved."

Nanetta took it in and seemed to think about it for a moment. "But he knows things about you, no? Things that you would be in trouble for?"

Quartz nodded her head. "If we don't do it, we'd be the ones going to jail."

"I *see*," Nanetta replied, nodding right along with Quartz. All the warmth she had slowly vanished from her eyes and with each nod, her face grew less and less amused.

"*Wait*, Netta—that's not what I was doing with you. I swear." She blurted it out quickly, then paused. "Well, just a little at first. I didn't even know for sure about LaGuardia or Kadouris. I was only guessing really. I…I just needed some help, Netta. I can't do this by myself."

"But your partners—your policemen. Why do they not help you?"

"They've already got their own assignments and they're as busy as I am. What I mean is—"

"What you mean is that there will be others like me," she said in a deadpan voice as she lit her first cigarette of the day. "Other *assignments*. How many will there be?"

"I don't know, Netta. We'll find out in less than an hour. But it doesn't even matter. The money—it's yours no matter what. Even if you do nothing but stand by my side and watch it happen."

She was trying to make the deal sound extra sweet but ended up sounding horribly desperate instead. Nanetta was still staring at her inquisitively and after a few drags off of her cigarette, her face softened slightly.

"Do not worry, Qiana, you have not offended me," she said, seemingly pleased with herself for the moment of drama. "I was your first choice, though. This is correct?"

Whether it was true or not, she knew the answer that was expected of her. "Absolutely. While the others were trying to think of the craziest, mad-dog killers they could come up with, I was thinking smart. I got the best one, too."

Nanetta's dirty little smile reappeared. "And why is it that are you so smart, Qiana?"

"Well," she replied, moving in close to her. "I knew that the perfect person would need to be intelligent.…"

She moved even closer.

"…and strong.…"

Quartz maneuvered herself in front of her, leaning back against the counter top.

"…and utterly fearless…."

Her hands were on that wickedly familiar skin again.

"…and devious…."

Quartz's eyes closed partly as a tiny gasp came from Nanetta.

"…and…"

She whispered a few choice words softly into her ear and dragged a loud moan from her. The sentence was never finished.

Damn, I'm good at this, Quartz thought, feeling shuttering skin beneath her hands, which were moving ceaselessly. *If this is all I have to do to get her to do things for me, I'm in business.*

It shouldn't have surprised her that her phone started ringing again.

Chapter 58

▼

"*Yeah, I'm here,*" Blash heard coming from his cell phone. She didn't sound entirely there though.

"Jesus, Quartz—let go of her for a second, will you? I just talked to Lou."

It seemed to bring her around. After a loud sigh—a pair of them actually—it sounded like he had her attention.

"*Should I be worried, Mike?*"

"Not about that guy. We probably could've all gone home and let him take care of everything. I'm not shitting you, Quartz. He covered that hotel problem and lined up those guys he was talking about."

Quartz remained silent and waited for the punch line. It didn't come.

"*Wait, you're serious. We're talking about Lou?*"

"What a trip, huh? He's out driving around, just killing time. I told him we'd hook up for breakfast in a little bit. How about that waffle place on East Grand?"

"*Perfect. Any word on Andrew?*"

"Nada," he replied. "And Lou hasn't heard anything either. I'm going to swing by his place and see what I can find out. You want me to kick him in the nuts for you if I see him?"

"*No thanks, I'll handle it. I'll...uh...I'll see you in just a little...while.*"

"Yeah, whatever, cutie."

Blash couldn't see Nanetta's busy hands, which had made Quartz's phone call nearly impossible, but he could imagine it quite clearly. He remained on the line silently waiting for her end to click off first. It took several seconds and a lot of banging around before the line went dead.

* * * *

He was still thinking about her when he pulled up in front of Daisley's apartment—both of the girls, actually. He couldn't wait to get a look at the French killer that was keeping Quartz so entertained.

Maybe she's on the level and she just let her crash on the sofa like she said. Maybe not, though, and that's what's giving me a boner right now. Why is that? I've always wanted to jump her bones myself and this certainly won't help things. Still...just picturing it...oh, she's right. I'm a total pig. It can't be helped.

"At least she won't be wasting any time on your ass, Daisley," he said quietly, stepping from the car.

He walked around the back of the building first and looked for Daisley's car. It wasn't anywhere to be found. He went up to the door and knocked loudly. Like the many phone calls he had made, there was no answer. He wasn't surprised in the least. Hitting the street again, he flipped open his cell phone and dialed Lou's number.

Chapter 59

▼

He pulled out his badge and flipped his jacket open slightly before the officer had covered the distance to the rear of the Porsche. Aside from the truth about Terrence Fisk, Lou wanted everything to be immediately clear to the approaching policeman.

"How are you doing today?" Lou asked with a smile that he thought was a little too bright. He never smiled so widely and felt foolish for doing so now. He stepped towards the officer with an outstretched hand and hoped for the best. Even with no makeup on, Lou thought she was very pretty.

The idea that the cop was a woman hadn't crossed his mind even after she had stepped from the car. She shook his hand firmly and met his eyes without looking up at him. He guessed her height at around six-foot four and her age around thirty-five. She looked like a linebacker—an extremely feminine one.

"I'm fine, sir. How about yourself..." She noticed his badge and gun in the same instant. "...Officer Poklatar?"

"Doing well. Is this a great morning, or what?"

Yeah, what lovely weather we're having. You're blowing it, Louis.

"I expect it is," she replied, not bothering to look at the bright sun or pretty clouds. Her eyes were glued to the Porsche. "My shift ends in half an hour, so I don't get a whole lot of working daylight hours. I was on my way back to the station when I saw you. It's pretty isolated out here—not a good place to break down. Is everything okay?"

Is it okay? I hope she's not asking me.

"Oh, it's great. My partner and I just got in from Fresno and we thought we'd check out the county." He couldn't help but notice her interest in the vehicle and answered the question before it could be asked. "It's just a rental. We can't check into our hotel room for another couple of hours anyway, and with a car like that…it'd be a waste not to drive it. This seemed like a decent place to let it cool down."

He was speaking too much and giving her way too much information. It was the kind of thing he would have noticed if he was the officer on the scene. For some reason, the guilty always felt the need to be chatty.

"I understand completely," she said with unhidden enthusiasm as she circled the car. "Is it a custom job? I've always wanted to drive one but my knees hit the dashboard.

"It's no picnic for me either," he admitted, growing more nervous with each glance she took of the interior. "My legs get in the way, too. It's a pain in the ass to drive if you're big. It corners like mad, though."

Jesus, Louis. Are trying to talk her into a test drive? It's already on her mind, or didn't you notice?

"Four speed?" she asked, dipping to a knee and looking underneath the rear end.

"Five, actually."

Tell her why you know and she probably won't be nearly as impressed.

No, she probably wouldn't, but he could always ask since his chattiness was giving no signs of letting up. "It's a funny story, really. When we switched off driving I didn't realize it was a five speed for almost an hour. Had it in fourth most of the time. Is that as stupid as it sounds—to you, I mean?"

Her face broke into an embarrassed smile. It was genuine and made him feel somewhat vindicated.

"That's funny. I did the same thing with my dad's first car. It was an old MG but it was his baby. It was a tiny little thing, too. I took it out one night when he wasn't home. I only had a learner's permit and I'd never been on the freeway before. Boy, did I kill that engine."

"Oh, you poor girl," Lou cried out, laughing loudly with her. Abruptly, he winced and lowered his volume, nodding towards his passenger. "Sorry, I should keep it down. We started out really early and he's pretty wiped out. So, what department are you with?"

Smooth, Louis. Now ask her if she comes here often…or better yet, ask for her sign. I'll bet she's a Virgo. And why don't you look at her fucking car if you want to know what department she's with. It's painted right on there, big guy.

"I've been with the Moreno Valley PD for a few years," she answered, removing her hat and shaking out her hair. "What's Fresno like?"

He shrugged his shoulders and took another glance at his surroundings. "It's a lot like this—on the outskirts, anyway. That's where I live. I'm not much for living deep in the city."

"Me neither," she replied, admiring the front end of the Porsche. "I like having some open space. I need it."

Fisk seemed to stare out at her through his dark shades. Occasionally, she stared back, which gave Lou the creeps. She moved her eyes to the tires and rims, poring over them as well. After another lap around the small automobile she shook her head and put her hat back on.

"Well, Officer Pok—"

"Call me Louis," he said immediately, throwing his hand out again.

"Okay, Louis. I'll tell you, if I wasn't on the job right now I'd want to take this baby for a spin. She's beautiful."

"She sure is. Maybe another time."

She started walking back to her cruiser. Lou followed.

I dare you to pinch her butt, came Fisk again, but it was obvious that he was joking. It would have been a suicidal move since she looked like she could easily wrestle him to the ground. Leaning into the driver's side window, she pulled out a small clipboard and started scribbling. If she was writing him a ticket, it was a very small one. It only took her a second.

"My name's Katherine Pearson," she said in a very businesslike manner, thrusting the slip of paper at him. "This is my number. There's a place about five miles from here where the locals drag race. If you'll be in town over the weekend and have the time, we could take her for a drive if you want and find out what she can do. How'd that be?"

She looked serious, wearing only half a smile as she eyed him. He blinked a few times before Fisk nudged him back into awareness.

You'd better take that from her. She's not going to hold her hand out there forever.

"I think that would be great," he replied, completely dumbfounded as he took her number. Almost immediately, the phone in his pocket began to ring. She was climbing back into her cruiser as he answered it.

"Lou here. Can you hang on for a sec?"

Receiving an affirmative answer, he covered the phone and returned his attention to Officer Pearson. She was already putting the cruiser into drive.

"When's a good time?" he asked, feeling sixteen years old. "To call, I mean."

"Any time after six in the evening, Louis," she replied straight-faced as she released the brake. "I'll look forward to hearing from you."

An instant later she was gone. He put the phone back to his ear.

"You're not going to believe this, Mike."
I can hardly believe it myself, Fisk uttered silently.

Chapter 60

"No bad news, Lou. Please,"

"Nothing bad, I swear, Mike," Lou assured him. "This great big, beautiful amazon cop just gave me her number. She says we can take my car for a drive and 'see what she can do'. That's not slang for something dirty, is it?"

"I don't know, Lou, but you're scaring the shit out of me. How did you happen to bump into a cop? I was just talking with you five minutes ago for God's sake."

"Don't worry. I didn't get pulled over or anything. I mean…I was already on the side of the road when she pulled up. She only wanted to check out the car."

"What car are you talking about?"

Yeah, genius. What car? You haven't shared that story with anyone yet.

"I got a rental," he said quickly, wanting to skip the explanation for now. "It's pretty cool. You can check it out when I see you. Where do you want me?"

"The waffle place. You remember where it's at?"

"Sure."

"Then we'll see you there in thirty."

After Blash signed off and hung up, Lou put his own phone away and returned to his passenger. He was preparing to pull him from the car again when Fisk interrupted him.

Hold on there, Louis. What do you think you're doing?

"Sorry, Terry, but all good things must come to an end. It's been fun, though. Thanks for keeping me company."

I should really let you do this, Louis. It doesn't bode well for me but it'll be even worse for you. Go ahead. Yank me out again and drag me behind a big rock. I'm sure it will be just fine.

"Okay, what am I missing?" Lou asked, tired of the games. He was on a schedule now.

I think you're missing about a gazillion brain cells. Do I have to explain to you what's going to happen when someone finds me? Because they will, you know. And on an isolated road like this, I can think of at least one police officer that will remember you being here. She might even remember me. You saw her looking at me, Louis. She could probably pick me out of a lineup.

"So I'll pick another spot," Lou said, buckling him up again, getting tired of the routine.

Where? It took you two hours to find this place. I don't suggest leaving me anywhere local. Hell, you could dump me in fucking Arkansas and someone would still find me. I don't mean to brag, Louis, but I'm a pretty popular guy. It's going to be big news when they find my bones. All it would take is for one old photo to flash across a TV screen. Next thing you know you've got some giant lady cop shooting her mouth off about what she saw.

She's got your name, Louis. First and last. She might even remember your badge number. Hell, she'll know even more than that if your weekend works out, Romeo.

"Why does everything have to be so damn difficult with you?"

I'm just covering your ass, Louis. Someone's got to.

"I have to be back in Corona in half an hour," Lou grumbled. He jumped back into the driver's seat and started the car. "What in the hell am I supposed to do with you now?"

Relax, Louis. You still have a motel room, don't you? I could use the rest anyway.

"Good thinking," Lou quipped, thinking the idea was splendid. He stomped on the gas pedal. "But this is the last time, Terry. You'll be gone before anything happens tonight. Gone for good, I swear. I'll think of something."

Just remember to hang the 'Do Not Disturb' sign on the door.

"I will," Lou replied quietly, heading back to the motel.

They made it with time to spare. It only took a couple of minutes to set Fisk up in the bed and put the sign on the door. It was time for some breakfast.

Chapter 61

"Here they are now," Blash said, craning his head around the large booth. "Only fifteen minutes late. I'm impressed."

Quartz and Nanetta had just walked through the door. Looking tired but alert, they made their way to the table. While Nanetta's eyes bounced back and forth between Lou and Blash, Quartz found it hard to make direct eye-contact with either of them. She took a seat next to Lou.

"Am I the only one who brought company?" she asked, finally looking up. "Mike, Lou—this is Netta…Nanetta…Nanette Lalonde…whatever."

She smiled blandly at them.

"Nice to meet you," they both replied at the same time. Lou nodded once to her. Blash's gaze lingered for a while longer. She was even more than he'd expected. She didn't look French, though.

"Sorry the rest of the lineup isn't here," Blash told them, though he didn't really think their presence was required at the moment. "Lou assures me that his boys are ready and willing. And Walter…I've got my own plans for him and I don't need him to hear what we're going to talk about."

"Damn, my guys too," Lou stated, whistling through his teeth and feeling very lucky that Alex Bautista and Joe Sheridan weren't present. "Don't worry, though. They're up to it. They just don't know all the details about what they're doing. You following me?"

"Yeah, I'm following," Blash answered, wishing he'd been told a minute or two earlier. It didn't take the women long to figure it out.

"She knows what's happening," Quartz jumped in. "I didn't have to lie to her. What did you tell your guys?"

Blash remained silent and looked curiously at Lou.

"I...uh...I kind of told them that Roche was a child molesting rapist baby-killer. It seemed like a decent reason. If Daisley would have given me the same crap story, I probably would have done it myself. What about you, Mike?"

"Well," he said, pausing as he took a deep breath. "We've had a few changes in the game plan. I ran by Daisley's place before I came here. You guys probably know that he flaked on us. You know that, right?"

He stared at them, knowing that they couldn't deny the truth for too much longer. Quartz and Lou nodded somberly.

"That leaves us with a bit of a problem," he continued. "If we don't hear from him, I'm going to have to assume that he won't be the first Corona detective on the scene. It's not a really big deal, but it means we just lost a little of our protection. We have to be extra careful not to leave anything behind since Daisley probably won't be the one scooping up the evidence."

"What about security?" Lou asked, thinking about what Fisk had said earlier. "Daisley was the one who knew what was happening at Roche's house. He had all that shit down. He knew the floor plan and how many people came by and how often. What if he's not alone? I've got to know this kind of stuff if I'm going to send two civilians in there."

"Me too," Quartz agreed. "I was picturing Netta walking up to his door with a gas can or a pair of jumper cables or something like that. He'd open the door for her. No problem. How could he resist that pretty face?"

Nanetta reddened slightly as she rolled her eyes in an attempt to reject the compliment. But it didn't work. The two men were already nodding in agreement. Blash even managed to look hopeful.

"That's a pretty interesting idea, Quartz."

"If he's alone he wouldn't stand a chance," she continued. "But if anyone else is there? Big trouble. Plus it's Friday. Who stays home alone on a Friday night?"

The two men raised their hands simultaneously. It drew a few chuckles before Blash spoke up again. When he did, he leaned in close to the center of the table and spoke quietly.

"If we do that, one of two things will happen," he said, not unhappy with how things were working out so far. "Okay, she goes to the door. Let's say he's all alone and he answers the door?"

"Pop-pop-pop," Nanetta stated softly, speaking for the first time since she arrived. "Qiana says we have a silencer, no?"

"That we do," Blash replied. "But here's what I'm worried about. Let's say she rings the doorbell and someone *else* answers? Now that shouldn't happen because I'll be watching the place all day. But if it does—"

"Then I will lead him to my car," Nanetta answered while stifling a yawn. "If he has protection, his protection will follow me away from the house. I will park down the street. Then it will be out of my hands."

Blash nodded thoughtfully in response. "And at that point, we just send in the next team. Lou? You tell me what happens next."

"If I see her leading someone away from the house, that's the queue to send in my guys," he answered, following the new scheme as if it was what they'd planned all along. "Bang, bang…my boys split. Is it really that easy?"

Quartz turned her eyes on Blash then Nanetta. "It just might be. But under that scenario we've got to be watching Netta like a hawk. If she's distracting some foolish bodyguard, he's not going to be happy when he hears gunfire. Won't there be one more of us?"

"Yeah, that'd be Walter," Blash answered hesitating, knowing they'd get around to him eventually. "He sticks by me. He doesn't carry and he doesn't get close to the action. He'll be an extra set of eyes and ears if they're needed. Quartz—you, me and Walter will watch your girl. We'll park at the north end—"

"Sorry, Mike," Quartz interrupted. "You and Walter can watch *me* and Netta. If she's going to the door first then I'm staying with her. Think about it. I'm not just a fucking getaway driver. It'll be safer anyway."

There was a silence at the table for a brief instant. Nanetta raised a single eyebrow and smirked at her. She hadn't expected any less and Blash wasn't going to argue with either of them.

"That's fine, Quartz. We'll park at the north end about twenty yards past the house. We'll make sure it's close to where you two park. I'm thinking Lou takes the south end. We keep in touch and stay out of sight as much as possible. Lou, make sure that your guys do the same. I'll want to talk to them beforehand and make sure we're all on the same page."

"No problem there," Lou replied. "I'll make that my first stop."

"Make it your second," Blash said. "We still have a case full of weapons to divide. Thanks to Fisk, we all get to use untraceable guns. At least that's one thing we won't have to worry about. Any questions?"

He felt funny even asking the question. Being the one who asked if there were any questions usually meant that you had the answers. It meant you were the leader. It felt strange.

"I've got one," Quartz said, lowering her eyes. "I hate to be the pessimist here, but this plan of ours—the one we just put together in, like, three minutes—it sounds good. I'm not kidding, it really does sound like a simple plan to execute. But what if it goes wrong? That's my question, Mike. What's our contingency plan?"

"Yeah, what about that?" Lou echoed.

"I don't think anything like that will happen," he replied, knowing the possibility was very real. "But if it does, everyone bolts. Get back to whatever car you came in and get the fuck out of there. Civilians too. Make sure you're gloved up so you can just drop your guns and walk away. I'll take care of the rest."

"What *rest*?" Quartz asked. "You'll clean up after us, or what? He's got to go. You know that, Mike. It *has* to get done."

"And it will," he replied calmly. "If it gets ugly, you guys beat it. I appreciate all the help but I'll grease him myself if it comes down to it."

The look he was getting from the others was the exact reason he didn't want to say anything in the first place. It wasn't a change of heart by any means and he was more than happy to let Quartz and Lou's candidates take a whack at it first. He just didn't want it hanging out there like an open wound. Wrong or right, for all their sakes, the job would be completed.

"Quit looking so surprised," he said as he picked up his menu and prepared to order some breakfast.

Chapter 62

▼

While the group of four ate waffles and drank coffee, Andrew Daisley was busy peeling himself from the floor of his bedroom. His eyes were blood red and his head felt like a saucepan simmering over a hot stove. He had many possible solutions for the pain but chose not to administer them.

Since a Bloody Mary or even some ibuprofen might have dulled his agony, they couldn't be considered. Pain was warranted, desired, and totally acceptable on all levels.

He had been stuck to his carpet since the knock at his door. At the first loud rap, his initial instinct was to hide, but since he didn't have the strength or will to sneak into the closet, he hit the floor instead. It was a pretty good impersonation of the way Terrence Fisk took a dive less than twenty-four hours earlier. He couldn't be sure how long he'd been lying there. It felt like a year but it was probably less.

Guessing that his problems hadn't solved themselves yet, Daisley waited for the answer to come. There was an easy solution but he was still busy pushing the thought from his head. As plausible as it had sounded while taking his fifth shot during the previous evening, the idea was inspired by drunkenness and he didn't quite trust it yet.

It would be a ballsy move for certain. More balls than he had at the moment...but there was an easy solution to that too. It was a shame he was all out of booze.

Just the same, the idea kept bouncing around his brain for some reason. Most likely, because there were no other contenders. He could have simply driven straight to Christian Roche's house right then and put a whole lot of minds to rest but it just wasn't going to happen like that.

He had to die, though. There was no doubt about that. He knew the truth as well as Christian Roche did. That's why he was targeted in the first place. As was Ratcliffe's standard procedure, he asked for the truth and got it. In giving it, Roche was at the mercy of the lawyer and should have realized right off that sharks were not exactly known for their pity.

Daisley remembered it clearly. From the first sentence, he knew how it was going to go.

✶   ✶   ✶   ✶

"Christian Roche—my, my, what a bad boy he's been," Donald Ratcliffe said as he looked over the papers in front of him. It was the first time that the lawyer had mentioned the name and Daisley assumed he knew why it was being mentioned specifically to him.

"What about him?"

"I'm covering him on this one," the lawyer replied with a strangely optimistic look.

"But you're changing teams in a couple of months. Why would you take on such a dog? I thought you wanted to go out a winner."

Ratcliffe knew it as much as Daisley did and he was right. Roche was as bad a case as one could hope for…or against, depending on what side you were playing for. According to the evidence against him, Roche's trial would be quick and clean. The jury would probably have a cup of coffee and vote unanimously guilty within fifteen minutes of leaving the courtroom. He didn't have a prayer.

"Oh, I'll go out a winner, Andrew. And I don't think it would be bold of me to go so far as to guarantee a victory." His smug face smiled across the table at the detective. "Well, maybe not a 'victory' per se, but I think a conviction will be out of the question."

"It says here they've got three of his street dealers and one of his distribution guys who delivers by the pound," Daisley noted, going over an unedited disclosure statement that had been illegally acquired from the prosecutor's office. "That's four guys turning on him. What are you going to do—call them all liars and hope the jury buys it?"

"It's down to two witnesses," Ratcliffe replied. "His biggest distributor and one of his street peddlers were found in Yorba Linda last night. The poor souls were all burned up in a car. It's a terrible thing, isn't it? A terrible, terrible thing."

It's a real shame for the prosecution and their case too. That's half of their witnesses in one shot."

He was smiling as he spoke. It was a creepy smile that only lawyers seemed to be capable of. Daisley thought hard before asking his follow-up question. "I don't suppose we know anything about how that happened?"

"The word was delivered from the man himself," Ratcliffe said, tapping on the paperwork in front of him. "At this rate, by the time we appear before the judge, the prosecutor's witness list should be pretty slim. It won't come to that, though."

Daisley readjusted his tone, struggling to bring back some of the authoritative resonance he once had. "Tell me we're not cleaning house for this fucker."

"Listen, detective," he replied, using the word *detective* with heavy sarcasm. "When I feel I need to *tell* you something, I will. Until then, don't *tell* me to *tell* you a thing. Are we understood?"

That was the most humiliating part of sharing a room with the shark. It was never satisfied with just being on a higher level than everyone else. It had to own the room and everyone in it. Daisley's reply was a quick, "Yes, sir."

"Then the answer is no. We're not cleaning his house. *He* is. As long as he knows who's on the witness list he can whittle it down to nothing for all I care."

"Witnesses aren't all they have on this guy," Daisley reminded him.

"We'll worry about that when he's done taking care of his own mess. After all the witnesses are gone, no one should be too surprised when he doesn't make his court date."

"Are you saying he's going to make a run for it? Why is he bothering to exterminate his crew if he's—"

Daisley stopped speaking as the shark's eyes rolled to the ceiling. "Oh, Andrew." He was almost laughing. "You don't have to play that game with me. This room is safe to talk in. You can speak as freely as you'd like."

A bad taste began to spread through his mouth. "It sounds like you're the one who wants to do the speaking...sir."

"How very attentive of you, detective. I've taken the liberty of compiling a list for you to look over."

"What's in it?"

"Every fuck-up I've had to keep out of jail for the last several years," he answered quickly, brushing a speck of lint off of his jacket. "Look it over. Tell me if you see anything interesting. Anything—or anyone—that might be used to rectify this situation we're currently in."

The situation that we're in? He knew immediately what the shark was implying as he pored over a list of almost a hundred names. There were names of people he'd been at the academy with and several he had arrested at one time or another. There were also many others that he hadn't heard of at all.

About three quarters down the page he discovered his own name.

He blinked slowly and reread some of the other names on the sheet, surprised and disappointed by the kinds of people he was obviously associated with. It felt a bit like wandering through a cemetery and finding his own name on a grave marker.

"Just let me know if anything jumps out at you, detective."

"I'll need some time, Don."

"Andrew, don't call me *Don*. And all I need from you right now is to go over that list and find me someone suitable. If you want to take care of this nastiness yourself you can be my guest. I suspect you won't, though. Something tells me you don't have the constitution for a job like this. You don't, do you?"

Daisley ignored the rhetorical question and continued to read. "I may see a name or two that I could consider but they're not going to work for free."

"I don't expect them too. There will be payment, Andrew—more than you make in a year—so it shouldn't be too hard to find someone with the kind of balls this will require. It's going to happen in your territory and there's no doubt that you *will* be involved eventually, so choose wisely. If you need any assistance you've got a sheet full of names in your hand to pick from. I suggest you use it."

"What if no one's interested?"

"Then I make a call to your old department in Chicago. Now, I don't think they'd be too interested in our dealings on the West Coast, but you can bet they'd be plenty interested in *you*. I know it's been a while, but I think they'll remember you Detective Daisley. Isn't it funny how these things always manage to work themselves out?"

Instead of insults, it was the threat of blackmail that he ignored this time.

"When everything's set up, what kind of resistance can I expect from this guy?"

"The worst kind is my guess. I wouldn't be lying if I said he was heavily armed and a bit paranoid. But that's your problem, detective. Isn't that why you get paid the big bucks?"

That was when he started laughing. It wasn't a light chuckle, but a huge gut laugh. It was directed straight into Daisley's face.

* * * *

Okay, maybe it's not so crazy an idea, he thought, suddenly finding the strength to climb to his knees.

A man as confident as Ratcliffe was most likely that confident for a reason, meaning he probably had a lot of information tucked away for leverage. Daisley could almost picture the safe deposit box or secret filing cabinet that the lawyer had stashed somewhere, jam packed with all kinds of incriminating goodies on everyone he'd ever done business with. That had to be the ace up his sleeve. The man obviously felt invincible and it made sense that there must have been a valid reason for it.

Killing Roche would only give Ratcliffe another huge chunk of leverage on all of them—he could see that now. It had definitely been the wrong route to go. And he knew that it still was.

Hell, I've nothing better to do today. It might not defuse the situation like I was hoping for, but it should at least keep me busy for a while.

Daisley rose to a shaky but standing position. It took him over a minute to walk to his kitchen and start a pot of coffee. He would consume six cups before making his way to the shower.

One didn't usually need to get clean before a fishing trip but this was a special one. He didn't need to dress warmly and he wouldn't need a rod, a reel, or even bait. All he needed was a gun. And a shark.

Chapter 63

Blash paid for breakfast and led the others to his car. After a quick check around the parking lot for prying eyes, he popped open his trunk. Another quick glance around was required before he opened Fisk's heavy-duty weapon's cache. The corners of Lou's mouth turned downward at the sight of what was inside. Nanetta's reaction was the exact opposite.

"I would like a quiet one please." She reached in and pulled out a small thirty-two caliber pistol. She tried two different silencers before she found one that fit.

"I thought you didn't talk to Andrew," Quartz jumped in, surprised at seeing the case in Blash's trunk.

"I didn't. I went by his office to see if he was there. He wasn't, but this was sitting on his desk. And I mean, *right there* in the middle of his desk where anyone could have opened the sucker up. I'm starting to feel better about his not being around, if you know what I mean."

They all seemed to know. Lou dove in next and pulled out two custom forty-fives.

"I guess these'll do."

"Quartz?" Blash said, nodding towards the case.

"I'm covered," she replied, pulling her jacket open enough to reveal the large forty-four that she'd left with on the previous day. "What about you?"

"I've got my own toys. Does everyone have their phones?"

He was treated to two nods and one blank stare. Since Nanetta was traveling with Quartz, she wouldn't need one of her own anyway.

"Okay, here's what happens now. Lou? I need you to make contact with your guys and call me as soon as you do. I'm going to hook up with Walter and make sure everything's cool on his end. Quartz? I'll be calling you when I know what's going on. And stay local, will you?"

"Where in the hell would I run off to?"

As he glanced back and forth between the two women, she got his point. He'd already been surprised by her once today. At this point, there was no telling what was going on in her head.

"Just stay nearby. I know I shouldn't have to say this, but if anyone happens to hear from Daisley, share it with me, okay?"

Once more, two heads nodded to him. There wasn't much more to say. Quartz and Nanetta were the first to leave.

Both men watched as they walked away and climbed into Quartz's Mustang. While Blash's eyes were pasted to the backsides of the two shapely women, Lou's concentration was on Quartz. He took a long concerned look and hoped that he would see her again. After they had disappeared in a cloud of rubbery smoke, Lou got a light elbow in his ribs from Blash.

"What do you make of that?"

"Make of what?"

"Our lady friends, Lou. Quartz and that Nanette girl."

"What about them?"

Blash only paused for a second. "Never mind, man."

So much for some heavy locker room talk with Lou, he thought sadly. Now probably wasn't the best time for it anyway. If all went according to plan, they'd have plenty of time later to talk and act like pigs. Lou was already retreating to his car.

"I guess I'll be calling you in a few," he said, watching Blash's jaw drop as he unlocked the door to the Porsche and jumped behind the wheel. He gunned the engine and backed out of his parking space before heading out to the street. When he took a final look in his rear view mirror, he could see Blash staring back at him. His mouth was still hanging open.

Fucking, Lou.

Twenty-five minutes later the Porsche pulled in front of a house in Costa Mesa. It was still early in the day but clouds were slowly stealing the sunlight. It smelled like rain.

Chapter 64

Lou explained it as it was told to him. He even drew a crude map of the street on paper for them and mapped out everyone's positions. The two young men looked equally nervous and excited as they huddled together in Joe's garage.

"Okay, the north end," he said, pointing to the top of his sheet of scribbled drawings. "Just ten or twenty yards past the house and around the first corner—that'll be two of our guys. They'll be pretty far from the action but they'll be watching everything really close."

"Why so far down the street?" Alex asked, trying to picture it in his head rather than count on Lou's horrible drawing.

"For one, they don't want to be seen—not even by you. The other thing is that they'll be watching the car that the girls will be driving. Now, up here even further away is where they'll park. They won't be *too* far away but they'll be on the other side of the street. They go first."

"So, we only move if they blow it?" Joe asked, tapping his fingers on the workbench.

"Kind of," Lou said tentatively. "If they walk up to the door and both come walking back, that means it's done. Forget about it and drive away. It's only when they walk back to the car with a person trailing behind them that you guys move. They'll be a good fifty yards away from the house by then. You'll have all the time in the world."

"Where do you want us?" Alex asked, looking at the bottom of the map.

"Right down here," he answered, pointing roughly where Alex had been looking. "The same position as the girls but on the south end instead. Get it?"

"And you?" Alex asked after a quick nod.

"Closer to the house…opposite side of the street. I'll be around the corner like the other guys, just out of sight. How's that sound?"

"Good," they answered simultaneously as Alex reassembled the shotgun, which they had just finished cleaning. He pumped and dry-fired it several times.

The noise it made as the mechanism slid back and forth was as scary a sound as anyone would hope to hear. With each cycle, Joe flinched visibly. Lou kept his flinches to himself.

"If we're cool, I've got a call to make," he said, pulling out his phone. "My boss may want to speak to you before we get started."

* * * *

Since all they could talk about over the cell phone was estimated locations, it was a fairly brief call. Actually, it was merely a confirmation. Blash wasn't entirely confident that Lou would relay the plan in the required detail but was pleasantly surprised. The man he had spoken with seemed to have it down solid. He knew what his role was, he knew where to be, and he understood his function completely. If he was correct, it was Alex Bautista he'd been speaking with.

Initially, he was leery of the softness in his voice. At no time did it rise in pitch or waver in the slightest. He knew that the man had to be feeling somewhat nervous, though it wasn't visible at all. It was the kind of coolness that Blash himself wished he possessed from time to time. Unfortunately, he was permanently stuck in "Blash mode" and made almost all of his thoughts public by the look on his face or the tone of his voice.

A second later, Lou was back in his ear.

"What do you think, Mike?"

"They'll do fine. At this point, they're strictly backup anyway. But listen, Lou…" Blash paused as he cleared his throat. This wasn't the kind of thing he was used to. "I just want you to know that I'm…well, Quartz too…we're real happy with all the work you've put into this thing. I'm just…well shit, Lou…I'm glad you're in on this with us and I feel better knowing you'll be there."

"Sure, whatever."

Though Lou sounded unsure of what to say about the kind statement, it was equally awkward for Blash, who had never given a compliment in his life—unless *'Nice tits'* counted. He didn't think it did, though, and felt badly that his initial opinion about the big man had been so inappropriate and unwarranted. "I'll be at Walter's in a minute, then I'll be heading over to the house to keep an eye on things. If I can help it, there won't be any surprises for us."

"Do we have a time yet?"

"I'm thinking some time after eight. It'll be dark by then and I'll have spent the day in front of the house doing recon. If there's anything weird going on, I'll know about it. And don't worry about an exact time just yet. We've all got phones and we'll know what everybody's doing at all times. We won't move until it's perfect."

"Sounds great. I'm probably going to hang around here for a little while, but I'll have my phone if you need me. And Mike...?"

"Yeah?"

"Thanks for taking up the slack. With Daisley gone, I was afraid that—"

"Shut up, Lou. Don't worry about it. I'll be back in touch once I'm in position. Don't let them out of your sight."

"I won't. We'll be talking to you soon."

They didn't talk again for several hours.

Chapter 65

Forced to choke down another few cups of coffee at Walter's house, Blash spent a good deal of time calming the little man down. It was much more time than he had intended but was acceptable since it took his own jittery nerves down a notch as well. It was way too early in the day to be as wound up as they both were.

"If you're telling me that everything's cool then why do we need all this stuff?" Walter asked, peering down into the large black bag that he had spent the night filling up.

"It's purely backup, Walt. We're talking a totally 'just in case' scenario here. Just keep your eyes open and do what I tell you. You're the last in line out of the seven of us and you really shouldn't have to do much of anything."

He nodded exactly as he had done each time it had been explained to him—and it had been explained to him three times now. Wound up tighter than he could ever remember being, each of Walter's sentences was followed by a heavy exhalation of breath. He wasn't shaking, though, and that made Blash feel slightly better since a certain amount of cautious nervousness was definitely called for anyway. He would have been more worried if Walter was totally at ease with the whole thing.

"Is there anything else we might need?" Walter asked, checking his inventory for the fifth time. "I mean *anything*, Mike. I can dash out and be back in a heartbeat if you happen to think of something. Just give me a shout."

"Man, if you hear me shouting then it's too fucking late already." The look on Walter's face quickly told him that his humor wasn't appreciated. "I'm just kidding, Walt. We've had this thing in the works for a long time now. Nothing will go wrong."

Walter nodded slowly again, taking him at his word. He was still nodding when Blash got up to leave.

"I'll be back to pick you up when it's time."

✱   ✱   ✱   ✱

From Walter's, it was only a ten minute drive to the place that Blash would spend his afternoon. Since their residences were in such close proximity, he would wait for both Lou and Quartz to get set up before returning to pick him up. Until Walter was in the car right next to him, Blash wouldn't feel ready to proceed. As far as he was concerned, Walter's presence was absolutely critical.

It was about eleven a.m. when he killed the engine in his predetermined location. Though he was down the street and parked on the corner of another residential neighborhood, the view was as good as could be expected. He estimated that Roche's house was no more than twenty yards away.

Since he had checked out Lou's position as well, he was confident that they had the area covered from both angles. Looking farther north up the street, he could see several ideal locations for Quartz and her redheaded counterpart to park. If Roche did have company and they were capable of being lured away by one or both of the women, the location of their car would put a safe amount of distance between them and the house.

That was the theory anyway. The important part would be keeping an eye on the girls if they happened to draw someone out of the house. He hoped sincerely that it wouldn't even get that far.

Settling in, Blash got as comfortable as he could and prepared for a long day. He'd been on many stakeouts and took part in many raids during his career but he suspected that this one would be something new. He turned his eyes on the house and waited.

Chapter 66

The sky had been darkening slowly throughout the day and it was now beginning to rain, which was a sharp contrast to the beautiful morning they'd had. Quartz and Nanetta looked to the clouds and let the rain fall on their faces for a good while before retreating back into the shelter of the apartment.

For the last couple of hours they had done very little aside from chain-smoking and staring awkwardly at one another. Though they had been relatively quiet, there was no discomfort in the silence. The thoughts they were sharing didn't need to be said out loud to be understood. They were simply preparing themselves for what lay ahead. It was closing in on one p.m. and their occasional glances at the clock served as a reminder that a countdown was now in progress.

They had already cleaned and double-checked their weapons of choice, which were resting between them on the table next to a rapidly filling ashtray. They hadn't uttered a word in the last fifteen minutes. It was Nanetta that finally spoke up.

"I want you to know I think it is sweet that you would walk me to the door, Qiana. It was unexpected, no? You were not planning for such a thing when you came looking for me."

She looked at Quartz with questioning eyes. Her gaze was returned for less than a second as Quartz chose to stare down at the table instead. She sighed heavily and pushed her chair back and scooted it closer to Nanetta.

"Stop looking at me like that. I feel like a piece of shit and I don't know what the hell I'm doing. I wasn't planning on anything…including walking you to the door. It just worked out that way."

"Then why is it that you are—?"

"Stop fucking looking at me," she said again, moving her eyes to any other location than the woman in front of her. Tears were developing and were in danger of streaking down her face.

Moving her own chair forward, Nanetta locked Quartz's knees between her own. She placed both hands on her thighs, massaging the tense muscles as she tilted her head in an effort to look into her face. Quartz twisted away from her each time.

"My God, Netta. What does this make me? What kind of people are we?"

"The kind that live longer than the people who get in our way," she answered, indicating that she had considered the question already—probably many times in her life. "Does it not please you to be so lucky? Would you rather it be you who were killed and not this man Roche?"

"Fuck that guy, Netta. A thousand guys like him could eat a bullet and it wouldn't mean anything to me. Not a goddamn thing. But you..."

Before she could finish, the first tear spilled over, leaving salty trail of wetness down her face. Nanetta quickly wiped it away as though it had no place there.

"Oh, my Qiana. You do not have to worry about me. It is silly for you to bother with such things."

"How can you say that? If anything happens to you it's my fault."

"Keep your pretty eyes on me, Qiana, and nothing *will* happen."

Nanetta smiled broadly and enveloped her in a tight hug. She ignored the flood of warm tears that were streaming freely down her neck and squeezed Quartz fiercely. It wasn't a ridiculously long embrace, but they took their time with it.

✴ ✴ ✴ ✴

"So, who's gonna puke first?" Joe asked, only half-jokingly. "I'll bet money that it's me."

Of the three of them, Joe was the only one looking a little green. He still wore a smile, though, and was hanging in quite well.

"That time sure is creeping up on us, isn't it?" Lou noted as they all instinctively looked at the clock. It read 2:34.

After going over the sole weapon they were expecting to use, Lou showed them the forty-fives he had picked out. It didn't matter which guns would be used since neither would leave any usable ballistics evidence. As long as they retrieved any spent shotgun shells, there wouldn't be a way to trace it back to them even if they did decide to hang on to it. Which they wouldn't, of course.

In the end, they decided to keep the shotgun and grab one of the forty-fives as well. Joe scooped up the custom pistol while Alex felt better hanging on to the bulkier and far uglier shotgun. They cycled each weapon several times, pointing them at the walls of the garage as though there were bull's-eyes painted on them.

Once again, Lou was drawn to the large, shiny objects that were stacked all around them and there were a few more now since they had finally finished unloading the back of the van. The gold colored, polished boxes and cylinders were simply too much to ignore.

"You like them?" Alex asked, noting his interest.

"They look expensive," he answered honestly, feeling like a child attracted to something he didn't understand. They seemed very well put together and he couldn't overlook the craftsmanship that went into them.

"They *are* expensive—that's no lie," Joe agreed, stuffing the gun in his waistband as he approached one of the objects. He ran his hand down the side of the gracefully etched copper alloy with a look of admiration.

"We've been swiping them from everywhere for about a year now," Alex explained. "I thought we had another few months of stealing ahead of us...then you showed up. That's twice, you know. We were working on the same thing when you surprised us in Fresno."

"What—all the wood and nails and shit?"

"Yeah. Aside from a bunch of six-inch wheels for the stands, we haven't paid for a damn thing. By the time we open for business I figure we will have spent about a hundred and twenty bucks for equipment. We've spent more than that on gas."

"How much are they worth?"

"About two or three grand a pop for a setup like this," Joe answered, looking at his own golden reflection in one of them. "They're all top notch and we've got sixteen of them now. We'll probably buy three more with the money you're giving us. We wanted to start with twenty of them, but nineteen's not bad. We'll make more than enough cash the first month we're in business. It's almost all profit anyway, right bro?"

"It's got a better markup than anything you can imagine," Alex confirmed. "If I wasn't sure about it, we wouldn't have even gotten started. I've got a degree in mechanical engineering, you know. And I'll make a lot more money doing this than I could building missiles for Raytheon."

Lou nodded with what he hoped looked like complete understanding and they nodded back to him. Joe took a quick look at Alex then turned back to Lou.

"You still don't know what they are, do you?"

Not unexpectedly, all he could do was shrug his shoulders. "Looks like a bunch of fancy water heaters to me. I haven't got a clue."

"They're espresso machines, Lou. You know…like coffee." Joe knocked lightly on one of the containers and listening to it clang almost musically. "You brew up the black stuff, blast some steam through a cup of milk, pour in some chocolate syrup or whatever, then mix it up and call it a latté. I bought one the other day and paid two bucks for it after waiting in line for ten minutes. Including the paper cup and little tiny straw, it costs about twenty-two cents to make."

Alex stepped in to give the details. He looked sufficiently proud of himself.

"We've got prime locations and storage for twelve portable rigs right now and we haven't even started on the marketing end yet. Seattle, Portland, San Francisco, Sacramento, San Jose…"

"…Fresno," Joe added. "Glad we went there, huh?"

"Yeah, that was a great fucking idea," Alex agreed with a sarcastic snort. "It was nicer than Bakersfield, anyway. The dollar figures we came up with—they're right off the damn chart. We've already got contracts with the owners of the property we plan to sell from and each stand is mobile so there's no rent to pay. We already have twenty-six cases of really expensive imported coffee beans and a ton of cups in storage. We got those for free too, so the only thing we have to worry about is minimum-wage employees and the dairy end of it, I guess. I'd hijack a whole damn milk truck if there was a way to keep it fresh. We should start seeing a profit about fifteen seconds after we open."

All Lou could do was stare at them with one of his many confused looks. The information that Alex had just given him sank in quickly.

He understood what they had been doing and, in a criminal's way of thinking, it made perfect sense. Alex had only been talking for a minute and had convinced him easily that their business would succeed. It wasn't an entirely legal endeavor but seemed incredibly smart regardless. Aside from the initial thefts to get the ball rolling, it could turn into quite the legitimate enterprise. He did find something troubling, however, and it didn't have a thing to do with coffee.

Only seconds after hearing their plans, they looked different suddenly. Both of them. Their faces…their voices…their auras…whatever. It was all different now and he couldn't see them in the same light as he did before. It was like taking off a pair of masks.

"You guys didn't kill Gabriel Marcos, did you?"

The three of them looked awkwardly at each other for several seconds. Lou seemed suddenly flustered as his eyes moved from Alex to Joe to the van then to the floor.

"I told you he still thought we did it," Joe said with a laugh.

"Yeah, you did. What's that about, Lou? We *told* you we didn't do it."

It was a sarcastic comment but didn't seem too funny at the moment. His two psychopath killers were nothing more than a couple of thieving entrepreneurs. Yet here they were, only hours from a job that Lou had sold them on by lying to them.

"Then…*why?*" he asked with a painful look.

Alex pumped the shotgun one more time. "Why not?"

*   *   *   *

It was almost four o'clock and Daisley knew he was still incapable of driving an automobile. The coffee had run through him and did a fairly good job of waking his body up, but he was left terribly dehydrated and his head still hurt. It was water he was drinking now as well as taking the ibuprofen that he had passed on earlier. Thoughts of torturing himself endlessly had gotten old after he threw up for the seventh time and he was dry heaving to the point where his head as well as his stomach muscles were screaming for mercy.

Alcohol poisoning was a very real possibility. He had drunk with such abandon that it could have been misinterpreted as a suicide attempt. That could have easily been the case considering his pitiful frame of mind, but he had a genuine purpose now.

It wasn't exactly a reason to live. It was just a really good reason not to be dead.

He considered it a project; not necessarily a mission or an assignment, but merely a project. It was also an experiment at the same time since he had no idea what the fallout might be from such a move since it wasn't very scientific and there would be no control groups. Regardless, there would certainly be results if nothing else.

If the lawyer did, in fact, have a safe or filing cabinet full of hardcopy evidence against everyone he had defended successfully, there would be a lot of unhappy people when he was gone. It wouldn't mean much legally since the double jeopardy rule still applied, but any improprieties would most likely be made public.

On the other hand, Daisley had seen Ratcliffe's list of clients and there was no information other than what had been recorded by the courts. If he needed dirt on any individual, he had to ask the lawyer himself for the details. If it was written down anywhere, Daisley suspected that Ratcliffe would have handed the paperwork over instead of wasting time answering questions.

It was the man's confidence that left Daisley feeling unsure. He had always assumed that the evidence was within arm's reach of the lawyer. If not for that fact, Daisley would have told him to get lost the moment he landed on the west coast.

Still, there was doubt. Unfortunately for the lawyer, doubts, suspicions, and uncertainties simply weren't going to play a part in Daisley's project.

For an instant, he thought about the three people that he had left hanging in limbo. Mike, Lou, and Quartz were bound to be angry with him. He hoped for their sakes that Ratcliffe wasn't holding any hidden paperwork with their names on it. He also couldn't wait to make the call to tell the others that they could forget about Christian Roche. Calling them now was an option but he wasn't about to go shooting his mouth off only to lose his nerve at the last possible moment.

No, he wouldn't make the call until the shark stopped swimming. If his head stopped pounding and his legs were solid enough to carry him, Daisley expected to take off around five-thirty or six. Depending on the traffic, he could expect to arrive in Los Angeles around eight p.m.

Chapter 67

Aside from several trips to pee in the bushes next to his car, Blash hadn't moved since he had parked. He knew every inch of the house that there was to see from his particular angle and had been staring at it for close to eight hours without the tiniest glimmer of what was going on inside. Until now, nothing had happened outside the residence either. A car had finally appeared from the south end of the street.

As he watched the large vehicle pull into the driveway, the hair on the back of his neck began to rise. It was a huge black Chevy Suburban with tinted windows. Its lights remained on and nothing happened for over a minute. It simply idled in the driveway.

As the automobile sat motionless, Blash pulled the nine-millimeter handgun from his shoulder holster. It was his favorite weapon, and like the others, it would never be traced to him unless he happened to die with the thing still in his hand.

Darkness was coming quickly, which made it even harder to see through his raindrop spattered windshield and even if the other car's windows weren't tinted, he wouldn't have been able to tell how many occupants it had. If he could see into the car and could positively identify Roche as the sole occupant, Blash supposed he would have shot him dead on the spot.

They all had to deal with the fact that once the bullets started flying, their only choice would be to flee as soon as possible. This wasn't a drug kingpin's palatial estate; it was an upscale residential neighborhood, meaning it wouldn't take long for someone to call 911 to report gunshots. It was imperative that they shoot straight and act very quickly.

He felt fortunate that Quartz had no problem being vocal about how she thought the operation should go down. It was a hell of a lot better than his own ingenious plan, which consisted of kicking the door in and chasing the man around in his own house. But with two beautiful women knocking at the door, there would be no kicking or chasing; just aiming and squeezing. He had to admit that it sounded pretty good.

The Chevy Suburban was still idling in the driveway when he reached for the phone. It was seven in the evening if his dashboard clock was correct.

* * * *

"Quartz here."

"Hey, cutie. How are you holding up?"

"Fine, Mike," she said with a shaky exhale. "We're just fine. What's the news?"

"It's about that time. Care to join me?"

"We'll be there in ten minutes," she replied, snapping her phone shut.

Less than a minute later, another call was made.

* * * *

"This is Lou."

Alex and Joe were on their feet before the first ring of the phone had faded. Joe dug the keys to the van out of his pocket while Alex hit the button that raised the garage door. They moved speedily as if they were beyond any form of distraction. To Lou, it looked like they had already rehearsed exiting the garage.

"You guys ready to move over there?"

"Well, we're moving now," Lou answered, feeling his stomach go into a knot. "I'm heading out now and the guys shouldn't be too far behind me. How are you doing, Mike?"

"Fucking peachy. Quartz should be here in a few minutes. When she gets here, I'll be picking up Walter, so don't go spastic if you don't see my car. You know where to go, right?"

"I sure do. We'll see you in…what…forty minutes or so?"

"More or less. It doesn't matter since nothing goes down until we're all here anyway. It's time to get started, though. Something's finally happening over and…shit, Lou…I've got to go. Call me when you're in your spot."

"No problem. Good luck, Mike."

He got no response. Blash had already hung up.

* * * *

"Hello?"
"*Jessica?*"
"Hello, Officer Blash. Are you coming by now?"
"*Yeah. He's still there, right?*"
"He's been out front for an hour," she answered, sounding only slightly nervous. If she knew what they were really walking into, she probably wouldn't have been so relaxed.
"*Tell him I'm on my way.*"
"I will. Just make sure you take care of him. If anything happens to my husband…I will definitely fuck you up."
"*Of course you will,*" he replied with a nervous laugh that was in danger of becoming an insane cackle. "*Just tell him that I'll be there in a flash.*"
"I'll do that," she replied with a sigh. "And this will be the end of it, right? Everything's even? No more worrying?"
"*That's right, Jessica. You won't have to worry anymore. This'll be the end for good.*"
He hated the way it came out.

* * * *

Blash folded up the cell phone as three figures were stepping out of the Suburban in Roche's driveway. One at a time, he sized them up.

The driver was a large fellow with long hair pulled back in a ponytail. His size and hard face looked intimidating, though they were mildly softened by the expensive suit he was wearing.

Another man stepped from the passenger's side and looked similar to the first. His hair was shorter and slicked back but that was where the difference ended. Aside from hair styles, they were very much the same; big, decked out in sharp suits, and serious looking. They were obviously professionals.

Somebody should have mentioned these guys to us.

Blash then watched the left rear door open. The man he recognized as Christian Roche was climbing out of the car.

Closing up his phone, he watched the three men head to the front door. One was out in front and one trailed behind. Their target was in the middle. He wore a suit as well.

If Blash had to guess he would have said that they looked like they were returning from a meeting with a lawyer or had even been to court. Since he knew that Roche wasn't scheduled to appear until Monday, a meeting with Donald Ratcliffe or some other bloodsucker seemed likely. If he had, in fact, been meeting with Ratcliffe, a little information from Daisley or the lawyer himself could have saved half a days worth of staking out an empty house.

It wasn't empty anymore, though.

Chapter 68

"Okay, guys, it's go time," Lou said, hoping to motivate them. It was unnecessary, however, since they were already climbing into the van and buckling their seatbelts. "Drive slow and take your time with this. We can't afford to get pulled over tonight. You know where to go. Got your phone?"

"Got it, Lou," Alex replied, holding it up for him. "We'll get into position and wait for your call. How's that sound?"

"Well, that's the plan, so it sounds about right. I've got a quick stop to make first. It shouldn't take long but it wouldn't surprise me if you guys get there a little bit before me. If you do, go ahead and call me and I'll let you know where the hell I'm at."

Yeah, guys. Just a little side trip to pick up a friend of mine. Don't worry, though. He'll be gone before the fun starts.

"All right, let's do this thing," Alex said, stepping on the gas pedal. "We'll be talking to you, Lou. Drive safe."

Lou followed the van out of the garage and watched the large door close behind him. By the time he was pulling open the Porsche's door, they were already out of sight.

"Keep your heads down, boys," he said quietly as he started the car and began what he hoped would be the last leg of Fisk's journey.

If things went his way, Lou hoped to have the hitman hidden permanently within thirty or forty minutes. It would be close, but he couldn't afford to let the others know about his failure in dealing with Terrence Fisk. He'd already taken a good deal of credit for it as it was and felt bad about lying to them. Even if he was a little late he knew they would wait for him.

* * * *

It had been about eight minutes since the three men had strolled into the house. Blash picked up his ringing phone quickly and put it to his ear. Quartz answered it before he even had the chance to say hello.

"Hey, good looking. Anything new?"

He quickly scanned the north and south ends of the street. "We finally have some company. And that's more than I could have said for the better part of my day. There was no action until I called you. There's three of them. Where are you, anyway?"

"Right here, Mike. What are you...blind?"

For a brief instant, two bright headlights lit the dark street. It looked like someone had snapped a photograph.

"*Jesus*, I didn't see you or hear you pull up."

They sat about twenty yards from him on Roche's side of the street and were right where he was expecting them to be. It didn't speak well for Blash, but he surmised that if he didn't notice them then nobody else would either.

"Yeah, we're a couple of sneaky vixens over here. We coasted in with the lights off. Should we take your spot, or what?"

"What for?"

"We can't see anything, Mike. I mean, we can see his roof, part of the driveway, and a little bit of the side, but we've got no angle on the front. Is that his Suburban in the driveway?"

"Yeah, that's the one," he replied as it occurred to him that he was the only one with a really clear shot of the house. "Don't worry about it. It'll only draw attention to us if we're pulling in and out a bunch of times. But you'll be able to tell if anyone comes or goes, right?"

"Sure, if they're going in or out of the driveway."

"That's good enough. Lou should be along pretty quick and he's mirroring me on the south end, so he'll have the same line of sight but from the other side. You shouldn't be able to miss him when he pulls up. If anybody *does* move, give me a call, okay? I'm off to Walter's."

"We'll keep an eye on things."

Blash's car came to life across and down the street from her.

* * * *

Even through the cool rain that was now falling outside and the windows that were rapidly fogging up, she could see Blash's car retreating from the area. Quartz folded up the phone, doing her best to appear confident and at ease as he pulled away. She knew she was failing miserably when the small device popped out of her sweaty hands like a wet bar of soap.

Nanetta rolled down her window and lit two cigarettes, handing one to Quartz. Her hand shook as she took it from her.

* * * *

"Is it my imagination, or did Lou look a little stressed out back there?"

"I don't think so," Alex answered, checking the traffic around him. "The guy's been a rock from what I can tell. But we don't know the guy. Maybe that's what he looks like when he's freaking out."

"How do *I* look?" Joe asked.

"Like you're freaking out—but I know you, so don't worry about it. He didn't notice anything weird about either of us, I don't think. I'll bet you I'm ten times as nervous as you are."

"Why's that?" Joe asked sarcastically. "It wouldn't be because you're about to shoot a guy, would it?"

"That might be it. How much longer do you think before we get there?"

Joe thought it was an odd and telling question coming from his best friend. Alex was never at a loss when it came to distances and time frames. "We've got a ways to go, bro. Lot's of time. And since you're doing the nasty part, I should really be driving, don't you think?"

Alex turned his head long enough to get a quick look into Joe's eyes. They were wider than usual and gave away his excitement as well as his anxiety, but his face had already lost the green tinge that it had while Officer Poklatar was present. It was a good thing that it did.

"I am driving, huh?" Alex noted, turning his face away. "I guess that means that you're the one who has to do shooting. Sorry, man, I should have told you the rules sooner." The words were said in the same sarcastic manner in which they had been speaking but there was a keen difference in the look on his face as he'd said it. The statement was capped with an uncharacteristically deep sigh as he stepped harder on the gas pedal.

"I think you're right," Joe said with a broad and horribly innocent smile. "*You* did the driving so I guess *I* should do the killing. That sounds about fair to me."

Though he had his own reasons for what they were about to do—reasons that had nothing to do with money—Alex was afraid he might not find the nerve. It was good to have friends.

Chapter 69

He was sitting on the curb in front of the house, his knees pulled up tightly to his chest. With the large black bag next to him, Walter looked like a kid waiting to be picked up for a sleep-over. He appeared comfortable but Blash knew from the man's own wife that he had probably been sitting in the same position for over an hour. He stood up when he saw the car approaching.

"Hey, buddy," Blash said, moving his phone and pistol off of the seat for him as he pulled up to the curb. "How are you feeling?"

He knew it was a dumb question when he asked it.

"I'm scared, Mike. How are *you* feeling?"

"Like I just got laid, man. Get in."

Walter complied and tossed his bag in the back seat. Buckling up, he stared straight forward as he waited for the car to move. Blash turned to him and motioned towards the front of his house.

"Say goodbye to your wife, Walt."

Jessica's pregnant silhouette was clearly visible in the living room window. She raised one opened hand and placed it against the glass. She didn't bother to wave. Walter mirrored her actions against Blash's window, swallowing loudly as they slowly pulled away from the house.

"Move it. Hurry up."

Though Blash was driving, he craned his head and watched Jessica's shadow disappear. Walter didn't. They were silent for a couple of minutes, waiting for one another to speak. Halfway to their destination they pulled up to a red light.

"She's pissed, huh?" Blash asked, knowing that she would be. He just didn't know who she was mad at the most.

"Nah, she's just worried." Walter reached into the back and pulled his black bag to the front seat with him. "And I'm not the most hopeful guy in the world either. She saw all this stuff and wanted to know why. So do I."

"You like westerns, Walt?"

Walter looked at him blankly, not knowing if he'd heard the question right.

"You know...cowboy movies...gunfighters...things like that?"

"Sure, I guess."

"Well, those gunfighters back in the eighteen-hundreds—the professional ones. They'd go from town to town, trying to show everyone what badasses they were. You know what I'm talking about?"

Walter nodded and shrugged his shoulders at the same time.

"I don't know if it was Bill Hickok or Buffalo Bill, but it was one of those famous guys, anyway. They used to bring somebody along with them...just in case, you know? The guy would travel around with him wherever he went. If the gunfighter happened to get shot—"

"Jesus, Mike, you're thinking of a *surgeon*," he spit out, finally understanding what his role was to be. "Those guys used to have a doctor on the payroll. I'm a nurse. I've never even worked in an emergency room. You think you're going to get shot? Is that what you're saying?"

If he had any composure to lose in the first place, Walter would have certainly lost it then. He was jerked forward as Blash applied the brakes.

"Hold on, Walter." He slowed and pulled the car to the side of the road. He put the car in park but left the engine running. "This is purely a precautionary measure. I've got five other people who are going to be in harm's way tonight. If anyone gets tagged, I know I wouldn't be able to do anything about it."

"And what the hell can I do?"

"I've seen what's in that bag too, Walt. You've got tourniquets, gauze, pressure bandages—all kinds of nifty shit in there. What did you think I wanted it for?"

It was easy to tell that Walter was searching for a way to play dumb. It was just his bad luck that Blash knew how smart he really was and what he was capable of.

"I thought you just needed someone to grab the stuff for you since I have access to medical equipment. I didn't know you expected me to be the one using it. You should have an ambulance on standby if you're so concerned."

"Sorry, man, no ambulances and no hospitals if we can help it. That's just the way it has to be on this one. But I'll tell you what; I've got an idea that might make you feel a little better."

Walter looked up as the bag was snatched from his hands. Reaching into his jacket, Blash pulled out his favorite gun and dropped it into Walter's lap. He stared down at it for a few seconds before picking it up.

"*I'll* be the doctor," Blash said as he unbuckled his seatbelt. "I don't know what I'm doing but I'm sure I'll figure it out as soon as one of my team gets shot in the face. I'll back *you* up, okay? Just take that gun...."

"Listen, Mike—"

"No, Walter, *you* listen. Just take that gun and put it in your shorts or something. I'll describe this fucking animal to you and when you see him...shoot him, okay? You'll want to be careful because he'll be shooting back at you."

Blash drummed his fingers on the steering wheel and stared out his window while he waited for Walter to speak. Giving him the opportunity to be the shooter instead of the medic seemed to put things in perspective. The silence only lasted until Blash felt the butt of his gun pressed up against his chest. Walter was holding it by the barrel.

"Take this thing," he said, holding onto his black bag like it was a life preserver. "Just make sure you're really careful. If you're counting on me to keep you alive, I suggest you don't get injured. I've never done anything like this before."

"Well, neither have I, dipshit."

Chapter 70

▼

It was a bad idea to be driving. His head was still throbbing, his legs were still wobbly, and his vision was a blurry mess. If Daisley hadn't already passed the halfway point to LA, he would have considered turning back. Even though it was raining, he rolled his window all the way down and let the wet wind slap him in the face.

It would also be convenient in the event that he needed to throw up again. At this point, he couldn't remember what it was like *not* to be throwing up. He felt better than he did in the morning, though, and that was good enough.

Twice, he had reached for his phone. Once, he'd actually got it flipped open. But he still didn't know who to call.

Ratcliffe was a possibility. Since he was going to his house to kill him, Daisley thought it would work out best if the man was actually home. Of course, a telephone call to him right before his murder wouldn't look too good.

His partners? He doubted that they would even accept a call from him. The same went for his ex-wife, both of his parents, and all of his friends. If he owned a dog, he wouldn't have called to it for fear that even *it* wouldn't respond.

He settled for talking to nobody and continued to drive north to LA.

Chapter 71

Driving up slowly from the south side of the block, Blash and Walter passed what would be Lou's end of the street. There were no cars anywhere near the spot.

"There'll be two of our guys in a van right there," Blash told him, pointing a finger at the vacant curb to his left. He drove another forty feet then jerked his thumb to the right. "And that's where the other guy will be. He'll have a clear view of the house and he'll make sure we know what's going on." They drove another twenty feet and Blash pointed to his left again.

"That's the house we're talking about. It's what we're here for."

Walter remained silent as they continued past the large but low profile piece of property that was the reason for all the excitement. They went another twenty feet then hung a right into a cul-de-sac. After flipping a quick U-turn, they pulled into the space that Blash had occupied all afternoon.

"Now, look to your right," he said, nodding towards the north end of the street on the opposite side. "We've got two more in that Mustang over there. Say hi."

He waved towards the car but couldn't see if anyone was waving back to him. A moment later, the phone nearly made a dead man out of him. When it rang, Walter tried to move through the heavy steel car door without bothering to open it.

"*Sorry*, man," Blash said with mildly sympathetic laugh. "I should really turn this thing down." He put his ear to the phone. "Mike here."

"*Hey, tough guy.*" It was Quartz and she was obviously trying to stifle two sets of laughter. "*Are you sure he shouldn't be on any prescription medication?*"

"Oh, you saw that, did you?"

Walter rubbed the side of his head as he watched Blash talk to the people who had just scared the hell out of him. It was pretty clear they were talking about him.

"*How could I miss it? I take it that's your boy?*"

"Nope, this is my good luck charm," he said, rubbing Walter's hair into complete disarray.

"*Well, good luck then. Nothing's happened in the last twenty-five minutes. Anything I should know?*"

"I'd say we're on schedule. The other guys are driving pretty far so I don't expect them for a little while still; not for at least another twenty minutes. We may or may not see them pull up, but we'll get a call when they're here. Let's keep it quiet until then."

"*We'll do our best.*"

Even while rubbing his soon to be bruised head, Walter continued to squint at the Mustang as his eyes slowly adjusted to the darkness. He would have given up long ago but he saw something that was making him curious. It was hair. Lots of it.

"You know, Mike—those people in the car over there…?"

"What about them?"

Walter took another quick glance at the car then turned to Blash. He covered his mouth with his right hand and lowered his voice to a whisper. "I think they're ladies."

Blash merely chuckled and shook his head.

"*Ladies?* Those two? I seriously doubt it."

Chapter 72

▼

As far as Lou was concerned, he couldn't get the key in the door fast enough. The *Do Not Disturb* sign was still dangling from the doorknob and everything looked cool from the outside. There was no reason it shouldn't.

"Terry?" he called out quietly and closed the door behind him.

He was completely out of breath for no apparent reason. The only place he had rushed to on two legs was the motel room door, which was about ten feet from the car. He guessed that he must have held his breath quite a bit during the long drive from Costa Mesa. Then again, it wasn't such a long drive considering he was doing close to ninety miles an hour the whole time.

His budgeted time was running out. Only after the door was shut tight did he dare turn on a light. When he did, he was relieved to see his good friend napping away.

So did you miss me, or what? It must have been a real chore going around all day without me talking sense into you.

"Yeah, it was a bitch. We've got to move fast."

Lou went straight for the bed. He stripped the covers off in one jerk and grabbed Fisk under the arms. A moment later he was draped over Lou's shoulder. Looking quickly around the room, he decided there was nothing else that he needed and took a peek through the blinds. There was nobody in the parking lot.

Look at your watch, Louis. There's no way you're going to have the time to do whatever it is you're thinking. There's no fucking way.

"I hauled ass over here and I'm way ahead of schedule now. Roche's house is only a couple of minutes away."

Why get rid of me now then? This thing might be over in twenty minutes, Louis. Then you'll have all night to dump me someplace.

"I already considered it," Lou replied, opening the door.

He removed the *Do Not Disturb* sign and tossed it on the floor. After another peek around the corner, he walked briskly to the passenger door and threw it open. Handling the large man was getting easier with practice. Fisk practically jumped into the seat for him this time.

Okay, you considered it. Can you finish a thought, Lou?

Lou started the engine and backed out from his parking space. He waited until he was on the main street before speaking.

"That hotel room is in Daisley's name. He reserved it for me."

Then you should definitely leave me there. He's screwing you over, isn't he? This is an opportunity that you won't ever get again.

"He'll show up, Terry. You'll see. The other guys think he split, but I think he'll come through for us."

Even so, Louis. You don't need to leave me there all night. Why don't you do your little job and then come back? It still doesn't make sense to ditch me now. We've got all night for Christ's sake. There's no reason.

Lou took a deep breath and prepared Fisk a mouthful of reasons. He was somber and loud in the same instant.

"What if I get blown away? What about that? This ain't like stashing all my porno before a big raid in case my parents have to go through my stuff if I'm killed. I'm responsible for you, okay? It's my job, Terry. *You're* my job. Now, what if I get myself killed?"

I wouldn't like that, Louis...and I know that you'd just fucking hate it. You shouldn't even think that way, big guy. Don't even think it.

"It's too late. I've already thought about it and I'm not going into this thing without at least *one* problem solved."

That's rude, Louis. I'm not just a problem, you know. Where are we going, anyway?

"Don't worry about it. I've got a spot all picked out for you...*whoa*...hang on, Terry."

Lou saw the mass of brake lights ahead of him and was forced to stop quicker than he was comfortable with. Instinctively, he threw an arm in front of Fisk's chest to keep him from falling forward, though he was buckled in tightly. They were in a line of cars at least a quarter of a mile long when they came to a stop.

"What is this shit? There shouldn't be any traffic at this time of day. It's Friday night, isn't it?"

That would be correct.

"Then why are we in traffic? This is bullshit…wait. Oh crap…I think it's an accident."

Leaning his head out the window, Lou tried to see what the problem was. There were several police cruisers along the side of the road and a large blinking sign. He couldn't make out what the sign read but he knew it was a little too late for roadwork. His forehead and neck began to sweat as they drew closer.

"*Shit!* Straighten up, Terry…*quick!*" Lou screamed, grabbing him by the jacket and violently shaking him into a halfway human position.

It was a losing battle as Fisk seemed intent on leaning awkwardly to his right. Vainly, Lou tried to pull him upright and keep his sunglasses on straight before they came to a stop. In the few seconds that they were stationary, Lou unbuttoned Fisk's top button and pulled on his tie until it hung loosely. He then let go of him and left him leaning against the door.

They were moving again, but only a few feet at a time. A minute later, they were at the front of the line of cars. The approaching policeman signaled for Lou to roll down his window.

"Good evening, sir," he said, shining his flashlight all around the interior of the car. "You haven't had anything to drink tonight, have you?"

Fortunately, the police officer didn't hear Fisk laughing at what he considered to be a wildly hilarious sobriety checkpoint. Lou heard it loud and clear, though, and came to the realization that they were doomed to be joined at the hip for a little longer than he had planned.

Chapter 73

"You know, maybe I *should* drive," Joe said, taking a long look at Alex, whose face was frozen in a permanent scowl. "You're not looking too hot, man."

"I know it," he admitted, making no move to pull the van off of the freeway. "I'm not feeling too hot either."

Joe was beginning to get the feeling that they had been driving too long. It wasn't that they had passed their destination or anything like that, but they were simply being given too much time to get there. If it was as easy as walking next door and shooting the guy, Joe suspected that Alex wouldn't be nearly as nervous. This was too much time, though. Too much time to think about what was going to happen next. It would have been better to shove the ugliness aside, but Alex was a thinker and Joe knew it. He just couldn't help himself.

Even when they were younger Alex had trouble letting things go. Whether it was something very good or something horribly bad, he had a tendency to over-think it. Usually, it worked out for the best, but he wasn't feeling as confident this time. It wasn't every day that Joe shared deep feelings with his best friend and he usually saved them for the most appropriate time available to him. Though sitting in the passenger's seat while they were on their way to a killing didn't seem ideal, it would have to do.

"You look worried."

"I am," he replied quickly, giving Joe an unsure look. "Don't get me wrong—this guy is going to eat shit in a big way tonight and I'm up for it. I want to do this, Joe. I *have* to. If I don't take it out on this sick motherfucker tonight then I might not ever feel right. Or worse, I might take it out on someone who doesn't deserve it at all."

"Taking *what* out? What do you mean?"

"Just stuff, man." Alex explained it in his usual soft-spoken manner, which Joe thought was a little creepy. When speaking of anger, one didn't expect the conversation to be so mellow. He wished, just this once, that Alex would scream it.

"It's nothing real specific, though. And whatever it is that you're thinking—you're wrong. I've been watching you, bro. I've been watching you look at me and it isn't what you're thinking."

Okay, maybe it isn't, Joe thought to himself, knowing he was often less than accurate while trying to read his friend's face. "I'm glad to hear it. I was starting to think that one of our teachers played with your nuts or something. But you're sure your old man didn't sneak into your room at night and bang your ass or anything like that?"

He was going overboard with it, but didn't want Alex to feel that he was being doubted in any way. The crude questions merely served as confirmation that Joe believed him with all of his heart…even if he didn't.

"No ass-bangings that I recall," Alex answered. "I'm pretty sure I'd remember that. It's a nice thing for you to think of, though. I feel really good knowing you've been picturing me getting sexually tortured as a kid. Thanks, man."

The sentences were laced with enough sarcasm to quell most of Joe's fears but the bitch of it was that Alex always knew how to play it. His expressionless face and quiet voice were simply tools used to conceal what was going on in his head. Joe knew first hand that there was a lot. He decided to drop the particular line of questioning and go for what was bothering him at the moment.

"So what's the problem then?"

"It's tomorrow that's bugging me."

"It's just another day, isn't it?"

"Not quite," Alex replied, gripping the steering wheel tighter. "I know how I feel right now. I *know* I can do this. But how am I going to feel tomorrow? What if I feel like I've done something real shitty? There's no going back on something like this."

"Well, that's true, I guess. But what makes you think you'll feel any different tomorrow? Maybe you'll even feel better."

"Maybe. But what if I don't?"

That was the question Joe didn't want to hear. If he couldn't figure it out, he knew for sure that Alex would go absolutely crazy without a logical answer. And there were no logical answers at this point. There was a simple solution, though, and strangely enough, Joe was the one who knew what is was.

"I'll handle it then. You just worry about getting us there and I'll take care of his stupid ass. It's no problem."

"*Bullshit*," Alex snapped fiercely. "I know we're in on this together but there's no way that's going to happen. Just forget about it. It's *our* job but this is *my* deal. I don't want you worrying about this shit."

"Hey, *you're* the only thing that's worrying me right now. I hear what you're saying about feeling like a turd tomorrow and I think you're right. Hell, I *know* you're right. But look at me, man. Do I ever worry about anything? Do you ever see me getting stressed out over stuff? I don't think so."

"That's different."

"It's not different," Joe countered. "It's the same thing. You'd dwell on it. I can see you now. You'd be sitting there everyday, crying on the inside and getting all torn up about it. Do you see that happening to me?"

"Maybe—I don't know."

"I'm not one-hundred percent sure either and I can't promise you that I won't feel bad in the morning. But I can definitely promise that *you* would. I know you, man. It'll eat you up."

Alex seemed to contemplate his partner's words as they drew closer to their destination. He sighed several times before turning back to him. "And you won't feel anything?"

"Man, I'm more worried about how much gas we have in the tank than all this other stuff. I'm telling you, I'll be fine with it."

"You're serious?" Alex asked through narrow eyes.

"I am," Joe replied with a solemn look. "You've already had to do most of the driving anyway. It wouldn't be fair for you to have to kill the fucker too."

Chapter 74

As he pulled into position, Lou's frustration was at its peak. He knew how it would look if the others knew he had a passenger and he hoped to keep it secret.

I can't believe we're finally here.

"No kidding," Lou replied tiredly as he picked up his phone. "We're running late. I wonder if anyone's heard from Daisley."

I wouldn't count on it, big guy. You should relax for a second and get your bearings before making that call.

"Why? We're where we're supposed to be and we're late."

Take a moment, Louis. I thought you were going to shit when we went through that sobriety checkpoint. And when that guy shined his light on my face....

"Don't remind me."

He didn't need a reminder since the whole thing had taken place only a few minutes before they neared Roche's neighborhood. Of all the disasters that had occurred since the previous day, Lou was most affected by the brief stop at the checkpoint. It felt like reaching the finish line only to trip and fall down just before winning the race.

It was no worse than anything else that had happened, but left a deeper impression because of the schedule he was on. Luckily, Fisk had played his role perfectly and remained quiet and still. As passed out as Fisk looked and as sober as Lou was, they cruised through the checkpoint unscathed, which left Lou howling with delight. His glee was dampened only seconds after they pulled away.

That was when Fisk had spoken up and told him what he already knew. They were going to be partners whether he liked it or not.

Maybe you should just ignore me until this thing's over. I know you've got a lot on your mind and I don't want to be a distraction.

"You're already distracting me."

I know, Louis. But try to keep your mind on what's about to happen. Try not to think about getting rid of me right now. I'm sorry the cop shined his light on me. I'm sorry he gawked at me so long and ruined your plans for me. I can't be held responsible for that, can I?

"I don't blame you, Terry. I don't blame anybody." He grabbed the phone again and flipped it open. "Don't worry—I'm not calling Mike yet. I didn't see my boys so I'm going to see what's up. Can I do that please?"

Give it a shot if you want. I'll bet they don't even show up. They're probably hanging out at the mall, Louis. Playing video games in the arcade and picking up girls.

"You want to bet?"

Fisk stayed quiet. Lou guessed that he was waiting to see if anyone answered the phone before he ridiculed him some more. It only rang once before Alex's voice was heard over the line.

"Yeah, I'm here."

"Where's here?" Lou asked, scanning the street ahead of him and behind him. He couldn't see a thing but the house. Quartz was parked too far away to see and he knew that Blash was tucked around the corner.

"We're still about fifteen minutes out."

"What did you do—stop for food?"

He instantly regretted the tone he had used. It wasn't their fault they were stuck in the van and didn't have access to a Porsche Speedster. They also didn't have badges to flash to appeal for consideration from fellow officers if they got pulled over for doing ninety miles an hour. Just the same, he was on edge and wanted to finish things up.

"Sorry, man, but the last thing you said to do was to drive slow. I'm guessing you're already there?"

"Just pulled up a second ago," he replied, realizing with his own words that they weren't too far behind him. "I'm going to make some calls and give everyone our status. How's it looking on your end?"

"We'll let you know once we're parked. It's all looking good, though. You want to try us back in a few or do you want us to call you when we're set up?"

"Call when you get here. And be ready. It won't be long."

"No, it sure won't."

Chapter 75

Walter only flinched mildly as Blash's phone rang again. He had turned the volume down to eliminate the possibility of his medic having a heart attack before he could patch anyone up.

"I sure hope that's you, big guy."

"Yeah, I'm here and the other guys are a few minutes behind me. Is everyone else here?"

Blash took a look down at the south end of the street. He couldn't see the Porsche from his current location and felt good about it. Though the neighborhood was lit about as well as any other, their locations were far enough apart not to draw suspicion.

"Yeah, we're all present and accounted for."

Aside from what they were about to do, Blash's final concern was communication since using their police radios was out of the question for obvious reasons. Of course, using their cellular phones was almost as dangerous to them and they all knew it. It wasn't too likely that some eavesdropper would be listening in and was even more unlikely that anyone would be recording any of the transmissions, but it was still a risk.

They all knew to keep it simple, though. Using names would be frowned upon, though they were way beyond worrying about trivial matters. They knew that if they were going to go down for any reason, it wouldn't be because of communications issues. It would be something far worse.

"What do you want me to do now?"

"Just hang loose until we're all here," Blash replied, hearing Lou's level of anxiety grow with each second that passed. "And just so you know, there's three of them. Our main guy and two serious looking friends. Make sure your boys know about them."

"Is that it?"

Blash could only hope. "I've been covering the place all day, but you know I can't guarantee anything."

"I understand. You'll hear from me once they get here."

*   *   *   *

Oh…you understand, do you? That's funny coming from you, Louis. The guy you were just talking to said he couldn't guarantee that there weren't any more people inside the house. I don't think you understand at all.

"We planned for it, Terry, and there are a lot of us here," Lou explained, staring at the house where their target was waiting patiently for them. "It'll be really quick I bet."

And if it's not?

"Then it'll be really long, people will get killed, and we'll all go to jail—except you, I mean." Lou's mood was darkening. He was beginning to fear what he might do if Fisk didn't turn down the volume on himself.

Shit, Louis. Maybe you do understand after all. I'm impressed with your appraisal of the situation.

"Don't be," Lou replied coldly. "Because I'm not impressed with *you*. You've done nothing but shoot your mouth off since I met you. It was nice being away from you, you know. All afternoon and not a word from you. I almost started feeling normal again."

You? Normal? I'd like to see that.

"And there you go again," Lou uttered through teeth that were clenching tightly. "I'm going to need one of two things from you from here on out. I need you quiet, Terry. If you can't do that then at least be a little constructive. That's it. That's all I need."

Constructive?

"Well, helpful at least. You know what I mean. I don't want any surprises popping up because you're bugging me."

I'll do my best, Louis, but let's get one thing clear.

"This ought to be good," Lou said, rolling his eyes to Fisk.

This is my game, big guy. Not yours. It's what I do for a living and I do it better than anyone here including the two guys that are babysitting Christian Roche right now. I'll try not to distract you, Louis. Just make damn sure that you don't distract me.

"Me distracting you? That's funny."

No it's not. You're going to need me sooner than you think. Your guys aren't going to show up, Louis. They're shit and they're going to leave you hanging just like....

Lou's phone began to ring. A thin but victorious smile appeared on his lips. "Yeah?"

"*We're here,*" came Alex's voice through the line.

Go ahead, Louis. What the hell do I know, anyway?

Chapter 76

▼

"It's good to hear from you."

"Likewise. You want us to go right now?"

"Nah, I need to send out the word that you're here. Take a couple of minutes to get yourselves together."

"Cool, we could use it."

"I should let you know this right off the bat," Lou warned, taking a deep breath. "Our man's here—it's him for sure. He's got company, though. I guess a couple of guys are hanging out with him."

I didn't hear you say the word "bodyguards", Louis. They don't know that Roche's pals are probably packing and looking for trouble. Maybe you should share that with them.

There was no concern at all in Alex Bautista's voice. *"And that's what the girls are for, right?"*

"Exactly right."

"Well, I guess we hang up now and wait for the word, huh?"

Lou scoured his brain for anything else that might be of assistance to them but came up empty. "Yeah, that sounds about right."

"Okay then. We'll be looking forward to your call."

They both hung up at the same time.

✱   ✱   ✱   ✱

It was only seconds later that Blash's phone sprang to life again. He answered it quickly, not bothering to guess who it was.

"Okay, we're in place. My boys pulled up a minute ago. We'll be ready to move when you say."

Blash paused as he turned to Walter and then to the girls in the Mustang. Though he couldn't see whatever it was Lou's boys were driving, he knew they were as ready as they were ever going to be.

"Damn, I'm glad I called when I did." He looked at his watch, noting the time of eight-fifteen. "I didn't know it would take us so long to get situated."

"Well, some of us haven't been trained for this kind of thing."

It was a vague statement, but Blash knew exactly where he was going with it. More than the fact that Lou's end of things was running behind schedule, it was clear he was worried about the two men he had brought into a mess that didn't concern them at all. His fear was justified.

"Don't worry, big guy. There's no real schedule for this. I only wanted to make sure it was dark but not too late for company. And I pulled the eight o'clock hour straight out of my ass if it makes you feel any better. We're right on time as far as I'm concerned."

"Are we waiting for anything?"

"Not any more. I'm going to send the girls up in a couple of minutes. Call me when you see them walking up to the house."

"Yes, sir."

Blash folded his phone up and turned to Walter, who was looking him in the eye. He appeared to be upset about something.

"What girls are going where?"

"Relax, Walt—we're all professionals here."

It was about to begin.

Chapter 77

▼

Quartz lit another cigarette while Nanetta pulled the clip from her silenced .32 pistol. After a final check of the weapon, she appeared satisfied that it was loaded. Whether it would fire or not was another story and she chastised herself for not test-firing the gun first.

"This will shoot, no?" she asked, holding it out for Quartz's inspection.

"Jesus, I hope so," she replied, trying to keep any worry off of her face. "The man we got them from doesn't…didn't screw around. I've got to admit we haven't tried them out yet, but I'm sure it'll put a few holes in something."

"They had better, or I will not be—"

Nanetta was cut off by the chirping of the phone.

Their eyes met for an instant before Quartz flipped it open. She took a last drag off of her cigarette and handed it to Nanetta, who took a final drag herself before tossing it out the window.

"Are you ready, Qiana?"

"Like I *wouldn't* be?" she replied with an anxious giggle, her voice a bit higher than she was used to hearing come out of her mouth. She put the phone to her ear and could almost hear Blash's chest heaving. "Time to go?"

"*Yeah, it's time. No bullshit, cutie—I want you to be careful.*"

"We will," Quartz replied, staring at Nanetta as she spoke. She gave Blash a few final words of encouragement. "And I swear to God you'd better not let anyone fucking sneak up on us."

The Ukrainian suddenly looked more intense than Quartz could have imagined her to be. Her breaths came long and slow as she slipped the gun into her right pocket and pushed her door open. She was standing outside of the vehicle before Quartz had even put her phone away. There was a coiled pair of jumper cables dangling from her left hand.

Quartz pulled on the hood-release then stepped from the car. After a brief wave to the men watching her, she walked to the other side of the car and joined Nanetta. They raised the hood into an open position and started walking.

* * * *

The call to Lou was quick and to the point. If Blash was speaking the truth to him then things were now in motion.

So, it's happening, Louis? All your bases are covered and they're just walking up to house now? Man, this is some exciting shit to be watching. I'm glad you brought me along.

Lou hung up and started dialing Alex's number.

* * * *

"I'm here."

"Good, they're on their way up." As Lou spoke, he watched the two women saunter slowly towards the house. "Let me know when they're in sight."

"I will if it's possible but we can't see shit from this angle. Are you hearing me, partner? We've got a pretty good view of the side but the slope of the street isn't working for us."

"No problem," Lou interjected soothingly. "I can see everything. Just stay with me and I'll let you know if and when you need to move."

Louis? Fisk chimed in, but was ignored completely. Now wasn't the best time to hear what the latest insult would be.

"Okay, they're just about to the driveway," Lou said, feeling like a very bad sports commentator. "They're moving pretty slow and damn if they don't look like a couple of girls needing a jump. It's perfect. I think this should work. I'll let you know in a few seconds."

Who's going to get it done? Will it be the girls or the boys? I bet you can't wait to find out. This is the best seat in the house, Louis. I can't wait to see the look on your face. This is going to be so....

"Shut up, Terry," Lou barked, covering the phone with his hand. "Later on, you can talk or yell or sing a fucking song if you want to. Just be quiet for a couple of minutes. Please."

He uncovered the phone and shared what he was looking at.

"They're walking up to the door. They're at the door, guys. They're at the door."

Chapter 78

They both looked up at the large archway they were walking under as they approached the door. Quartz wiggled her nose around and scrunched her face up a few times in an attempt to relax the muscles and get rid of any visible lingering tension that might give her away. Nanetta didn't require such an exercise as her face was already the picture of perfect calm. Her face wasn't expressionless by any means but contained the right amount of desperation a person might have if they were forced to knock on a stranger's door and ask them to help start a stubborn car. Quartz tried to match her expression but found it difficult.

Without pause, warning, or any announcement that she was about to do so, Nanetta stepped forward and rang the doorbell. Surprised by the sudden move, Quartz gasped slightly then covered her mouth as though stifling a cough.

* * * *

"Okay, Walt," Blash said, throwing his door open and stepping out to the curb. "Watch the house. If anything's going to happen, it'll happen there, so keep your eyes open. If anyone so much as scrapes their knee, I want you on them. Get them back here to this car. If they can't move, pull them into the back seat. Got me?"

Walter blinked a few times and nodded. He looked dazed like he had just woken up from a long night's sleep. The black bag was pulled closely to his chest.

"I'll be right out here, just a few feet away," Blash explained, making sure his gun was ready to fire. "If anything happens, I'll be the first one in there, so you might want to keep an eye on me too."

Any nerves that Blash had were suddenly replaced by a rush of adrenaline that left him mildly dizzy. A slight grin graced his face as he closed the door and poked his head back through the open window.

"Ain't this some shit, Walter? Don't tell me you're not having a good time."

"Wait, Mike. Don't...."

He stepped away from the car and moved out of sight.

"...leave me alone."

* * * *

The door was pulled open quickly, though only twelve inches at the most. The man who answered it stared cautiously at the two women, his face wearing a blend of curiosity and annoyance. He looked each of them up and down then pulled it open a little wider.

"Can I help you ladies with something?"

It wasn't Christian Roche. This man was bigger than she'd expected and his hair was pulled back in a ponytail. Quartz eyed him with what she hoped was a look of embarrassment as she shifted her eyes to Nanetta. She was surprised when the woman opened her mouth.

"We are very sorry to be bothering you, sir," she said with a heavier accent than Quartz had heard her use so far. It was lower, huskier, and sounded like something one might hear from a phone-sex line. "The car...our car...it is not starting. We have these...jumping cables...but...."

The man stepped out of the doorway and pulled the door shut behind him. He glanced at both women then out towards the street.

"Where's your car?" he asked, looking left then right.

"It is just down from the street...four...five houses away. If we could put these..." she paused as though searching for the words, looking down at the cables in her hand. "...to your car...then to our car. This is possible, no? We would be *very* grateful to you." She shifted her eyes to Quartz than back to him, running her tongue over her teeth. "Both of us."

Quartz watched the man think about it and could practically feel him getting erect right in front of them, but his response was too slow in coming. She could have easily jumped in and tried another angle to coax him from the property but at this point she was afraid to speak. Since Nanetta was playing the ignorant horny foreigner, it would have looked strange if Quartz broke her silence and started speaking clear English.

"Wait here a second." He walked back into the house and closed the door behind him.

Quartz and Nanetta looked at each other and waited, both taking several heavy gulps of air while they still had the opportunity. A moment later, the door reopened. The man walked out and pulled the door closed behind him, stepping quickly between them. He looked anything but helpful.

"Sorry, ladies, I think Triple-A is who you're looking for. This is private property so I'm going to have to ask you to leave." He then placed a heavy hand on each of their backs and manually walked them from the entryway.

Since a tug or jerk in the wrong direction might have jeopardized their status, they allowed the man to handle them. He wasn't being rough but simply pushed them with enough force to keep them moving forward at a faster pace than they wanted to go. When they reached the edge of the driveway, he stopped and looked to his left. The Mustang with its hood up was barely visible. He gave them one more light shove and began his retreat back to the door.

"I am sorry?" Nanetta said with a confused and bitter look, spinning around to look at him. "I do not understand. The car…it is there. You can make it work, no?"

He put on a cold smile and turned back to them. He shook his head slowly as he neared them and looked ready to push them both off of the sidewalk. Stopping just short, he folded his arms and stared down at the two women.

"I'll say this again since your English doesn't sound so good. *Move along*. Do you understand *that*? Because if I have to tell you a third time—"

Quartz was surprised when he stopped talking so abruptly. A thousand things had been going through her mind at the moment and she didn't even notice it when Nanetta pulled out her gun and put it to his head.

Chapter 79

"Oh my God, she's going to shoot him right in the fucking driveway," Lou yelled, causing Alex to yank the phone away from his ear.

"Isn't she supposed to do that?" he asked in reply, unsure of what everybody else's roles were.

"No, it's not him! She's got the wrong guy! She's—"

"Stop freaking out and tell us what to do, man." Alex's voice remained steady and smooth. "We're ready to move. Where do you want us?"

There was a long break in the conversation as Lou stopped narrating. When he came back on, Alex was glad to hear he wasn't yelling anymore.

"Hold on, guys. Just hold on."

Oh, go ahead and send them in, Louis. What could it hurt?

* * * *

Blash watched from less than twenty feet away and his first instinct was full of typical Michael Blash ingenuity. With the one man held at bay, he was tempted to rush the door and take his chances with the two inside. Common sense talked him out it, however, as he took in the scene and watched the women work.

Even from his current distance, he could see the look on Nanetta's face. He could see that she was itching to shoot the man. If she wasn't then she was one hell of an actress. The man with the ponytail could see the look in her eyes as well and most likely wasn't going to try anything. It would have been suicidal in any event.

Blash didn't move. For the moment, he was comfortable and ready for whatever came next.

✶　　✶　　✶　　✶

Why not, Louis? Give it a try. The redhead's about to empty that guy's skull onto the concrete, which would leave two inside. That's one for each of your guys. Send them in, I dare you.

"Hang tight and don't do anything," Lou said into the phone, knowing that it wasn't time yet. "We're halfway there, guys. Just don't do anything."

Chapter 80

"Keep your fucking mouth *shut*," Quartz growled as quietly as she could while she dug into his jacket. "Not a word. You understand me?"

He nodded while Quartz yanked a nine-millimeter semiauto from his shoulder holster. Then, moving two fingers around his belt line, she pulled a revolver from the small of his back. She completed the search without finding a third gun down by his ankle where she had expected one to be.

"Start walking," she said from behind him and gave him a shove towards the car.

He moved a few inches forward but didn't begin to walk as instructed. After a look into Nanetta's eyes, it was clear why. He could see as easily as Quartz could that Nanetta didn't want him to walk anywhere. She just wanted him to fall down and bleed from whatever hole she put in him.

"Let's *go*, sweetie," she said with a mildly frightened and panicked look, motioning towards her Mustang. After getting no response, she held up her hand and tapped on her watch. Time was definitely an issue and they were now on someone else's schedule. They had no idea when another person might come walking out the door.

It was almost thirty seconds later that she finally lowered the gun and slid behind him next to Quartz. The harsh scowl disappeared. She was wearing her dirty little smile instead.

"Walk, pig," she said, smacking him in the back of the head with the gun. Letting out a shaky sigh of relief, Quartz winked at her and gave the man a nudge.

He walked briskly this time but by the time they had him behind the Mustang, he wasn't very eager to get into the trunk. Even though it appeared he wasn't about to receive a bullet within the next few minutes, he still looked unhappy with the alternative they were offering. He climbed in slowly and remained totally silent as they slammed the trunk on him.

"*Jesus*, Netta."

They were all the words she could come up with.

* * * *

"Okay, I think we can stop shitting our pants," said Lou, who was only seconds away from having to wipe his own ass. "That's one down and…and I don't have any idea what happens now."

Send them in. Don't be a pussy, Louis.

"I've got to sign off for a second, guys." Lou didn't wait for a reply. He hung up and dialed another number.

* * * *

"What the *fuck* was that about?" Blash asked of whomever was on the other end of the line.

"Don't ask me, man. I just need to know what to do now."

It was Lou and he was damned glad to hear from him. He needed some quick answers rather than more questions, but he supposed hearing a friendly voice was far better than watching a man get his face shot off. He was frustrated nonetheless.

"There's two more of them and I don't know if it's safe to send the girls back in. That guy didn't just come bopping out the door; he went into the house before coming back out. He must have said something to somebody."

"So, another knock at that door might be bad news."

"I agree," Blash said quickly, realizing he was taking way to much time thinking about it. "Let me scream at the girls for a minute. I'll call you right back."

They disconnected and he dialed Quartz.

* * * *

"What the *fuck* was that about?" he said again, knowing exactly who he was speaking to this time. She and her Ukrainian sidekick would have heard a lot more from him if they could have managed the time.

"Don't ask. I think it was just an attention getter."

"Well, it got mine for sure," he replied harshly, though he wasn't at all unhappy about the man who was busy relaxing in her trunk. "How would you feel about going in again?"

"Unthrilled—but I can think of at least one person who'd be more than happy to go kicking down doors and jumping through windows with you. She's a girl after your own heart, Mike."

"Thanks, but it looks more like she's after yours. I need to figure out what we're doing next. Are you up for this?"

"I know she is…and I'm with her, so…whatever you think, Mike. Whatever."

He honestly didn't know what to think or what to do. But like everyone else involved, she was waiting for an answer from him.

He ended up making an executive decision.

Chapter 81

Do it, Louis. This'll be great. They're just sitting there, waiting to be used. You were going to use me, weren't you? They already took half the money…just like me. That's the deal, Louis. If you take the money you do the job. Send them in. This is killing me!

Lou stared straight forward doing his best to block the words out, but it wasn't any good. He knew the phone was going to ring in a couple of seconds. It had been way too long since he'd talked to Blash.

At least it took him a while to decide. That's got to count for something, right? He's spent a whole forty-five seconds picking your guys for the suicide dash. What a fucking sweetheart.

Here it comes…

Wait for it…

The phone in Lou's hand began to ring.

And there it is.

"I'm here. What are we doing?"

Blash was already firing the words out quickly. *"Are they ready to go?"*

He didn't even bother to say hello first. That's sad.

"They're ready to roll. Should I send them up?"

Oh please, oh please, oh please…

"Yeah, big guy." Blash said with a strange pitch to his voice. His usual cockiness seemed to be on vacation for the moment. "Send them on over. Here's how it's going to happen…"

Do you want to tell them, or should I?

* * * *

"Yeah?" Alex asked pensively into the phone, watching Joe handle the shotgun.

"Okay, you guys are up."

Alex could sense his nervousness, though Lou's tone was quite a bit different than what he had been expecting. Sounding much more relaxed than he had in the last several minutes, his voice was practically buoyant. Apparently, their plan had changed radically in the last half of a minute.

"And you're gonna have some company."

"Oh, are we?" Alex asked in reply.

"Yeah, you'll have three of us on the north side of the house. The girls and the boss will be just past the entryway, about ten feet away from you. As you're walking up, you'll see two sets of garage doors on your right. Just past there and around the corner on the left is where they'll be. You're covered on the way in and your back's covered if you have to make a quick exit. What do you think?"

"I think it's time to get moving," he answered. "We can go now if you want."

"Let's do it then. Be careful, guys. I'll talk to you when it's over."

"Yeah, when it's over," Alex echoed. "We're on our way." He clicked off the phone and turned to Joe, holding Terrance Fisk's custom forty-five caliber handgun out to him. "Give me the shotgun and take this."

Joe couldn't hide the broad smile that appeared on his face. "Change your mind about how you'll feel tomorrow?"

"No, you're just enjoying this too much." They exchanged guns. "The first one to shoot him wins. What do you say?"

Joe nodded his approval. "Cool."

* * * *

It was the last call Lou hoped to make tonight. The next time he listened to words from the tiny little phone, he prayed that it would be a call from Blash telling him that it was all over and time to go home.

"Yeah?"

"They're on their way," Lou said, hardly believing that it was really happening. "Keep your eyes open."

"We will."

Blash, Quartz, and Nanetta were moving into position.

Chapter 82

▼

They stepped from the van and faced each other, quickly checking their clothes. Both in white shirts and black ties, they swapped coats since Alex would once again be holding the shotgun. Their hair was combed neatly and their clothes still looked pressed. They looked like they were going to church.

"I'll do the talking," Alex said. They started to walk.

They covered the distance to the house without breaking stride once. Like a pair of horses dragging a sulky behind them, each step was committed to what lay ahead. Not too fast and not too slow, it took about thirty seconds to reach the driveway. It felt like an hour.

Not even bothering to look to their right, where they knew their backup was waiting, they walked straight to the door. Joe reached out with a gloved hand and rang the doorbell. Turning to Alex, he whispered into his ear.

"If he asks 'Who's there?' I swear I'm gonna kick your ass."

They heard footsteps approaching.

The deadbolt was unlocked.

The door was pulled open.

In front of them stood a man in his mid-forties wearing an expensive suit, looking surprised, confused, and very unhappy to see the pair on his doorstep.

He looked past the two young men and examined the street behind them. The only expression he wore was one of complete suspicion. After several seconds of uncomfortable silence, he said hello in his own special way.

"It's a little late for this shit, isn't it fellows?"

The greeting was less than cordial but Alex smiled at him anyway. It was an easy thing to do since he had been preparing for the moment for the last twenty-four hours. In fact, it was even easier than he thought it would be.

Though he was seeing the man's face for the first time, he could tell just from the look of it that this was the pedophile baby-killer he'd been dying to meet.

He looked his target dead in the eye.

"Are you Christian?"

The one question seemed to make him even more unhappy than before. His rude, dismissive behavior was ignored and the question was put to him again.

"Are you Christian?"

He paused for a moment and seemed to ponder the question before answering. Looking angry and completely out of patience, he finally did.

"Yes, I suppose I am. Now get the hell off of my doorstep before I—"

He never got to say what is was he was going to do.

He was blasted right out of his shoes instead.

*   *   *   *

Keeping their guns out in front, they took a moment to look over the man who was now a full six feet further from them. He was flat on his back with a large hole in the middle of his chest. Wisps of smoke were rising from the wound.

With their fingers on the triggers, two pairs of eyes darted around the interior of the house as they waited for a second man to appear. If he was there, he was taking his time or just hiding in a closet somewhere. Ten seconds, then twenty, passed before they started backing out the door. Their job was finished and there was no point in hanging around waiting for trouble.

Alex took a final glance at the body before him and felt like spitting on it. He resisted the urge since nothing in the world was more solid than DNA evidence, but it didn't matter—he'd already killed the man and that was enough. He had killed him brutally, slaughtering many of his own demons at the same time.

Staring down at what he knew to be a child-molesting sociopath, he didn't see Christian Roche at all. He saw something else; something different. Some*one* different. And as he took a final look at the smoking dead man, he was sure for the first time that he wouldn't feel bad tomorrow morning, if ever.

Before he knew it, Joe was pulling him from the doorway.

"We're done here. Let's go."

Their pace back to the van was as even as when they walked to the house. The walked with the same determination as before, though they were slightly more determined now that they were fleeing the scene. As quickly as they'd arrived, they were back in the van.

They made a U-turn and cruised slowly away from the neighborhood.

"Well, that went pretty good," Joe said, pulling the handgun from his pocket. "We're lucky you were carrying the shotgun."

"Why's that?"

"Because I didn't even get a shot off," he replied, laughing nervously. "I think I left the safety on."

Chapter 83

It had been a long couple of minutes waiting. When Blash's phone rang again, he practically ripped it from his pocket to eliminate the sudden noise. The three of them had been huddled together on the north side of the house since Blash had come up with his latest plan of attack. It had been several minutes, and though they were mostly obscured, they were still vulnerable if anyone decided to go poking around on the side of the residence.

"What's taking so long?" he asked in a harsh whisper. The line was quiet for a moment. He could hear breathing in the earpiece.

"Is that you, Mike?"

"Of course it's me! What the fuck are they waiting for?"

"What are you talking about?" There was a ten second pause as the breathing got heavier. *"What are you doing?"*

"Is that you, big guy?" he asked, praying for it even though the voice in his ear didn't sound a thing like Louis Poklatar.

"No, Mike, it's Andrew. What in the hell are you doing?"

"Daisley?" A wide range of emotions filled Blash's head upon hearing the voice, though he had no idea what to say to the man right now. Just saying his name made him mad enough to want to strangle his own cell phone.

"Jesus, Mike. Please tell me you didn't—"

"This ain't the time, Daisley. We're up to our asses in work right now, you motherfucker. Thanks for all the help. What do you want?"

"God, Mike. You've to stop what you're doing."

It didn't sound like an order and Daisley didn't sound like himself—his old self, anyway. His tone was resigned and his voice wavered with each word.

"We can't stop it now," Blash replied, trying to keep his anger in check. "It's happening right now and we've already taken the first step. There's no stopping this thing now that—"

"Donald Ratcliffe's dead."

Blash paused, letting the words sink in, though he wasn't exactly sure of what to believe at the moment. "What the fuck are you talking about? You'd better make it quick."

"He's dead, Mike. I'm looking at him right now. I came up here to kill him."

"Jesus, man—we're on cell phones for Christ's sake," Blash uttered, knowing it was too late now if anyone was listening in. "You killed him? You killed the lawyer?"

"No, I was about to. I was a few seconds away from it when these two guys came walking up. They blew him right the fuck away, Mike. I saw it happen. They were twenty feet from me. A couple of younger guys. That was about a minute ago. Stop whatever you're doing, Mike. Please. You don't have to do it."

"Two guys? What—? Oh, no. *No, no, no.*"

He killed his connection to Daisley with the press of a button. He punched in Lou's number.

*   *   *   *

"I'm here. What's going on?"

"Where are they, big guy? Where are they at?"

Lou wasn't sure if he was hearing things right, but he could have sworn that Mike Blash sounded scared. It was a bad thing to be hearing at the worst possible time. Especially since his two young civilians were probably only a few seconds from their big moment.

Who is it, Louis? Is it Blash? Is it Daisley? What are they saying?

Lou did his best to ignore the assassin's ramblings as he tried to quell the waves of panic that he could hear coming off of his team leader. "Sorry, man, I don't know what's taking them so long. They haven't even walked by me yet."

"But you said they were on their way." And there it was again—that unsettling fear in Blash's voice. "They're on their way—that's what you said."

"That's what they told me. Listen, they probably just have cold feet or something and they're—"

"Shut up! Look down the street. Do you see their car?"

Lou did as he was told even though he already knew the answer. "No, it's out of sight, just like you said."

The van, you mean? Fisk inquired. *Is he asking about our boys?*

"*Jesus Christ! Start your car and don't bother looking for them.*" Blash was done being quiet and Lou's ear was suddenly full of him. He yelled loudly this time. "*We're pulling out and you're pulling out! Get the fuck out of there!*"

"What's wrong?" Lou asked. "What's happening?"

Ha, ha, ha, ha....

"What's going on?"

"*No time, man. Just go. Get out of here.*"

Blash's voice disappeared as the line was disconnected abruptly. Lou stared down at the silent phone, then turned to Fisk.

Ha, ha, ha, ha. Oh, Louis. Louis, you poor man. I'm sorry. Ha, ha, ha. I'm really...really...sorry.

"Okay, I give up. What is it?" Doing as he was told, he started the Porsche's engine as fresh beads of sweat dripped into his eyes.

Don't be pissed, Louis. I already told you....

"Told me *what?*" he screamed, grabbing Fisk by the collar.

That I snuck one by you, Louis.

I did, you know. Right fucking by you. Do you still feel like you're the one in control? Well, do you? Do you? Ha, ha, ha, ha....

He didn't. He couldn't even fake it. It was true.

He had never even mentioned the city of Corona to Alex Bautista or Joseph Sheridan. Not once. He had sent the two of them deep into Los Angeles instead and he knew it. Though he had no recollection of writing Donald Ratcliffe's address down for them, he was aware of just how easily it had been done.

Ha, ha, ha, ha....

He clicked on his phone again.

Ha, ha, ha, ha....

Chapter 84

Alex answered it and spoke immediately.

"We're almost to the freeway," he said, realizing that several people had probably been waiting for a report from him. "We never did see the second guy you warned us about, but it all went as smooth as can be."

He didn't understand why it was so important considering they had been watching them the whole time. Alex guessed they just wanted to make sure that they had made it safely out of the neighborhood. He thought it was nice that they were concerned.

"What should we do now?"

"You say you're almost to the freeway?"

"Yeah, we're getting on I-5 right now. We should be home in about forty-five minutes. What do you want us to do?"

He thought very hard about it. He had asked them to do a job and they had done everything they were told. There was really only one thing to say to them at this point.

"It's done—go home. You guys did great. We'll take care of the clean up. It's out of your hands and it never happened."

"That's it?"

"That's right. Never happened."

"There's still the matter of the five thousand," Alex reminded him.

"I've got your address. You'll get some mail in a couple of days and you'll be happy with what you find. Other than that, my advice is to forget about all this. Forget it. I can honestly tell you that you did a real important thing tonight."

"He was a real monster, huh?"

"You got that right." Though he had only known him personally for a couple of days, Alex had never heard the cop speak with such sincerity. *"You both take it easy, okay? If I don't talk to you anymore, just know…just know that I wish you guys the best."*

"You too. Take it real easy and…wait a sec…Joe says bye."

"Tell him the same for me."

He would never speak to either of them again.

CHAPTER 85

Call Blash back. Let him know we're on our way in.

"Wrong, Terry. We're on our way *out*. Ratcliffe's gone. We wouldn't be here if it wasn't for him and now there's no reason to stay. Blash told us to beat it and we're beating it."

Have they left yet? Do you see their cars tearing out of here? Call Blash, Louis.

Lou ignored him. Instead of making another call, Lou put the car into first gear and stepped lightly on the gas. He was easing out of his spot when Fisk grabbed his attention yet again.

STOP!

* * * *

"What the fuck is he doing now?" Blash asked, watching the Porsche come to a slow stop just short of the house. He should have been cruising past them by now.

He had been waiting for over a minute for Lou to leave and just when it looked like the man was finally going to do what he was told, he stopped in the middle of the street. Louis Poklatar was a man that Blash would never understand; not in his lifetime.

"Why's he stopping, Mike?" Quartz asked in a whisper, pressed to the side of the house, shoulder to shoulder with Nanetta.

"I don't know. I told him to—"

Blash stopped talking. He was scanning the street from south to north. Starting with the rough location of where Alex and Joe should have been, he moved his eyes to the spot that Lou had just pulled out of. He looked at Lou's idling Porsche, then to the Mustang behind him.

Something was wrong.

He looked at his own car and found what it was. It was Walter. He was banging on the windshield of Blash's car from the inside. He appeared to be yelling something frantically.

* * * *

Move, Louis! Go!

Fisk had been screaming at him for the last several seconds and it was obvious why. Two men were now standing outside the door, cautiously making their way to the driveway.

"What do I do?" Lou screamed back at him.

The pair reached the driveway and were looking up and down the street, most likely searching for a man with a ponytail. Finding nothing else of interest, both sets of eyes landed squarely on the Porsche that was idling in front of the house. They were staring at the shiny red vehicle. A moment later, they were staring at Lou.

Two guns came out.

As they stepped forward, Lou noted that the man on the left was Christian Roche. He had finally laid eyes on the man that had started all the trouble for them. It wasn't entirely his fault, but the felon was the main reason for their participation in the day's events.

What do you think? Fisk asked, sounding like he was finally done horsing around. *They're walking this way and they don't look too happy. Are you going to wait for them to get right up to the window, or what? You've got to do something, Louis. Whatever it is, you'd better do it now.*

He didn't have to. The men stopped suddenly and spun around, distracted by something behind them.

You know what they're hearing, don't you?

"Yeah, I guess I do," Lou replied, pressing harder on the gas pedal. The engine began to whine.

* * * *

"Jesus!" Blash whispered loudly through clenched teeth. He had surmised from Walter's screaming that the two men were there, but he didn't actually see them until they cleared the driveway and started walking towards Lou.

It was Christian Roche in the flesh as well as half of the protection team that he had seen earlier in the day. He guessed that they must have come out looking for their misplaced bodyguard. They seemed to be looking to Lou for his whereabouts.

"Get out of there, Louis," Quartz said quietly, peering around Blash's shoulder. "Why's he just sitting there, Mike?"

He had no answers for her. He only had questions and they were all about Lou.

It actually surprised him when they opened their jackets and removed their firearms. Until now, he didn't think they'd be willing to pull them out in the middle of the street. But he shouldn't have been surprised. It was a move of pure desperation and a result of constant paranoia. He was familiar with it.

It was only a second or so later that the phone in his hand began to ring. He knew it was Daisley calling back to see why he had been hung up on so quickly.

Even sixty miles away in LA, the detective was still fucking things up.

* * * *

Walter saw it happen and knew exactly what had occurred. It was crazy for the guy to go sneaking around while carrying his phone. He knew it the second Blash had stepped out of the car and left him alone.

As the two men crept towards the side of the house, he decided that banging on the window and screaming weren't working out at all. They would round the corner in a few seconds and the fireworks would then begin. He had no doubt who would come out on top, though. It was simple arithmetic.

Three guns was greater than two guns; therefore the side with three guns should technically win in such a shootout—but that wasn't all there was to it and doing the subtraction made the outcome a little more clear.

Three guns *minus* two guns equals one gun, making his team still the winner…but with only one player left standing. It wasn't nearly good enough odds and Walter wasn't even sure if he could stitch one person up, much less two.

No, he wasn't going to sit back and watch the show. Walter stopped banging on the glass and stopped yelling. He flipped on the headlights, leaned on the horn, and put his head down.

* * * *

"Oh my God," Lou moaned, looking up and to his right. "What now?"

The two men were immediately drawn to the loud, blaring horn and sudden brightness, though it was only for an instant. Rather than make a choice as to which distraction to pursue, they stopped.

After a moment of looking up and down the street then looking at each other, the two men raised their guns. Christian Roche, who was on the left, aimed at the northern corner of his house where the first noise had come from. It was pretty much the spot where Blash's head would be if he even so much as peeked around the corner.

The other one pointed at the ugly sedan with the bright lights and blasting horn.

They both looked back briefly the idling Porsche then concentrated on their two targets. Without a word to each other or even a nod, they began shooting.

Chapter 86

"Down, Netta!" Quartz screamed, even though she was already pulling the woman down with her. Sliding against the house until their asses hit the ground, there was no room or time to return fire. All they could do was cover their heads as an unseen barrage of bullets began whizzing by them.

A moment later, the rounds were coming straight through the wall that they were leaning against. The man that they came to kill was firing his weapon into the stucco of the front of his own house, amazingly adept at figuring out where the bullets would exit on the other side.

Quartz and Nanetta squeezed closely together and did their best to get as small as possible. They were forced apart for a moment from an explosion of debris between them, but fell back together quickly. When they did, there was a warm, wet stickiness as their arms made contact. There was hardly any pain at all.

Though she was completely soaked in panic, Quartz looked to her right and felt suddenly envious of the man next to her. While she and Nanetta were paralyzed with their backs to the wall, Blash was much lower and seemed to have found a good position on the ground.

It only took her a second to realize that he had been shot.

* * * *

Each explosive blast was punctuated with a bright flash of light. Every round that Lou heard lit up the interior of the Porsche with a strobe light effect, sending everything into slow motion. Up to that point in his life, it was the most horrifying scene he had ever been witness to.

We're all that's left, Louis and we've got to move now! If Blash or the girls poke their heads around that corner, they're dead. That car's taken about twelve shots and whoever's in it isn't going anywhere. That leaves us. Now, let's see those balls of yours, Louis. Step on the fucking gas and let's get into the middle of this thing.
Do it, Louis! DO IT!!

He didn't know what he could possibly accomplish but he knew that Fisk was right. Before he knew he was doing it, the pedal was pushed to the floor and the clutch was released. Smoke filled the air and screeching tires filled every ear within a two block radius. The car lurched forward violently.

His first instinct was to run the two men over. They were close enough to each other to take them out with one swipe, but they were also too close to the house to go barreling through them without crashing into something very large. Putting his instinct on standby and letting Fisk handle the driving duties, Lou sensed his foot lifting off of the gas and pressing down hard on the brakes. He felt the tires lock up as the tiny car skidded halfway up the sidewalk. The noise was deafening.

They came to a stop directly between the shooters and Mike Blash's newly pockmarked vehicle. That was when time stopped.

Chapter 87

Quartz ignored the flying strips of wood and paint as she struggled to drag Blash further from his unprotected position. It was made nearly impossible by the fact that Nanetta was trying to pull her away at the same time.

Blash was grimacing with pain and pulling his right leg up into his chest, his eyes rolling back while his head swayed back and forth. A long gasp of agony was the only sound coming from him, though it was blocked out quickly by a loud noise that even obscured the gunfire around them.

To Quartz, it sounded like a woman screaming.

* * * *

He was scared beyond anything he had ever imagined but felt relatively safe. As long as the man firing bullets wasn't walking up on him at the same time, Walter figured he was better off than the people across the street. He was covered in glass and pieces of rubber and plastic as he stretched himself out across the bench seat as flat as he could. For the first time in his life, he felt lucky for being small.

He flinched at the sound of each gunshot, but it was the big noise that scared him beyond almost all muscular control. The screeching sound filled his ears until he thought his heart would explode.

It reminded him of one of his cases on the fourth floor. A favorite patient of his was the sad victim of Tourette's Syndrome. She screamed like that all the time.

* * * *

In contrast to the continuous thunder of gunfire from Christian Roche and his associate, the two relatively quiet reports coming in rapid succession of each other sounded like a couple of balloons popping.

They brought a sudden end to all the noise. The silence was so abrupt it was frightening.

* * * *

Quartz was the first to look around the corner. Nanetta had an arm around her waist, ready to pull her back if she got too cocky, but she didn't need to. Quartz blinked her eyes a few times and looked again at the two men who were face down in the driveway. Neither was moving. The Porsche was a mere fifteen feet from her and Lou was behind the wheel.

They had all seen Louis Poklatar with some strange expressions on his face but this was a new one. He was just staring out the window at her. Even as Walter ran up to them and grabbed Blash under the arms, she couldn't tear her eyes from the shiny red sports car in front of her.

Though Blash had a one inch hole in the center of his knee cap, he found the strength to stop long enough to take a look for himself. As Walter threw his arm over his shoulder and grabbed him around the midsection, they both paused and stared.

Lou was facing them but not looking directly at them. He appeared very ready to lose his mind. The .45 caliber pistol was slowly pulled back into the car.

Neither of his hands were on it.

Chapter 88

The passenger door creaked open and Terrence Fisk stepped out onto the pavement. "We've got about thirty seconds to get out of here unless you all want to go to jail."

They jumped when he spoke.

The infamous killer walked shakily to the other side of the car and rested his hands on the hood for a very short moment. Pushing himself back up, he took a deep breath. He spoke rapidly.

"You," he said pointing a finger at Walter while nodding towards Blash. "Get him back into that piece of shit car and get out of here. You'd better hope it starts. If it doesn't, we'll see you in prison."

"And *you*," he was pointing at Quartz this time but his eyes shifted between both women. He was rubbing the back of his head with his hand while he spoke. "Whichever of you can still drive…do it. Be gone. The cops will be here before you know it. You're bleeding, by the way, and don't forget about the guy in your trunk."

He then turned to Lou and pulled open the car door.

"Get out. I'm taking it. Grab a ride with anyone who'll take you."

Lou shuffled out as quickly as he could considering his current state. He hadn't even blinked since the Porsche squealed to a stop. It was strange that he was the only one with the guts to speak.

"You can't take the car," he said tentatively, swallowing very hard. "It's not mine. It's a—"

"High Performance Rentals," Fisk cut in, wearing his first smile in many, many hours. "I know, buddy. I'll return it before I fly out of LA so don't you worry about it."

The group stared with disbelief at him as he climbed into the Porsche and stepped on the gas. Letting it drop to a quiet idle, he looked back at Lou, who was still gawking at him.

"Louis?" he said, beginning to chuckle. He started to speak three times before the words would come out. "You...I mean...*Louis*. Jesus *Christ*, man. We're going to have a talk one day, you and me. It's been a real treat, big guy. Take care."

He threw it into reverse and stepped on the gas before pausing once again.

"One last thing," he said, making direct eye-contact with each person present to let them know he was speaking to all of them.

"Somebody owes me fifty grand. I'll be in touch."

Chapter 89

Jessica Van Staadt could only stare in amazement as she brought the group of five another pot of fresh coffee. It was the pregnant woman's third trip down to the basement since they had all came stumbling into her house a couple of hours earlier. Aside from the fact that most of the blood had stopped flowing, nothing much had changed since then.

Three of them were still huddled around a police radio scanner, listening intently for some kind of news about one thing or another. Apparently the news was good. They looked like they were finally beginning to relax.

Two of them were women, which surprised her. They were both wearing bloody clothes but had already been bandaged up by her husband. They got seven stitches each and looked strangely happy with what would probably be matching scars. There was something else about the two women that she couldn't quite put her finger on.

The policeman she had met before looked quite a bit worse than the rest. He was stretched out on a table that Walter had cleared off. They were still arguing and it looked like Officer Blash was about ready to give in.

It didn't happen very often but she loved watching her husband be assertive.

* * * *

"That's all I can do," he repeated for the fifth time in a tone of sheer frustration. "Your patella is shattered, Mike. You've got to go to the hospital. *Any* hospital. I don't even know if you'll be able to walk on this thing ever again."

"Aw, come on, Walt," Blash whined with a pleasantly buzzed grin. "I trust you. Just yank the bullet out of there and throw a fucking Band-Aid on it. I'm sure the swelling will go down real soon."

His knee was the size of a cantaloupe and all of the skin around the bullet hole was puffy and was already changing colors. If not for the few shots of local anesthetic that Walter had administered, Blash would still be screaming in pain. The homemade opiate cocktail he was currently stoned on helped as well.

"Listen, Mike. I know you're a cop and a report has to be filed if you go to a hospital, but you need treatment. Make up some bullshit story if you need to. I know you're good at that."

"I am, aren't I?" he quipped, then turned to the others. "What's the latest over there?"

Quartz, Lou, and Nanetta looked up. They had been watching the small police scanner as though it was a television set.

"Two DOA's and a shitload of holes," Quartz replied with a hopeful smile. "That's it so far. They got a positive ID on Roche—nothing on the other asshole who was shooting up the street."

"What about the guy in your trunk?" Blash asked.

"We dropped him off a few miles past the the middle of fucking nowhere. He'll be walking for a while and I'm fairly certain we won't be hearing from him again. As far as Roche's street goes, there were no witnesses or anything that I can tell. Not even a plate number. Someone would have called it in by now and we'd have heard something about it. We didn't leave any prints and we know we didn't leave any slugs or shells behind. You have to actually fire a weapon to do that." She'd mentioned it twice now, and all of them rolled their eyes uncomfortably to the ceiling or walls each time she did. "How did none of us get a single shot off?"

As before, she received no answer.

Nanetta was watching Quartz as she spoke and seemed to enjoy listening to her flowing in and out of cop mode with each shift in the conversation. Every now and then, they would meet eyes then look down at their bandages. They had something new to share.

"What's the matter, Lou?" Quartz asked, noting his tense look. He was the only one who hadn't seemed to relax once they were in the shelter of Walter's basement.

"It's a couple of things," he replied, shifting his eyes around the room. "How long do we have to wait before we can stop shitting about the cell phones?"

They all knew what he was referring to. It was on all their minds, but shoved towards the back. Most of them were still busy celebrating simply being alive and weren't going to stress about any potential fallout until it was necessary.

"You can worry about it for the rest of your life if you want to," Blash answered, wincing as he shifted his body to look at Lou. "But I'm not going to think about it after tomorrow. If anyone was picking it up and could make sense out of our ramblings they'd call it in as soon as they see the story on the news...or even sooner. We could sweat for a few days but I'm not gonna. What else is bugging your ass? You're making me nervous."

It was a lie. He had never been so at ease in his life.

"The lawyer," Lou replied, looking down at his shoes and hoping that they would be gentle with him.

"What lawyer's that?" Quartz asked with squinty eyes, motioning towards Walter, who she guessed didn't really need to know about another murder. Lou caught the look and put a hand to his mouth.

"Yeah, what lawyer?" Walter asked.

"Oh, don't worry about it," Blash replied belligerently, seemingly speaking to the whole room and possibly even the people next door. "If I thought the guy had anything on paper, I'd be worried about it. But think about it, guys. Anything he had lying around could be used against him just as easily as against us. I hope that's the case because Lou didn't check with anyone before he fired our favorite attorney. Ain't that right, Lou?"

So they weren't going to be gentle on him. He knew it would get worse before it got better and they hadn't even gotten around to the whole story on Terrence Fisk yet. He wasn't anxious to go over it; at least not until he was sure what had actually taken place. Much of it was still a mystery.

"Sorry, guys. I didn't plan it, you know? It...uh...kind of snuck right by me."

"Like a typo?" Quartz asked, bursting out laughing.

"Yeah," Blash agreed, laughing painfully. "It was just a few numbers and letters—and *cities*—in the wrong place. No big deal, right?"

Even Lou started to chuckle as he found the will to look up.

Everyone's laughter died quickly, however, as Quartz gasped loudly and dove for the police scanner. After knocking it around clumsily, she found the volume knob and turned it way up. The room grew silent as the radio picked up a transmission. It was regarding the strange shootout that had occurred in a neighborhood only a few miles from where they were currently resting.

It wasn't what was being said that grabbed Quartz's attention. It was who was saying it.

"*Jesus*...that's Andrew," she said, listening to him speak to another Corona police officer.

Even hauling ass from LA, there was no way he could have been the first on the scene, but he had made the trip anyway and it sounded like he was the detective in charge now. They all listened and breathed simultaneous sighs as a series of commands were given by a man who'd spent the prior evening laying in his own vomit while avoiding the people he was responsible for.

Amazingly, he sounded like a detective again. There were still no guarantees, but the detective had the ability to make the scene look like anything he wanted. Anything but the truth would do just fine and they suspected that Daisley was thinking the same thing.

Growing bored with whatever it was that was so exciting to the police officers, Nanetta nudged Quartz lightly and held her tiny paper cup out to her.

"I am thinking I would like to freshen my breath again," she said with an uncharacteristic giggle. "You will serve me, won't you, Qiana?"

Of all the cylinders hanging on Walter's wall, the oddly flavored parsley brew seemed to be the most popular. Quartz took the cup and filled it then poured herself one. Handing it back to her, she leaned down and whispered something into Nanetta's ear. Based on the dirty little smile that followed, it appeared that something would indeed be served.

While they all listened to Andrew Daisley rattle on like the detective that he was, Walter began digging through one of his drawers. When he found what he was looking for he held it up and nodded to Blash. Blash nodded back and pushed himself up into a halfway sitting position as he shifted his eyes to Lou.

"Can you guys turn that down for second?"

The volume on the police radio was lowered and Walter approached Lou. Blash looked at him with an uncomfortable smile. "I think it's time to hear about your friend Terrence."

Lou's face went red and his eyes shot straight to the floor again. "Okay...here's what happened. Wait..." He cleared his throat several times and searched the room for something that would pass for an adequate response. "Just wait a sec. Now, Daisley was the one who checked his pulse...and...well. Okay...wait a sec...."

"Hang on, Lou," Blash said, cutting off his embarrassed babbling. He looked to Walter, who had moved next to the big man. "Walt?"

Walter didn't answer him. Instead, he unscrewed the lid from a tiny bottle and brought it up to Lou's face. "Open up."

A single drop of Walter Van Staadt's *Phase Three* tumbled onto Lou's tongue.

"Okay, big guy," Blash said, looking at his partners, who had no clue what was going on. "I want to hear all about Fisk. Give it a couple of minutes and try it again." Not having the slightest clue as to how Louis Poklatar would react to the dose of illegal hyper-awareness, he looked ready to burst. "This is gonna be so fucking funny."

Chapter 90

The Porsche Speedster purred as it made its way north up Pacific Coast Highway. It was a cute little car but Terrence Fisk liked his own Jaguar better. Speed and handling were great but comfort was what he was all about.

It had been painful to watch the big cop banging his knees into the dash repeatedly—almost as painful as listening to the Porsche's engine while it was in fourth gear for an hour on the previous day. Even bashing his head into the table had hurt less than that; at least he thought so. He couldn't be completely sure.

He remembered getting caught up in something on the floor. That part was clear.

Then he remembered being horribly embarrassed as his arms began to flail. That was when he decided to fall. He didn't mean to smack into the table, but sometimes a swift tumble looked a whole lot better than a long, pathetic, drawn out attempt at righting oneself. He figured he was going to hit the floor anyway, so doing it quickly with as little fuss as possible made the most sense.

The next thing he knew, the lead detective of their sad little crew was laying fingers across his trachea, the boniest part of the entire throat region; a rigid structure that wouldn't produce a pulse on the best of days. He had considered startling the man and humiliating him in front of his group, but decided against it. He was glad that he did.

The conversation that followed was just about the most amazing example of bad judgment and complete ineptitude that he had ever had the honor of listening to. If he had heard them correctly then the group of dirty cops was actually going to attempt to recruit replacements for him.

Replacements? For me? Silly policemen.

Furthermore, they were drawing their applicants from a pool of people who were so poorly equipped to commit crime that they had already been arrested at least once. Even while laying on the floor as his head swelled, he'd found it hard not to laugh.

He decided to play along, though. There was no reason not to. Even at the risk of losing the fifty grand promised him, he simply couldn't help himself. If screwing with cops was a sport, Fisk knew that he would be considered a professional athlete. Perhaps even the best in his field. He had been doing it his whole life.

He had a friend back east who claimed to have played dead for over sixteen hours one time. He couldn't wait to call him up and let him know who was the king.

It wasn't all a cakewalk, though, and there were some tense moments where he almost gave up the ruse. Fortunately, the man they had left to deal with him was right out of his mind…or he was in a *fragile emotional state*, rather. Either way, he was only going to put up with a certain amount of physical abuse before he unexpectedly rose from the dead. Luckily, he never had to.

The mild slapping he received in the posh hotel room was no big deal to him and he didn't really mind. Though he did feel foolish letting the big man play with him like a puppet, he sensed that Officer Poklatar wasn't a bad guy at all. Not bright, but not bad. Aside from getting tossed on the ground a bit, he thought they played well together.

It was the talking that drove him crazy.

Though it was obvious that some pretty heavy dialogs were going on between himself and the cop, Fisk felt left out because he didn't know what his lines were. It was only after the officer had responded to something that Fisk could venture a guess at what prompted each response, so things were a little backward most of the time. He supposed he picked up about ten percent of what was being said and it was more than enough to know that Louis Poklatar was a good guy…but slightly unbalanced.

He had only expected to spend a few minutes with the man; not almost two whole days. After listening to their conversation while stuffed in the hotel closet, he thought for sure that he was going to be tossed into a dumpster. It would have been messy but ideal. He could have simply showered, changed, and had the job done before the sun went down. Instead, he felt like the big dumb cop was taking him on a vacation with him.

It wasn't all that bad.

He got to be chauffeured around in a nifty little Porsche and had gotten more sleep than had been afforded to him in recent weeks. He even got to go to a fight. Aside from killing the two idiots who had been spraying bullets around a residential neighborhood, the fight was his favorite part.

Watching Officer Poklatar and the two kids had almost been as good as watching the boxing match itself. From three rows behind them, Fisk had watched them yell and scream and laugh together like an uncle with his nephews. They were his two killers; his replacement shooters. It was stupid and ludicrous and insane and he loved it. On top of all that, it really was an exceptionally good fight. That kid Gianni Costa could really throw some punches.

All in all, it was a fine experience. He wouldn't really miss any of the players but knew that he would think of Officer Poklatar from time to time. The crazy man nearly made him laugh at least fifty times during the ordeal.

As he made his way up the coast, Fisk took his time thinking about the money. Fifty-thousand. It was a decent chunk of change and he was still debating whether to go after it or not. He gathered from various conversations that the half of the money given to him by Ratcliffe was now divided between several people. The other half was apparently unreachable as well since Donald Ratcliffe had been whacked by Louis's two young men.

Though Fisk had always considered himself to be a man who knew what was going on at all times, he had to admit that he had no idea how *that* had happened.

He was already going to kill the cocky lawyer anyway—that much he had decided shortly after his embarrassing trip to the floor. With the three cops forced in on his job from the start, he already had more get-out-of-jail-free cards than he needed. The lawyer was a dishonorable snake and would have come back to haunt him as he had apparently done to each of the police officers that were involved. The man seemed to live and breathe blackmail but hadn't intelligently considered the risks involved.

Donald Ratcliffe had asked and paid for a quick and clean hit that would occur in a timely manner, which was exactly what he got. It was just ironic that two kids hired to replace him did the truly important killing instead. Unfortunately, this also wiped out his payday and brought him to his current dilemma.

He knew the truth, though. Embarrassing as it was, it was all his fault. If he would have never fallen in the first place, no one else would have been brought in to replace him. And if everyone involved wasn't so damned stupid, they wouldn't have given away half of his money and killed the wrong man, effectively erasing the other half of his money. Of course, the right man did get killed—both of them in fact—just not by all the right people.

It was all very confusing and made his head hurt worse than it already did. He didn't like being confused about anything. It made him think of Louis Poklatar and all the quality time they had spent together.

Maybe he would miss that guy. Just a little.

Money isn't everything, Terrence. Maybe we should sleep on it.

"Yeah, let's do—" He almost finished the sentence before catching himself. "Great, now *I'm* doing it."

0-595-32225-5